THE ASPECT OF ESSENCE

THE AELFYN ARCHIVES
BOOK ONE

SAMANTHA AMSTUTZ

STARLIGHT FANTASY PUBLISHING LLC

The Aspect of Essence

Copyright © 2023 by Samantha Amstutz

All rights reserved.

No part of this publication may be reproduced, distributed, or transmitted in any form or by any means, including photocopying, recording, or other electronic or mechanical methods, except for brief quotations in reviews, without the prior written permission of the publisher, except as permitted by U.S. copyright law. For permission requests, contact author.samantha.amstutz@gmail.com.

The story, all names, characters, and incidents portrayed in this production are a work of fiction. No identification with actual persons (living or deceased), places, buildings, and products is intended or should be inferred.

ASIN : B0C2VNS1T1

ISBN : 9798218253301, 9798989789603

Developmental Editor and Proofreader: Hannah VanVels Ausbury

Line and Copy Editor: Michelle Hope

Cover Artist: Jeff Brown Graphics

*For anyone who feels at home behind the pages of a book.
You're not alone.
This fantasy world is for you.*

CONTENTS

Author's note … vii
Guide … xi

Chapter 1 … 1
Chapter 2 … 13
Chapter 3 … 23
Chapter 4 … 31
Chapter 5 … 37
Chapter 6 … 49
Chapter 7 … 60
Chapter 8 … 65
Chapter 9 … 69
Chapter 10 … 81
Chapter 11 … 91
Chapter 12 … 97
Chapter 13 … 110
Chapter 14 … 122
Chapter 15 … 130
Chapter 16 … 142
Chapter 17 … 149
Chapter 18 … 159
Chapter 19 … 170
Chapter 20 … 176
Chapter 21 … 182
Chapter 22 … 190
Chapter 23 … 200
Chapter 24 … 217
Chapter 25 … 227
Chapter 26 … 242
Chapter 27 … 251
Chapter 28 … 262
Chapter 29 … 267
Chapter 30 … 278
Chapter 31 … 285
Chapter 32 … 294
Chapter 33 … 300

Chapter 34	310
Chapter 35	320
Chapter 36	328
Chapter 37	335
Chapter 38	347
Chapter 39	362
Chapter 40	375
Chapter 41	385
Chapter 42	389
Chapter 43	394
Chapter 44	398
Chapter 45	407
Thank you for reading!	411
Acknowledgments	413
About the Author	415

AUTHOR'S NOTE

As an author, the last thing I want to do is cause a reader distress. Please be aware that this novel is intended for adults with darker themes some readers may find triggering or disturbing.

Please consider your mental health before diving into this story if you have any concerns about the following content warnings.

This is by no means an exhaustive list or arranged in any particular order: panic attacks, death, violence, eugenics, trafficking/forced servitude, racism, infertility, brainwashing, dubious consent, off page rape/sexual assault, adult language, sibling death, DID, uncontrolled switching, involuntary body modification, attempted suicide, bullying, substance abuse/addiction, emotional trauma, loss of body autonomy, choking, vomiting, blood/bleeding, absent parent, emotional/physical manipulation, physical/emotional abuse, death of animals.

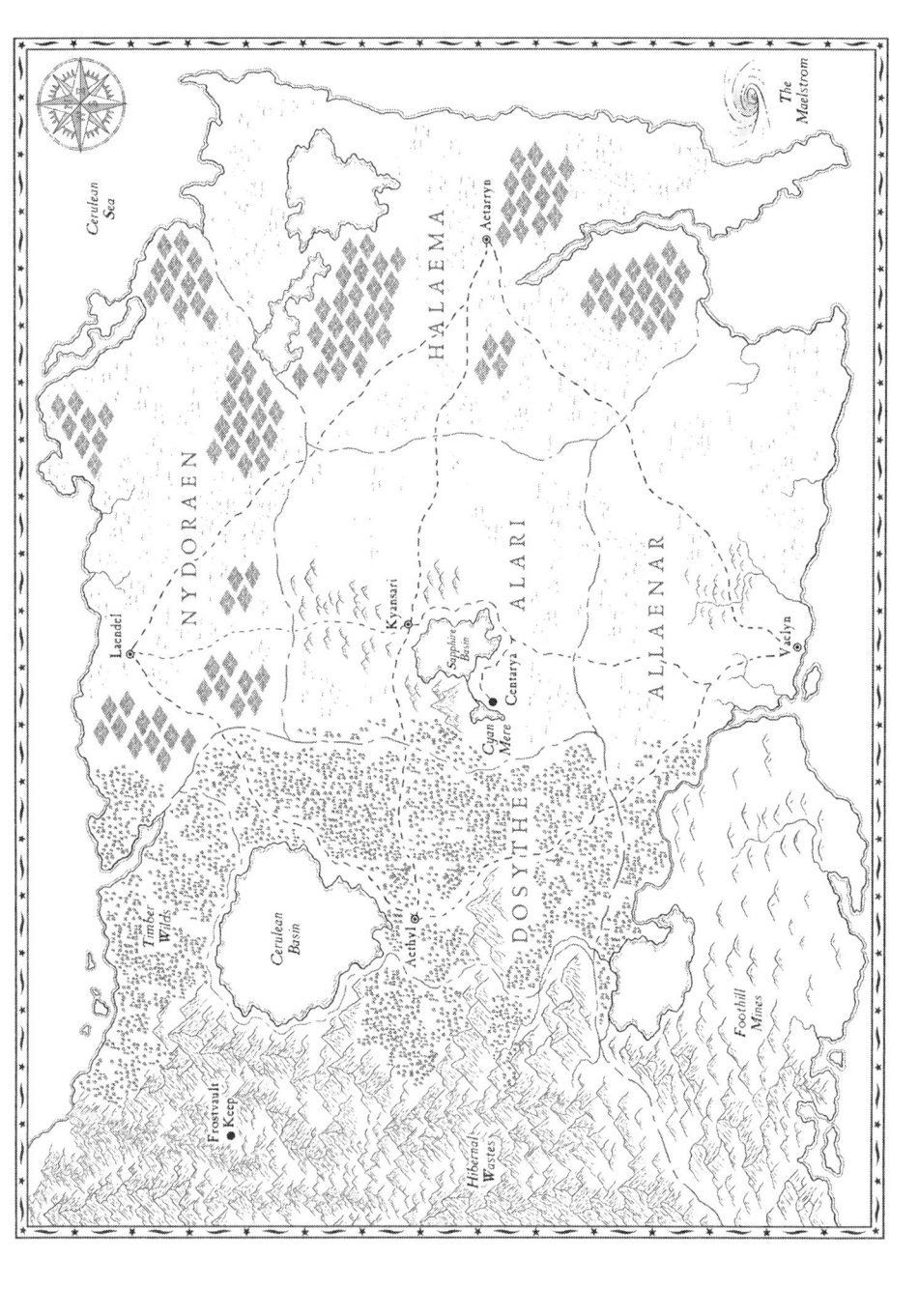

GUIDE

Prominent characters
Serenna (Sir-REN-nah) - Princess of Allaenar
Jassyn (JAS-sin) **Raellyn** (Rae-ELL-in) - a mender and researcher at Centarya, half cousin to Vesryn
Vesryn (VEZ-rin) **Falkyn** (FALL-kin) - prince of Alari
Elashor (e-LASH-or) **Vallende** (Val-LEND-e) - Serenna's father and Alari's General
Velinya (Vel-LIN-ya) - Serenna's elven-blooded handmaid and friend
Lykor (Lie-CORE) - wraith leader

Minor Characters
Queen Arianna (Air-E-un-a) - elven-blooded queen of Allaenar, Serenna's mother
Magister Thalaesyn (THAL-Aye-Sin) - Mender at Centarya, Jassyn's mentor
Galaeryn (ga-LARE-rin) **Falkyn** (FALL-kin) - Elven king of Alari, Vesryn's sire
Ayla (EYE-la) - An initiate at Centarya, half niece to Jassyn
Ceryn Raellyn (SER-in)- Jassyn's half sister, sits on the High Council
Kal (CAL) - A wraith and Lykor's captain

Lady Farine Vallende (Fa-REEN) - Elashor's mother and one of Jassyn's contract holders
Aesar (ACE-ar)- Vesryn's twin brother who perished in the first wraith attack
Queen Maraelyn (Ma-REL-in) - Vesryn's mother who perished in the first wraith attack, half sister is Jassyn's mother, Ceryn
Saundyl (SAWN-dil)- Serenna's bother, heir and prince of Allaenar

Places
Centarya (Sen-TAR-e-ah) - the elven-blooded military academy
Alari (a-LAR-e) - Elven realm
The Terminal - a growing elven-blooded city below Centarya and a waypoint for traveling to campus
Kyansari (KEY-an-sar-e) - Elven capital

Human Realms
South - **Allaenar** Al-LAE-nar
    Capital - **Vaelyn (**Vey-LIN)
North - **Nydoraen (**Nye-DOR-ain)
East - **Halaema (**Ha-LAE-ma)
West - **Dosythe (**Do-SITHE)

Races
Aelfyn (ALE-fin) - The elves' ancestors
Elves - arch elves can control the entire spectrum (all eight elements) of Essence
Elven-blooded - those with any amount of elf blood mixed with human blood
Half-breed - a derogatory slur for elven-blooded
Humans - natives of the mortal shores
Wraith - a secretive, monstrous race that appeared within the last century intent on destroying the elves

CHAPTER 1

JASSYN

Jassyn wanted to vanish. Disappear into a zephyr of shadows like a wraith. Anything to avoid this new assignment—his fate dictated once again by the High Council. Illusions of freedom were ridiculous, considering how effectively the elves had uprooted his life.

In the courtyard near the Portal Platform, Jassyn absently fiddled with the golden rings looped through his pointed ears, awaiting the arrival of General Elashor's delegation. Regardless of his distaste for his new responsibility, he focused on appreciating the pleasant autumn morning. A breeze fluttered through the plaza, prompting him to shake back the raven curls dangling haphazardly in his face.

He didn't bother growing his hair longer to plait in intricate braids, like the trending male fashion. Jassyn told himself it was because he wanted to embrace his differences, if only to set himself further apart from the elves.

But he'd learned being unique only made him stand out more as a novelty.

Now, his only concern was that his shaggier hairstyle concealed the newest white-inked tattoo mottled across his forehead.

Unfortunately, the circular trail of his thoughts dragged him back to the present. The brief respite of marveling in nature did little to ease the dread expanding in his gut. Standing idle, playing a pawn in the court's politics, and being forced into this new position—he despised the elves using him in such a way.

Jassyn shifted his weight, his traveling boots scraping against the cobblestones. He couldn't wrap his head around General Elashor's unrelenting determination to assign him to a human court. *There are plenty of other half-breed spawn like me he could choose from instead to tutor the princess.*

The elven council dictated every aspect of Jassyn's life. It hardly mattered what the previous fifty years of his research at Centarya had amounted to. Here he was, hauled away from his studies, moments from traveling to one of the four mortal realms.

A hand clapped him on the shoulder, jerking him out of his gloomy thoughts. Jassyn tensed at the overfamiliar and rather unwelcome touch. Suppressing a defeated sigh, he turned to face who was undoubtedly his cousin, Vesryn.

The prince.

Who had an aggravating habit of invading his space.

The white peaks and glass spires of the elven capital, Kyansari, framed Vesryn like a court painting. Every building the elves constructed gleamed in snowy tones arranged on precisely gridded streets. Whether it was because they perceived the absence of color to be a symbol of wealth and power or because the architecture had been inspired by an ancestral desire to capture the light of the stars, Jassyn couldn't say.

"Were you going to slink through the capital without even saying goodbye?" Vesryn asked with mock scandalization.

"That was the idea," Jassyn muttered, shrugging his cousin's fingers off. He restrained his irritation.

"Well, no matter." Vesryn straightened, like he was trying to stretch himself to Jassyn's height. "I've come to see you off instead."

"How uncharacteristically thoughtful of you." Jassyn's frayed nerves and ruminative thoughts wouldn't win him any duels if the prince insisted on engaging in their typical verbal sparring.

"I'm curious." Vesryn's jade eyes glittered. "How did you get your hands on a half-breed princess? Stars, *I* don't even have a princess!"

Jassyn's cousin flashed a grin that was all jagged edges and vicious delight. Like other pure-blooded elves, the prince's angular features and silvery hair, tied into a rather outdated half knot on top of his head, framed a visage too appealing for his own good.

"I'll be *tutoring* Princess Serenna," Jassyn corrected, stopping himself from grinding his teeth. "My assignment in Vaelyn is nothing more."

Vesryn's obsidian leathers strained across his chest as his fingers drummed rhythmically on his crossed arms. He emitted an amused grunt. "That's not how I heard it."

The prince was out of place among the elegant nobles, especially with the hilts of his twin glaives peeking over his shoulders. Jassyn's lip unconsciously curled when he studied the frayed threads of the prince's dragon sigil stitched across his armor. But Vesryn was a singularity, operating within his own parameters, seemingly unconcerned with replicating expected royal behavior.

"Since you have a seat on the High Council," Jassyn explained in a practiced lecturing tone, "you're well aware the general's personal wishes are not the will of the realm. I'll be preparing his daughter for life in Kyansari in the event he brings Serenna to the elven courts."

"How many offspring does he want you to produce with this Princess Serenna?" Vesryn asked, cocking his head, like the question was the whole purpose of seeking Jassyn out. "I can only assume that's his stipulation before you can return to your studies at Centarya. It's no secret Elashor has apparently deemed you a *worthy* match for his half-breed daughter."

As the prince's eyes danced with self-satisfied humor, Jassyn willed stoic indifference into his features. Vesryn had a unique way of nearly riling him into violence. It took Jassyn all his restraint to stifle the urge to smack that idiotic smile off his cousin's face. He refused to give the prince a reaction, despite his blood boiling at Vesryn's usage of the derogatory term "half-breed."

Jassyn's voice sharpened. "I have no intention of siring any more offspring outside of my *required* contracts."

"Well, what's the fun in that?" Vesryn asked as if he couldn't comprehend such a concept. "Do your voracious females keep you too busy, then?" The prince slapped him on the back, like they were sharing a joke. "I figured all of that coupling would have unwound you a bit by now."

Jassyn flinched from the sting of the verbal blow, his shoulders curving in. His tentative composure wavered. *I've said too much. I don't know why I bother explaining myself.*

Like a shark scenting blood, Vesryn lunged, propelled by eliciting a reaction. "Did you get a new tattoo?" He swiped at Jassyn's curls, peering at his forehead, before Jassyn could react and swat his hand away.

If he had any choice in the matter, Jassyn would have refused to wear the inked sigils of his four contract holders like he was some prized cattle. And, of course, "Lady" Farine felt the need to brand his head for the world to see. *No wonder she produced an offspring as detestable as General Elashor.*

"Ah, Lady Farine finally laid a claim on you." Vesryn swept his eyes over Jassyn with an exaggerated appraising look. "Word has it the general's mother has even more insatiable appetites than he does. She's been after one of those spots on your contracts for, what? Sixty years now?" Vesryn cackled wildly. "I'll be dying to know your experience fucking both Elashor's daughter and mother."

"You're revolting." Jassyn admonished his cousin with a scowl but shrank back from the humiliation flooding his veins.

Jassyn's thoughts flashed back. Even weeks later, his first compulsory visit at Farine Vallende's estate had him retching when he woke in the middle of the night. The crisp air winding around the courtyard did nothing to prevent his body from springing with anxious sweat at the reminder. Jassyn sucked in a ragged breath. The memories of those three nights he was contractually obligated to service Farine had panic threatening to claw out of his lungs.

As one of the initial elven-blooded birthed, Jassyn was bound by the will of the council to sire the children of prominent elven females who clamored for the opportunity to bear offspring since they no longer could reproduce with other pure-blooded elves.

Decades ago, Jassyn had mistakenly revealed his turmoil concerning the coupling contracts to the prince, which he immediately regretted. Since then, Vesryn had gone out of his way to torment him by jerking the shackles of his reality, taking a personal delight in Jassyn's discomfort surrounding his responsibility to the realm.

Now, Jassyn knew better than to seek any measure of solace in the elven courts in the supportive sense—especially where the prince was concerned. *Why did I ever expect him to care?* Unlike humans, definitions of familiar kin carried little value or meaning among the elves.

Jassyn's own conniving pure-bred mother had secured a prestigious coupling with a human king with the intention of binding her offspring's "services" to the realm in exchange for a seat on the High Council. Jassyn's half sister occupied that position now, while the elves forced him into servitude to apparently pay that debt indefinitely through access to his bloodline. All the while, the council reaped yearly payments and favors from those who'd purchased one of those four coveted spots on his contracts.

Yes, it's my duty as a half-breed to personally see to it that the elven race doesn't die out. I should feel so honored to have this required purpose. But why stop at four handlers? Why not have an auction and send me somewhere different every night?

Jassyn's mind repelled against the idea, swinging his awareness back to the capital. He blinked, dissolving those thoughts, realizing his glower only made Vesryn's grin widen further.

Smoothing his features, Jassyn drew in a calming breath through his nose. Levelly meeting the prince's gaze, he dismissively flicked the wind-blown curls out of his eyes.

"The humans are rather conservative with how many partners they take, are they not?" Vesryn asked, unsheathing a dagger at his belt. "I suppose you'll have to fabricate excuses about your obligations to your elven females." He idly flipped and then snatched the dagger out of the air. "You wouldn't want this Princess Serenna to get jealous."

"Serenna just came of age." Jassyn clenched his fists in a renewed effort of restraining his hands from throttling the prince. "She's hardly older than a child."

The prince *knew* the council had excused him from servicing his contract holders during the duration of his assignment in the southern realm. Traveling back and forth wouldn't be practical.

Jassyn experienced an odd blanket of emotions threaded with anxiety at the new situation but also a sense of relief at the reprieve from his duties to Alari.

"Elashor mentioned his daughter turned twenty-five. You half-breeds are considered adults by then." Vesryn waved his blade dismissively. "It doesn't take you a century to mature like us pure-bloods."

"And some of you obviously require longer than that," Jassyn snapped. "If you're so invested in the general's family, why don't you volunteer in my stead?"

Vesryn arched a brow as he tossed his knife into the air again, and then caught it while holding Jassyn's scowl. Jassyn only rolled his eyes at his cousin's display. *I know he's fully dedicating himself to my embarrassment.*

Motion behind the prince snagged Jassyn's attention. His gaze flicked over his cousin's head, noting more nobles gathering in the courtyard. Jassyn's stomach churned, sensing the time of his departure approached, as inevitable as the rising sun.

Distracting himself, Jassyn veered his attention back to the prince, interrupting whatever Vesryn was getting ready to say. "The realm is *quite* aware of your reputation among the females of court. I understand the king is looking to secure you an elven-blooded match to ensure the succession of your line."

For a moment, Jassyn thought he might have something akin to an upper hand when Vesryn's empty fingers twitched at his side. The prince had evaded his sire's demands of securing a suitable consort. Whispers circulated in court about King Galaeryn's fury that Vesryn had forced him to intervene on his behalf.

The prince sheathed his blade with a frown. Locking his spine, Jassyn held his ground as Vesryn barged uncomfortably close. He patted Jassyn's cheek. "Oh, I have no doubt *you'll* be an excellent present for the princess."

Resisting the urge to retreat, Jassyn channeled all of his willpower into not allowing his stony exterior to crack.

The prince clicked his tongue, like he was disappointed he hadn't elicited a reaction. "Anyway, I'm off to hunt a group of wraith. Those beasts intercepted a shipment of the western realm's lumber headed for the Terminal, so I suppose this is farewell."

"Interesting." Jassyn crossed his arms, unable to comprehend why his cousin attempted to engage in further conversation. They weren't close. For obvious reasons.

When he didn't provide any parting words, Vesryn reached out to ruffle his curls like he had for the past eighty years. Jassyn's flinch had Vesryn flashing a grin before he pivoted on a heel, sauntering away. The prince gave Jassyn a parting wave as his offensively scuffed boots clicked on the white stones.

Vesryn strolled to the center of the Portal Platform, the designated place in the capital for opening traveling gateways. He blatantly ignored the surrounding nobles bowing their respects before they scurried out of his way in a flurry of pastel silks.

Essence ignited, swirling around the prince when he extended a hand. Magic warped the air like a heat wave, shimmering above the cobblestones. A flash of green light sliced through space like a rip running through fabric. The rift expanded to open an inky portal.

Vesryn disappeared into the gateway with feline elegance and the carefree gait of a male born into privilege, as if the responsibility and demands of the realm held no sway over *his* life.

Jassyn trembled as he released the taut tension in his shoulders. Holding a breath to the point of discomfort, he counted the heartbeats knocking against his ribs while the frustration in his chest uncoiled. Moderating his reactions brought no significant sense of relief, though the controlled action allowed his mind to settle. Somewhat.

And breathing is the only thing I seem to have any power over.

Jassyn blew out a long exhale. *Who am I kidding?* His excuses to Vesryn about tutoring General Elashor's daughter sounded feeble when voiced. Jassyn knew the general could care less if anyone educated Princess Serenna.

Elashor used his influence to twist the High Council to his will, and they assigned Jassyn to the southern realm. Conveniently, with the excuse that Princess Serenna needed an elven tutor before the general brought her to Alari. *Well, they assigned a half-breed tutor at* least. A pure-blooded elf would never lower themselves to live among humans.

Jassyn couldn't fathom what he was supposed to do in their courts, where he wasn't permitted access to magic because the mortals had no knowledge of the elves' power. Lounging about didn't suit him. He wanted to be doing something meaningful with his time, have a purpose beyond this forced duty of procreating and "tutoring."

Perhaps most importantly, he couldn't help further his mentor's research investigating elven infertility. If their studies at Centarya could reverse the affliction, surely the council would release him from their mandated directives of siring children.

The only progeny pure-blooded elves could bear were with humans or elven-blooded, like him. Pure-bloods had been unable to reproduce together for over two hundred years. The sterility curse seemingly didn't affect those with any amount of human blood in their veins. For whatever reason.

Not all elven-blooded living in Alari were subject to the same fate. Jassyn's misfortune stemmed from being born into one of the most powerful elven families. His line, the Raellyns, was riddled with arch elves, masters of the entire spectrum of Essence. Despite having a human sire, Jassyn retained a notable magical proficiency.

His bloodline and the ability to produce offspring with pure-blooded elves made a tie to him highly desirable. To the point where the High Council drew up breeding contracts for notable elven-blooded males in Alari to ensure the proper distribution of their "services."

As if that weren't degrading.

A deep voice rolled over him. "Ah, Jassyn," General Elashor said, marching through the gathered crowd. Ten members of the general's personal guard flanked him in elaborate snowy armor that appeared more decorative than functional with all the whorls and lacquered plates.

Despite Elashor being a head shorter than him, the general's dominating presence always made Jassyn feel smaller. Elashor's burnished hair grazing his shoulders reflected nearly as much sunlight as his shining longsword strapped to his side. Jassyn suspected the weapons were more for displays of intimidation towards the humans rather than defense against potential ambushes from the wraith.

Elashor was King Galaeryn's right hand, and gossip behind closed doors suggested the king held him in higher regard than his son, Vesryn, Alari's heir.

As a pure-blooded elf from a family of significant standing, Elashor periodically visited the human southern realm. Somehow, he had convinced the elven-blooded queen to bear children for him. *Well, it's no wonder, considering those in the mortal realms believe it's an honor to be selected by an elf for coupling.*

"We're about ready. Are you tethered?" For confirmation, Elashor's sapphire eyes roved over Jassyn's golden jewelry, suppressing his magic.

Jassyn swallowed a bitter taste of shame when the general smirked upon noticing his mother's sigil tattooed across his forehead. Elashor lazily dragged his gaze down the length of Jassyn's body.

Evaluating him.

The hairs on the back of Jassyn's neck lifted as he tracked the motion of Elashor's fingers stroking the hilt of his sword. Jassyn's skin crawled, reliving the memory of Farine's hands working his body in the same suggested motion.

Swallowing so he wouldn't be sick in the middle of the assembled crowd, Jassyn dropped his gaze, knowing Elashor was goading him with a silent insinuation. The Vallendes made him feel as helpless as a sheep cornered by wolves. Fear threatened to constrict his chest. *Stars, please don't let the princess be the same*, he begged.

"Come." Elashor's mouth twisted with amusement when Jassyn braved meeting his gaze. The general jerked his head in a command to follow. "You're the man of the hour."

His feet dragging with dread, Jassyn waded alongside Elashor through the current of the gathered crowd to reach the Portal Platform. The nobles paid their respect by placing a hand over their heart and bowing.

The aristocrats didn't rush out of the way like they did for Vesryn. No doubt they wanted to give the prince's unpredictable conduct a wide berth. Jassyn frequently heard about his cousin's tendency to obliterate the wraith that terrorized Kyansari in vicious raids. He could only hope one of these days those beasts would bring Vesryn to his knees.

Just enough to deflate the prince's ego.

"Serenna is going to be thrilled when she sees you," Elashor said. "My daughter has always been fascinated by her elven heritage. She's been hounding me for a tutor from Alari for years."

Like tutoring is why I was hand-selected. "My research will stall without Essence in the human realms," Jassyn pointed out. He knew the objection against the general's self-serving desires was useless, but some small part of him wasn't prepared to surrender so easily.

"As you know, the humans and half-breeds living outside our realm are unaware of our magic." Elashor's greedy eyes dallied on the nobles as he spoke. "Have patience. Everything will change soon."

Jassyn didn't have time to wonder about what the general meant. Elashor halted when they passed a group of prominent arch elves. The general exchanged pleasantries before commenting on how ravishing they looked.

One woman, who unsurprisingly knew Jassyn by name, was bold enough to grab his hand, inviting him to seek her out when he returned.

Assaulted by her cloying cloud of perfume, Jassyn suppressed a wince. Anything related to his birthplace made his stomach roll into a knot. He wished he could sink into the stones or rip his arm out of her insistent grasp, but instead, Jassyn plastered a practiced congenial look on his face, as was expected of him.

This kind of sudden intimacy was one of the numerous reasons he avoided Kyansari unless his presence was required by his capital-dwelling contract holders. Despite growing up in the palace, since his mother was the late queen's half sister, Jassyn had abandoned his life in the city as soon as he was of age to attend the remote academy some fifty years prior.

The attention of the courts never suited him, but he could hardly go anywhere in Alari without the citizens recognizing who he was. It didn't take Jassyn long to discover the elves were only interested in him because of his bloodline. They had no desire to discuss his research or learn anything about him.

Not that there's much to say.

Elashor eventually lost interest in leering at the gathered nobles and steered Jassyn toward the traveling grounds. "Think of this venture as a holiday. If you manage to get Serenna with child, I'll see that the High Council assigns you back to your research at Centarya."

It shocked Jassyn when the general didn't puff up like a rooster, proud of crowing about such blatant manipulation. Instead, his gut twisted into an icy knot, knowing Elashor's obsession with extending his line was the *actual* reason for his assignment.

Jassyn knew he could slip into the role of tutor, but decided his theatrics would end there. He wasn't bound by decreed obligations beyond teaching Serenna. If Elashor believed he could pressure him into impregnating his daughter, he would be disappointed. Jassyn banished the thought, appalled by the general's intentions.

"I don't see how another descendant will make any difference to your line," Jassyn argued, regaining his composure. There was no doubt Elashor had more elven-blooded children and descendant offspring than any other elf. It appeared the general's aspirations were to couple with as many elven-blooded as possible for reasons Jassyn couldn't fathom.

The thought disgusted him—Elashor using the mixed-race elves as if they were his personal breeding stock. He suspected there was more to the situation than he was aware of.

"This is my only line in the human realms," Elashor said with a pointed look as sharp as the sword at his side. "You might not be informed, as this is your first visit, but humans aren't as accepting of our ways. Queen Arianna is unaware of my offspring in Alari." The general's eyes narrowed. "I plan on keeping it that way."

Shaking his head, Jassyn glanced away. If given a choice, he wouldn't be inclined, like Elashor, to scatter his progeny over the realm as if sowing seeds to the wind. No, this was far from any life he wanted.

"Power has been shifting in the courts of late, Jassyn," Elashor said.

"I'd hate for you to be on the wrong side of it." The general strode ahead to the edge of the Portal Platform.

Jassyn heard the unspoken threat, but his interests didn't lie in playing politics, even though the council controlled every facet of his life. They made his purpose in the elven realm quite clear.

The pure-blooded arch elves retained the most power and influence, since they had the most magical abilities at their disposal. But they wouldn't rule forever. Not if the pure-bloods spiraled toward extinction, as they had been for the previous two hundred years. Elves lived multiple human life spans, but they didn't live indefinitely. Some believed they used to, before the fall of their Aelfyn ancestors, but immortality was a dream of the ancient past.

From his towering vantage point, Jassyn watched Elashor spin a portal. One step through the gateway would save them three weeks on the road. Of course, their delegation brought along packhorses, providing the illusion they had traveled overland from Alari. The elves didn't lower themselves to ride the beasts, as the humans did; only a select few rangers even flew on the dracovae. *Appearances need to be kept. The elves wouldn't want their human chattel to startle by revealing their magic.*

Jassyn waited his turn to travel through the gateway. He didn't possess the portaling ability, so he would be stranded in the southern realm until the general deemed his return fitting.

Shoulders slumped, Jassyn approached the looming portal. With a defeated sigh, he stepped through.

CHAPTER 2

JASSYN

A single step spirited Jassyn from Kyansari to the grassy countryside of Allaenar. To the west, rolling hills rippled out in waves from stony mountain ranges. The highlands contained extensive networks of mines yielding various types of ore.

The metals were the southern realm's most prominent export. Each of the human realms channeled specific goods to Alari, unburdening the elves of having to procure resources themselves.

Jassyn scanned the horizon, the air hazy with heat and humidity. He squinted in the blinding sunlight, momentarily stunned by the striking turquoise waters glittering in the distance. Having spent his entire life landlocked in the elven realm, he'd never laid eyes on an ocean before.

A gray stone castle perched on a cliff overlooking the sea. Vaelyn, Allaenar's capital, surrounded by a village. *Stars only know how many years I'll live there.*

"Like Alari's borders, we have this designated portaling area shielded with deterring wards," Elashor explained, slipping golden rings onto his fingers. "So we need not worry about wandering humans. I imagine the peasants will greet us in the village before we reach the castle. We'll meet privately with their half-breed queen when we arrive."

Jassyn gave a curt acknowledging nod, unsurprised by the general's disrespect toward the monarch.

He loosened the laces on his tailored tunic, attempting to unearth some relief from the sultry air smothering him. *How is it this hot with winter approaching?* It was ludicrous the soldiers wore steel armor in such oppressive humidity.

Or at all. Jassyn had heard the humans were thoroughly cowed and intimidating displays seemed unnecessary. In fact, throughout their occupation on the mortal shores, the elves had never needed to subdue something as minor as a riot.

"You received your instructions from King Galaeryn?" Elashor asked, angling them toward Vaeyln's castle. Small clouds of dust puffed under Jassyn's boots as they traveled down a worn dirt pathway.

"Do you mean his coercion?" Jassyn fired back, his mouth working before his mind. He wiped the beading sweat from his brow, straining to reel in his agitated nerves. It wasn't like him to react so rashly.

"The king requires those spending time among humans to be compelled by his will," Elashor chided. "We can't allow elven secrets to reach human ears. We've kept them sheltered for centuries for good reason."

Jassyn had been unaware King Galaeryn was capable of such telepathic power. The king's coercion was presumably a type of magic only he could manipulate due to the magnitude of Essence required to influence another being. No other elf came close to possessing the same strength in power.

It's unnatural, but that's why he's the king.

Even in the searing heat, Jassyn suppressed a shiver skating up his spine, unnerved by the monarch wielding so much control over another. While forming a telepathic link and channeling Essence, the king constrained Jassyn completely to his will.

This binding rendered Jassyn unable to divulge information. King Galaeryn's limitations pertained to the secrets the elves concealed from the humans. Most notably, knowledge of their magic.

Jassyn's knees locked midstride as he remembered the eerie power winding around his mind like a noose. *Can the king bend others to his will beyond forcing their silence?*

"How do I instruct your daughter accurately with the restrictions he placed on me?" Jassyn asked, shaking the unease out of his shoulders.

"You'll figure it out." Elashor shrugged like the thought never crossed his mind. "Relax, don't take your role here too seriously. And remember, it's up to you when you return to Centarya."

The general lengthened his pace to stroll ahead with members of his personal guard. His snowy plated armor clinked with each step as if reminding everyone of his importance.

Elashor added over his shoulder, "I'm confident Serenna will be all too willing to tumble in the sheets if you show her any interest. That is, if you can bring yourself to set aside tutoring and accomplish something *important*, you'll be back at the academy in no time."

With an irritated scoff, Jassyn dismissed the notion, shoving errant curls out of his eyes. The thought of emulating the general's behavior was the last thing on his mind. Even if it meant remaining tethered in the human realm for the foreseeable future without his magic.

He imagined Elashor would eventually bring the princess to Kyansari. *Why else would he concoct this whole tutoring charade?*

Without the coupling contract's demands looming overhead, perhaps he could find some sense of purpose in preparing Serenna for life in Alari. Like him, she was also of mixed descent, a disadvantage in the elven courts.

Jassyn remained silent for the rest of the journey, taking in the landscape. The delegation eventually approached the sprawling human village on the outskirts of the castle walls.

The local peasants appeared to reside in slumping thatched-roofed hovels. Their homes weren't so different in structure from the jumbled stacks of firewood leaning against their cottages. Disbelief had Jassyn's eyes popping.

Even the stabled dracovae live better than this.

Why hadn't the elves taught humans how to construct tiled roofs or build their dwellings from stone? It wouldn't have taken any effort to marginally improve their living conditions, judging from their ramshackle houses.

The party entered the outskirts of the village. A dirty-faced woman in a tattered linen dress knuckled the small of her back after stooping to draw a bucket out of a well. *Stars, do they not have running water?*

Jassyn tugged his boots out of the suctioning mud, cringing at the squelch. His nose wrinkled. From the persisting stench of waste, it appeared they didn't have sewer systems either.

By the time they reached the first dwellings on the puddled path meandering through the town's center, the entire village had assembled to welcome the delegation. Compared to the elves, the crowd was an unexpected sea of diversity, cheering and tossing flowers, gazing upon them with haggard faces but reverent eyes.

Do the peasants not realize they toil their whole lives so the elves don't have to?

By the time the fanatical greeting ushered them into the castle walls, Jassyn could only stare ahead, bile creeping up the back of his throat. His breath came shallow as he swallowed disbelief that the humans lived in such squalor. He had heard stories from his peers at the academy, but seeing it for himself chilled his blood. The poverty was a sickening contrast to the bottomless riches siphoned by Alari.

Small ponds dotted the castle's entrance, partially hidden by reedy grasses and dainty fronds. Jassyn supposed they were artfully arranged. White paving stones formed paths through the sand, shaded by thin branches of towering palm trees.

Portions of the elven delegation split away to greet Vaelyn's aristocrats in the courtyard. The human servants busied themselves with familiar tasks: stabling the horses, delivering the elves' gifts to the court members, and preparing their rooms.

It was obvious the silk-attired nobles lived in far more comfortable conditions behind their stone walls. Shining ringlets coiled around the women's heads, pinned back with decorative clips studded with pearls. Their golden jewelry glittered in the sun.

Jassyn determined the nobles were elven-blooded, as indicated by their pointed ears. The elves had been diligent in only interbreeding with influential members of human society this past century, ensuring the elven-blooded ruled over the peasants.

Elashor spared no time before ushering Jassyn into the keep. They weaved around the stony but surprisingly airy and bright interior of the castle. Two guards in leather armor permitted their entrance to the queen's throne room with a salute. The general afforded them no more attention than the rugs on the floor.

The receiving hall was modest but elegant, decorated with sheer curtains undulating in the breeze curling through the open windows. Sunlight streamed in, accenting the monarch's bronze features. Alone in the chamber, Queen Arianna sat poised on her throne, ready to receive them.

With her red silk dress and straight-backed posture, the queen exuded a regal presence. Appearing of equal age with him, similar to humans in their late twenties, Jassyn assumed she was also decades older.

Of course, every piece of her jewelry was solid gold. The elves had conditioned the elven-blooded outside Alari to wear the metal to tether their magic well before they would have manifested any abilities. Even their infants wore golden studs pierced into their ears.

What would happen if these elven-blooded discovered their powers?

Queen Arianna and Elashor nodded to each other cordially. Jassyn bowed in elven fashion, unfamiliar with human customs. He glanced toward Elashor, waiting for an introduction.

"I'd like to present Tutor Jassyn, one of our scholars in Alari." Elashor extended a hand to him as if offering a delicacy on a platter. "This court visit is a perfect opportunity to discuss Serenna's future. It's time we expand her education beyond the human basics of reading and writing. I can think of no better person for the job."

The queen inclined her head. "I can agree with that. Serenna would benefit from more structured duties to keep herself busy." Arianna's dark eyes evaluated Jassyn. "You're a half-breed as well, are you not?" Her attention lingered on his pointed ears.

"Yes, Your Highness," Jassyn said, heart sinking like a pebble skipped into a pond. He assumed those in the human realms didn't realize the term was demeaning. Perhaps he could reduce the use of the word in Vaelyn with time. "I was among the first generation of elven-blooded born in Alari."

"We have a similar ancestry, then," the queen commented, a small smile forming. "I am among the first generation as well, albeit from the mortal realms. Tell me, what manner of research is your specialty?"

Jassyn dragged his fingers through his curls, uncomfortable with lying. "I specialize in medicinal plants, but I am a student of all subjects." At least, it was as honest of an answer he could provide, given the king's coercion prevented him from sharing details about magic.

Jassyn darted his gaze toward Elashor, and with a little rebellious thrill, he added, "It would be my honor to tutor your children, or *any* children, who wish to further their education."

Perhaps a less intimate setting with more pupils would establish a clear boundary between him and the princess.

Elashor took a daring step closer to the throne, cutting off any opportunity for Queen Arianna's reply. It was obvious the general regarded his position as more significant than this elven-blooded monarch.

"My intention was for Jassyn to be Serenna's *personal* tutor. I will take her to the Kyansari courts once our son secures your line's succession with his future offspring—which should be within the coming months."

The queen allowed her disapproving silence to saturate the hall while she considered Elashor with an unreadable gaze. "We have not discussed this path for our daughter. It was my intent to keep Serenna by my side as a lady of the Vaelyn court now that she has come of age."

"My queen, dear Arianna," Elashor said with his teeth bared in a semblance of a toothy smile that made something at the back of Jassyn's neck crawl. "Those in Alari would covet Serenna's impressive bloodline. She would provide exceptional heirs to either the elves or the half-breeds in our courts. Her duty is with her people."

The implications weren't lost on Jassyn. He could only assume what favors the general would reap if he offered yet another direct tie to his bloodline through his offspring. *And I doubt the queen is aware he brought me with intentions other than tutoring.*

"Serenna's people are *here*," Queen Arianna challenged. Her fierce eyes landed on Jassyn and the ridge between her brows softened. "Forgive me, Tutor Jassyn. Elashor and I will discuss these matters *privately*. I welcome you to my court. We will prepare quarters and offices for you, whatever you require."

Queen Arianna beckoned to a guard and relayed instructions to retrieve Serenna's attendant.

"Serenna has been…difficult lately," the queen admitted, smoothing the silk of her dress. "It's the age, I fear, where she believes she knows better than her mother. Having a mentor will do her good."

The queen addressed a blonde elven-blooded woman sweeping into the throne room, spreading her airy skirts in a curtsy. "Velinya, this is Tutor Jassyn. He is joining our court. Please introduce him to Serenna. Inform her that her father has arrived. Report to the chambermaids after to coordinate his living arrangements."

Jassyn bowed his farewell. He glimpsed Elashor distractedly surveying the young woman with an avaricious gleam in his eye. Burying his revulsion, Jassyn trailed Velinya out of the chambers.

The throne room opened to a hallway lined with open windows, permitting the sea breeze. Jassyn marveled at the unlit torches affixed to the walls, realizing the humans must use fire as a primitive light source since they didn't have illumination at their disposal.

Life in this castle would be quite an adjustment from the luxuries he was accustomed to—especially considering his origins from Kyansari's palace. *I'm sure Vesryn would be delighted by my discomfort here.* Navigating unpleasant thoughts away from what the absence of running water meant, Jassyn riveted his attention instead to the glimpses of the ocean through the gaps in the stone.

As they walked down the corridor, Velinya periodically tilted her head to stare up at him. Her gaze didn't make him uncomfortable. Jassyn had become desensitized to curious looks, considering he had what the prince claimed was a "wraithlike" height. At least she didn't feel the need to amuse herself by skimming her fingertips across his skin like the nobles in Alari. The contrast in Vaelyn slackened the constriction in his chest.

When Jassyn glanced in Velinya's direction, her eyes, hazel flecked with color like her golden earrings, danced when she said, "We don't entertain many visitors from Alari for an extended time. I trust you won't find our hospitality lacking." She provided him with a smile not quite as shy as he expected until he broke their gaze. "If you do, it'll be my *pleasure* to see that all of your needs are met during your stay here."

Jassyn suppressed a defeated groan. Redirecting her, he responded with something as bland as he could think of: "I know it will be pleasure enough to tutor the princess."

Velinya tucked her curls behind an ear, her fingers trailing down from the pointed peak to her neck. "I'm sure she'll be eager to meet you. The princess is at the beach. This way."

Velinya hurried off, tossing him another demure smile over her shoulder. She led the way down a winding stone staircase, out of a tower, and down the cliff. When the grassy lawn morphed into sandy dunes, she kicked off her sandals.

Jassyn frowned at the peculiar behavior but didn't see the harm in imitating her, slipping out of his traveling boots and socks. The novel sensation of the coarse grit under his toes only reminded him how far away he was from everything familiar. He gawked at the unending expanse of crystal water.

Jassyn's eyes found the princess sitting on a rocky pier, dangling her feet in the gentle waves. Hesitation to follow Velinya had his feet sinking in the sand before he trudged toward the white shores, escorted by cries of gulls circling above.

Velinya introduced him to the royal guards. She then abandoned all protocol and cupped her hands over her mouth, calling and waving frantically when Serenna looked their way.

The princess rose and glided toward them. Her flowing amethyst dress billowed around her legs like the crest of the waves rolling against the shore. Velinya relayed the news of Jassyn's and Elashor's arrival in a flurry of breathless words.

Serenna regarded him with clear sapphire eyes—Vallende eyes that made him want to avert his gaze. The princess shared more characteristics with her mother than she did with her sire. Despite her human influences, Jassyn imagined any elf in the courts would appreciate her features. *Since physicalities seemingly have nearly the same importance as bloodlines.*

He didn't bother spending the energy dwelling on preferences, not having the option. However, he reached the conclusion that basing someone's value on their bloodlines or superficial attributes, such as appearances or gender, was preposterous.

"Your tattoo is beautiful," the princess said, her attention fixed above his eyes. "Is the flower a trillium? Do all elves have such markings?"

The wind flipped Jassyn's hair, his forehead burning like a brand. He barely stopped himself from unleashing a barbed remark as he rearranged his curls. The breeze made concealing the tattoo pointless. *She's innocent,* he reminded himself. *Her question isn't cruel.*

"It's…personal," he managed to say while determining the best way to defend himself in this new situation.

His short answer didn't deter her. She gripped her golden necklace while studying him. "You're to be my tutor? To prepare me for Kyansari's courts?"

"I am at your disposal, Princess." Jassyn bowed in elven fashion with a hand over his heart.

Serenna's eyes lit up like the sun dancing across the waves. She shared a look with Velinya, giving her attendant an unrestrained grin, before fastening her gaze back to him.

"When do we start? Will you be escorting me to the capital? How long until we leave? I just turned twenty-five, so I'm considered of courting age in Alari as a half-breed, right?"

Jassyn blinked, momentarily stunned, while he processed the sudden burst of rapid questions. He was familiar with the elves keeping their emotions obscured as if it took them significant effort to bring passions to the surface. He had heard humans were more free with their feelings.

Serenna's eyes sparkled with curious wonder at every question he answered. She didn't know how ruthless the elves could be. And the king's will prevented him from divulging the secret truths of his realm.

A surge of loathing had Jassyn detesting Elashor even more for forcing him into this situation. Once in Alari, he knew the general would manipulate the princess into bearing offspring from those of his choosing. *If he ever relinquishes the idea of having it be my duty.*

Judging from Serenna's expectant, radiant face, Jassyn already knew he would have to break her heart.

CHAPTER 3

SERENNA

King Galaeryn is searching for a suitable match for the prince, Serenna eagerly thought while her chin slipped into her palm.

Upon hearing the rumors gathered by Velinya a few weeks prior, Serenna could think of nothing else. *And he's choosing a half-breed consort to ensure the Falkyn line endures. I'm a princess, surely I would be an ideal candidate. Perhaps I'll make Prince Vesryn's acquaintance soon since Father is taking me to the capital.*

Although infrequent, her father made appearances at her mother's court to celebrate special events. The recent birth of her nephew, Elashor's first grandchild, prompted a visit. The southern realm expected the general's delegation to arrive any day now.

With her nephew having guaranteed the succession of her brother's line to Vaelyn's throne, Elashor intended to present her to the Kyansari nobles. Serenna's heart rate doubled in time, fantasizing about her introduction to the elven prince.

She imagined the prince to be regal, dressed in luxurious silks and garnished with dazzling gems. He would have the fine manners of a courtier, bowing and gracing her waiting hand with a soft kiss of his lips. Would he be as tall as Jassyn, but strong like her father? Or perhaps—

The sudden snap of Jassyn's fingers in Serenna's face had her blinking the glaze out of her eyes, wrenching her awareness back to his office.

"What?" she snapped, straightening at her desk, irritated that he'd jarred her out of a daydream.

"Oh, the princess has graced us with her presence." Jassyn's mouth thinned in annoyance. "Did you have a pleasant visit among the stars?"

Serenna scowled at her tutor, who hovered like a persistent cloud. *Fantasies about the eligible elven prince are more interesting than history lessons.*

Despite originating from Alari, Jassyn adopted the fashion of the men in her mother's court. The nobles wore airy cotton trousers gathered around the ankles to help offset the sweltering days. A soft breeze ushered in by the windows tugged at the open laces of his azure tunic.

Serenna glanced at her notes. "You were speaking about the Aelfyns' arrival?"

"Yes," Jassyn clipped, striding back to the writing board. He clasped his hands behind his lanky form. His foot tapped expectantly. "And?"

After spending the previous six months in private lessons, she knew all too well that Jassyn would require an answer.

"The Aelfyn arrived on our shores over a thousand years ago," Serenna recited, already slouching back into her seat with boredom. "The humans welcomed and worshiped their race. In turn, the Aelfyn shared their wisdom and knowledge with the mortals of the past."

Sunlight streaming in through the open windows illuminated Jassyn's ebony curls to a midnight blue, his hair reflecting the ocean outside. His office contained traces of his elven heritage. Various tomes, scrolls, vials of potions, tapestries, and—of course—plants decorated the meticulously organized space. He was nothing if not a perfectionist.

"What happened in the centuries following the Aelfyns' arrival?" Jassyn asked, his spine as straight as an arrow. Nearly two heads taller than her, he had to duck through most of the castle's doorways.

Serenna twirled a feather-plumed quill in her fingers. "The Aelfyn guided the primitive human race toward civilization and established the four mortal realms that exist today."

It was common knowledge humans owed more to the ancient Aelfyn than could ever be repaid. All humans proudly paid homage to the elven realm, Alari. Without the elves, the humans would likely still be wandering the wilderness, unenlightened.

Jassyn nodded and strayed to an open window, peering out toward the sea. "The Aelfyn arrived significantly more advanced than the native inhabitants." Resting an arm on the windowsill, he traced the raised patterns on the stone ledge. "They established farming and agriculture, helped construct the mortal capitals, and created trade routes leading to Alari, cleverly positioned in the center crossroads of the four mortal lands."

"Why do we refer to the Aelfyns' descendants as 'elves' now?" Serenna asked.

As Jassyn faced her, an array of lights scattered off the gold-plated cuffs ornamenting the tips of his ears.

Sometimes, Serenna sensed a silent melancholy shadowing him. With how reserved he was, she suspected there was something more to him than he allowed everyone to see. *Maybe he's just homesick and feels out of place around us.*

"As we know it, the Aelfyns' homeland is across the Cerulean Sea," Jassyn said. "A fleet of their ships wrecked off of Halaema's coast, stranding a portion of their population on this side of the world permanently." Jassyn returned to his desk and fiddled with the leaves on one of the many plants arranged in his office.

"We call their living descendants 'elves,' as the passage of time has simplified the term. We have no information as to what happened to the rest of the Aelfyn separated from us by the ocean."

Serenna didn't dwell on the possibilities of what could exist on the other side of the world. Instead, she eyed the waxy-leafed plant warily, recalling the mortification of learning which ailment *that* one cured when crushed and infused into a tincture. Jassyn brought a variety of healing herbs from the elven realm and used those plants to concoct potions to treat minor nuisances like cuts, bruises, headaches, and upset stomachs.

Jassyn noticed her attention on the leaf. His mouth quirked into a smug expression, likely remembering the sparked memory.

As much as Serenna appreciated his gesture after the fact, a sour taste of wine still crept into her throat. She had lost interest in the finer elven vintages after that incident. Memories dredged back into her mind from the Winter Lunar Solstice festival, a celebration held a few weeks after Jassyn's arrival.

Disconnected flashes of inebriation filtered through her thoughts, but she *clearly* recalled Jassyn ushering her into his office under the guise that he possessed a remarkable vintage from Alari.

He then presented her with a vial of an unnamed liquid, the one crafted from *that* plant. As soon as the vile potion settled in her gut, Serenna promptly ran—well, stumbled—to the window and vomited all the wine she had consumed that evening.

Her initial reaction was an eruption of outrage, but she quickly recognized Jassyn's guile was a favor, and she registered the deceptive act as overprotection.

Without his intervention, Serenna could only imagine how she would have embarrassed herself with her foolish consumption of drink. Something between them shifted that night, and she anchored her trust in him.

Serenna trailed her fingers over the grainy wood of her desk, unable to stay focused on Aelfyn history with her father's impending arrival at the forefront of her mind.

"Do you think your council will allow me to wed a pure-blooded elf?" she casually asked, still preoccupied with what her father's visit meant for her future. She would be one of the few inhabitants of the human lands who earned the privilege of dwelling within the borders of Alari.

"I see we're not going to make any progress with your history lesson today." Jassyn sighed, flicking the curls out of his face. "I can't speak for how the council may rule, but I'd *like* to believe your sire has suitable males selected for a pairing."

Jassyn's eyes darted around the room, avoiding hers. "We've discussed this before—*marriage* between mortal men and women is a human construct. Many elves, though not all, aren't so inclined to form"—he twisted a wrist in the air as if he could corral the words—"*permanent* commitments. The royals wed their lines together for a show of solidarity to tie bloodlines, but it's not a common practice."

Serenna shrugged, not overly concerned by their cultures' differences. She was unsure where she would fit in among the elves, but as the superior race, they were obviously more civilized in their ways. She was keen to embrace their customs and shed her human-influenced inclinations acquired from living her entire life smothered in her mother's castle.

In fact, her parents weren't *married*, so perhaps she was romanticizing the mortal practice. If her options were an arranged marriage in the human realm or a loose commitment in Alari, she would rather accept whatever agreement the elves contrived so long as it meant leaving Vaelyn.

"Do you think my sullied blood will make me less desirable?" Serenna asked, lifting a strand of her mahogany hair, grimacing at the human-colored hue.

"Sullied?" Jassyn questioned, disapproval dripping from the acid in his words. "There's nothing *sullied* by having human blood in your veins."

His tone made Serenna hesitate. "I...I don't want to be at a disadvantage in Kyansari."

What if no elves desire me because I was raised like a human? Would they return me to the mortal realms?

Serenna's only redeeming quality was her potential to increase the elven population. Otherwise, they wouldn't permit someone of lesser upbringing in their courts.

The rigid lines in Jassyn's features softened, but he didn't offer any reassurances to quell her unease. He circled behind his desk and leaned forward, gripping the back of his chair. Oddly enough, this stiff-backed stance was notably more relaxed than when their lessons had started. *At least he's not standing as stoically as a sentinel anymore.*

Serenna probed further to settle her mind. "Has your academy's research made any progress in discovering the cause of the elves' sterility?" Infertility had afflicted the elves for nearly two hundred years. During the last century, they interbred with humans in an effort to save their dying race.

"Not yet." Jassyn retrieved a paper displaced by the breeze fluttering around the room. Groups of fluffy clouds gathered on the horizon, likely accumulating for an evening spring storm.

Nearly ninety years ago, an elven male selected Serenna's grandmother, a human queen, to pair with. The arrangement wasn't a *marriage* by any means. Instead, it was an honored and prestigious coupling intertwining their races with successive offspring. *I'll be the first of my line to live in Alari.*

As Serenna understood it, the elves didn't breed indiscriminately with humans like domesticated animals rutting around in the pastures. They curated couplings based on noble blood. Being chosen to couple with an elf was one of the highest honors *any* human could hope for. In fact, most accepted the proposal graciously, seeing it as an opportunity to aid the elven race. *Now they have half-breeds to choose from so they don't have to mingle with the humans anymore.*

Attempting to pry something else out of Jassyn, Serenna asked, "Do you think a pure-blooded elf will be interested in me?"

Jassyn's brows rose as he weighted the papers on his desk with a heavy tome. "Is that what you want? You do know pure-bloods are going to be over two hundred years old, right?"

"So? I thought pure-bloods took a century to mature anyway. *And*, like my mother, you're in your eighties, and you look no older than me."

Jassyn frowned. "That doesn't mean you'll have common ground with someone *centuries* older than you, no matter if they appear your age."

"*We* seem to get along just fine," Serenna said, crossing her arms stubbornly.

She thought her relationship with Jassyn was slowly evolving beyond this whole mentor-student division he was determined to keep them partitioned in. Over the previous six months, she'd worn him down with the persistence of water eroding stone with her questions about his life in the elven realm. Jassyn *finally* began to relent and converse with her beyond the content of their lessons.

If anyone asked, Serenna would deny having any interest in him. Her stomach twisted with embarrassment that he didn't return the same feelings. Jassyn was always polite, but warded off her advances.

Multiple times.

He had proper mannerisms, as if he was raised in court, and it was difficult not to be drawn in by his gentle personality. With his soft raven curls and kind amber eyes, Serenna wasn't the only person in the castle who thought he was definitely the most handsome half-breed to grace their halls.

Serenna supposed her infatuation stemmed from Jassyn's foreignness, inspired by her longing to gain a deeper connection to her elven heritage. She knew her tutor wouldn't always be there to instruct her when her father relocated her to Kyansari, but she at least wanted to develop a friendship with him, even if he desired nothing *romantic*.

Jassyn tossed his hands in defeat. "We've deviated enough from today's lesson."

Serenna chided herself for losing what progress she'd made involving him in conversation beyond their lectures. Driving a hand through his curls, like he could reassert his usual seriousness with the force of the motion, Jassyn readied another question.

Before he could voice it, a knock sounded at the door and Velinya entered the room.

Velinya originated from a line of the queen's most trusted advisors. Her duties included arranging Serenna's schedule and running errands. Unofficially, Serenna tasked her with gathering gossip. Even though Velinya deferred to her, both women had become close growing up together in court.

"I apologize for the interruption, Princess," Velinya said, curtsying to her before she turned to Jassyn. "Tutor Jassyn, a matter requires your immediate attention. If you'll follow me?"

Serenna perked up. "What is it?"

Velinya winced, drawing her teeth over her lower lip. "I apologize, Princess, but I cannot say. This is for Tutor Jassyn alone."

"He's *my* tutor," Serenna protested, a spark of possessiveness flaring. "What could possibly require his attention?"

Velinya hesitated, eyes bouncing between them before she

answered, as if choosing her words carefully. "There is a matter concerning General Elashor's arrival. I'm afraid it cannot wait."

Serenna's gaze flicked to Jassyn, who went rigid. She frowned as his face drained of color, but waved a hand in displeased dismissal, unsure why Jassyn would need to be involved with the incoming delegation. Surely there were others who could handle the details so as to not cut their lesson short. *His time preparing me for life in Alari is more important than that!*

Velinya led Jassyn to the door and added, "Queen Arianna will see petitioners within the half hour. She sends a reminder that your attendance is required."

Serenna groaned, stretching her arms over her head, gold bracelets jingling. "That's today? I swear we just had a session." She tucked a strand of breeze-blown hair behind her pointed ears.

"Yes, my lady," Velinya answered noncommittally, hurrying out of the office.

"We can continue our lecture tomorrow," Jassyn said. He distractedly blinked before rubbing the trillium tattoo on his forehead, treading out the door.

"As you wish," Serenna said to his back, annoyance rising like a jagged peak from the exclusion. *What good is having a title if I'm not even aware of what goes on in the castle?*

She glanced at the mechanical elven timepiece hanging on the wall. Muttering irritably under her breath, she unfolded herself from the chair to attend her mother's court.

CHAPTER 4

JASSYN

With a fortifying breath, Jassyn steadied himself. His legs threatened to quake as he followed Velinya into Elashor's guest suite. The general's arrival was earlier than the court anticipated.

With a flush to her cheeks, Velinya curtsied. Jassyn bowed in human fashion, cognizant of how human customs grated on the male.

Jassyn's nerves started humming upon noticing Elashor wore no gold. *He's untethered. Has something changed?*

Elashor's eyes grazed the tattoo on his forehead as if purposefully bringing Jassyn's attention to the marking, reminding him of his servitude and inferiority. The general didn't meet his eyes, not bothering to give Jassyn his full attention while he continued sorting through parchments.

Elashor's eyes inevitably slid to Velinya. Lingering indecently.

I see some things don't change, Jassyn peevishly thought. The male had no shame, unhindered by any sense of a moral conscience.

Jassyn tried to see a glimmer of good in everyone, but Elashor consistently fell short. From the condescending way he spoke to the arrogant smirk to the way he took perverted amusement toying with Jassyn and other elven-blooded, the general appalled him.

Velinya beamed when Elashor gave her a nod. "Inform Queen

Arianna I will be at her disposal this evening," he said. "You may leave us."

The door clicking shut sent Jassyn's heart hammering. Unease scurried under his skin at the sudden vulnerability. He hadn't felt this dismantled and exposed while in Vaelyn.

Why should his indifference intimidate me? Jassyn knew his sole purpose revolved around waiting for others to have a use for him. The general was the one who'd summoned him, but now forced him to wait until he deemed Jassyn *worthy* of his time.

The lack of additional seating in the room didn't surprise him. Elashor did nothing without intention, and this meeting already had the air of an interrogation, questioning Jassyn's *value*.

Apprehension vibrated through his bones. *I doubt this will be pleasant.* Relaxing his posture, Jassyn rested a hand on a hip and left the other loose at his side.

"We have much to discuss and limited time to finalize preparations," Elashor finally said, lifting his eyes.

The general's head tilted in a predatory fashion, his attention focused on Jassyn—a cat amusing itself with a broken-winged bird trapped in its claws. "Have you bedded Serenna yet?"

While expected, the question still fractured Jassyn's composure. He unconsciously stiffened when a breath locked in his chest. His crafted illusion of relaxed confidence fragmented, chipping his spine. Drawing in on himself, Jassyn folded his arms around his middle defensively.

Jassyn's reply was toneless. "No."

This was the same conversation they'd had a few months prior when Elashor had previously visited. The stars-cursed menace knew how to humiliate him. The general had no reservations about twisting the knife deeper into Jassyn's gut. He failed to dodge the jab of Elashor's sharpened gaze while his mind replayed the previous bombardment of questions.

Why don't you have any interest in bedding Serenna? Is she not to your liking? Would you prefer to entertain my son instead? Your handlers are missing you during your assignment. My mother is looking forward to your visit upon your return and has quite the event planned in your honor. Would you—

Jassyn squashed the angry swarm of questions stinging his mind.

The past barreled over him, reawakening memories he suppressed of those mandatory couplings during his required time in Kyansari. The wake left Jassyn reeling, anxiety battering against his chest.

It had been six months since he was required to perform his *duty* to the realm. He didn't realize how much he took the reprieve for granted. Unable to access his Essence while tethered was a small price to pay for the lull in fulfilling his contracts—despite feeling like he was wasting his time not contributing to the research at Centarya.

Elashor steepled his fingers under his chin, leaning forward to study him.

Shifting his weight, Jassyn remained silent, knowing he was toeing the line of disrespect. But how could he not? Chilled by dread, he clenched his jaw to prevent himself from trembling.

Jassyn focused his attention above Elashor, studying the approaching clouds through the window in the distance, not willing to meet the general's penetrating stare. The freedom of the gulls gliding above the waters had him enviously wishing for wings.

Elashor chuckled to himself. "I know you are...resistant to your duties coupling with your assigned females." Jassyn flinched, and a cutting smile knifed its way over Elashor's face. "One might think you're as modest as the humans."

Oh yes, I'm well aware of my flaws.

"I have a proposal for you that would free you from these...*responsibilities*," Elashor said, flicking his wrist.

Considering he would sacrifice a limb—and more—to have his contracts dissolved, Jassyn still had no interest in finding out what the general had to offer.

Gathering what evaporating respect he could manage, Jassyn gritted out, "The High Council dictated my duties are to tutor your daughter...unless those requirements have changed? Is your council commanding me to couple with her now?"

"No one is *commanding* you to do anything." Elashor's chiseled jaw tightened as Jassyn gathered courage to meet his icy stare. "I have a solution. If you can bring yourself to produce *one* offspring with Serenna, I'll see that the council releases you from your other *obligations*. A complete dissolution of your existing contracts."

Disbelief hollowed out his mind. Jassyn's eyes widened automatically. *He's serious?* Jassyn couldn't imagine what his life would be like without those demands shadowing him.

Could he actually figure out what he wanted to do instead of waiting in perpetual dread for his handlers' summons? Even his research into discovering more about elven sterility revolved around the situation the realm forced on him—fettered him to.

But Jassyn couldn't determine why the general was so obsessed with him and Serenna producing offspring.

It wouldn't be too difficult, though. He had barely kept the eager princess at arm's length ever since she'd shown an interest in him. Serenna had finally relented on that front, but still acted half starved for his attention and approval.

He would only need to let her believe he harbored similar feelings and invite her—

Jassyn halted his sequence of thoughts. His stomach roiled with mortification for even considering Elashor's offer. *Scorching stars, what is wrong with me?*

It was a selfish desire, a fleeting temptation. A wave of distaste rose bitterly in the back of his throat. He wouldn't be able to live with himself if he used Serenna in such a way, dragging her down with him to reproduce for the elves—not even to free himself from the realm's demands. Jassyn wouldn't wish anyone to be shackled to the same fate.

And he didn't want to think about what would happen to the child. Though most of those subject to the coupling contracts were from the first generation of elven-blooded born in Alari, Jassyn's assumptions only led him to believe that Elashor intended to force their offspring into the same breeding situation.

Jassyn refused to play any part in the general's plan. Like a rotten egg exploding, something foul would surely hatch from Elashor's schemes.

Does he truly believe his empty promises will persuade me? There would always be another requirement of him—even if he followed through with the general's wishes.

There was no way Elashor's mother, Lady Farine, would relinquish her spot on Jassyn's contracts and retract her claws now that she had them sunken into his flesh.

"Unless, of course, you enjoy being whored out to those in court," Elashor added with a disinterested shrug as Jassyn's silence stretched between them. "I don't judge. Many of you half-breeds relish the honor."

"I perform my duties as required." Jassyn's stubbornness was his only restraint from imbuing the words with revulsion. "Until the contracts include *servicing* the princess, I must respectfully decline."

Despite his unreadable features, Jassyn sensed Elashor's displeasure cocooning them in silence.

"Very well," the general finally said. "I have other plans for Serenna. However, I would have *appreciated* a guarantee that she can produce offspring. If you change your mind, you have my assurance we will handle it discreetly. Any progeny would be cared for by fosters."

Jassyn stared ahead and fused his teeth, letting obstinance mask the disgust congealing under his skin. Elashor's plan was to barter Serenna's offspring? For what? Court favors? *Doesn't he wield enough power?* But such was the way of greed—it always demanded more.

The unfortunate part of the whole situation was he could see himself *liking* the princess. Not romantically. No, he doubted he would ever be capable of having feelings of love. The realm had ensured he was too broken for that.

Jassyn nearly admired the princess's defiance, despite her attitude's need for tempering. He was attempting to hone her emotional approach in a different direction, away from eruptions of anger. But she never hesitated to question others or assert herself.

I wish I could do the same.

It was unusual for someone to engage with him with no ulterior motives, and Serenna was the first person he'd met who regarded him without judgment—unaware of his contracts or the power behind his family's name.

Of course, the princess's belief concerning elven superiority exasperated him, but that wasn't necessarily her fault. She was raised in such a manner, and didn't know any differently. Unfortunately, she would discover that having mixed blood meant the elves would never regard her as one of their own.

Because of that, every interaction and lesson buried Jassyn in a grave of guilt. Serenna would learn the secrets of the realm when she accompanied Elashor to the capital, but what would she think about him as her mentor for keeping so much concealed? The magic restricting him from informing her of the truths threatened to suffocate him with remorse.

He wanted to tell her, share his knowledge of Essence with her. Instead, he had to drone on about how great the elves were and how the *noble* Aelfyn ancestors colonized human civilization.

He had hoped their lessons would open her eyes to the discrepancies between humans and elves. He wiggled in as much of his disdain as he could, but his efforts were falling on deaf ears.

Jassyn senses blared in alarm, recognizing a vibration of power. His attention soared to the general. Essence swirled around Elashor like a gossamer curtain. Even tethered, Jassyn could see the magic circling and shimmering—he just couldn't access his own.

Panic erupted like a flow of magma in his chest when Elashor rose and rounded the desk, approaching him. Completely defenseless, Jassyn dropped his arms and balled his hands into fists at his side, steeling himself, waiting for the general's move.

Elashor smirked and trailed a finger across his forehead's tattoo. Jassyn inhaled a jagged breath, disoriented like vision blurring under seawater.

The binding coercion unraveled, releasing him from the king's embedded secrecy. Jassyn freed the air locked in his chest as a tightness in his mind relaxed, like threads unwoven from a spool.

"Let's get comfortable," Elashor said, striding to the adjacent sitting room. "We have much to discuss concerning the changes at Centarya."

CHAPTER 5

SERENNA

Lounging on her gilded throne, Serenna's chest heaved with an exaggerated sigh. She *dreaded* attending these weekly petition sessions. Her velvet-lined seat flanked the left side of her mother's elevated position on the dais, where both women listened to the solicitations.

Well, Queen Arianna listened. Serenna traced the decorative whorls winding up her armrest while her thoughts dwelled on how her life would unfold in Kyansari.

She briefly gathered today's docket of petitions contained rather dull content—as expected from the usual insignificant matters the *humans* faced. This session had already resolved several petitioners' requests.

The queen granted approval for the final list of supplies required to repair the road to Alari's borders. She confirmed a proposal for Nydoraen's cloth exporters to outfit their vessels with sails. To begin the construction of a small harbor along their coastline, she procured lumber from Dosythe's mills.

Now, a band of grubby men in earth-stained linens were lamenting over a collapsed mine. The laborers begged for a redistribution of resources and aid for their injured. At least this was the last item for today's session.

Finally.

The only interesting detail of a collapsed mine is that it happens to be a gold mine. Serenna's attention drifted to the rings encircling each of her fingers. Gold wasn't quite her preferred metal to adorn her body, but the elves placed a high value on the material and outfitted themselves with such accessories.

As a noble, it was imperative for the royals to curate appearances to display wealth, so, of course, she wore what they expected.

Her attention now on her jewelry, Serenna absentmindedly raised a hand to trace a plated ear cuff curved sharply to accent her tipped ears. Upon realizing what she was doing, she mindfully halted her finger's journey. *Could there be anything less interesting than listening to these meaningless problems?*

"What would you suggest, Serenna?" Queen Arianna's question rang through the air, yanking Serenna out of her thoughts.

Serenna's eyes snapped toward her mother and then flicked over the cluster of gathered miners. It was typically her brother Saundyl's responsibility to be the one offering *his* suggestions and opinions, but he'd spent time away from his duties these past few weeks to attend to his wife and newborn son. Serenna was here because of her mother's force of will, not of her own accord.

Serenna blinked, oblivious to the finer details of whatever the petitioners droned on about to the queen. Something about hearing "voices in the rocks" before the collapse. As if anyone would destroy their most valuable mine.

Does she actually believe this nonsense? The miner's wits were most likely addled by a pocket of noxious gas while they tunneled like grubs through the earth.

"I trust your wisdom, Queen-Mother." Serenna dipped her head and hoped a show of deference would excuse her from having to pay heed to these trifling matters.

She wanted to separate herself from the mortals, not jump like a toad to solve all of their grumblings. *Why couldn't I have been born in Alari?* Jassyn was proof she would have had an honored place—even as a half-breed.

Worry collided against insecurity inside Serenna's mind that her wasted years under human influence would embarrass her father because she'd never learned the intricacies of elven culture. The council granted her the privilege of living with him in Kyansari, but she feared he would come to realize he'd made a mistake including her in their courts.

Arianna's unamused stare indicated she knew full well Serenna's mind had wandered again.

"It is settled, then," the queen declared after holding Serenna's gaze, ensuring her dissatisfaction was known.

Arianna gracefully turned to face the expectant miners, assuring them that their injured would be cared for. "Redistribute the salvaged resources to the iron mines. They have been long overdue for replenished supplies. I will inquire if General Elashor can spare any of his soldiers to aid in the investigation to determine if an unknown foe indeed caused this collapse."

"Thank you, my queen," the miners said, bowing before they exited the throne room.

As soon as the doors closed behind the petitioners, the queen smacked her palm against her throne's armrest. The *crack* from her hand reverberated around the chambers like a slap of thunder. The remaining guardsman snapped to attention.

"It would do well, daughter," the queen spat, facing Serenna, "if you could at least feign interest in these matters. I include you because you may find yourself in a similar position someday."

Serenna rolled her eyes, dismissing the notion. *Ruling grimy peasants is the last thing I want to do.* "I hardly see the point of participating since father will escort me to Alari in a matter of days."

The queen's dark eyes turned icy, chilling Serenna with her glare. Unfortunately, Serenna had inherited her mother's swift temper, another human shortcoming, and likely the reason they collided as furiously as two warring storm clouds. *If she didn't insist on being so domineering, our relationship wouldn't be so strained.*

"Speaking of your father," the queen said, rising from her throne and smoothing her dress. "He arrived this morning and will join us for supper in the private dining chamber. Be on time," she said over her shoulder, exiting the hall with her silks whispering on the floor behind her.

A surge of eagerness coursed through Serenna, despite a thread of annoyance lacing her anticipation for the evening. Her mother had obviously withheld this news from her.

Rising, Serenna considered seeking her father out beforehand so her mother's presence wouldn't cast a shadow on their reunion.

During Elashor's previous visit to Vaelyn, he was most interested in how her studies with Jassyn were progressing, and Serenna was anxious to prove how much she'd prepared.

Perhaps he'll be interested in discussing the elven suitors he's selected. Serenna glided from the throne room, heart soaring at the prospect.

Two of her personal guards turned from their posts to trail at a respectful distance.

Serenna's escort was another area of contention between her and the queen. Just because a chambermaid walked in on her and a rather enthusiastic half-breed guard in a compromising position, her mother felt the need to replace every younger man around her with those who were nearly withered and gray.

On multiple occasions, Serenna had considered bedding one of the older men solely out of spite to prove to her mother that she couldn't meddle in every area of her life. *Even the elves consider me an adult, for stars' sake!*

Life in the castle was simply suffocating, but at least the queen permitted Jassyn's presence. Not that her tutor would ever participate in any *improper* activities. Serenna had a difficult time simply conversing with him beyond their lessons.

Velinya accompanied her in the breezeway and matched her stride. Serenna doused the usual sparks of envy when she evaluated her friend's appearance, most notably Velinya's honey-colored elven hair.

It wasn't like Serenna always craved what others possessed, but it would have eased her mind if she went to the elven realm looking more the part. Even so, Serenna was certain she would regret having to leave Velinya behind when she departed for Kyansari.

"I had the pleasure of meeting with General Elashor," Velinya chimed, always eager to relay any news. "He made quite a fuss about your nephew. I didn't realize an elf of his station would show such delight—you know how reserved they are." Velinya shot her a knowing smirk. "Well, outside of the bedroom that is."

I wouldn't know, thanks to the queen's diligence in my guard.

But thinking of her newborn nephew spawned a worm of jealousy, burrowing its way through Serenna's thoughts. Of course, visiting his grandson was the first order of business her father attended to. *Is there a reason he hasn't given me the same priority?*

"I should thank Saundyl for reproducing," Serenna said, concealing her disappointment with deflection. "I'll never understand why he stayed in Vaelyn when Father offered him the opportunity to court nobles in Kyansari."

Velinya brushed wind-blown curls out of her face. "It's obvious he's been smitten with your sister-in-law ever since they were children. He had no reason to seek another."

Open windows overlooking the sandy white shores lined every wall in the corridor. The sun's rays fought a losing battle bleeding through the gathering clouds.

Serenna still couldn't believe her brother had chosen *love* instead of pursuing a more well-bred match. His wife hardly had elven blood in her pedigree! Not to mention he'd married, which wasn't aligned with elven customs. *What does our father think about that?*

"At least they've cleared the way for me to leave this dreadful court." Serenna idly twirled a strand of hair. "I'll try to secure you a position once I'm situated in Kyansari. I'm sure there'll be more interesting duties for us than overseeing mining operations."

The women whisked through the hallway, soft slippers padding on the violet rugs carpeting the marbled floors. Serenna loved gazing at the artwork lining the corridor. Oil paintings and woven tapestries depicted the Aelfyns' arrival. Ethereal beings extended their hands to a starry sky as if touching the galaxies themselves. *Or perhaps they're pleading for a deliverance from the mortal shores.*

Serenna imagined the stranded Aelfyn experienced the same sense of displacement she did. They could never return to their homeland across the ocean because of the traveling Maelstrom, a stormy anomaly in the Cerulean Sea, that ensnared and destroyed their vessels. As a broken people, they didn't possess the resources to build new ships or have the knowledge of how to avoid the tempest.

At least hope was on her horizon since she was leaving the mortal realms behind.

But Serenna had no time to contemplate the past with her pressing future. She breezed toward her tower, the generous apartments overlooking the crystal sea. Velinya dwelled in rooms across the hallway.

"Have you visited your nephew recently?" Velinya inquired, still fixated on the subject, apparently.

Serenna sniffed, disinterested in the conversation. "Only when I suspect my mother is close to commenting about my lack of involvement."

"You do know the elves will expect you to pair with a male and produce heirs in Alari, right?"

Serenna knew Velinya found it liberating that the elven race didn't conform to the same rigid constructs as the humans did for coupling. Her friend always made it a point to distinguish that they had the option to choose partners of any gender—even multiple, if they so desired—if the gossip from Alari was to be believed.

"I'll delay that *responsibility* for as long as possible," Serenna said, ignoring the bowing guards stationed outside of her living quarters. "I'd rather enjoy what the elven courts offer and take my time selecting an appropriate match. We'll have centuries to get to childbearing, won't we?"

"I suppose we'll find out," Velinya said, following Serenna into her chambers. "We are among the first few generations of the mixed races. The elves can live for nearly a millennium, so I imagine some portion of that longevity will pass on to us."

A thought drifted into Serenna's mind. "Was my father's early arrival the reason Tutor Jassyn was summoned away?"

"Yes." Velinya eyed her warily as if expecting to be on the receiving end of her ire.

Serenna bracketed her hands on her hips. "And you didn't find it fitting to inform me of his presence?"

Velinya winced and slipped into a formal tone at the chastisement, her words tumbling out. "I apologize about the secrecy, Princess. Queen Arianna forbade your knowledge of his arrival until after you attended the petitioners. She didn't want you"—Velinya looked down as if she found the woven rugs interesting—"distracted."

Serenna scoffed her irritation. "I see."

How long would her mother continue to tangle the strings of her life? The queen didn't even *permit* her awareness of her father's arrival? Serenna clenched her teeth, rankled by the thought. This was another reason to leave Vaelyn. Surely her father wouldn't impose upon her to this great of a degree.

Serenna dispatched Velinya to solicit Jassyn for his expertise, needing his insight to help prepare her for the evening in appropriate elven fashion. She wanted everything to be perfect when she met with her father. In the meantime, Serenna busied herself with dictating preparations to the chambermaids.

Taking a moment to relax and quell the excitement buzzing through her veins, Serenna stepped out onto her balcony. She rested her hands on the parapet's cool stone ledge, gazing at the sea. Scattered light from the setting sun trickled through the cloudy sky, igniting the turquoise waters with a green fire. She closed her eyes as the shift of the breeze stirred to kiss her skin.

The alluring pull of the ocean had always captivated her. There was something primal about the unpredictability of the wind and the crash of waves. The estate's private beaches at the bottom of the cliff were a favored place of her childhood, containing fond memories of swimming in the tide's salty embrace. But once she matured, Serenna realized such reckless activities weren't proper for a princess.

She turned to her sitting room when her chamber doors swung open. The guards in the hallway nodded to Jassyn. He lingered near the entryway, clearly hesitant to enter her rooms, judging from his shifting eyes and stiff stance.

Serenna's maids were bustling about; it wasn't as if anything was *improper* about his presence in her apartments. *It doesn't matter what my mother thinks.*

She accepted that Jassyn didn't want to be romantically involved, but would he ever view her as more than a pupil? *I don't understand how being more than acquaintances clashes with his stringent concerns for etiquette.*

Jassyn was the only gateway in her life to Alari and true knowledge of the elves. He was significantly more educated than anyone else she was *allowed* to be around. He actually knew what living in the elven realm was like.

Does growing up in the human lands make me so glaringly different from him?

Serenna's heart dropped with the weight of concern. Perhaps he didn't want to be associated with her in Alari if her upbringing was an embarrassment.

"I apologize for the delay, Princess," Jassyn said. A muscle strained in his jaw. "Velinya had to extract me from a meeting with your sire."

Serenna crossed her arms, like she could shield herself from the persistent feeling of dismay that her father hadn't sought her out. The birth of his grandson may have prompted his visit, but he was only here to take her with him to Kyansari.

"How has the entire court, aside from *me*, already secured an audience with my father?" she asked.

"Don't worry, Princess." Jassyn clasped his hands behind his back. "He'll have time for you and the queen tonight."

Serenna released an exasperated huff. "Can you help me select attire for the evening? I have a few dresses my father gifted me these past few years, and I need help deciding what would be suitable."

Jassyn thumbed the bottom of his chin, surprisingly providing her with a slight tilting of his lips. "I suppose I do have a weakness for the fashions and the finer things the capital offers."

"Just help me appear like I *belong* in the elven courts," Serenna pleaded, holding herself back from hauling Jassyn along into her dressing room. "I want to prove I can present myself appropriately."

She needed to make a worthy impression and demonstrate to her father that she was prepared for life among the elves. Growing up in the mortal realms presented an obstacle, but she wanted to show she could overcome the shortcomings of her human heritage.

Jassyn gestured for her to lead the way into the dressing room. His attention drifted to her displayed diamonds. Serenna presumed he preferred wearing gilded ornaments, judging from his ear cuffs, rings, and the studs strewn across the borders of his pointed ears. From his collection, he must have been wealthy too, even if he was a scholar.

"Do all elves wear as much jewelry as you?" she inquired.

"Some do."

Serenna tilted her head at him expectantly. To see if he would elaborate, she asked a frivolous question. "Do you have a preferred accessory?"

"I am partial to ear cuffs," Jassyn admitted. Glancing down at his hands, he added, "Rings, not so much."

"Why do you wear so many, then?" Serenna asked.

He tugged at a golden loop in his ear. "Appearances," he muttered.

"Oh. Because the High Council dictates how you should present yourself in your position?" Serenna trailed her fingers along the gems in her display case. "I understand how important impressions are."

Jassyn didn't meet her eyes. "It's…something like that."

They wandered over to the dresses her maids had arranged, where Jassyn, unsurprisingly, selected a modest lavender gown with airy sleeves and recommended which cosmetics would be appropriate.

"You never talk about your life in Kyansari," Serenna commented, settling in a chair so her attendants could pin, braid, and weave her hair around her diadem.

She was hesitant to further pester him with questions. Since Jassyn seemed to be sharing more than usual, she waited to see if giving him the option to speak would prompt more conversation. He didn't rush out of her chambers as she'd expected after helping select her evening attire.

As a foreigner, Serenna imagined Jassyn felt isolated and out of place in Vaelyn. She knew she would be lonely in a strange land, not knowing anybody. *Wouldn't he want someone to talk to?* Engaging with him was her attempt at making his assignment in the human realms more enjoyable. After all, he was taking time away from his important research to tutor her.

And she couldn't help but try to pluck every scrap of elven knowledge out of his head.

Jassyn appeared momentarily lost in thought while gazing out the windows overlooking the sea. "I don't exactly have fond memories aside from my life at Centarya."

Serenna's disbelief unfolded like a moonflower at night. Living in Alari with the elves was her *dream.* Processing Jassyn's admission put her wariness on edge; she was so distracted, she didn't even chastise her attendant for poking her scalp with a pin.

"Why didn't you enjoy your time in the elven courts?" Serenna held her breath, waiting for Jassyn to close himself off.

Instead, his shoulders slumped as if something pressed on him. "I was among the first elven-blooded born in the realm. Life…wasn't easy growing up different. Lesser to the elves."

"Lesser?" Serenna asked, her uncertainty spiraling in a whirlpool of unease.

The thought of the elves treating him in such a manner made her heart twist. *His mixed lineage shouldn't matter—that has nothing to do with who he is.* Surely customs in Alari had changed by now.

Jassyn stared at his hands, spinning a ring around a finger. Serenna didn't think he was going to answer. Stilling her legs so she wasn't twitching in her seat, she kept silent, not wanting to pressure him if he was having a difficult time voicing his thoughts.

"The elves constructed Centarya specifically for the elven-blooded," he finally said. "A place to separate those of mixed descent."

Incredulity had Serenna gaping. The elves were the ones who honored select humans to intertwine their races. It made little sense why they would treat their own offspring differently.

"I don't think any less of you because you're a half-breed. Technically, I am too." Serenna wanted to voice the distinction since the elves' actions obviously bothered him—even if she did have more elf blood than him.

Jassyn sighed. "'Elven-blooded' is the *polite* phrase to use." It wasn't the first time he'd corrected her.

"Half-breed" was a confusing term anyway, since not everyone was necessarily half human and half elf. Serenna herself was three-quarters elf—a fact she was most proud of.

"But I've heard my father—"

Jassyn cut her off. "Your sire isn't the example you should follow."

Serenna leaned back in her chair, stunned by his vehemence. Jassyn swiped curls out of his eyes in an unusual show of frustration before seeming to collect himself with an audible breath.

"I only mean, as a pure-blood," Jassyn said gently, "he isn't as sensitive to those who grew up in a different world."

"I see." Serenna held a hand mirror a maid presented, inspecting her woven hair. "Why do you always refer to him as my 'sire'? Is that the proper phrase among the elves?"

Jassyn rolled his shoulders. "I find 'father' to be the more appropriate expression to use when someone takes an active role in your life."

Serenna didn't believe it was her father's fault he hadn't been a more prominent presence through the years. After all, he was King Galaeryn's *general*, and it was still baffling he even bothered visiting her family.

Jassyn glanced at the darkening sky again. "I think it's past time you're expected at dinner. I'll see you in the morning." He bowed before his long strides carried him out of her chambers.

Serenna bit the inside of her cheek, chewing over their conversation. *Did I say something wrong?* If she couldn't earn Jassyn's approval after months of trying, she didn't have any hope of gaining her father's.

But Jassyn had shared more of his life with her than she expected. Serenna wasn't sure what had prompted the change, but she appreciated the conversation nonetheless. If the elves treated him so poorly in Alari, she could understand why he appeared forlorn and sealed off.

She still didn't believe Alari was as horrible as Jassyn made it seem. Serenna mulled over Jassyn's comments, but the comforting thought of the elves being more accepting filled her with relief. *The elves' attitude must be changing, otherwise they wouldn't permit my presence in their courts.*

She should have remembered that Jassyn preferred the term "elven-blooded." His speech always came across as careful and calculated. Words spouted out of her mouth like a geyser of thoughts before coalescing in her mind.

Such behavior wouldn't do in the elven realm.

Serenna squared her shoulders, rising to change into her gown, determined to prove to Jassyn—and her father—that she could do better.

CHAPTER 6

SERENNA

The queen's guards bowed to Serenna as she swept into the dining chamber. Distant lightning at the edge of the horizon flashed through the windows. Heavy air gusted through the room, carrying the promise of an evening storm. Rushing to close the shutters, the servants flitted around like dragonflies.

Serenna focused her attention on her father, seated beside her mother. The walnut table complemented the wood paneling concealing the stone foundation of the room. Golden candelabras and iron sconces affixed to the walls flickered with dancing flames.

Elashor wore what Serenna assumed was formal elven court attire—a dark swallow-tailed vest covering a white billowy-sleeved undershirt. Draped in her favored crimson silks and golden diadem, the queen conversed with him in what appeared to be an unpleasant conversation, judging from her mother's scowl.

Spine straight, Serenna glided toward the dining table. She could replicate the queen's commanding presence without a second thought. The confidence in her bearing gave her the power to captivate an entire ballroom, lest anyone forget her elevated rank. When she approached, her parents abruptly ceased their discussion.

"Father." Showing the same regard as she would toward her mother in a formal court setting, Serenna greeted him in the elven fashion, with a hand over her heart and dipping her head in reverence. "Your presence honors me." She cringed inwardly at the ceremonial formality and could only hope her desperation for any hint of his approval would go unnoticed.

Her father nodded at her with the shadow of a smile. Like other elves, General Elashor Vallende lacked facial hair framing his heavy jaw and dimpled chin. His golden mane draped past his shoulders, and intricate braids outlined his pointed ears.

Jassyn's instruction for the maids to style her hair in the same manner had Serenna sighing with relief. Besides flaunting her elven ears, she wanted to show she embraced the appropriate fashions.

Elashor's elevated cheekbones drew attention to his sapphire eyes, an elven color she fortunately shared. A thin silver circlet concealed faint lines etching the evidence of age across his forehead. At a century old, pure-blooded elves were considered adults. Once they matured, the rate of their aging decelerated rather dramatically. Five centuries rendered Elashor of age with a forty-year-old human.

Serenna settled into a seat facing her parents. Silver plates, utensils, and crystal goblets decorated the table. Servants fluttered about, filling wine glasses and arranging the dinner courses.

"Leave us," the queen commanded once the staff had organized the meal. Scents of the sea fare, Vaelyn's staple food, wafted up from the steaming dishes. The servants bowed their respects and closed the heavy wooden doors behind them.

A surge of excitement sped through Serenna's veins as if racing the arcing lightning outside. *So, we are going to discuss private matters.*

Though already knowing the answer, Serenna wanted to seize the reins to steer the conversation toward her departure.

Feigning interest, she asked her father, "Have you visited your grandson yet? I do hope Saundyl's family will join us for dinner one of these evenings before we leave."

Queen Arianna shot Serenna a flat look, evidently seeing through her subterfuge. Yes, she felt fondly for her family, but she would rather do, well, anything else than be around a fussy infant.

Elashor nodded. "I am pleased your family's line has ensured a stable reign for Allaenar. It is encouraging we continue to see successful couplings between half-breeds." While he filled a plate with clams, scallops, and mussels, Serenna registered the unusual absence of golden jewelry on his hands. "Hope is blooming in Alari now that we see a future of our race that ensures elven bloodlines."

Shoulders relaxing that he viewed the elven-blooded as part of his homeland, Serenna took a hesitant sip of the red wine while he spoke. The vintage was rather dry, making her mouth pucker. She tried not to gag on the liquid, recalling the last time she'd consumed such drinks.

Elashor focused on selecting a roasted flounder. "With Arianna's line secured, that brings forward another reason for my visit."

With all of her attention on her father, Serenna nearly tipped over her wine in her haste to deposit the glass on the table. The excited smile spreading across her face was impossible to contain. *This is it!* This was the moment she'd spent the past six months fantasizing about ever since he'd suggested she was eligible to court in Alari.

All etiquette evaporating, Serenna's enthusiasm sprang a fountain of questions, engulfed by anticipation. "Do you have news of the potential houses you'll introduce me to? Will we leave at once?"

She scribbled the familiar sketch in her mind. Her father, King Galaeryn's general, a trusted and respected advisor, parading her among rich and powerful elves. And if the latest gossip could be believed, Prince Vesryn. At last, *she* would be the one in control of weaving her destiny. The floodgates now open, Serenna failed to stem the tide of questions streaming out.

"Have you met any of the suitors? Are they pure-bloods? Will you be introducing me to the prince?" She would have continued the barrage, but her father held up a hand, halting her verbal assault.

Though a flush of embarrassment singed the tips of her ears, Serenna couldn't mute one final comment. "It would be an honor to serve the Vallende line. I have been waiting for this opportunity for so long."

Serenna spared a glance at her uncharacteristically quiet mother, who normally dictated the direction of the conversation. The queen disinterestedly prodded the oysters on her plate, seeming to find the food more interesting than sharing in Serenna's excitement.

Doesn't she realize this is the most important moment of my life?

"I'm afraid introducing you to suitors will have to wait," Elashor said.

Serenna's attention flew back to her father, searching his face. Her heart plummeted like a star falling out of the sky. "What…what do you mean?"

Did he already determine I'm not worthy of the elves? I haven't even had a chance to prove myself yet! Serenna blinked back frustrated tears, slumping in her chair.

Her father, seeming far less disappointed, paused from portioning his flounder. "The elves have been addressing a developing threat endangering our existence."

Serenna straightened. *That's hardly any information at all! Isn't infertility the greatest danger to the elves' survival?*

"A threat?" she asked, stabilizing herself by placing her palms on the table. "What threat?"

"We've sheltered those living in the human realms from certain aspects of the elven civilization." Elashor shifted in his seat. His broad frame dwarfed the dining chairs, and the wood creaked in protest. "My people determined some information was better kept concealed in order to safeguard the humans. I'm going to share with you secrets that haven't left Alari's borders. You need to understand the dangers that surround us all."

Forgetting her manners, Serenna gripped her fork like a fishing trident while she processed her father's words. She bristled. *I'm not human. I just have the misfortune of living in a* human *realm.*

But her father thought she was ready to learn elven secrets. Serenna's gaze flicked toward her mother, assuming that's what they were discussing before she arrived. Her fingers relaxed on her silverware, realizing he was sharing information with her. *That's a good sign,* she assured herself.

"Nearly a century ago, we imprisoned a population of dangerous creatures we call the wraith," Elashor said with a grimace. "They attacked Kyansari in a vicious raid and killed Queen Maraelyn and Prince Aesar." He cleared his throat. "And also one of my brothers."

Serenna's fork clattered to the table as her heart launched itself against her chest. *Something can kill the elves?*

"We hoped, and tried, to reach an understanding with those monsters, but they're mindless beasts. We failed to grasp the extent of their corrupt nature." Elashor retrieved his wine goblet, swirling the vintage as he turned pensive. "The details evaded us, but the wraith escaped from their imprisonment nearly twenty years later, brutalizing the capital's citizens while they fled."

An icy fear chilled her marrow. *What kind of monstrous race attacks the elves?* It was inconceivable. Serenna covered her mouth, staring at her father as he continued his story.

"My people were already vulnerable and terrified because of the infertility crisis beginning a century prior. Unwilling to endanger our dwindling population, the council decided not to pursue the escaped wraith. Prince Vesryn has spent nearly every waking moment avenging his twin's death, hunting those monsters, but his efforts haven't been enough." Elashor shook his head. He clicked his tongue before drinking from his glass. "In hindsight, it was a mistake to not trust the humans to lend aid. We kept silent, fearing any intervention would have prompted the wraith to retaliate and target the mortal cities."

Serenna frowned as this new reality crystallized into a nightmare. "But if the wraith escaped over eighty years ago, how does that affect us now?"

But she really wanted to ask, *What does this have to do with me not going to Kyansari?*

"Through the decades, the wraith have made a habit of terrorizing our capital and dragging off its citizens." Elashor set his wine down and returned his attention to the flounder. His knife *clinked* against the plate. "However, their raids have become more frequent in recent years. The creatures are spreading out, increasing in number, and attacking our supply lines to Alari. It's well past time we take the fight to them."

Serenna had no desire to touch the food before her. *How does he even have an appetite?* She imagined her father was simply accustomed to the horrors the elves sheltered the mortals from. A sense of foreboding loomed like the storm whirling toward the castle.

Serenna pondered his words. "I haven't heard of this 'wraith' race before. The mortal realms surround Alari. Wouldn't the humans have seen their armies?" *Jassyn never mentioned these monsters either.*

"The wraith have abilities we can't explain," Elashor said, lifting a shoulder. "They can bend shadows to cloak themselves and disappear. We never know when they're going to appear until it's too late."

"How can they disappear?" The idea was absurd. Surely her father didn't mean the wraith *literally* vanished.

Serenna pursed her lips when Elashor raised a palm, demanding her silence and attention.

"We've bolstered our military training and presence in the capital, but it's nearly impossible to face a foe we can't prepare for. Dosythe reports they've had supplies of lumber stolen. Livestock has disappeared from the farms in Nydoraen. We believe the wraith are also responsible for stealing ore and collapsing mines in this realm. Left unchallenged, it's only a matter of time before those monsters directly target the humans."

"I don't understand why the elves have held back in seeking them out," Serenna said before considering every pure-blood killed was one who would never be replaced. *Their race is in danger of extinction.* "Why haven't your people said anything about the wraith moving within the mortal borders? Can't the humans help?"

Serenna realized her question was absurd. *If those monsters can kill a superior race, what good would mortals be against them?*

"We've begun mobilizing troops to prepare the human populations." Elashor waited for a roll of thunder to finish rumbling. "Thanks to our population of half-breeds born this past century, we have been able to establish a small standing army in Alari. The elven military of pure-bloods has always been minimal because of the peace and stability we've brought to these lands."

Serenna eyed her father's empty wine glass, and, with no servants present, she rose from the table, taking it upon herself to refill the goblet. As an afterthought, she replenished her mother's as well.

"Our deployments will ready the humans to rise to our aid," Elashor said, nodding his thanks.

"We were discussing the logistics when you arrived," the queen said. As if Serenna's presence had interrupted something important.

"So, I'm needed here, then?" Serenna asked, glancing between them. Her heart felt as heavy and hollow as the chalice she placed back on the table. "To help prepare the *humans* to address this conflict?"

Elashor shook his head. "We need you, but not in Vaelyn." Serenna settled back into her seat as he continued. "We found it prudent to establish an academy for the half-breeds born in Alari. Around the same time the wraith escaped their prison, we completed the construction of Centarya in a place that is wholly impossible for anyone to breach."

"Jassyn has told me about Centarya," Serenna said, eager to show she'd heard about the prestigious research facility. "But what does the academy have to do with the wraith?"

"Centarya's…priorities have shifted beyond education." Elashor drummed his fingers on the table. "The wraith have backed us into a corner. We are out of options. The High Council decreed we must assemble all mature half-breeds from the human realms."

Elashor paused while the shutters rattled from the wind howling outdoors, announcing the storm's imminent arrival. "In efforts to preserve our pure-blooded population, we need to utilize any advantages over the wraith. This begins with including your generation in our academy's training."

"Training…what exactly?" Serenna inquired, hesitation escalating at what he *hadn't* said.

Elashor extended a hand. She gasped when the surrounding air rippled with motion, unlike anything she'd ever seen before. A glowing orb as bright as the sun sprang to life, hovering above his palm. "We'll be teaching you how to invoke the blessing of the elves, your *Essence*."

Serenna's heart skipped a beat when the light flared in his hand. Curiosity shattered the wall of her unease. Leaning forward, she studied the flickering sphere as if her eyes could drink in the amazing summoned glow.

A palpable silence followed, like the air tensing after a flash of lightning. A tidal wave of confusion swept Serenna's thoughts into a swirling eddy of questions. She glanced at her mother, who didn't appear surprised or awed like she was. *Does she already know Father can…summon light? They hid this from me?*

Serenna hesitantly met her father's eyes, the words knotting in her throat. She didn't want to admit the truth. "But I don't have any of these…powers. I didn't know the elves possessed such abilities either."

"It has been my people's greatest secret. When the Aelfyn landed on the mortal shores, they found it prudent to conceal their magic." The small sun in his hand flickered out when he pulled his arm back. "Our ancestors wanted to prevent any hysteria from spreading, especially since the human population was so vast. The Aelfyn were wary the mortals would seek ways to seize their powers. However, the elves are desperate, and the time for secrecy has passed."

Serenna's mind spun like a leaf caught in a breeze. When the ancient humans met the Aelfyn, they'd immediately abandoned their primitive worship of nature's elements. If the elves had displayed their magic, she couldn't fathom the extent of the mortals' idolization.

Dragging her thoughts away from the past, Elashor said, "We've confirmed half-breeds, even those with traces of elven blood, can call upon these powers and manipulate Essence, although to varying degrees."

"If that's true, then why don't I have any abilities?" Serenna had yet to experience any whispers of power. Maybe her father was mistaken, and she didn't have their magic.

"Gold," Elashor replied with a shrug. "We conditioned half-breeds in the human realms to wear it from birth. It *tethers* your abilities, stifling them. If the metal touches your skin, you cannot access or even perceive your powers. The elves wear the ornaments around humans to prevent any lapses in judgment of revealing our power."

Serenna jumped at a crack of thunder. Something about the cacophonous noise ignited a blast of resentment in her veins. Her skin crawled under the golden jewelry, the reminder that everyone saw it fitting to control her life. She couldn't understand why the elves didn't permit at least the elven-blooded to know such things.

Don't I have the same rights since I share their blood? I have magic, but my powers have been suppressed because I live in a human realm?

"So, you chained me?" Serenna asked, her indignation warring with her disbelief. Her voice rose in pitch. "Like a rabid *dog*?"

"Serenna!" her mother scolded, apparently taking an interest now. Serenna ignored her.

Elashor held up his hands, the gesture doing nothing to ease her frustration. "It was to keep the mortal realms safe until we knew the lasting effects of uniting elf and human blood."

Serenna tossed a strand of hair over her shoulder with a scoff. *So, if you're born in Alari, you're allowed to have access to your magic. Why didn't Jassyn tell me? He must have these powers too.* His deception stung like a bruise blooming over her skin.

"My delegation has spent the past month traveling to the human realms and meeting with individuals containing any traces of elven blood." Elashor drained another goblet of wine. "We've relocated those of age to Centarya so they can join Alari's half-breeds in their military training. The human population outnumbers our own tenfold, making them ideal as our foot soldiers. The half-breeds will be their commanders, wielding Essence against the wraith."

Serenna fumed that he appeared so relaxed while her world crashed down around her. Crossing her arms to keep her hands from trembling with the anger of betrayal, Serenna turned to her mother. "Do you have this power as well?"

The queen lifted her chin before she answered. "Yes, but this isn't my path, nor your brother's. Those few remaining in the human lands will stay tethered for everyone's safety. I have decided Saundyl and his family will remain by my side in court. I am dispatching every half-breed adult to Centarya if they have no dependents or if they are not vital to the daily functioning of the realm. Including you. This is not negotiable," her mother finished, leaving no room for objection.

Shock careened through her. Serenna's sheer disbelief threatened to capsize her composure. In a matter of moments, she went from being a princess to…*what*? Someone who wasn't essential? Someone *disposable*? Her fiercest desire was to live among the elves. But not like this. Not at some *academy*.

"I don't understand," Serenna said, dismissing her mother and focusing her attention back on her father. "Am I to study at Centarya to learn about magic? Do I need an elven education before I'm allowed to court suitors?"

That's not terrible, I suppose. It would make sense if prominent families want me to have a proper *education.*

"Unfortunately, we have to put your courtships on hold until we eradicate the wraith," Elashor said with a frown. "But that doesn't mean there won't be opportunities to meet others of your kind at Centarya."

My kind. Like she was separate from the elves. *Because I'm lesser?* Serenna swallowed back a rising bitterness that scraped her throat. *Jassyn was right.*

Elashor smoothed his silk vest with the flick of a hand. "As an initiate, you will learn to hone your magic. The academy will prepare you to join the war front as a soldier."

It took Serenna a few heartbeats to process the entirety of what her father had said. "A *soldier*?"

Serenna shot to her feet. Her chair screeched when the abrupt movement flung it back. "I don't want to be a *soldier*." She articulated in exaggerated syllables. "I'm a *prin-cess*." Outrage stole all respect from her tone. "I refuse to be sent to this…this…this *half-breed's* academy!"

The queen's palm cracked against the table. "Serenna, sit down!"

Serenna spun to her mother, her voice rising above the ringing in her ears. "You agreed to this?"

Serenna smacked her palms against the wood in return, leaning forward towards the queen, bracing herself. The flames in the table's candelabras seemed to flare in time with her wrath. "You want me to become a *soldier*? I have no training in weapons, marching, or whatever it is that *soldiers* do."

Nothing would be more humiliating than leaving her home as a princess and being demoted to a soldier. *Does she really care so little for me? I'm not important like a pure-blood, so I get to be fodder for the wraith?*

The queen drew herself up. A thick layer of tension strung out between them like a mooring line. Her mother spoke rather coolly. "You will do your duty, daughter. As we all do. The realms are bigger than you, and this war will affect us all."

Rancor had Serenna panting through her nose as she combated her mother's frosty gaze. Her senses buzzed with a crackling energy, skin prickling as it pebbled. A shift in the wind blew an errant breeze through a hastily closed shutter. The current slashed through the chamber, extinguishing the candles between her and the queen. Serenna held her mother's gaze, clenching her teeth to bite back a remark.

I'm not going to win this. Her fate was beyond her control now.

Serenna straightened, pivoted, and stalked out of the hall. Ramming open one of the dining doors, she slammed it with all her strength behind her. The boom echoed with the resounding thunder rising in the gathering storm.

CHAPTER 7

SERENNA

Serenna stormed out of the dining chambers, oblivious to her guards trailing behind her. Her sandals slapped against the stone as she stomped down the stairs of the keep. Her only concern was escaping the confines of the castle. A tide of shock and anger swelled inside of her chest.

Lightning from the tempest flashed, darting through the corridor. A squall was brewing, fitting for her blustery mood.

Rational thoughts skittered away, like the webs of color crawling across the sky. Serenna didn't have a destination in mind. She let her feet carry her to the beach.

The warm pressure of the air mobbed her in the courtyard, guaranteeing rain was not far off. Fine, salty mist collected as watery beads on her dress.

One guard shouted between the rumbles of thunder, "Princess, the storm!"

Spinning toward him, Serenna shrieked, "Leave me!"

Her guards halted their approach, permitting her to trek alone toward the water. When her feet met the sandy shores, Serenna yanked off her sandals, abandoning her shoes on the dunes.

She approached the turbulent waters. Tremors from the crashing waves vibrated through her legs, striking her bare feet. Her anger kindled to a white-hot flame. Serenna choked out a gasp and finally permitted her tears to fall.

Staring off into the distance, her vision blurred as the lightning fractured between the rolling clouds. Gusting wind flung her hair like lashing eels, but the breeze did little to cool her ire.

Her parents had usurped her right to become a lady in the elven courts in exchange for becoming some *soldier*. This was the destiny they'd assigned to her. She would never get the chance to court suitors, attend elegant balls, or live the lavish life she'd pictured in Kyansari.

That destiny was gone, like ashes spiraling in the wind. Her dreams disappeared like a plume of smoke. *How am I supposed to be a soldier?*

A lump of fury burned Serenna's throat like swallowing a hot coal. The tides of her fortune had changed. How had she been so misled about everything in the world beyond the castle walls?

The elves chained me my whole life, and I didn't even know it.

With that thought, Serenna balled her hands into fists and shrieked at the sky. A strike of lightning cracked in front of her, briefly stealing her sight. The blast of the answering thunder drowned out the howls of her outrage, echoing with her pounding heart.

Ripping the diadem off her head, Serenna hurled it into the sea. Unburdening herself of her jewelry, she threw her golden rings, earrings, and priceless necklaces. She channeled her hysteria into the devouring waters.

Everything she knew was a lie. Her entire existence had been a cruel joke. And for what? For the elves to keep their secrets until they had a use for her?

What am I now? Just a body to sacrifice on the war front?

A tiny truth revealed itself. She was expendable. Disposable. Not even worthy of knowledge. She had magic, but that component of her life had been concealed from her too. *What gave the elves the right to hide everything from me?*

She was a naive fool, allowing herself to be so unaware of the world, trusting everyone so blindly. Why did she have to fight the wraith? How was that *her* responsibility? The whole situation was unjust.

Anger fueled her assault. Serenna continued the barrage of casting every golden item into the crashing waves, freeing herself from her shackles. Like the storm promised, a deluge descended.

Serenna tore her last necklace off with a shriek, trembling with blistering outrage. Rain sluiced down her skin in rivulets, soaking through her dress.

She planted her feet and jerked her arm back to fling the final piece of jewelry against the howling vortex of wind. When she angled to lurch into the throw, a soft hand hooked on her wrist, halting her motion.

Startled by the intervention, Serenna spun around. Her gaze collided with Jassyn's. Lightning illuminated the concern of his features, but his eyes were steady on hers.

"Easy," he said, almost too quietly to be heard above the roar of the storm. His soothing tone only invoked her wrath. Like he *pitied* her.

Serenna's attention latched onto his fingers, devoid of golden jewelry. His pointed ears were uncharacteristically bare of rings and studs.

He's untethered; he has magic too.

Jerking her arm out of his grasp, Serenna directed her anger at him.

"You knew! About everything! This whole time!" Still clutching her necklace, she swung her other hand to strike him across the face.

Faster than the arcing lights darting across the sky, Jassyn halted her arm midswing before the blow could land. Serenna shrieked, her rage imprisoned in his hold, having no place to go.

She screamed at him, hoping every word cut deeper than a knife. "You lied to me! Did my *father* send you to retrieve me? How many other lies have you told me?"

"I never lied to you," Jassyn calmly replied, but he didn't deny her father dispatched him.

"Then what do you call what you did?" Serenna seethed, shaking the pelting rain out of her face. "You knew I was going to be sent to Centarya, and yet you said *nothing* this whole time. You led me to believe you were preparing me for life in Kyansari. How could you? I *trusted* you!"

Serenna struggled against him to pull her arm out of his grasp. "Stars scorch you, let me go!"

Jassyn released her and retreated a step, brushing rain-slicked curls out of his face. "I didn't know you were going to be sent to Centarya until today. I wanted to tell you more these past six months, but I couldn't."

Clenching her hands into fists, Serenna dug her nails into her palms around the necklace. Her throat tightened, leashing tears at the sympathy in his eyes.

"What do you mean you *couldn't*?" Her voice broke, a stifled sound escaping. "Am I not deserving of the truth?"

Jassyn's brows fell, his eyes reflecting her anguish. He hesitantly touched her shoulder as if he were questioning if it were the right action. It was featherlight, an offering, one that she could move away from or into.

Serenna's chest trembled, tightening to where it ached, when she inhaled a strangled breath. The knot in her throat untangled. She released an unbidden sob, covering her face in dismay.

Arms wrapped around her. When Jassyn pulled her in close, Serenna succumbed to her weeping. He held her while she poured out her misery and frustration. Her confusion and anger festered like an infected wound.

Hot, angry tears mingled with the cool rain streaming down her face. Emotional anguish surged through her like the roiling sea. Serenna trembled in racking waves. She couldn't see through the murky haze of her grief, couldn't process the despair overwhelming her.

Distantly, she knew Jassyn wasn't at fault. He was a scholar. It was the elven council that dictated the realms' decisions.

"Why didn't you tell me?" she wept into his chest.

"Magic enforced my silence." Jassyn's arms tightened around her. "Your sire lifted the restriction today. It hasn't been easy for me either. Knowing what exists beyond the human borders, but forced to keep secrets until the council decided otherwise. It's been…" He trailed off. "I wanted to tell you more."

Jassyn pulled away, giving her shoulders a reassuring squeeze. Serenna studied the jewelry in her hand, recognizing it was a piece gifted by her father. *Of course.* The final link of the tethers she so blindly wore.

Releasing more than her hopes and dreams, Serenna's fingers went limp. The chain tumbled to the sand.

She wasn't a princess anymore. Her family had turned against her, relegating her to another life.

Like a falling tide, her tears and unsettled emotions slowly receded.

A green burst of light flickered on the edge of her vision.

Jassyn pivoted in the direction of the flare. A violet wall slammed in front of them as a radiant sphere ignited in his palm to illuminate the beach.

Serenna tensed, not expecting to see magic. "What is it?" she asked, startled by his alarm.

Her body tingled with a static buzz as she experienced an overwhelming sensation that something unseen lingered nearby.

"I thought…" Jassyn squinted down the shore. "I thought I saw a portal opening."

"A portal?"

"Let's get you back inside." Jassyn's magic dissipated as he steered her toward the castle and nodded to her guards. "It's probably just light from the storm."

Serenna's limbs went numb from both the shock and the chill. The rain had thoroughly soaked through to her skin. She dragged her feet toward the keep, reluctant to accept her new life.

CHAPTER 8

LYKOR

Alone in the wraith's war room, Lykor reviewed the day's reports. He made a mental note to inform his captain the northern realm's spring apples would be ripe for harvest.

Lykor let his second-in-command handle the inconsequential details of the raid so he wouldn't have to fuck around with it himself. For whatever reason, Kal jumped at the opportunity to rotate warriors through the rosters.

AND FENN IS EVEN WORSE, Lykor thought. STARS, HOW DID KAL MANAGE TO RAISE A SON MORE EAGER THAN—

Lykor seized. An unpleasant jolt, like talons slicing into his chest, shredded through the fibers of his being. He thrashed, buckling in his chair, feeling as if a wave of lightning electrified his body. With a grating screech, his clawed gauntlet dug furrows into the table as he flailed against the current searing him from the inside out.

A barrage of emotions blasted through his defenseless mind. Anger. Fear. Sorrow. But they weren't his own.

Not this time.

His instincts took over.

Before realizing what he was doing, Lykor scanned for the foreign presence that so suddenly sprang into his awareness.

AFTER ALL THESE YEARS...COULD IT BE HIM? DO BROKEN BONDS EVEN REFORGE?

IF SO, I'LL FUCKING KILL HIM.

Perhaps he'd finally be free from the wretched magic compelling his mind.

After several minutes of searching, sensing, and casting out his awareness, he finally determined the location of the connection. Anticipation had his chest heaving, senses firing like sparks igniting from flint striking steel.

Seizing Essence, Lykor split a fissure before him, lacerating the air with a gateway. He shrouded himself in shadows. Coercion had him stalking through the rift with murder on his mind.

On the other side of the portal, rain pelted him, battering him from every angle. Two figures embraced near the water's edge, a hundred paces down the shore. A male spun toward Lykor's concealed location with a shield igniting and illumination blazing in his palms.

ELVES, Lykor thought, a low snarl reverberating in the depths of his chest. Unraveling the gateway, his bared fangs elongated even farther with conditioned loathing upon seeing magic. His malice transformed into a maelstrom of volatile emotions, springing to life in a violent hurricane.

The coercion plaguing his mind demanded the destruction of *him*.

A frenzied and desperate need to kill consumed Lykor in a fiery explosion, like a comet plummeting to the earth. He wanted to destroy them. Shred them. Siphon the blood from their veins. And pluck every bone from their bodies.

Rending shadows whipped from the sand, surrounding him in a black fog.

But he wavered, clutching onto a sliver of awareness, hovering on the precipice of lashing out. His crimson eyes darted over the figures on the shore, recognizing that neither of them was the one he had been compelled to kill—the one the magic demanded annihilation of.

Lykor drew in sharp breath from the agony of the command, but he maintained control of his fragmented mind.

This time.

The other entity in his head stirred awake as if summoned by Lykor's pestilent thoughts skittering around *him*.

DRACOVAE'S TITS, Lykor swore upon rousing the other presence, peaking the other being's meddling interest.

Gasping, he spasmed like a drowned man, twitching in the throes of death, when the opposing entity confronted him. Lykor doubled over as they grappled for control of their body.

Concealed in shadows, Lykor furiously wrestled the intervening presence back into the dark recesses of their mind. They'd perceived each other decades ago, and had both discovered there could be no harmony between them.

With a crack of his spine, Lykor straightened and rolled his shoulders, reasserting control over their body.

His body.

The elves had disappeared by the time he'd asserted his dominance and shoved the other entity into a corner of his awareness.

With an irritable swipe, Lykor scraped rain-plastered hair out of his eyes.

The black night and downpour obscured his vision on this foreign shore. Lightning cracked like a whip across the sky, allowing him to discern a stone castle next to the sea. He'd never ventured this far south in the human realms before. Perhaps he'd soared these skies on Trella, but that was a lifetime ago.

Rejecting the other being's past, Lykor had renounced those memories. They weren't his anyway.

The presence of elves outside of their realm made little sense. Lykor knew they would never lower themselves to live among the mortals. Unless…

DID THEY MIX WITH THE HUMANS?

That was the only explanation; merging their races for the elves' survival was discussed a century prior. The other entity was aware of that. Lykor had only discovered the elves' true intentions for melding the races while imprisoned in their dungeons.

THESE TWO MUST BE OFFSPRING FROM THOSE UNIONS.

Steel creaked as the plated joints in Lykor's clawed gauntlet articulated, crushing into a fist. His simmering wrath accelerated to a rapid boil upon realizing what the tugging on his perception meant.

THIS STARS-CURSED CONNECTION HAS TO BE WITH ONE OF THEM.

He nearly obliterated the castle out of spite, but he knew the other entity would only stop him. *I CAN'T AFFORD TO PUT THE WRAITH AT RISK WITH THIS FUCKING BOND.*

Lykor extended a hand and twisted a portal, ripping a rift through the realms to transfer him back to the wraith's war room. He needed to think of a way to eliminate the hovering link of magic straining to form.

THIS CHANGES EVERYTHING.

CHAPTER 9

SERENNA

Serenna collapsed onto a stool across from Jassyn. The stone walls of the stark kitchens were as gray as her mood.

After she finished changing into dry loungewear and brushing the tangles out of her damp hair, she wandered to the main level of the keep. Resigned to the fact that her dreams of her future were just that.

Jassyn thanked and dismissed the staff after they arranged platters of bread, cheeses, olives, nuts, and figs. Not familiar with spending any amount of time where servants prepared the castle's meals, Serenna glanced around, eyes flitting over the wooden cupboards, hanging cured meats, and jars of spices.

She considered the dried herbs, assuming the plants were the variety Jassyn had instructed the kitchen staff to brew into teas for healing minor ailments. He spent his free time in the village surrounding the keep and had developed a mentoring relationship with one of the local midwives, teaching the woman how to use the medicinal plants he'd brought from Alari.

Serenna frowned while Jassyn cut his figs into precisely diced portions, eating the pieces with a fork. Perhaps the elves were more particular about their arrangement of food than the elven-blooded in her mother's court.

Blinking through the grainy fog of emotional exhaustion, Serenna recalled Jassyn was the one who'd invited her to the kitchens after inquiring if she'd eaten at dinner. *Is he going to tell me more about magic?*

Even though her stomach sank with dread, she would have to learn about her powers to survive. A new door had cracked open to an entire world she knew nothing about.

"The plants sent to you from Alari," Serenna began, "do they have magical healing properties?"

Jassyn paused with the utensil halfway to his mouth. He followed her gaze to the decorative ceramic pots dotting the windowsills before returning his silverware to the plate. "The plants themselves don't have magic, but one of my peers at Centarya studies their healing qualities. I turned that knowledge into a…personal project while I was here."

"Why?" Serenna assumed Jassyn had an eccentric fixation with plants, but she'd never understood his peculiar habit of spending his leisure time among the peasants.

"I didn't realize the way humans lived until I visited Vaelyn," he said, pouring a cup of steaming tea. "Just in the surrounding village, I witnessed the townsfolk suffering from illnesses. Illnesses that don't exist in Alari—an elf wouldn't be debilitated for even an hour without seeking mending. I'm still disgusted that I was *prevented* from healing those afflicted with such simple ailments."

Jassyn spooned an alarming amount of sugar into his teacup with excessive force. Liquid sloshed over the side. Pursing his lips, he retrieved a napkin to wipe the scattered droplets off the cup.

"Compared to life in Alari…the differences here are unacceptable," he said. "We don't think twice about mending such minor inconveniences with our powers. Why should we withhold our gift from those who need it?"

Running a finger around the mug's rim, he stared into the tea. "In addition to my research, I'm also one of the campus healers. I… wanted to make the villagers' lives easier. It's almost laughable, but it was the only way I knew how."

Serenna wasn't sure why she'd never asked Jassyn about his interest in helping the locals before. Perhaps she dismissed them as beneath her because she thought she was *special*. What a fool she was for assuming being three-quarters elf put her at an advantage. No, being *special* earned her a trip to Centarya to be trained with *her kind* to fight in the elves' war against the wraith.

Focusing her attention on her hands in her lap, Serenna blinked back the tears welling in her eyes, emotions solidifying in her chest. *Is this why Jassyn never opened up to me? Why would someone so selfless like him want to know someone so self-absorbed like me?*

"I'm sorry I…" Serenna's voice faltered, unable to find words amid the reality crushing her like a mountain toppling over her head. "I'm sorry I refused to see. You must think I'm horrible for being so selfish."

Serenna swiped at a stray tear, attempting to swallow the constriction in her throat while her bleak thoughts accumulated like snow. She couldn't meet Jassyn's eyes. She wasn't sure why his approval mattered.

Maybe it was because she'd never had to earn anyone else's favor and Jassyn didn't automatically offer his like everyone else in her life. He was her direct connection to the elves, and what did that say about her potential if she couldn't even gain his regard after six months of trying?

A claw of sadness wrapped around her heart. Her father kept secrets from her too, but surely the council had their reasons. Elashor was also subject to the will of his realm. She obviously knew nothing about the world beyond the castle's walls.

Perhaps the elves had justification for their silence, and she didn't have the entire painted picture yet. They had their dwindling race to worry about. They couldn't address every worldly problem overnight.

Maybe after eliminating the wraith, the council would have more resources to focus on correcting the discrepancies in the human realms Jassyn was upset about. As someone from both worlds, Serenna wondered if her place would be helping bridge that gap. Would the knowledge at Centarya allow her to do something to actually make a difference in the world?

If I don't die in the war first.

Thinking about her forced attendance at the academy rooted a snarl of fear, which sprouted into a thorny tangle of anxiety. Living a cushioned life in her mother's court, she'd trained to be a noble, a lady able to navigate the courts. Not someone who brandished weapons or magic at a foe. Most of the elven-blooded in the human realms were from royal lines. She imagined everyone else was experiencing the same sudden shock.

"I'm terrified I won't be able to fight," Serenna admitted, twisting the linen napkin in her lap. "If it does come to war."

"The frequency of the wraith attacks is concerning, but you won't be alone learning about your power." Jassyn's eyes softened in the flickering candles when she gathered the courage to look at him.

"Your sire expects nearly a thousand initiates will attend from the human realms. It'll take time to train all the recruits in combat and magic. You're going to be pushed, but I think you'll be able to adjust to life at Centarya."

Jassyn rubbed his temples as if he were trying to expel an unpleasant thought. "But I imagine the quiet setting I was accustomed to will be *quite* different now that the academy is a military institute."

Looking up to the ceiling as if the surrounding stone could provide a sense of comfort, he blew out a breath and said, "The king assigned Vesryn as the military commander over operations at Centarya. Stars help us all."

Serenna nearly choked while taking a sip of water. Immediately perking up and straightening in her chair, she sputtered out a cough. "The…the *prince*?"

Rolling his eyes, Jassyn said, "Ah yes, the *noblest* and most eligible bachelor in the kingdom. His personal crusade of hunting the wraith is the only thing important to him." Jassyn crumpled his napkin into a fist. "He's ruthless and absolutely detestable."

Serenna's stomach leaped off a cliff of delight, ignoring Jassyn's obvious distaste for his royal. The only piece of information she registered was the fact that the elven *prince* was going to be at the academy. And he was the commander, no less.

"Is the prince an instructor too?" she excitedly asked.

"I wouldn't give him that much credit." Jassyn flicked curls out of his eyes. "He's filling the role of the rending magister. And, yes, rending is as unpleasant as it sounds—that magic is essentially the inverse of healing." Jassyn's face pinched as if he'd swallowed something foul. "Vesryn possesses unnatural talents in that regard. It's vile power and should be outlawed."

Serenna's eyes unfocused. Tendrils of thought stretched, drawing the outline of a plan. *Will I be under the prince's instruction?* If she mastered this rending power, surely Vesryn would notice her. Hope expanded in her chest like an inhalation of breath amid drowning; she'd never envisioned such a possibility.

For the first time since the disastrous dinner, Serenna saw a glimmer of hope. A few hours prior, she assumed her father would present her to members of the elven courts and, if she was lucky, the prince. She never imagined living at the academy would *increase* her access to Vesryn.

Jassyn's scoff rudely yanked her out of her thoughts. He gawked at her. "I know what you're thinking—it won't work," he chided in a clipped voice. "Do you want the attention from someone who has the reputation of bedding half the realm?" He punctuated his words with a jabbing finger. "Vesryn is married to his vengeance, seeking the death of every wraith. He'll disappoint you. And besides, he's beyond arrogant."

Jassyn said everything as if it were a simple collection of facts and common knowledge. Serenna didn't care about *arrogance. What royal isn't full of themselves?*

"Your efforts would be better spent elsewhere," Jassyn said as if he would allow no argument.

Serenna scowled until a ripple of recognition washed over her. He spoke about the prince with a peculiar familiarity. "Do you know Vesryn? Will you introduce me to him?"

Jassyn's mouth went slack. After a lengthy pause, he set his jaw. "Did you not hear everything I just said?" A muscle in his cheek twitched. "No, I won't."

Jassyn folded his arms, the action suggesting she wouldn't persuade him.

At Serenna's squawk of protest, he added, "I'm not important enough to introduce ladies to the prince."

Serenna refused to be dissuaded so easily. "Does my father know him?"

Jassyn covered his face with his hands and shook his head with a frustrated sigh. "If you're so star-bent on meeting him, then *yes*, your sire knows him. They're both on the High Council."

"Excellent!" All she needed was a proper introduction, and then she could devise a strategy to draw the prince's gaze. *Would I have a chance of being selected for his consort?*

Serenna's stomach grumbled, reminding her of missing dinner. Now, feeling more fortified with her emotions after the initial shock of the night wore off, she found the energy to fill her plate.

"Do you enjoy living at the academy?" Serenna asked, hesitantly curious to hear more about Centarya. The news of Vesryn's attendance vastly elevated her mood.

Jassyn arched his brow suspiciously before indulging her inquiry. "Centarya is my home." He plucked cheeses from the arranged assortments. "It's the only place where I feel like I belong."

Maybe I'll feel like I belong too.

Serenna contemplated the extent of the mysterious abilities she might wield while Jassyn meticulously stacked the selected rinds of cheese on slices of flatbread. He could summon light and heal others, and he mentioned the prince's rending power.

Serenna nodded at the unlit hearth the scullions didn't have time to rekindle. "Can you start the fire with magic?"

"Not with this." Jassyn summoned a sunny orb like her father had at dinner. "Illumination is only a pretty light. Though it is useful for replenishing someone else's drained Essence."

Studying the light, Serenna tilted her head, not understanding half of his words. "So, what can our magic do?"

"Our magical abilities originate from the stars, where the elves believe their powers came from." Jassyn's light morphed and swirled around his fingers like an aurora waving across the sky. "We have no control over the elements of the physical earth: fire, water, wind, lightning, and the like." His eyes glowed with the reflection from the gleaming stream that wrapped around his hands. "Those were perhaps abilities belonging to the human shamans of the past."

Serenna assumed ancient shamans allegedly having powers was folklore crafted by the peasants to pass the time. She was familiar with hearing the stories of shamans manipulating the earth to heal, strike lightning, and hurl balls of fire.

But Jassyn was a scholar and a student of magic with knowledge of the bigger world. *He believes shamans had powers too?* Perhaps she should also give credit to the humans' tales.

Something captivating in Jassyn's tone grabbed her attention and piqued her interest. Serenna recognized a whisper of his enthusiasm, an undercurrent of a distinct passion evident by the telltale sign of his gestures becoming more animated, like his hands weren't able to restrain themselves from the stir of excitement.

Serenna straightened and brushed crumbs of bread into her napkin, eager to learn more about what the council didn't permit him to share until now.

Recognizing she might wield some type of magic, she asked, "What abilities do we have, then?"

"We refer to the blanket term of our power as 'Essence.'" Jassyn wove the river of light around them. "There are eight categories that comprise our magic: force, telepathy, illusion, mending, rending, shielding, illumination, and portaling."

Serenna's eyes went round at the sheer scope of the magic's possibilities. "You have control over that much power?"

"Not quite. I only have the abilities of mending, shielding, illumination, telepathy, and illusion." Jassyn let the radiant ribbon dissipate. An imprint of the light lingered for a few moments in the air between them, like the image of the sun burning behind closed eyes. "The abilities we have are innate—specific talents aren't something you can learn how to control."

Serenna leaned closer to him with a flourishing interest, hoping she had the same abilities as the prince so she could insert herself in his presence. If her father were in a position of power, surely he must have significant magic at his disposal. *Did he pass along his magic to me?*

"How do I find out which abilities I control?" she asked.

"Our talents manifest near the time when we reach maturity and when the aging process comes to a relative halt." Jassyn picked through a bowl of olives, focusing on choosing a select few with a fork. "In your case, I'm not exactly sure how prolonged tethering will affect access to magic—if it does at all."

Serenna didn't consider the implications of having her power suppressed. *Will I have trouble summoning Essence?* Noxious weeds of doubt germinated with her thoughts.

She wilted like a parched flower, eliciting a wince from Jassyn, but he reassured her by adding, "You've only reached your maturity. I wouldn't worry too much about it. Everyone from the human realms will be in the same situation. We have an ancient Aelfyn relic that unveils which abilities you'll have at your command—even if you haven't manifested those powers yet."

Serenna blinked in disbelief when Jassyn put his elbows on the table. Seeing him relaxed for once was like unearthing a different layer of him.

"You at least have illumination, the gift of the stars," he continued, returning to the arranged food to collect chocolate-coated pecans this time. "Everyone with elf blood shares that ability."

While reassured she shared at least one power with the elves, Serenna hoped her inherent capabilities extended beyond simply conjuring dazzling lights.

"Did this relic show you which powers you controlled? Or did you already manifest your abilities since you weren't tethered?" There was no malice in her tone, despite the resentment polluting her chest.

"As you summon magic more frequently, manifestation occurs organically. The Heart of Stars, the ancient artifact, revealed two abilities I had yet to uncover when I was sent to Centarya." Jassyn focused his attention on spreading honey over a wafer. "As a magus, I report to the mending magister—the magisters are the primary instructors. We assist with guiding talents and helping students access their Well."

"Their Well?"

Jassyn gestured with a flick of his hand. Light appeared again, blue this time, suspended over the table in the shape of a long circle. "Think of a reservoir where your power collects—literally like a well. With overuse, your magic will deplete and run dry." The sphere in the air hollowed out until only a ring of light remained etched above them.

"So your magic isn't infinite," Serenna commented.

"No, Essence has limitations. If you exhaust your power, you won't be able to access any of your abilities until you replenish your Well by regenerating. It's easiest to restore our magic by meditating under the stars." Light flooded to fill in the shape, like a tide rising on the shore. "If you don't utilize your power consistently, your Well also withers from underuse and you won't have as much magic at your disposal to draw from."

Serenna sensed Jassyn showing off with his animations. The image in front of them shriveled like a raisin and *popped* like a bubble, disappearing.

"Your Well is like a muscle, requiring exercise to maintain its functionality," he said.

Serenna put her chin in her palms, mulling over the new information, not understanding why Jassyn would suppress his powers to tutor her. Or perhaps he was just that kind of person—one who didn't hesitate to help others.

Realizing Jassyn was going to be a familiar face at Centarya provided her with the reassurance that she wouldn't have to encounter this foreign place alone. In the morning, once the news spread, Serenna decided to inquire if Velinya had been conscripted as well. *If the queen determined she was expendable like me.*

Serenna's mind wandered back to the knowledge Jassyn had concerning the prince. "What else can you tell me about Vesryn?" she asked.

Jassyn rolled his shoulders as if releasing a coiled tension. "It's late and well past the time we should have retired for the evening." He rose, dismissing any further questions. "We'll be departing in two days, and I'm sure you'll have much to prepare in the meantime."

Serenna rose to follow him, preparing to object to the finality, but paused instead, reflecting. Despite her assumptions that her father had pressured Jassyn into retrieving her, Jassyn had been supportive. To a degree more than he needed to be.

She'd pestered him with questions concerning the prince and should've recognized the way he closed himself off.

"Jassyn, wait," she pleaded before he left the kitchens.

He turned toward her with a sigh as if surrendering to the prospect of additional harassment.

Feeling awkward and uncertain, Serenna floundered to find the right words. *How do I acknowledge what he did this evening?* Her heart reached for him, appreciating his concern and for towing her away from the brink of despair.

She needed to make amends for her actions on the beach. "I'm sorry I tried to slap you. My behavior was uncalled for."

Jassyn shrugged off her apology but gave a nod.

"Thank you. For being there tonight," Serenna hurriedly added before he walked off. "I'd like…I'd like to hear more about your life sometime since you're allowed to talk about it now. If that would be something you're willing to share with me?" She clutched the sides of her dress, wringing the material. "I hope we can stay…acquainted? When we go to Centarya? If that wouldn't be inappropriate for your position."

Thumbing his chin, Jassyn considered her. "If you're interested in healing others, I'll have a few aiding positions to fill in the Infirmary—if you have the mending talent. You'll know your abilities shortly after we arrive at Centarya."

I could be a healer? Under Jassyn's offer of continued mentoring, she could learn more about her magic. Serenna couldn't help but think this opportunity was Jassyn's way of meeting her in the middle. He wasn't under any obligation to continue associating with her.

She nodded eagerly. "Yes, thank you." *Surely the menders won't fight the wraith.* "I'd like that."

Jassyn offered a small smile. "Of course. Good night, Princess."

"Serenna," she said, following him to the doorway.

He stopped in his tracks, angling back slightly.

"Just…Serenna," she repeated.

Splitting ways with Jassyn, Serenna ascended her tower to return to her chambers. She paused briefly outside of Velinya's door to see if her friend had heard the same news, but hurriedly entered her quarters instead when she registered rather animated moans of pleasure from within.

From what sounded like more than two people.

Shaking her head, Serenna wondered who Velinya had invited to her bed from her father's delegation *this* time. *I'm sure I'll hear more than I care to in the morning.*

The rain had roamed inland, and Serenna stepped out onto her balcony to the roar of the ocean. Thoughts swirling like the departing clouds, she wrapped her arms around herself to stave off the cool, lingering breeze.

The heavy weight of inevitability settled on her shoulders. She accepted that attending the academy was unavoidable now. Instead of allowing the elves to dictate her entire destiny, a part of her wanted to steer her time at Centarya in a direction more significant than simply learning how to wield her magic as a weapon.

Would it be possible to learn how to heal—and potentially avoid combat or, better yet, get closer to the prince? If he were looking for an elven-blooded match, Serenna didn't see why he wouldn't consider her. *Unless I appear too human for his liking.*

She balked at the thought of being involved in battles, but if Vesryn was a warrior, she imagined learning how to master her magic would impress him.

She had no illusions; living a plush life at court had made her soft. If forced into any physical activity, she would be pathetic. But still… surely her strong elven bloodlines, her royal heritage, and her father's position would set her apart from everyone else.

Something tickled the back of her mind, like a brush of a feather. A breath halted in her chest.

Serenna spun, facing the direction of the cliffs across the bay. She noticed nothing unusual besides the unexplainable sensation of being watched. Just like she experienced down at the beach.

With a shake, she knew Jassyn was right. It was late. The events from the evening had made her weary.

Perhaps she would prove herself at Centarya. In a way she didn't expect, she *was* getting the opportunity to live in Alari. The elves were the majority of her heritage, and she yearned to learn more about them.

And Prince Vesryn was going to be *at* the academy. The unexpected twist of fate might not be so bad, after all.

CHAPTER 10

SERENNA

Serenna and Velinya ceased their discussion about the prince's presence at Centarya when Elashor appeared in the courtyard. Taking a deep breath, Serenna pressed her hands to her middle to calm a steady fluttering.

Her father's unblinking soldiers ensured absolute compliance of those conscripted. Like her mother had stated, no one would be excused from their duty.

The elves must be desperate if they're relying on untrained nobles to fight their war.

The morning sun crested over the wall of the castle's courtyard, staining the sky with streaks of red and gold. Serenna wiped sweaty palms on her lilac traveling dress as Kyansari's warriors approached, their boots stirring up sand.

Both formidable and regal in his pearly-plated armor, Elashor extended a hand. The space in front of him undulated like a curtain rippling in a breeze. The gathered court gawkers expelled a collective gasp at seeing their first glimpse of magic.

A light slashed through the air, expanding until it formed a gaping hole, large enough for three men abreast to walk through. A glimmering green line outlined the portal, the surface rippling as if it were a disturbed pool of ink.

Elashor nodded, and Jassyn took the first steps forward, disappearing through the gateway with long, sure-footed strides.

No turning back now.

Hefting the pack onto her shoulders, more so to dispel jittery nerves than the need to readjust, Serenna looked toward her mother, who didn't glance her way. *I guess this is it.* Despite her reservations and blossoming anxiety about attending the academy to become an Essence wielder, a part of her was relieved to leave her stagnant life in Vaelyn behind.

As each conscripted court member vanished through the gateway, Serenna closed the gap to the waiting rift. When it was her turn to travel through, she trailed her fingers over the midnight expanse. A slight tingle numbed her outstretched hand.

Magic is real.

The thought, so foreign and incredible, filled her with an exhilarating wonder now that she had time to process the new world she was about to step into.

It could be hers.

The power of the elves.

Since becoming untethered, Serenna had perceived nothing different. She strained to hear a whisper of her magic—as if something inside her would echo with the portal before her.

With another steadying breath, Serenna closed her eyes, taking the first step forward into her new life.

A windless roar, like the sound of a conch shell held to the ear, engulfed Serenna's senses. A heavy pressure squeezed her body as if she had dived into the deepest depths of the ocean. Icy waves vibrated through her bones, rattling her clenched teeth. Time stretched and the space between her heartbeats lengthened. The feeling of eternity spread out before her.

A bright wave of light warmed Serenna's skin when her foot landed on grassy earth. Her eyes flew open to greet the first glimpse of opportunities, unfolding like a dusting of stars.

Gone were the familiar palms, ocean, and sand. Blinking against the sun, Serenna studied the countryside. The unexpected crisp air contrasted with the humid atmosphere in Vaelyn. *I can't believe I can move across the realms with one step.*

Serenna's sight snagged on an enormous landmass *hanging* in the sky. Her stomach lurched, shock stealing her breath. She stumbled backward, mind spinning at the disorientation, attempting to make sense of what she was seeing.

Centarya was a floating island.

"Serenna!"

Forcibly peeling her eyes away from the hovering isle, Serenna detected Jassyn beckoning to her from where the court members gathered. Drifting toward the group, her attention was determined to stay fixed on the bizarre impossibility.

Her steps turned choppy, like her legs were preparing to flee, while her mind expected the island to come crashing to the earth at any moment.

"Magnificent, isn't it?" An uncharacteristic wide grin lit up Jassyn's face.

I'm here, in the elven realm. Serenna couldn't help but smile back, feeling like she'd been reborn into a better place. Already, their lands contained evidence of the inconceivable.

The ground below the floating island shimmered. Serenna's attention drifted upward to watch water tumbling *from* the isle, cascading down as waterfalls to be collected by the lake below.

"How is this possible?" Velinya asked, gaping alongside the court members, who were staring in disbelief and awe.

"Centarya's creation was a massive project involving scores of elves wielding force abilities," Jassyn said. "Tearing into the earth, they uprooted the landmass and cast it into the sky. Elves remained on the isle during its ascent to open the first gateways. Tying off their magic, the architects used the ground as an anchor to ensure the island would remain a permanent buoying structure. Every few years, the magus reestablish the magical moorings to stabilize the connection."

Jassyn pointed at the water. "The crater left behind is a lake, the Cyan Mere."

Serenna glanced toward the portal as Elashor strolled through. The traveling rift flickered and faded when he approached the group.

"We'll travel by foot the rest of the way, so you have time to see the Terminal," he announced, striding off.

Serenna hurried to her father's side. She had profusely apologized the previous day for her display at dinner. He'd understood the sudden news devastated her but encouraged her to do well at the academy.

Now presented with the opportunity to integrate herself more into her father's life, Serenna spent the dark hours of the night contemplating the best way to develop a relationship with him. She already considered ways to redeem herself to gain his approval. She wouldn't want to shame him by being a failure among so many who knew him. Even if she would never be a pure-bred elf, she still wanted to cling to every thread of similarity between them.

Her link to him was her access to the elven realm beyond her temporary duties at the academy. Once they subdued the wraith, her father had assured her she would remain in Alari with him. *And then I'll finally have the chance to meet suitors in the capital.*

Well, that is, if my efforts with the prince don't succeed and the wraith don't finish me off first.

"Father, may I propose something?" Serenna asked. When Elashor nodded, she said, "With your permission, I'd like to take your name and formally be known as Serenna Vallende. I have no claims in Vaelyn... There isn't anything left for me there."

Serenna assumed sharing her father's name would carry more weight since he was one of the most distinguished elves in Alari— aside from the king and prince. *I want every advantage I can get.*

"It's customary for elves to take whichever family name is more prominent when they reach their maturity," Elashor said, glancing in her direction. "It would be an understatement to say 'Vallende' is one of the more notable houses, so it would be an appropriate change."

While he strode through the meadow, Elashor rested a hand on his longsword's hilt at his hip. His eyes tightened and slid over her as if he were studying her from the inside out. Serenna sensed he was ordering and cataloging all of her inadequacies. The tension in the silence had a trickle of sweat rolling down her spine.

"If you can offer me reassurances that your *future* actions won't reflect poorly on my family name," he finally said, "then I will make arrangements."

A wave of happiness wrapped Serenna in a comforting embrace. She clutched the straps of her pack, restraining her eagerness, but animatedly reassured her father she would master her magic and do her best to live up to the Vallende name.

They walked together through the expansive prairie. The soft, swaying grasses tickled her sandaled feet. Wildflowers bursting with a rainbow of colors danced in the sun, ushering the group with their floral scents.

"Is that a town?" Serenna asked, shading her eyes upon seeing white buildings near the water's edge.

"It's the start of one," her father answered. "The Terminal is still under construction, but the new dormitories on campus are complete."

Even considering the sun's movement across the sky, the settlement would never be in Centarya's floating shadow positioned at the southern end of the lake.

Elashor released a disbelieving grunt, pulling her attention away from the Terminal. "Of course, we've had a few setbacks in construction with the wraith pilfering supplies."

"What do the wraith look like? Have you fought them?" The only description Serenna had of the creatures was their ability to disappear into shadows.

"Wraith are aberrations, a mockery of intelligent life," Elashor nearly snarled, "sharing nothing of the beauty the elves hold in high regard. The monsters are gaunt, looming over us. They might as well be beasts with their fangs and claws." He directed a glower toward the horizon. "They're grotesque with skin like midnight ash, eyes the color of blood, and hair as black as any human's." With a jerk of a shoulder, he added, "They don't have Essence at least—that would be the greatest offense of all."

With a wince, Serenna pulled her hand away from her dark locks and glanced over at Jassyn's raven curls. She'd wished for the elves' light-colored hair for as long as she could remember. She recalled how she tried to scrub the color out of hers with the beach's sand when she was a child—even spending hours outside did nothing to sun-bleach her hair.

But comparing a race as monstrous as the wraith to the physical similarities found in humans or elven-blooded had her cringing. *Surely the wraith killing Alari's monarchs and his brother is more grievous than what color their hair is.* Locking the thought away, Serenna didn't give it voice, not wanting to misstep again with her father so soon.

She regretted asking about the wraith, now having a clearer picture of the monsters she would be training to fight. Elashor continued to answer the rest of her question.

"I haven't faced the wraith in combat, but Prince Vesryn has killed more of those creatures than anyone else combined." A peculiar smile drew across his face, like the idea of the prince slaying so many of the beasts delighted him. "He must be close to a thousand now—almost repaying the same number they've taken from our capital this past century."

Speaking of the prince…that brought up Serenna's next request, and she'd much rather discuss her prospects with Vesryn than the horrors of the wraith.

"Would you be able to introduce me to Prince Vesryn?"

Out of the corner of her vision, Jassyn's head swiveled toward her, mouth thinning. But he remained silent, his disapproval radiating like the steam curling over the Cyan Mere. Serenna held her breath, dismissing his annoyance.

Elashor's eyes glittered in the sun while he considered her request. "I don't see why not. By now, I'm sure you've heard King Galaeryn intends to bind the Falkyn line to a half-breed to ensure their reign's stability."

His mouth twisted into something resembling smug amusement while he entertained the notion. "Perhaps if you can distinguish yourself, you'd be an acceptable contender for the prince's hand."

With a rush of excitement, Serenna's heart swelled at the possibilities unfolding for her—she had an introduction to Vesryn now. She brushed off her father's usage of "half-breed." *The world can't change overnight.* Grasping how crucial it was to succeed at Centarya, determination solidified Serenna's intention of wielding her hidden power to impress the prince.

They traveled past a massive multileveled structure with arched windows towering over them near the lakeshore. Vaelyn's castle would have been swallowed up inside the rounded white stone building. Unlike the other half-built projects coming into view, this one appeared completed.

When Serenna inquired what the construction was, Elashor said, "I don't want to spoil the surprise. Prince Vesryn will go into detail about Centarya's Coliseum. Let's just say you'll get a taste for the entertainment we have in Alari and the chance to make a name for yourself."

Allured by another way to differentiate herself from the other recruits, Serenna turned to Jassyn to glean more information about this elven recreation. For whatever reason, he hung back and kept his distance from her father's delegation, conversing with members of Vaelyn's court instead.

Humans roamed about when they entered the outskirts of the Terminal. Serenna stared in disbelief at seeing the mortals. Hundreds attended to their tasks like ants crawling with a purpose over a hill. They appeared to be working under the direction of elven-blooded who were intermittently flaring bursts of blue magic to hoist lumber or arrange large stones. Evidently, their power was no longer a secret.

"Why are the workers constructing a town?" Serenna asked.

"With the exponential influx of half-breeds attending Centarya, the council deemed it prudent to establish an outlet for the initiates," Elashor explained while they strode down the main street. "Right now, there are only a handful of taverns and a winery." He pointed to the buildings on their left. "We have plans to add familiar comforts as found in the capital: shopping, fine dining, hot springs, music halls, entertainment centers, and the like."

"And humans are permitted here too?" Serenna asked, swiveling as she attempted to take in the sights. They passed workers arranging cobblestones, organizing timber, and situating a tiled roof on top of a building.

"We've relocated peasants from both Dosythe's lumberyards and

Halaema's foundries to aid in the construction," Elashor said. "The half-breed architects organize and oversee the project, but we've relied on the mortals to assist with the labor. The council is even contracting a few families to open businesses and remain in town for general maintenance."

Serenna chewed her lip, studying a group of men repairing an axle on a broken cart. *It seems the elves are keeping their distance while they use the humans and elven-blooded for all the work.*

Historically, the elves had only permitted the mortals access to checkpoints near Alari's borders to deliver the realms' goods. Their current presence was an obvious shift in leniency, but Serenna wasn't sure how to decipher the change.

The sounds of hammering, sawing, and stone hitting stone escorted the group farther into the budding city. Paved cobblestones lined the streets, providing a stable footing. Jassyn eventually wandered beside her.

Serenna asked, "How much of the Terminal is new since you've last been here?"

A pained shout and a string of curses drew their attention to humans on scaffolding, hammering framing around the skeleton of a building.

"The whole town is," Jassyn said, stooping to retrieve a fallen hammer. "For those of us who don't have the ability to portal, the waypoint for traveling to Centarya was previously in Kyansari."

Upon handing the tool back, Jassyn paused. His attention hooked on the man's smashed joint and bruising nail. After some encouragement and reassurance, the human descended the ladder and permitted Jassyn to heal his hand.

The man trembled like a saddled colt, looking like he wanted to bolt. But Jassyn's steady words eventually relaxed the human's stance.

Serenna's eyes widened when magic fountained around the pair. Like a braid of rope, a red network of strands enveloped the worker's fingers. Something about Jassyn's obvious compassion made her heart squeeze in admiration.

Shrugging off the human's thanks and Serenna's praise, Jassyn picked up their conversation as if nothing had happened. "I won't mind bypassing the capital if it's now an option."

Serenna couldn't imagine why he wouldn't want to spend time in Kyansari. *I wonder when I'll get to see the city.* She didn't have a chance to ask when her father spoke up beside her, his attention aimed at Jassyn.

"I suspect you'll receive a summoning soon," Elashor said, his brows furrowing as he watched the humans working. "Now that you're back in Alari and no longer excused from your *obligations*, Magus."

Jassyn stopped in his tracks, his face draining of color. Serenna glanced between him and her father. *What other responsibilities would Jassyn have besides his research?*

The tension hovering between them vibrated like a strummed chord until a voice called out, "General Vallende, welcome!"

A woman wearing…*pants* busied herself with bowing to Elashor. Serenna assessed the elven-blooded's peculiar clothing—white leather armor. Chevron-shaped pieces of leather overlapped to cover the woman's chest and shoulders in sharp angles, leaving her arms bare. Silver grommets and heavy stitching held the leather segments together in a tight-fitting, intricate design. Buckles and straps running down the sides of her ribs kept the tunic in place.

Are they always battle ready?

Dresses were the appropriate wear for women in her mother's court. Serenna goggled at the exposed shape of this woman's legs. She averted her eyes, realizing she was staring.

"Magus," her father said in acknowledgment. "I bring court nobles from Vaelyn. We expect to have the remainder of the southern realm at Centarya by the end of the week."

"Thank you, General." The magus scribbled in a leather-bound book resting on a podium. "As you know, most of the initiates are already in attendance. Classes will formally begin once Allaenar finishes recruiting."

Despite Jassyn's assurances everyone from the human realms wouldn't be any more prepared than she was, Serenna stifled waves of unease at being behind the other recruits.

Tearing the paper free from its binding, the magus rolled the sheet and opened a portal the size of her hand. She sent the parchment sailing through and closed the rift in a fluid motion, nearly faster than Serenna could register.

Without missing a beat, the magus strode to the center of the white cobblestone ring and created another gateway with a flash of green light. This rift was large enough to accommodate even someone as tall as Jassyn.

She gestured at the group to travel through. "Magus Nelya will meet you on the other side. Welcome to Centarya."

CHAPTER 11

SERENNA

Another journey by gateway transported Serenna to the island in the sky. Before she had time to observe her new surroundings, a man's voice called, "Off the Portal Platform!"

The elven-blooded speaking to her wore the same leather armor as the magus below. He waved everyone to the side as soon as they stepped through the gateway. Serenna shuffled over to where the rest of the southern realm gathered.

The entire premise of portaling fascinated her. The platform provided a central traveling point, and groups of people waited on both sides to enter and exit the floating isle. Gateways appeared to work from either end, but they failed to open if more than one activated within ten paces of each other.

Jassyn explained magus and their aides staffed the area to provide portals for those who didn't have the talent. Except for the initiates, who weren't allowed to leave the island without an escort. And even then, they were only permitted to travel to the Terminal. Serenna wasn't sure how they would keep track of the recruits who had the portaling ability.

The pristine beauty of Centarya eclipsed everything she'd ever experienced. Like the town below, seamless limestone and marvelous arched windows appeared to be the common design of the buildings on campus.

The soft wind rippled the grasses of the manicured lawns. Towering birch and willow trees outlined white stone pathways. Curtains of vines bursting with hundreds of violet, pink, and yellow flowers dangled from branches and swayed in the breeze like ribbons of color. A rushing stream glided over flat rocks alongside the Portal Platform, flowing through the center of the isle.

Serenna's breath caught when she studied a structure reaching to touch the sky. Her head angled toward the clouds, seeking the top of the winding white tower dominating the island.

"That's the Spire," Jassyn explained from beside her. "The ground level contains the cafeteria. A floor above is the gathering hall for assemblies. Guest rooms and the magisters' apartments take up the remaining levels."

Across from the traveling grounds, practice yards with recruits locked in combat jerked Serenna's mind away from admiring the architecture and back to the reality of joining the elven military. A botanical isle that looked so much like a paradise seemed at odds with its new designation of training Essence-wielding warriors.

"Ah, here is Magus Nelya," Jassyn said.

Another woman wearing white armor, which Serenna now understood was the magus' uniform, approached them. The thought of parading around in a similar fashion didn't thrill her. *But I'm sure my wardrobe will be the least of my worries.*

Magus Nelya, a short, olive-skinned woman with a head of loose-knit curls, gave the group a warm smile. Her presence immediately put Serenna at ease. *Maybe the academy won't be so bad if everyone here is just as welcoming.*

She appraised Nelya. *Surely this diminutive magus isn't a cold-blooded killer.* Serenna couldn't picture someone like Jassyn engaged in any type of confrontation either. *Well,* Centarya *used to be a place of study, it's not anymore.*

Nelya addressed Jassyn first, clasping his hands in greeting. "It's good to see you again, Magus Jassyn. We're happy to have you back on campus. Magister Thalaesyn should still be in his office if you wanted to catch him before the midday break."

With a small smile in Serenna's direction, Jassyn departed, picking his way to a stone pathway, leaving the group.

Nelya laced her fingers in front of her, addressing them. "I am Magus Nelya, a mender and researcher under Magister Thalaesyn. There are over a hundred magus on campus, and we are here to guide and mentor new initiates. Follow me. I will settle you into your living quarters."

Elashor called Serenna before she was swept away following the group. "Let's go see the prince. I'd like to know your abilities before I depart."

Serenna skidded to a halt, her voice squeaking. "What?" She blinked at her father. *"Now?"*

"Come," he said with a smirk, striding off toward the Spire.

Serenna's heart galloped against her ribs as if suddenly running a race. Velinya offered to take her pack, while the rest of the southern realm's recruits followed Nelya for a tour around campus.

After her friend left, Serenna tried to untangle the panic twisting in her chest. *I'm severely underprepared for my first meeting with the prince!* She straightened her hair with her fingertips, and frantically brushed at her traveling clothes. *Stars, I'm not even wearing a fine dress!* Not to mention she was going to have her power tested in his presence. This was all too sudden for her liking. *What if I embarrass myself?*

Realizing that dismay rooted her in place, Serenna persuaded her feet to move. Half jogging a few paces to catch up to her father, she asked, "Are you sure the prince isn't too busy?" Maybe she could delay meeting Vesryn until she was more composed. "I don't want to be a burden on his time." *I haven't thought about what to say to him!*

"Nonsense." Elashor gave a dismissive wave. "A personal introduction is befitting for your station. And besides," he added with a wink, "Prince Vesryn will always have a moment to meet beautiful ladies."

A flash of annoyance seared through Serenna's thoughts, even though she knew her father meant to reassure her with a compliment.

Yes, she wanted to stand out, but she refused to compete for the prince's attention like some harlot displaying their wares for coins. *I'm a princess. I'm more dignified than that!*

Walking over one of the many latticed white bridges to cross the stream, Serenna searched for the origin of the rivulet. Waterfalls cascaded from the upper levels of the winding Spire. Her eyes followed the flowing water to the uppermost peak of the building. She gaped.

. There was a gateway in the sky.

"The *portal* brings water in?" she asked.

Elashor glanced up. "When engineers constructed Centarya, they realized a water source would be practical and beneficial. Near Kyansari, they opened a permanent rift in the Sapphire Basin. A continuous supply pours in through the portal."

Her father steered them to an outdoor set of spiral steps, bypassing the Spire's main entrance. "Cisterns collect and store the water. Anything surplus flows through reservoir channels and other features around campus, eventually circulating off the island as waterfalls."

What else have the elves thought of? All that she had witnessed today was both foreign and marvelous, and it kindled a sense of curiosity to discover more.

Serenna's astonishment came to an abrupt halt upon realizing the elves had concealed such knowledge from the mortals. *Why didn't they share these wonders for everyone to enjoy? The elven-blooded had magic in the human realms this past century, but they left us unaware.*

Squaring her shoulders, Serenna refocused on the opportunity she had in front of her. She had the chance to get to know her father. That, she could work with—she had control over that. *I'm sure the elves had their reasons.*

Serenna had prepared questions she assumed her father would enjoy answering, since he was involved in the military campaign. She still hadn't been able to determine what his regular duties were.

She asked, "What will you be doing after you're done recruiting?"

"Much of my time will be spent with the nobles in the mortal capitals dictating King Galaeryn's instructions," Elashor said. "The aristocrats will be prepared to utilize the humans under their rule. I'll be reporting the realms' progress to the High Council as we mobilize the war effort." He angled the hilt of his longsword so the scabbard wouldn't strike the marble as they ascended the Spire's steps. "We'll begin training human scouts to comb through the lands while you're learning how to master your magic. If all goes well, it won't be long until we discover the wraith's stronghold."

"So, you're overseeing the war front?" Serenna held up the corner of her dress so she wouldn't trip climbing the stairs.

"In a way." Elashor shrugged. "I'll be representing the king and the prince so they won't have to abandon their more important duties."

Through an arched white oak door, they entered the Spire, weaving around the interior chambers of the building. Serenna felt as if they glided through clouds. The structure was airy, dazzling with white walls. Bright sunshine glinted in through the windows. After the first few twists and turns, she was lost, but her father was pursuing their destination like a hound on a trail.

"Where are we going?" Serenna asked.

Her legs burned from the never-ending stairs. She experienced a peculiar pulling, like a weight dragging on her chest and couldn't quite put her finger on the sensation. *I'm probably just getting lightheaded.*

"The prince's quarters are on the top level. The magus at the traveling grounds reported he's currently on campus—we'll see if he's in his office."

Serenna panted her question in between sucking in air to douse the fire burning in her lungs. "Why don't we portal and save the trip?"

"As you'll learn from your classes, portaling can be dangerous. We have designated locations where portals are permitted in public areas," Elashor said, straightening one of the steel plates on his shoulder. "It's mandated that those are the only places we create gateways. Let's just say if you create a rift and someone is in the way, they may be a few limbs short by the time you finish opening it."

Serenna shuddered the disturbing image out of her thoughts. "I see."

Stationed outside a door, two towering guards in black-plated armor stared ahead when Elashor strode between them. Serenna warily eyed the longswords hanging at their sides. The warriors were hulking elves, even more intimidating than Elashor as they stood unblinking, not even glancing her way.

Serenna tucked her disheveled hair behind her ears before following her father into the room to meet the prince.

CHAPTER 12

JASSYN

With Elashor's taunt still ringing in his ears, a shadow of dread surrounded Jassyn, swirling like a veil of toxic fog. Returning to Centarya's refuge was supposed to envelop him in relief. But now, his emphasized *duties* loomed over him like an approaching squall.

Even after his assignment to Allaenar, Jassyn had kept both his living quarters and his office space in the Infirmary. During his six month absence, laborers constructed additional wings in the magus residence hall to house the influx of new assistants.

Now open to the human realm's elven-blooded, Centarya accounted for the fourfold increase in recruits. Jassyn intended to check in with Magister Thalaesyn after he situated himself back in his chambers.

Jassyn hadn't quite worked through his thoughts surrounding the upcoming war. As a mender, he knew he would have a place on the battlefield, but his usefulness ended there—not having offensive talents such as force or rending.

I doubt I'll be called to arms if they're going to position the humans on the front lines. But if the wraith are dragging off elves who have Essence, what hope do magicless mortals have?

Taking two steps at a time in the magus hall, Jassyn forced himself to smile and greet the handful of peers he passed. He supposed he could consider a few of them friends, or at least acquaintances. Nelya and he had worked closely together over the years.

But lingering gazes on his tattoos always drove a silent wedge between him and everyone else. As if everything unvoiced held enough space for their differences.

The ink he was forced to change every time his contracts switched hands was a symbol to the pure-bloods. He was someone the council had deemed coveted, *desired*. A bloodline the nobles should compete for.

But to other elven-blooded, the markings were a line drawn in the sand.

He was different.

On the way to his suite, Jassyn overheard gossip of the wraith attacking orchards and slaughtering a population of villagers in the northern realm. *Why have they attacked humans now?* The creatures were content enough over the previous century to only drag off elven citizens in Alari.

A tingling rush streamed through Jassyn's fingertips when he waved a hand in front of his apartment door to reveal a violet shield. An inversion of illumination twined with shielding magic rendered the ward invisible, but anyone with Essence could sense the hum of power if they approached.

Six months tethered took a greater toll on his abilities than he'd expected. His Well didn't hold nearly as much Essence compared to his former reserves. He would have to put in an effort to refortify his magical stores.

Draining and restoring his Well daily would be a start to stretch the amount of power he could draw from. Considering the addition of combat and rending classes, Jassyn suspected he would have ample opportunity. *I'm sure we'll be spending more time mending recruits than we ever have before.*

Like unwinding a coil of rope, Jassyn extended a tendril of Essence. He flared his shielding ability to unravel the ward on his rooms. The tied-off magic hadn't degraded since his absence.

Locking his apartments had nothing to do with his trust in the other magus. He simply preferred the comfort and security of his privacy. Others could untangle his shield if they put in the effort, but he doubted anyone would have any reason to go into his chambers.

Aside from his former rooms at Kyansari's palace, this was the only space that had ever belonged to him. He wasn't exaggerating when he told Serenna that Centarya was his home.

Once inside his suite, Jassyn busied himself with removing the furniture's dust covers and opening windows to usher out the stale air.

While he knew the academy was a place to stow the undesired elven-blooded, the elves had spared no expense in Centarya's construction. The architecture's seamless angles and the excessive use of glass were just as pleasing as the buildings in the capital.

He despised appreciating something the elves had created.

While filling the hanging sconces throughout his apartments with globes of illumination, Jassyn decided he would decorate with plants to bring life back into his chambers.

There was a certain solace to be found in keeping himself occupied, a comfort in staying busy so his mind didn't have time to dwell on his other obligations. Perhaps he could distract himself with delusions of having a normal existence. If he could control something as simple as decorations, it would craft a sliver of satisfaction—even if everything else was out of his hands.

Tucking away the few sets of clothing he'd brought from Vaelyn induced a feeling of finality to his chapter there. If anything, he would actually miss the distance from Alari. Looking back, he would gladly sacrifice his access to Essence if it meant living on his own terms.

He wanted to believe he'd left something good behind—helping the less fortunate peasants was the least he could do to atone for the elves' oppression. And perhaps someday, Serenna would align her thinking to the reality in front of her instead of the fantasy she desired.

Defying Elashor's obscene request of impregnating her only proved that the realm didn't dictate his every action. Jassyn's thoughts skipped over the general's proposal of dissolving his contracts if he submitted to his will.

He didn't know who to trust, but he knew Elashor wouldn't be his savior even if he followed through with his wishes. Acid churned in his stomach for even contemplating such an idea.

Why does producing offspring with Serenna matter so much? Jassyn was unable to comprehend why one child was worth the dissolution of his contracts.

The council couldn't pretend the coupling arrangements were about preserving their numbers as a race anymore. The population of elven-blooded already rivaled that of the pure-bloods.

So why won't they release me?

Was it simply for the nobles to have unfettered access to his line, the Raellyns? The council received payment or bribes every time his contracts changed hands to a different family. *Is everything about accumulating their wealth?*

He wondered when Elashor would pressure Serenna into whatever couplings he deemed fit. If he could ever work up the courage to have the discussion, Jassyn hoped to open her eyes just a little to what life as an elven-blooded *really* meant.

Now that the general would be a more present figure, Jassyn felt inclined to protect Serenna from her sire's influence. She deserved to have the freedom to make her own decisions and not be an unaware pawn in Elashor's schemes. Her heart was already in her eyes every time she looked at her sire, too enraptured by his presence to realize he would tear her to shreds to get what he wanted.

Changing back into his magus armor, Jassyn studied his appearance in a dressing mirror. He swapped out the gems at the tips of his ears for his preferred silver-plated cuffs. His hair mostly concealed the white-inked tattoo on his forehead, but his eyes still lingered on the sigil.

How long did he have before his handlers caught wind of his return to Alari and summoned him like Elashor so bluntly reminded him? Refusing to dwell on the inevitable situation, Jassyn rearranged his curls as if he could obscure the brand and conceal his bleak thoughts.

Opening a drawer in his dresser, he shifted a hidden compartment to retrieve a handful of small knives, the steel handles cool against his fingers. The golden blades reflected shards of sunlight as he tilted the daggers to inspect their edges. Metal leaves and vines wrapped around the hilt as a decorative grip.

Lacking offensive talents inspired a certain creativity to compensate for his magical deficiencies. The thought of being completely helpless at another's hand had panic gnawing away at his insides.

He'd already experienced enough vulnerability in other areas of his life.

Jassyn had never used the weapons to tether anyone. But he wasn't sure what to expect at Centarya anymore. Possessing the additional defense provided him with what he assumed was a false sense of reassurance.

In recent years, he hadn't honed his skills throwing knives like he did in his youth under the instruction of the palace's weapon masters. Perhaps it was time to polish those rusty abilities.

And to think that he once wanted to be a warrior, hunting down the wraith.

Like his cousin.

As if Vesryn were someone to look up to.

Growing up, Jassyn used to beg for stories of Vesryn's adventures whenever the prince returned to the palace. But Vesryn had dismissed him as beneath his notice—only taking an interest in Jassyn when he was mature enough to decipher and react to ridicule.

Like poking and prodding a *half-breed's* human emotions was a form of amusement, a game that provided the prince with some sick little thrill.

At first, Jassyn couldn't control his outbursts elicited by the prince's jeering, but he learned any reaction only evoked more taunts. He closed himself off and suppressed his feelings after that.

He would never understand why some people delighted in the suffering of others. *Maybe they're so miserable themselves that projecting their pain is all they have left.*

Jassyn's hand trembled around a dagger until he willed his fingers to relax, swallowing the jagged edge of his dissected memories. Perhaps he'd been desperate, grasping at a ledge, attempting to cling to *someone* who would see him as more than a half-breed with a singular purpose.

He just put his hope in the wrong person.

Even after all this time, a petty part of Jassyn resented admiring his cousin. Vesryn radiated a different flair of nobility. He was one of the few pure-bloods who actually did anything of note. After his twin's death, the prince established the rangers and pursued the wraith relentlessly.

Jealous. That's what I am. Vesryn had the freedom to do whatever he wanted. The thought stung like a dagger dragging over skin.

Jassyn wondered what new gambits the prince would devise to make his life more miserable now that he managed operations at Centarya. *I'll be shocked if I can avoid him.*

Shaking his head, Jassyn slipped the knives into the hidden seams of his leathers, wishing he could bury his unwanted memories in the same way.

Departing the magus' quarters, Jassyn wandered along the shaded pathways back to the Infirmary. Taking his time, he appreciated the excessive beauty of the impeccably pruned flower beds dotting the cobblestone trails. Blankets of color bloomed from spring flowers in lawns edged so sharply, the ground looked as if it could slice through his boots with its immaculate angles.

Filling his lungs to near bursting, Jassyn reveled at breathing in the familiar crisp air. Centarya hovered half a mile in the sky, and the island smelled refreshing, not having the oppressive cacophony of scents like Kyansari.

At the same time, his mind shied away from thinking about how high up they were. Jassyn's stomach rudely reminded him with a nauseating roll.

Daydreams of joining the rangers defined his adolescence. Jassyn recalled the giddy excitement of being included in one of their scouting missions—before he was sent to the academy. If things had been different between him and Vesryn, it was possible he would have chosen that path instead.

But that was a time before the weight of his contracts began strangling his autonomy. He later grasped that entering their ranks meant enduring even more of the prince's vicious behavior.

And besides, if Vesryn hadn't pushed him off of a flying dracovae during his first flight, Jassyn doubted excessive heights would make him break out in a sweat. *Who does that?*

The prince had ultimately halted his plunge to the ground, but not before Jassyn had snapped into his shielding ability moments before he thought he would splatter across the earth.

And Vesryn had laughed and congratulated himself on driving Jassyn into his power. Like it was some grand achievement to incite trauma.

Stumbling, a wave of vertigo split Jassyn's skull. His head spun like a tornado, recalling the terror of plummeting from the sky as the edge of his vision darkened.

Clutching the doors of the Infirmary for support, he gasped, closing his eyes to steady himself. The sudden flash of memory dredged up frenzied panic. Jassyn grappled against his senses to remain calm. Inhaling gulping breaths, he waited for his head to stop whirling.

Breathing in through his nose and releasing the air out of his mouth.

Desperately attempting to settle his racing heart, Jassyn tore himself away from his unwelcomed history and refocused on the present. He latched his awareness to his feet on the ground, the smooth wood gripped under his fingertips, and the lavender scents wafting up from the flower beds.

Breathing in through his nose and releasing the air out of his mouth.

Scorching stars, get yourself together.

With one final stabilizing breath, Jassyn straightened, unnecessarily readjusting his leathers. Regaining his composure, he swung open the double doors of the Infirmary and wove his way through the healing wing back to his mentor's office.

"Magister Thalaesyn?" he asked, knocking on the propped door.

Jassyn's awareness ricocheted around the chambers when he entered. He gaped at the state of the magister's study, nearly incapable of thought. Tomes, random artifacts, and clutter he didn't even have a name for engulfed every surface, submerging the space into chaos.

This was the room of a madman.

Jassyn avoided drawing attention to the psychological decline he noticed in Thalaesyn over the years. His mentor had always been unorganized and aloof, but the current disarray of his office severely contrasted how it had looked before Jassyn's departure.

Sunshine filtering in through the diaphanous curtains outlined the window behind a sofa and scattered dust motes in the streams of light. Wading through the chambers, Jassyn discovered Thalaesyn passed out on a raggedly upholstered couch. His mentor's rumpled and stained robes only stressed his disheveled state.

Seriously? Jassyn snatched a wine bottle in danger of slipping out of the male's grip and placed it on a shelf, shoving back what he assumed was a vulpintera's articulated skeleton to make room.

This is worse. Much worse. Jassyn made a mental note to ask Nelya if this current behavior was becoming a trend.

For the sake of his mentor, he hoped it wasn't.

Jassyn knew a turbulent history existed between Thalaesyn and King Galaeryn. The discord resulted in the magister's dismissal from the king's service around the time the wraith killed Queen Maraelyn and Prince Aesar. The king exiled Thalaesyn from the capital to continue his research on Centarya once the construction was complete.

Perhaps the shift of the academy toward a military operation was the cause. Jassyn could think of no other recent changes.

Opening his perception, like a blossom unfolding in the sun, Essence surged through Jassyn's senses. His awareness buzzed with the static charge of his magic. Like a vine coiling around a branch, he hesitantly extended a tendril of unformed power to assess his mentor.

Thalaesyn was unsurprisingly drunk, as Jassyn had already deduced from the dredges in the wine bottle and the sour scent of alcohol stirred by snores.

Delving deeper with the wave of power, Jassyn sought to discover if anything else would explain the magister's deteriorating behavior beyond consuming drink.

One of Thalaesyn's toes was inflamed. *Most likely from stubbing it in a stupor.* Jassyn healed it anyway.

His mentor's cognitive function appeared as expected for a drunkard. Except...Jassyn's mouth pinched when he perceived a drug in his bloodstream.

Thalaesyn was dabbling in Stardust.

That's a slippery slope.

On the walk to the Terminal, members of Elashor's delegation had discussed Vesryn banning Stardust at the academy since assuming command. Which was a wonder, considering the tales Jassyn heard of the debauched parties the prince had thrown at the palace in his youth.

But there had to be something else. *Would Stardust cast him into such a downward spiral?* The drug was supposed to induce ecstasy, but Jassyn knew little of it beyond sensing it.

He tunneled his perception further.

His instincts were right. There was a...foreign abnormality on the magister's brain, like a barnacle latched onto a shell.

Jassyn failed to recognize the irregularity. A flicker of unease chilled his blood while he analyzed the snare shrouding Thalaesyn's mind. The singularity reminded him of an infection, a contagion that didn't belong.

Transforming his power into one of his talents, his mending ability, Jassyn poised a hand over his mentor's skull. Red light pulsed from his fingertips while he cast magic to prod at the anomaly like the push of a goad.

The abnormality appeared as if filaments of Essence tangled together into a thousand intricate knots, covering the magister's mind in an insurmountable web. Jassyn frowned, realizing it was a coil of telepathy.

An eerie awareness prickled over his skin, spiking every hair in alarm.

Coercion. It has to be.

The magister stirred on the couch with a murmur concerning someone named Mara. Releasing his power, Jassyn left Thalaesyn to his stupor.

Thoughts spinning like dust trapped in a whirlwind, Jassyn wandered back to the comfort of his office, drifting in a sea of thoughts. *Why is he compelled? What secrets would need to be concealed at Centarya?* As far as Jassyn knew, King Galaeryn was the only one capable of binding anyone to his will with telepathic power.

That level of control imposed on others had apprehension snaking up his spine.

Is Thalaesyn consuming Stardust as a release from the weight of the magic?

Questioning his mentor wouldn't work. The coercion likely prevented the magister from discussing whatever the king had veiled from his mind. Could there be a way to study the restricting power? Or untangle such a colossal labyrinth of telepathic Essence?

The task would be daunting. Jassyn knew he didn't have the skill. Not yet. But Elashor had the knowledge and unraveled the coercion the king had placed on him. *Maybe it's like pulling one specific thread to release a knot.*

Would the king know if someone tampered with his power? Or is the coercion like a shield? Magic to be tied off and forgotten about?

Jassyn entered his office, situated in an alcove on the main level of the Infirmary. It was just as he'd left it. Upon seeing an envelope on his desk covered by a white trillium flower, Jassyn's knees jerked until they locked, every muscle frozen in place.

His heart smacked into his stomach on its plunge to the floor.

Stars, no, he pleaded.

Jassyn rushed to the missive with panic climbing into his throat. Crumpling into his chair with a subdued whimper, he recognized the script of his name.

Familiar echoes of despair reverberated through his mind, embedding a tremor in his hands. He unconsciously traced the ink on his forehead.

Like leaves of a tree shriveling in a frost, Jassyn collapsed in on himself. *Scorching stars. She couldn't have waited for me to settle in first?*

He drew a hand over his face. Dismay weighed on him, dragging him down like an anchor in an ocean of dread.

Jassyn's hearing muted to a droning buzz while he read the

summons to Lady Farine Vallende's estate to celebrate her seventh century. His nose wrinkled at the rancid perfume emanating from the letter. His gut roiled as his mind dredged up memories like vile sludge.

Before realizing what he was doing, he had the parchment shredded into a dozen pieces.

Defeated, Jassyn placed his head in his hands, his chest tight as he swallowed back a strangled gasp. A few days. He had a few days before he had to leave and perform his *duty* to the realm.

If he could even pretend what Farine forced him to do at her estate had anything to do with the survival of the elven race with all the males and females she made him service.

Later. I'll deal with this later.

Paralyzed with distress freezing the marrow in his bones, Jassyn wasn't able to move from his desk. A thought niggled at the back of his mind, like a fish hooked on a line.

No. I'm better than that. I won't do it...

But will it help?

His mentor certainly had a supply in his office, judging from the amount swimming through his bloodstream.

Putting no more thought into it, Jassyn shot out of his chair, speeding to the magister's study. Shutting the door behind him, he ensured Thalaesyn was still unconscious.

Where would he put it?

His desk, obviously. Hiding in plain sight. As if anyone could even find anything in the mess of this room.

Heart thudding a frantic rhythm, Jassyn rifled through the drawers, all the while keeping one eye on the sleeping elf.

He retrieved a hand-size box and flipped the lid open.

What am I doing? I'm not actually considering stealing and fouling myself with a drug, am I? He studied the luminous blue powder, never having indulged in mind-addling substances before.

Stardust, crafted from Essence-infused salts, was a relatively new form of recreation this past century, commonly used among the wealthy. It had only increased in popularity in the courts for its ecstasy-inducing effects.

It was also highly addictive, interfering with accessing and regenerating magic.

Jassyn snapped the container shut. He tucked it under his arm, hurrying back across campus to his living quarters.

Time trickled like sand falling in an hourglass. Jassyn couldn't say how long he sat alone at the table in his chambers, staring at the glowing powder. Considering and weighing his options, wondering if he could escape the hopelessness of his reality.

I can be careful. I'll take a small dose when I arrive at Farine's estate. Shouldn't that be enough to ease my mind while I'm there? I just want to control something in my life.

I can handle this.

The indecision crawled through his thoughts, sinking in barbs of doubt. His resolve to destroy the drug was being tested, but his preconceived concerns started to fray the more he contemplated the presented escape.

Jassyn wanted to put on a brave face before resuming his duties, refusing to let his obligation to the realm drag him down a well of misery.

But it wasn't easy.

There was no point in dreaming about realities that didn't exist—having a life that was his own.

Every time his handlers summoned him away, Jassyn descended further into something unrecognizable. The masks he had to wear, the illusions he had to curate to survive, none of it was him. And he loathed everything about it.

He was losing sight of who he was and who he wanted to be. He hadn't had the choice in decades. All that existed was the time between filling one contract and the next. His *duty* shackled him to the realm, tainting every moment of his existence.

The weight of his circumstances caved in around him. He was drowning. Capsizing in the sea like a ship with a broken hull.

I'm so tired of feeling.

He wasn't sure what he would decide to do. For now...for now, he would let his composure fracture so he could put the pieces back together.

Or try to.

Like watching a vase slip off a counter, Jassyn allowed himself to shatter. Bracing against a surge of grief, talons of despair pried open his ribs, scraping over his heart.

Jassyn sank into his misery, letting the gloom swallow him. He dropped his head into his arms, and with an anguished sob tearing free from his chest, a piece of him sundered and slipped away.

CHAPTER 13

SERENNA

Serenna had a vague notion of what she expected the prince to look like. She anticipated meeting an impressively dressed male. One who was imposing, radiating a regal aura.

But the elf in rugged leathers lounging in the center of the chambers wasn't quite what she had in mind.

Utterly at ease, the prince leaned back in a chair with his booted feet sprawled over his ebony desk. Vesryn's eyes were on them before they entered the doorway, but then flicked down, seemingly engrossed with trimming his nails with a knife. His gaze lazily lifted again when Elashor's boots echoed on the marble floors as they approached him.

"General," the prince said, more as a statement than a greeting.

His silvery hair spilled over his shoulders, glowing with a luminosity, convincing Serenna the shine had nothing to do with the sunlight streaming through the arched windows behind him.

A stitched dragon lurked on the chest of his armor. Based on the tapestries decorating his office, she assumed it was his sigil.

Raising a hand, Vesryn inspected his nails before he seemed satisfied. He lazily flipped the blade three times before sheathing the dagger at his waist with a whisk of metal and leather.

Serenna flinched, slightly unnerved by the display.

Vesryn's chair dropped to all fours. Feet swinging to the ground, he stood in one fluid motion. The prince's gaze flitted over her dismissively before he addressed Elashor.

"This must be your daughter from the *human* realms?"

Serenna's heart dropped, even though she'd predicted her origins would be a disadvantage.

Surely King Galaeryn would scour the lands beyond Alari for a suitable match for his son. Willing an iron confidence into her attitude, Serenna lifted her chin. *The king has to see the wisdom in choosing the prince's consort from outside the elven realm.* Such an arrangement would only be strategic in binding the lands together.

Elashor nodded and gestured to her. "Prince Vesryn, I'd like to introduce my daughter, Serenna Vallende. I was hoping we could use the Heart of Stars to unveil her abilities before I depart."

Serenna wrestled down a surge of pride when her father claimed her with his name. And then blinked, realizing she should say something.

Vesryn's jade eyes bored into hers while she appreciated the sharp angles of his unimpressed face. Like a bird trapped in a cage, Serenna's heart flew with a frenzy within the confines of her chest under the attention of his gaze. Her mouth went dry, and she forgot every curated court pleasantry she was ever taught. She gripped the sides of her dress to steady herself while she stared stupidly at the prince.

Bright stars, no one has a right to be that attractive. Serenna's mind blundered, still not prepared for the moment, until finally tendrils of cohesive thoughts crept together to form the semblance of rational words.

Stop drooling over him, you stargazer. What kind of impression are you making?

She hunted down her sensibilities.

Serenna cleared her throat. "Prince Vesryn." A mortifying heat rushed to the points of her ears. "It's…it's an honor," she stuttered, inclining her head. *Thank the stars I didn't curtsy like a human.*

"Pleasure," Vesryn said, even though it sounded like anything but. His eyes, sharp like sea glass, narrowed and threatened to slice her with his piercing gaze.

An eerie sensation, like a hook pulling on her spine, persuaded Serenna that if she closed her eyes, she could point to where the prince was in the room.

Stop being an idiot. He's just handsome and you're just flustered.

Vesryn fastened his attention back to Elashor, tapping his fingers over his arms. "As I'm sure you're aware, the magus use the Heart of Stars when they register new initiates." The prince sounded as if the topic thoroughly uninterested him. "But I suppose I can spare a moment to satisfy your curiosity."

Serenna's brows rose. Despite being the academy's commander, Vesryn didn't appear busy. A manicure was apparently the only thing on his list of things to do. *There aren't even papers on his desk!*

Elashor bowed. The prince pivoted on a heel with a predatory lethalness and stalked to one cabinet along the perimeter of the room.

His obsidian leathers did nothing but accentuate his striking figure. Vesryn obviously spent more time in the sun than her father, judging from his golden skin. A weight she didn't realize she carried, lifted from her shoulders as she suddenly felt less self-conscious about not having a luminescent, elven complexion. *I suppose I won't be out of place among the other elven-blooded here—even the prince looks the part.*

Though not as broad, Vesryn was taller than her father. From the width of his chest and the definition in his bare arms, Serenna determined the prince was as strong as any warrior, despite his lithe appearance. His leather pants were obviously crafted to display every muscle in those sculpted legs, and still somehow allowed motion despite how snug they were.

Serenna shamelessly stared, torn between watching the prince prowl across the office and smothering the anxiety kindling in her middle. She stood there awkwardly, unsure of what to do with her hands.

Tearing her fingers away from twirling her hair, she clasped them at her waist. *No, that's too matronly.* Folding them under her breasts seemed too stiff. Holding one arm was too timid. Behind her back was too formal.

Stop it. Focus.

By the time the prince retrieved a container no larger than a jewelry box, Serenna's skin felt too tight and uncomfortable, arms dangling ungracefully loose at her sides.

Vesryn flicked a hand. A network of purple webs surrounding the container ignited with a burst of light. The magic dissipated in strands, like tongues of flames burning through wicks.

Serenna's attention latched onto the power, eager to see more of Essence's capabilities. She assumed whatever the prince did unlocked the box because the lid opened with a *click*.

Vesryn retrieved an object shrouded in a snowy cloth. Uncovering the top, he displayed a triangular, crystal prism.

The corded muscles in his forearms flexed with the motion. An intrusive thought sprouted, and Serenna wondered what those ridges would feel like under her fingertips.

Stars, now isn't the time to be distracted, she berated herself.

One side of the prince's mouth quirked, like he knew what she was thinking. His gaze pinned on Elashor. "Wouldn't it be...a *shame* if your daughter fails to possess a fraction of your abilities?"

Serenna's shoulders cinched with tension. His tone was difficult to interpret. She glanced at her father for reassurance, even though the prince's words felt like a taunt directed at her.

"What determines how many abilities you can control?" she asked. "Is the magic passed down from your parents?"

"One does not inherit the sum of the control their predecessors have over each talent," Elashor said. "We believe our ancestors were all arch elves—those able to manipulate all eight abilities." He nodded to the prince. "Prince Vesryn and I are both arch elves. But this is only the case for about twenty percent of the population. And only purebloods retain this type of governance over magic. Essence mastery appears to be decreasing."

Serenna's heart raced in anticipation. She didn't want to disappoint her father if her magical capabilities were lacking. And she certainly didn't want to embarrass herself in front of the prince.

"And the number of talents you possess determines your strength —thus your station in the realm," Vesryn said blandly, idly picking at the dragon's stitching on his chest.

So, the more abilities I have, the stronger and higher ranking I'll be. If I only have the illumination talent like all other elves, I'll curl up and die.

Studying the prism dwarfed in the prince's hand, Serenna asked, "And this...piece of glass will show which powers I have?"

"This *piece of glass*," Vesryn mimicked, "is the Heart of Stars and is perhaps the most ancient artifact the Aelfyn brought across the Cerulean Sea."

Serenna frowned at the condescension dripping from his tone. *It's not like I knew anything about the elves' secrets until a few days ago.*

"The relic resonates with your magic and will shine specific colors to indicate which abilities you have," the prince said. He tugged the cloth from under the prism and tossed the fabric onto his desk.

As soon as the crystal touched his bare palm, a dazzling array of shimmering lights radiated from the uppermost point. A rainbow of colors glittered around him in a halo. "The entire spectrum of the Heart illuminates for an arch elf."

With an unreadable look, Vesryn nodded in invitation and extended the shining prism.

Serenna's senses tingled as she took a hesitant step forward while the prince tracked her with the calculating intensity of a hawk, his gaze siphoning what shreds of confidence she fiercely clung to.

So as not to drop the priceless artifact, Serenna focused on stilling her quivering hands as she reached out to cradle the offered Heart. The opportunity to hold an ancient relic her Aelfyn ancestors had deemed important enough to carry across the sea had her breathless with reverent awe.

When her palms lifted the surprisingly warm exterior, a spectrum of colors shot up from the peak, bright in her face. Serenna inhaled sharply through her teeth, relief sweeping through her that more than one color sprang to life.

Vesryn peered at the glimmering halo and clicked his tongue. "Let's see...mending, illumination, portaling, shielding, force, and rending."

The lack of emotion in his voice detracted a little from her satisfaction. Surely having six abilities was an achievement, especially since she wasn't a pure-blood. *Well, he is an arch elf, so it makes sense if he's hard to impress.*

The talents at her disposal were more than she expected. Serenna's mind raced in every direction like a fracture spreading across ice. *I have the same rending power as the prince.* A thrill bloomed now that she would have the opportunity to distinguish herself with her magic. *And have the chance to spend more time with Vesryn during his classes.*

She nearly bounced with excitement, hardly able to restrain herself from running down the stairs of the Spire to tell Velinya and Jassyn about her abilities.

"Impressive." Vesryn's voice channeled Serenna's attention back to him.

Their gazes tangled as she met his eyes. A warm flush, like the sun igniting across her skin, had Serenna beaming while she basked in his praise.

The prince smirked. "For a half-breed."

Serenna's mouth went slack. Her father grunted in amusement beside her.

"What?" Squinting at the prince, she scoffed at his slur.

Vesryn was training her kind at the academy and would be betrothed to a *half-breed*. She considered throwing the relic at the prince's head to knock the smug expression off his face.

As if provoked by the thought, the Heart flared in Serenna's hand, shooting a pulse of heat into her arm, straight into her chest. Her spine went taut like a bowstring when a low, guttural voice uncoiled in her mind.

> *Greetings, young draka, hear our plight,*
> *New hatchlings from earth and starlight.*
>
> *From distant galaxies did the whelps arrive.*
> *They stole our magic and left us deprived.*
>
> *They used five Hearts to bind our power in chains:*
> *Earth, Fire, Lightning, Wind, and Rain.*

The balance of earth, it must be restored.
The Hearts must be returned to where they were forged.

But the Hearts were hidden by the thieving hands,
The cunning ones from otherworldly lands.

Bring us the Hearts so we can restore
The harmony as we had before the war.

Young draka, heed our call,
For this balance of nature affects us all.

Releasing a shocked gasp, Serenna shoved the Heart into Vesryn's waiting palm. He arched a brow. She looked frantically between him and her father. *Am I the only one who heard that voice?*

Apparently, she was.

Effectively excluding her, they engaged in their own conversation, discussing some matters of the council.

Wrapped around the relic, Vesryn's hand glowed in the artifact's rainbow light. The prince remained focused on Elashor, but his eyes darted to her. Twice. The movement was so subtle Serenna wasn't convinced it happened, even though her stomach flipped when she sensed the weight of his attention.

She ground her teeth. *No one dismisses me like this! Don't either of them care that I have six abilities?* A tremor twitched a muscle in her cheek. *Why did I want to meet this...this...pompous prince? This isn't an introduction at all!*

Taking a stabilizing breath, Serenna calmed her emotions before they spiraled out of control. The previous few days had been beyond stressful, exhausting, and overwhelming—leaving her more wrung out than clothes drying on a line. Perhaps she simply misinterpreted the purpose of the meeting.

Elashor's proximity didn't exactly set the tone for more intimate discussions with the prince. It wasn't fair to expect Vesryn to engage in any personal conversation with her father hovering. *Now that Vesryn knows me, I'll just linger after his classes to converse.*

Letting her attention drift, Serenna considered the voice speaking from the Heart. *Was it magic from the relic?* The words floated away as she tried to commit them to memory before they evaporated from her mind. She expected the prince would have reacted if he'd heard the same thing when he touched the crystal, but he didn't appear concerned.

Serenna's attention flew back into focus, meeting Vesryn's stare burning into the side of her face.

"I'll be instructing rending classes in the evenings if I'm not hunting the wraith," he said, closing the chest around the Heart. He tossed it onto his desk. The box skidded across the wood.

Serenna stared in disbelief at the prince's derelict behavior, mishandling the elves' most precious relic.

Well, she certainly wasn't going to ask *him* anything about the voice. She didn't need Vesryn or her father thinking she was some foolish initiate if she mentioned something so absurd.

Surely Jassyn would tell her if the relic spoke to those holding it. He would be more reliable anyway, being a scholar. *And he never belittles me for asking questions.*

"You're one of the ten percent on campus who have rending at their disposal." Vesryn crossed his arms and considered her.

Serenna's pulse spiked to alarming levels when their eyes collided. A flush creeped up her neck to scorch her face the longer the prince held her gaze, like he was waiting for her to look away.

Balling her hands into fists, Serenna denied him the concession of submitting. He picked her apart like she was one of those frayed threads on the dragon stitched across his chest, but she refused to yield by averting her eyes.

The right side of Vesryn's mouth twisted higher the deeper her nails furrowed into her palms. Like getting a reaction out of her amused him. Serenna's nostrils flared when her discomfort swelled into a tide of annoyance in the silent battle of wills.

"Perhaps you'll surprise me," Vesryn said at last, turning away.

Serenna's chest loosened with her held breath. *What was that about?*

She didn't bother listening to the rest of the conversation and couldn't recall if she even supplied Vesryn with a farewell when they exited his office. He certainly didn't offer a kiss to her hand like a *proper* royal would.

Serenna skirted past his threatening guards, following her father down the hallway.

I don't know what I was expecting. Why would meeting a princess from the human realms impress the elven prince?

Jassyn was right. Vesryn definitely wouldn't be worth her time. Judging from his obvious scorn, she could already tell he looked down on her. *Is it because I'm of mixed descent?*

No, I'll prove him wrong. Only twenty percent of pure-bloods have access to the entire spectrum of Essence, and they're not even the ones training their powers. I can still master my magic.

Pulling her out of her thoughts, Elashor said, "I think the prince liked you."

A shill laugh spilled from Serenna's lips, echoing in the stairwell. "What?" *Did he not see the way Vesryn sneered at me?* "I don't think so."

"Don't disregard him." Elashor strode down the serpentine staircase with ease. "I've watched hundreds of males and females throw themselves at him over the years."

Hundreds? Like the number was something to be proud of. "And why should I be one of them?" Serenna frowned. "I'm sorry I wasted your time. This introduction was a mistake."

"If you were smart, you'd put in the effort to attract his attention." Elashor's forehead formed a ridge, sharp like his words. "I'll give you some advice. If you want anything from this realm, earn it."

"Earn it? How?" Serenna stared at her father's back as he outpaced her. She tripped and refocused her efforts on descending the stairs. "Jassyn says the prince refuses to even think about taking a wife until we eradicate the wraith—that's why the king is intervening to select a match for him."

"Of course Jassyn would say that," Elashor muttered. "You don't need to be the prince's *wife* to find yourself in his favor."

Serenna returned to her father's side as they reached a landing. *Are we...discussing what I think we are?*

"Becoming close to the prince would be a wise move if you can do it sensibly." Elashor ran a hand over the whorls of the marbled railing.

"If you were a clever woman, you would see the value of positioning yourself closer to power."

Biting the inside of her cheek, Serenna debated if she even wanted to spend more time with Vesryn after their interaction. *Maybe the prince acts differently when his subordinates aren't around.* Her father reported to him, after all.

Serenna was familiar with the intricacies of the court, but she wouldn't have *this* discussion with her father. She attempted to steer the conversation in a different direction. "Since I'm from the human realms, do you think I would even be considered as a potential consort?"

"There are better matches if you want to consider the purity of bloodlines, but you have an advantage that pure-bloods don't." Elashor raised his brows, giving her a sideways look.

Serenna stopped in her tracks. *Oh, he's definitely discussing what I think he is.*

"You don't have to be a *consort* to provide the prince with heirs."

"But that..." Serenna tripped over her words, tangling her like thorns. "But that wouldn't be proper," she protested. She wanted to find an acceptable match in the elven courts, not...gallivant from bed to bed. "Why would I want to have the prince's children?"

"The elves have different ideas of what is proper than what you were taught in the *human* realms," her father said, reaching the next landing. "You should embrace the ideals of your heritage. The Falkyn line is the most powerful in our realm, and any offspring would be remarkable. From what I gather from court gossip, coupling with the prince would be...memorable."

The tips of Serenna's ears radiated with flames of embarrassment as they passed a handful of servants carrying linens. Disbelieving, she gaped at her father's back. He condoned her wiggling her way into the prince's bed and had heard enough about Vesryn's so-called reputation to claim the act would be *enjoyable? Is that supposed to tempt me?*

These elves had drastically different principles than those in the human realms if they didn't perceive the whole situation as scandalous. She knew and accepted that elves didn't marry.

Jassyn didn't prepare me for this. I thought the court members would choose someone as a life partner. I didn't realize you were expected to pick a rotating bedfellow.

Serenna had no intention of throwing herself at the prince, amusing him for an evening and walking away bearing his spawn like some broodmare.

But despite their different interpretations of the word "proper," Serenna didn't want to misplace the momentum of the conversation. She hardly had any experience talking to her father, and she didn't want to disappoint him with her *human*-influenced differences.

"I'm sorry," she apologized, rushing to catch up to him as they entered the sunny lawn of the Spire. "Everything the past few days has been such an adjustment, and I'm trying to keep my head above water. The prince is very attractive, but I'm…unsure of how to proceed."

Serenna's throat stung with the bitterness in her voice. "Mother never permitted me to court suitors. I'm out of my depth with the elves, and I don't want to embarrass myself—or you."

She hesitated, blinking away a burn in her eyes, unwilling to admit an elf from Alari already didn't find her desirable. But she could be honest with her father, since he was giving her advice. "When…when I tried to gain Jassyn's favor, he only discouraged me."

Elashor's armor clinked when he suddenly stopped. He turned to her slowly, with a dangerous glint in his eye. With what emotion, Serenna couldn't say, but the redness in his face hinted at anger.

He voiced a scathing question. "Jassyn…*discouraged* you?"

Serenna retreated a step from her father's bared teeth, unfamiliar with seeing any expression from him. Mortification and shame spiraled through her. She wasn't brave enough to meet his glare.

"I'm not quite sure what's proper with the elves." Serenna studied the grass under her sandals, blinking back the tears threatening to steal her vision. *Well, beyond their promiscuous behaviors.* "If I'm not worthy of their attention because of my human blood, I can understand. But I feel as if…as if I won't be good enough for any of them."

Serenna tensed and glanced up when her father tipped her chin. "You've been given an advantage with the Vallende bloodline and have a substantial number of abilities," he said with a reassuring smile that softened his rugged features. "Immerse yourself in your studies and master your power. I know you will impress the prince, especially since you're one of the few with rending." Elashor's face contorted in a scowl. "And *Jassyn*," he snarled, dropping his hand. "That half-breed is a lost cause. His inaction has nothing to do with you. I can promise you that."

Serenna stiffened, but her father smoothed his features the next instant, his emotions receding. "You'll make me proud if you bring honor to the Vallende name. Follow the prince's lead."

He gave her shoulder a reassuring squeeze before breaking away and gesturing to the building he led her to. "This is your residence hall. You can find your room on the third floor. I arranged for you to stay with your handmaiden so you had a familiar face nearby. We'll talk the next time I visit." Elashor nodded at her and strode off toward the traveling grounds.

A bubble of hope rose in Serenna's heart at the possibility of developing a relationship with her father, even though she still had reservations about his wishes. Now, more than ever, she wanted to make him proud regardless of the human blood in her veins.

CHAPTER 14

SERENNA

Velinya met Serenna in the dormitory's courtyard. Each realm had its own building, and unsurprisingly, the initiates from Alari maintained the prime location in the island's center while everyone else had to trek across campus.

Already settled into their chambers, Serenna's friend led her around their new accommodations. Velinya couldn't restrain her curiosity and demanded a recounting of her meeting with the prince.

Serenna hadn't sorted through her feelings concerning Vesryn. He had been condescending, dismissive, and—not to mention—disdainful toward *half-breeds. But maybe he has to keep up appearances as the commander in front of other elves.*

Not wanting to ruin Velinya's excitement, Serenna kept those observations to herself. She appeased her friend by describing the sharp points of the prince's ears and how his muscles bulged in his sleeveless leathers.

Like with Jassyn, Serenna asked Velinya to drop the formalities surrounding her title. She didn't believe revealing her position as a princess from the human realms would do her any favors with the other recruits—especially since they were all now the same rank.

Passing through the white doors of the residence hall's entryway, the common room opened to a vaulted ceiling. After pining over the prince, Velinya provided commentary on what she'd learned during Nelya's tour.

According to her, the elves' system of *running* water was their most impressive feat. Both women sighed in relief at not having to lug buckets around for washing. *It would have been nice to have these comforts in the human realm.*

The term would start in a matter of days. Velinya relayed Nelya's advice to attend regeneration sessions in the evenings to begin perceiving their power. Much to everyone's dismay, Nelya also encouraged them to begin physical conditioning under the supervision of the combat magus.

Bright light trickled in through an expansive wall of curved windows in the lounge. Translucent curtains billowed in the breeze. Richly carved tables, bookcases, and even a wine bar outlined the perimeter of the room. Serenna wove around a cluster of plush chairs, following Velinya up a spiral staircase.

Serenna expected the new accommodations at the now designated military academy to be stark and dismal, but to her delight, she was wrong. Like the ground level, the third floor contained many windows saturating the hallways in sunshine.

In their apartments, a white oak table arranged for four sat under a crystal chandelier Serenna assumed was to be filled with illumination lights. She trailed her fingers on the armrest of one of the velvet chairs, the soft fabric rippling under her touch. On either side of the room, doorways led to private sleeping chambers.

Their quarters impressed Serenna more than her residence in Vaelyn's castle. "At least we won't be bunking," she said, satisfied they had their own space. Each bedroom contained a generously curtained four-poster bed, armoires, and full-length mirrors.

Velinya reviewed the locations of their classes. Serenna was already aware mending was taking place in the Infirmary. The Citadel held their other indoor subjects: telepathy, illusion, and illumination. And the rooftop was used for regeneration. The outdoor practice fields allowed more room for rending, force, combat, shielding, and portaling.

Even with the added luxuries, Serenna knew life at Centarya

would be an adjustment. Thrust into this new duty, the swiftness of the change didn't allow her any time for the shock to settle in. While ready to embrace the unknown, she still wondered why the elves never shared their comforts with the rest of the world.

Even before the term officially started, Serenna remained occupied. At the recruit's initiation ceremony, the Heart of Stars unveiled everyone else's abilities.

Velinya had portaling, force, telepathy, and illumination. To Serenna's disappointment, they shared no classes together during the first term—Serenna only had illumination, combat, mending, and rending since there wasn't enough time to fit classes for all of her abilities into the day.

Much to Serenna's alarm, no one mentioned hearing the voice from the Heart, but she didn't inquire either. *The stress of meeting the prince just had my imagination running wild.*

Taking Nelya's advice, Serenna and Velinya both attended evening regeneration sessions. On overcast nights, they learned that limited starlight made replenishing magic problematic—not that either of them had a need to restore their power since their Essence hadn't manifested yet.

Joining them one session, Jassyn had mused that perhaps the extinct shamanic powers could push back the clouds, but the elves' magic didn't have the same capabilities over the elements.

But this evening, the stars and the two rising moons, both crescents, glittered down on the assembled recruits. Serenna's battered body screamed in protest while she adjusted her seated position on the rooftop of the Citadel.

Running a hand along the complaining muscles of her leg, she grazed the chestnut-hued leather. *Am I ever going to get used to these trousers? At least the leathers don't smell like the insides of whatever animal it came from.*

The most troublesome part of the initiate's attire was putting on the top portion. A sleeveless leather bodice covered a white chemise.

Down the front, Serenna had to zigzag laces through loops to secure the material.

Naturally, the men's uniform was simpler and cinched together with clasps and buckles like the magus' armor. While more comfortable in dresses, Serenna enjoyed the familiarity of keeping her arms bare as she had in Vaelyn's warm climate.

Even though she knew she should have been focusing on the lecture about regenerating magic, Serenna couldn't stop replaying her disastrous day in the Combat Yard. A female magus with a mohawk had *backhanded* her for speaking out of turn.

Wincing, she touched her face, knowing that a bruise painted her cheek. Disgusted by Serenna's lack of abilities, Magus Kieryn voiced she expected the general to produce better offspring than the likes of her. The magus had assigned Serenna to "basic conditioning" for the foreseeable future.

The term hadn't officially begun, and she'd already embarrassed herself under her father's name. But Serenna decided to stubbornly return to the Combat Yard tomorrow before she met with Jassyn to tour the Infirmary. *I'll never improve otherwise.*

Serenna had no desire to be eviscerated by a wraith or to disgrace the Vallende name. Recruits from Alari were ahead of those from the human realms, having the luxury of being aware of their magic. Some initiates had been at Centarya for years *before* it was a military operation.

After another failed regeneration session, where Serenna was unable to sense her power, she and Velinya ambled back toward their residence hall, enjoying the stillness of the evening. They passed a cluster of Alari recruits sprawled out on a lawn passing around bottles of wine.

I'm sure the elves want us to lower our inhibitions so we're more likely to engage in coupling. Serenna still couldn't believe her father had encouraged her to find a way into the prince's bed.

It's lunacy.

No, the elven culture differs from what I'm used to, she corrected herself. *It doesn't make it wrong...just foreign.* But she wasn't sure if she would be comfortable with the notion—even if her father had her best interests in mind.

Serenna didn't point, but she nodded toward a curvy, pale-skinned woman who appeared to be the center of the group's attention. Orbs of illumination twinkled around her cascading hair, alight with the colors of flames and the setting sun.

Whispering to Velinya, Serenna said, "Look at her hair!"

"I didn't know *red* was a hair color," Velinya said, her eyes popping.

The initiates halted their revelry to watch them pass. The recruits from Alari stayed together in a pack, while those from the human realms had mingled. *Surely those from the elven realm aren't that different from everyone else.* They all were attending Centarya for the same purpose, after all.

Serenna was never one to pay compliments, especially to a stranger, but she experienced an impulse to do so. Perhaps it would be possible to befriend someone from Alari aside from Jassyn if she took the first step.

Halting near the group, she addressed the scarlet-haired woman. "Your hair is beautiful. I've never seen such a shade before."

The heart-faced woman paused with a wine bottle halfway to her parted lips. She assessed both Serenna and Velinya with a measured sweep of her gaze. Striking against her dark brows and lashes, she pinned her azure eyes on Serenna before taking a deep drink.

Ignoring Serenna's comment, she asked, "And which *human* realm are you two from?"

"Allaenar," Velinya said, quick to answer.

The flame-haired woman scoffed dismissively. "I suppose those from the southern courts have seen little of the world. Tell me, is it true you actually live underground in the mines?"

The Alari group burst into fits of exaggerated laughter.

Taken aback, Serenna sifted through the woman's words and tried to grasp the quip's meaning. *Was I rude to comment on her hair color?*

The nobles of her mother's court always treated her with respect, even if she misspoke. In fact, Jassyn was the only person who didn't hesitate to speak his mind around her. But she didn't appreciate the insinuation they were so backward in the human realms. *It's hardly our fault the elves kept secrets.*

Velinya chimed in again while words wedged in Serenna's throat. "We're from the Vaelyn court, and you're addressing the *princess* of the southern realm."

Serenna cringed. She knew her friend meant well, but she wanted to keep her royal ties to the mortal lands quiet—especially around those from Alari.

The red-haired woman pursed her pouty lips. She held the wine bottle out as if expecting someone to take it from her. Which, they did. Unfolding her legs, she stood gracefully, as sinuous as a viper slithering across sand. Serenna was forced to crane her neck to meet her gaze.

"I heard one of my sire's human offspring was in attendance," she said with a sneer. "I didn't expect to encounter you so soon. I'm Ayla Vallende of the *Kyansari* courts. If you've spent any time in Alari, you would know that my mother, Ceryn Raellyn, has a seat on the High Council."

A heavy silence suffocated the courtyard.

Serenna blinked as shock careened through her thoughts. *I have a sister? And she's related to Jassyn?*

An unexpected sting sliced through her chest. She glanced at Velinya for support, only to see bewilderment marring her friend's features as well.

Ayla tittered with delighted glee. "Oh, of course you're unaware. Why would our sire tell you?"

A blonde-haired woman rose to join Ayla, positioning herself almost defensively next to her.

Ayla addressed her. "Mishryn, aren't humans so quaint? It's best to keep them sheltered." She patted Serenna's head like a dog, receiving more laughter from their peers.

Serenna recovered her wits, backing away from Ayla's reach. "I'm not a human."

Ayla's grin spread wider, flashing perfect white teeth. *She's elven-blooded too!*

"No, but you might as well be. I'm assuming you were oblivious to magic until you came here. Isn't that right?" Ayla flicked her scarlet hair over a shoulder. "You know nothing of the elves. It's rather embarrassing opening Centarya to ignorant half-breeds."

Ayla cocked her head at Mishryn. As if in unspoken communication, they both extended their fingers. Blinding lights burst from their palms. Serenna and Velinya staggered and shielded their eyes from the sudden wave of brightness.

Peering down her nose, Ayla asked, "Have you even sensed your magic yet? With the power in our sire's bloodline, it would be a disgrace if you haven't."

Ayla held out her hand for the wine bottle, then paused to take another long swallow when it was returned to her. "Out of all the initiates, Mishryn and I have the most abilities. Seven, in fact. Nearly arch elves," she said smugly. "How many do *you* have?" she asked, jabbing at Serenna with the drink.

Serenna shuttered her expression, denying Ayla and her friends the satisfaction of seeing her dismay at the revelation that her father had other offspring. She'd had quite enough of this charade.

How can I hope to compete with Ayla, who already had access to her powers? Her sister even looked like a pure-blood with her near-luminescent skin and striking hair. Serenna's thoughts darkened, her heart sinking with her shortcomings.

Jassyn didn't speak about his family, but on more than one occasion, her father had mentioned the Raellyns were also among the most powerful bloodlines in Alari. *Alya is from both Vallende and Raellyn lines? Of course she has the most potential.*

Serenna couldn't think of anything clever to say to recover from the conversation. "I wouldn't want my presence to disturb someone with such a high standing," she said, assembling strings of composure before jealousy frayed her. "Don't choke on your wine. *Sister.*"

Serenna spun and stalked toward the southern dorms. Velinya scurried to catch up to her.

Ayla's parting taunt rolled over them as laughter from the group followed them. "I trust you'll learn that the elves from Alari are your betters. You wouldn't want to embarrass yourself any further. What would our sire think?"

Serenna trembled from the disbelief settling into her limbs. "Why didn't my father inform me I have a sister?" she asked, swallowing a bitter taste of jealousy. "Do you think my mother knows he has other offspring?"

Sharing her shock, the news had also rendered Velinya speechless.

Serenna's throat tightened with dismay, threatening to spiral into a gale of choked emotion. Her father had to be aware she'd uncover the truth. *Ayla knew about me. Why am I undeserving of knowing about her? Maybe I'm not worthy yet since I have so much to prove and live up to.*

But he had let her take his name. Surely that meant something.

Like a breeze howling around a crag, Elashor's words rushed back to Serenna. Her father had informed her that she'd have to earn whatever she wanted from the realm—the elves wouldn't hand it to her.

Why should they?

Serenna ground her teeth so forcefully, she feared they would crack. She would *earn* her place in Alari and prove to him that she was worthy of belonging as much as anyone else. *Why should Ayla get everything I want?*

With the wraith now attacking defenseless human villages and continuing to drag off elves from Kyansari, it wouldn't be long before Serenna had the chance.

CHAPTER 15

SERENNA

A few days before the term began, Serenna trailed Jassyn while he toured her through the Infirmary. She loved everything about the sharp angles and the vaulted ceilings of the limestone buildings—even their clinic was an architectural feat. Through the open windows, scents from the lavender hedges wafted in on a breeze.

"Since classes haven't officially started, it's been fairly quiet," Jassyn said, straightening a pillow on one of the empty beds. "But once the recruits start beating the stars out of each other, I imagine it'll get quite chaotic."

Serenna nearly groaned, not looking forward to more bodily abuse. "I'm just sore from running laps around the island."

No longer in Vaelyn's court attire, Jassyn's height had him appearing formidable in his white leathers. Along with his added accessories of plated ear cuffs, the armor and calf-high boots suited him, she decided. The dark circles under his eyes had Serenna believing the morning training Vesryn required of the magus had left him as weary as her.

Eager to learn more about mending under his guidance, Serenna agreed to spend an hour in the afternoons aiding him between her other classes. Judging from her failures in the Combat Yard, she assumed the Infirmary would be a haven. *Maybe I'll be more useful as a healer and not be dispatched to the front lines to fight. Will we even be able to control our powers yet if war comes soon?*

"What kind of work will I be doing as your aide?" Serenna asked.

"Until you manifest your mending power, you'll mostly be following me around." Jassyn led her deeper into the building. They wandered through a curtain-partitioned alcove. "I'll have tasks for you, like cutting bandages and mixing potions."

"Potions?" Serenna asked skeptically. "Won't you use magic?"

Jassyn released a derisive scoff. "Our noble commander ordered the magus to limit using Essence for healing unless it's absolutely necessary—life-threatening or debilitating. We're not *permitted* to heal cuts, scrapes, and bruises." Jassyn showed her into Nelya's alchemy lab. "The prince expects us to keep our Wells fully primed in the event the wraith organize any escalations." Under his breath, he muttered, "But I'm sure Vesryn simply delights in building character with pain."

Scrutinizing the variety of splints, bandages, and shelves lined with tiny vials of prepared medicines, Serenna imagined graphic injuries, each worse than the last.

She touched her yellowing cheek. "Do you think we'll be hurt that much in training?"

Jassyn's gaze lingered on her bruise, but he didn't comment on it. "Let's hope not, but I have a feeling you'll experience harsher methods than Centarya previously employed."

"You're not making me feel any better," Serenna grumbled, crossing her arms.

"You know where to find me if you need mending." Jassyn surprised her by giving her arm a comforting squeeze. "And it's not like I'm excused from combat either since Vesryn is having the magus train together as a unit," he said, guiding them into a darkened drying chamber where rows of herbs dangled from the ceiling in bunches.

"From what I gather, the war strategy involves Centarya leading the assault once the humans locate the wraith." Jassyn pinched off dried heads of echinacea flowers and instructed her to do the same. "But we won't be facing the creatures alone. Your sire commands the elven-blooded army, but the mortals will be the bulk of the fighting force."

The prince and her father were the few pure-bloods involved in addressing the conflict. *It would make more sense if those in the capital with stronger magic lent their aid.*

But then again, the elves' numbers had dwindled to a few thousand. The mortals outnumbered them ten times over, so she recognized the advantage of using the humans' vast population. But no one had any guesses on how numerous the wraith were.

Unwilling to discuss the horrors of the coming war, Serenna asked, "Didn't you say there was a greenhouse somewhere?" She was familiar with the gardens scattered around campus but had yet to discover the glass structure Jassyn endlessly spoke of.

His eyes lit up, like the sun mirroring off water. "Do you want to see?"

Without waiting for an answer, Jassyn snatched Serenna's handful of collected flowers and dumped them onto a counter's drying racks. He whisked out of Nelya's lab, his boots echoing in the silent corridor. Serenna rushed after him.

Out of the things she mentally cataloged, she'd only discovered a few items evoking such excitement from Jassyn. Plants contended for a spot near the top of the list, right beside the most sickeningly sweet desserts, and perfectly dyed book spines—lavender of all shades.

Leading them up a spiral staircase, Jassyn's long strides—taking three steps at a time—promptly had Serenna gulping in air. The exertion of the labored breaths bit the back of her throat. Serenna's legs rudely reminded her of the torture they received throughout the week with their own screaming protests.

"What is it with elves and their insistence on constructing these dizzying stairs?" she gasped. The castle at Vaelyn had a few similar staircases, but those were nothing to comment on.

"It's only a few more levels to the top," Jassyn assured her.

Serenna groaned, gripping the metal railing and hauling her burning muscles up another step. She glanced sideways at him. "May I ask you something?"

There wasn't any way to bring this up obliquely. At his nod, she asked, "Did you know my father...had other offspring? I ran into one of your relatives—my half sister, apparently."

Jassyn halted at the top landing as her question hung between them.

"I'm sorry," Jassyn said finally, with a sigh. He pushed open a door to the roof. "I should have prepared you. Ayla has been on campus for a few years now."

A few years? But why is he apologizing? "It's hardly your fault," Serenna protested. "My *father* should have been the one to inform me."

A complicated knot of jealousy and disappointment tangled in her heart when Jassyn informed her of Elashor's other offspring scattered around Alari. He wasn't aware of the exact count of her siblings, but his estimates indicated she had an alarming number of kin in the elven realm.

Serenna meandered to the roof's edge, overlooking the grounds, her limbs numb with disbelief. Jassyn didn't join her, mumbling he disliked heights. She leaned over the parapet to watch the activity in the Combat Yard. A scattered assortment of recruits and magus ran through sparring exercises.

"How are you related?" Serenna asked after taking a deep breath to ease her frustration. Prying her clenched fingers off the railing, she forced herself to relax and not dwell on what she couldn't control. She hoped her other siblings weren't as unpleasant as Ayla.

Jassyn's eyes unfocused on the horizon. "Ayla's mother, Ceryn, is my half sister. I was already at Centarya by the time Ceryn was born." He idly ran his fingers along the stars tattooed across his hand. "Anyway," he said abruptly, squaring his shoulders. "You're going to find out soon enough, so I might as well be the one to inform you. Vesryn and I are...cousins. Half cousins."

Serenna's jaw dropped. She released a thrilled laugh. "Are you elven *nobility*, then?"

"Hardly." Jassyn brushed curls out of his eyes. "I wouldn't want any titles, even if they gave them to us *half-breeds*."

"Elven-blooded," Serenna scolded, joining him in the middle of the roof to jab at his arm. "Don't forget your own lessons. Why didn't you say anything before?"

"I could hardly keep your attention on your studies as it was." Jassyn rolled his eyes. "Do you really think you would've focused on *history* once you knew of my relation to the prince?"

"Okay, fine," Serenna said, conceding. She couldn't smother a guilty grin, knowing he was right. "But for the record, I like you better than Vesryn, anyway." Following Jassyn to the greenhouse, she added, "My father introduced me to him."

Jassyn snorted his amusement. "Isn't that what you asked for?"

"Well, I'm having second thoughts."

Mentioning the meeting with Vesryn reminded Serenna that she wanted to question Jassyn about the strange relic. "Does the Heart of Stars speak to those who touch it?"

Jassyn's hand hovered above the door's latch before he frowned. "No? It only glows with light, depending on which abilities you have."

"Oh." Serenna bit her lip. *The voice seemed real, though.*

"Why? Did it…say something to you?" he asked, swinging the greenhouse door open to reveal a lush jungle inside.

Serenna inhaled the earthy woodland, the humid air erupting with scents of soil. Her eyes popped as she tried to identify the different plant species.

Tables and shelves overflowed with countless varieties of herbs and flowers, as if an uprooted garden had been stored into pots. Vines trailed to the floor from planters suspended from the ceiling, giving the impression they'd stepped into a tropical rainforest.

"I…I think so?" she said, accompanying Jassyn inside the bursting botanical thicket. "I'm not sure now. I can't imagine a more awkward introduction with both my father and Vesryn there observing the relic illuminating for me."

Jassyn's raised brows indicated he believed as much. "Honestly, I wouldn't be surprised if Vesryn manipulated you telepathically to elicit a reaction."

Serenna groaned. *Like I need something else to worry about.*

Jassyn wandered to a corner of the greenhouse. Serenna accompanied him, reading a few of the plant names scrawled in tidy handwriting on the pots. While he didn't have any other guesses about the voice she heard—aside from blaming the prince—bringing up the Aelfyn artifact prompted him to share his research.

"My personal project is more a working theory than anything else." Jassyn shrugged. "Unfortunately, my studies are stalled until I can uncover new material. I proposed to Magister Thalaesyn that the elven sterility is a curse. The idea intrigued him, and he invited me to join his collaboration."

"So you think the elves' affliction is magical in nature?" Serenna asked. *Who could have cursed the elves? The wraith have no powers.* Glancing through the glass of the greenhouse, she watched the sun disappear under Centarya's floating horizon.

"My theories began when I lived in the palace," Jassyn said. He extended a hand, and two spheres of green light sprang to life, hovering to illuminate the darkening space. "Growing up, rumors were still whispered among palace staff of King Galaeryn flying into a rage when Aesar and Vesryn stumbled upon a particular tome in their youth. The king nearly destroyed the entire royal library."

"And you suspect he was hiding something," Serenna commented, pulling back a leafy vine cascading down from the rafters to follow Jassyn deeper into the building.

"I asked Vesryn about the texts they discovered, but he…doesn't talk about his brother. I think Aesar's death in that first wraith attack invokes too much pain." Jassyn caressed a white mushroom in a trough of loam. The velvety cap flared with a dim blue light under his fingertips. "All the information I ever wrung out of him was that the destroyed tomes pertained to the downfall of our ancestors in a war with the druids across the Cerulean Sea."

"Druids?" Serenna asked with a frown. "Are they different from the human shamans?"

She had no knowledge of the conflict between the Aelfyn and these druids, having never heard of them before. Aside from what she'd previously assumed was folklore pertaining to elemental shamans, the only ancient history she knew came from Jassyn.

There had been no recorded strife since the Aelfyn arrived on the mortal shores. *That our history remembers.* The elves' past before crossing the ocean was as mysterious as their ancestral lands. But she recalled the Heart of Stars mentioning there was harmony "before the war."

Jassyn nodded. "The druids are an extinct magical race that we don't know much about beyond their conflict with the Aelfyn. Over the years, I eventually collected scraps of knowledge from historians, but much has been lost to time."

Jassyn studied the morels under his hands like he found something interesting in their scales. "Some archivists believe the druids were responsible for the way gold suppresses our magic and may also be to blame for the loss of our immortality. I deduced, or rather theorized, that the ancient druids sacrificed themselves to curse the Aelfyns' fertility."

His brows drew together when he drifted to moss hanging from suspended sheets of bark. "I don't know why the curse took a millennium to go into effect or why the druids would do something so extreme. Unless eliminating the Aelfyn was the only way they saw to protect the humans. The druids' extinction may be related to their efforts in the war." Jassyn retrieved a watering can to irrigate the moss. "I believe they must have used their life force, combined with their power, to curse the elves so completely. The pure-bloods are going to die out if nothing changes. Vesryn and Aesar were among the last few born."

Serenna watched him work and mused, "The druids probably didn't expect the elves to interbreed with the humans as a final resort."

Jassyn agreed, leading them to a sandier section of the greenhouse containing desert-dwelling plants. Serenna recognized a few species of yellow-flowering cactus that grew along the dunes in Vaelyn.

"Magister Thalaesyn believes we'll see reproductive incompatibilities if the elven-blooded become too closely related to the elves," Jassyn said. "But if the elves are destined to die out, I don't think it'll be difficult to create a brighter future for the humans."

He studied the illumination lights floating around them. "That's also why I'm assisting with Nelya's projects. We're hoping to cultivate and distribute medicinal plants to human villages—to make their lives easier and leave something good behind."

For someone who grew up among Kyansari's royals, Jassyn behaved differently than Serenna expected. He certainly didn't exude an arrogant demeanor like the prince. *How did he become so concerned with the welfare of others?* Perhaps he felt he had a foot in both words, like she did. But he actually took action, caring for the villagers in Vaelyn.

Jassyn stooped to snap off a spiky leaf belonging to a rosette plant. With a squeeze, he collected a drop of sap in the hollow of his palm.

"The aloe should help ease the bruise." Jassyn reached out to gently spread the gel over her cheek.

Serenna winced at the slight flash of pain but didn't recoil from his touch. A cooling tingle fanned across her skin. "Thank you," she said, his kindness warming her heart.

"Over the years, I've come to believe maybe the world would be a better place if the pure-bloods did go extinct," he said softly.

Serenna froze as Jassyn's admission cut through the air, cleaving the silence between them. Her eyes went round, disbelieving he would vocalize such an opinion. *The elves are his heritage too.*

She attempted to voice a defensive argument but only got as far as opening her mouth. Words evaded her.

Jassyn sees through what I've let myself be blinded by.

He had exposed the glaring discrepancies found right outside her mother's castle—how the peasants labored and perished in the dangerous mines.

Serenna had lived her entire life willfully oblivious to the injustices surrounding the keep. As the privileged princess, content living in the lap of luxury, she was indifferent to the grueling lives of the villagers she was supposed to help rule.

How am I any better than the elves?

Jassyn's amber eyes flicked to hers as if expecting a reaction. His stripped expression revealed nothing, as if he left a blank canvas, letting her determine the next strokes. For the first time, he'd spoken to her not as a mentor.

I've been waiting for him to open up. What he voiced wasn't a frivolous conversation debating which metal should craft plated ear cuffs

—which he had strong opinions about. Serenna knew the discussion was something more.

"I…understand the humans would have a chance to thrive if their resources remained in their own lands," she admitted. "You've helped me recognize that the elves view the mortals as expendable." *Like us.*

Serenna didn't believe their conversation was over. "Do you think we can make a difference? Once we eliminate the wraith, won't there be an opportunity to correct those wrongs?"

Jassyn halted in front of hanging vines and extended a hand. "If the elven-blooded return to their homes with a knowledge of magic after the war, I want to believe they'll use their power to help their subjects." Tendrils of fresh growth reached for him, like he was a sun they were stretching to. "But the elves had a thousand years to do the same on these shores, and they oppressed the mortals instead." The vine twined around Jassyn's finger like a chameleon's tail gripping a branch. "Maybe enough people will find the differences unacceptable."

The world pressed in on her. *I'm only one person and I haven't even sensed my magic yet.* Before worrying about anything else, Serenna knew she needed to focus on learning more about her power. The elven realm hurtled them toward a war. Like a river chiseling a stream, she was as helpless as the bank.

They left the humid greenhouse, greeted by the cool air of the night. The two waxing moons gleamed above the island. Streaks of stars shimmered in the ebony sky. Upon hearing a violent clashing of steel, Serenna returned to the railing to observe the after-hours training.

A crowd congregated near a flurry of motion. Glowing spheres sailed and revolved around the ring, bathing the sand field in light.

A black whirlwind wielding twin glaives clashed with nearly a dozen magus, churning dust into the air. The cacophony of clanging metal flowed up to the rooftop. Blades against glaives—no one used magic tonight.

"Who is that?" Serenna asked, leaning over the parapet.

Jassyn clutched the railing next to her. With a disgusted exhale, he asked, "Who do you think?"

Serenna tracked the sparring group as intently as an eagle

arrowing to the ocean in a dive. The curtain of silvery hair whipping in the frenzy could only belong to the prince.

She cursed to herself, hating how Vesryn impressed her by seamlessly flowing from one form to the next in a tempest of steel. *What did I expect? He has killed more wraith than anyone else.* The prince was a blur, a streak of midnight slicing through the ring.

When a magus dropped around him, those from the sidelines dashed into the yard to replace their fallen comrades' places. Red light blooming like bursts of flame gave away the presence of healers. They rushed to drag the battered fighters off of the field to mend their wounds. *I guess he's out for blood tonight.*

Vesryn didn't appear to be flagging. Judging from the crowd, they must've been skirmishing for quite some time. From the vantage on the roof, Serenna watched his arms flex in a way that made her inhale sharply and suppress a shudder winding up her spine.

"Does he do this every night?" she asked breathlessly.

The prince lunged forward in a spin, taking an even more aggressive offensive against the pack of magus. As if the glaives were extensions of his hands, he battered away every countered attempt.

Similar to small pikes, the shafts of his weapons were of length with his arms. A wicked curve of black steel lashed out like the strike of a scorpion's tail.

Doubting he even needed the blades to disable those sparring against him, Serenna watched in fascination. The prince effortlessly maneuvered around the yard with the glaives whirling in his hands. *It's hardly a fair fight.*

"I thought you weren't interested in him anymore," Jassyn challenged in a teasing tone.

Indifferent, he turned his back to the activity in the ring, leaning against the railing. He busied himself with splintering illumination into a cluster of raindrop-size globes. With a flick of his hand, he sent the glowing droplets swirling around them, changing their colors as they spun.

"I'm not. I—" Serenna's voice faltered when the prince deflected three attacks simultaneously. He kicked a magus in the stomach, sending her sprawling. Serenna nearly cheered like the onlookers when she recognized Kieryn as the person he'd knocked down.

Vesryn's head snapped up to where she stood on the rooftop.

Time tripped over itself.

The prince's eyes latched onto hers, and a strange pulling sensation evoked a flutter in her chest. Serenna's heart spasmed, clawing into her throat. Everything around him faded like no one else existed.

The moment was as brief as a star streaking across the sky. With no warning, Vesryn sprang into another attack, a dark figure spinning nightmarish glaives of death.

I imagined him looking at me.

Serenna wrenched her eyes away from the ring while her heart hammered for all the wrong reasons. "I think I'm going to take *your* advice about Vesryn instead of my father's." She released a disbelieving laugh, turning away from the practice yards. "He wants me to *sleep* with the prince and bear his children."

Serenna gasped, clamping a hand over her mouth as if she could shove the words back in, horrified she'd mentioned such a thing to *Jassyn*.

Jassyn, who was the example of proper. *What was I thinking?* Just watching the prince had reduced her to a brainless chit. She hadn't even worked past her unease and gossiped with Velinya about her father's wishes.

Jassyn went rigid like a statue. The surrounding illumination halted their dance.

Heat scorched Serenna's face while she apologized for her indecent remark.

A muscle flickered in the profile of Jassyn's jaw. "There are… certain aspects about the elves I'm not comfortable discussing. Your sire's…*inclinations* include that." Slouching, he added more quietly, "The elven culture disgusts me, and I'm ashamed to be a part of it."

Serenna placed a hand on Jassyn's arm. He flinched under her touch. The lights disappeared, submerging the rooftop in darkness.

"Sorry," she said, drawing back awkwardly for startling him. "You shouldn't be ashamed of what you have no control over. I think the world needs more people like you."

As silent as the moons above, Jassyn stared at his palm. Serenna squinted, thinking she perceived a shimmer around him like steam rising from hot stones after a summer rain. The space above his hand flickered like a sputtering candle. With a shuddering exhale, Jassyn reignited the lights.

Recovering from her embarrassing statement, Serenna trailed after him while they descended the stairs. Bidding him a good night, she opened the Infirmary's door.

Jassyn spoke up behind her. "I've been summoned to Kyansari for a few days."

"You're leaving before the term starts?" Serenna asked, turning around. "Why do you have to go to the capital?"

Jassyn avoided her eyes. His hand drifted to his forehead, grazing the trillium tattoo. "I have…personal matters there I'd rather not discuss. I'll send for you when I return."

After seeing his vacant expression, Serenna decided against the temptation of questioning him further. Jassyn's shoulders slumped as he released another heavy sigh, trudging toward his office.

CHAPTER 16

SERENNA

Apparently, the prince was late.

To his own assembly.

Two mornings after touring the Infirmary, Serenna stood at attention between the surrounding columns with the other thousand initiates assembled in the Spire's Grand Hall, feeling like a fish trapped in a shoal.

Colossal pillars larger than tree trunks stretched from floor to ceiling in the marbled chamber. Sunlight filtered in from the windows overlooking gardens, providing the illusion they were in a forest grove.

Each of the magisters dutifully chipped away at a chunk of time, crafting impromptu speeches to introduce themselves, their respective magus, and their hopes for the next four seasons at the academy. Various Kyansari nobles attended the formal ceremony to oversee a new era of Centarya's military future.

Serenna shifted her weight back and forth. She understood this was a historic moment, but the morning was dragging out. Velinya nodded off—while standing—and Serenna nudged her friend's shoulder.

Maybe if she didn't stay out so late at the Terminal's wineries, she wouldn't be so tired.

The monologues had lost Serenna's attention. She directed her gaze at the elven nobles. This whole affair appeared to be in their honor. They received updates on the measures implemented at Centarya to prepare the elven-blooded for war.

She assumed the aristocrats funded the operations at the academy or had a personal stake in the governance of their *half-breed* army. *I'm sure they feel like our benefactors.* Serenna knew they wouldn't be taking an interest otherwise.

The elven females wore shimmering dresses of unrecognizable fabrics dyed in luxurious pastel colors, uncommon in her mother's court. The materials shone like glossy satin in sky blues, amethysts, and blushing pinks.

Jeweled diamonds netted their sun-colored hair. Matching gems infused with illumination glittered along the lengths of their ears and rested in delicate chains on the bare portion of their breasts. Serenna imagined the lavishness drowning the nobles had more value than the combined riches of the southern realm.

The males and females were all disgustingly beautiful, each almost ethereal like they were birthed from stars, with radiance shimmering under their powered skin. Serenna's gut churned with envy, longing to look like them, knowing she would be out of place standing among their number.

The entry doors crashed open, interrupting a magister's droning.

The booming noise elicited a collective jump from the attendants. Gasps and a few startled shrieks echoed around the cavernous room.

"It's an honor to be Centarya's commander in this new era at our academy," Vesryn said, boots striking the marble floor. Each step resonated more ominously than the last as the hall went as silent as a tomb.

Serenna stood on her tiptoes in an attempt to see over her peers. The prince loomed over those in attendance while he strode down the center aisle. The sun glinting off of his bound hair made each strand appear to glow from within.

The prince stomped past her row of recruits to the front of the chambers, crossed twin glaives strapped over the length of his spine. He wore the same obsidian leather uniform she'd met him in, with additions of spiked vambraces and shoulder pads. Two bandoliers brimming with silver knives formed an X across his chest. *Why isn't he dressed like a noble?*

Paling, Serenna realized why those in the back of the hall had screamed.

Wrapped around one of his hands was a bundle of black hair coiled like a rope. Her stomach gave a sickening lurch upon seeing what could only be three wraith heads dangling from his fist.

Vesryn ascended the dais and tossed the severed heads down the steps toward the aristocrats. Like he was a proud castle cat presenting a vanquished rat. Smearing a black trail of blood, the heads tumbled down the stairs before rolling and landing with an appalling, squelching noise.

More than one noble fainted. The staring red eyes in the creature's obsidian faces had Serenna's vision pulsing white around the edges. She wobbled on her feet, her lungs pulling in air too fast.

I will not swoon over a monster's head! What would the prince think? Gritting her teeth and brushing clammy hands down her leathers, Serenna stubbornly battled her body's reaction to pass out.

"I trust you'll excuse my delay." Vesryn wiped a blood-caked hand on the front of his chest. Black flecks splattered his arms like someone had shaken a paintbrush at him. "I was…occupied." He glared at his nails before scrubbing his fingertips across his leathers.

Focusing his attention on the crowd, his lip curled somewhere between a snarl and a sneer.

"I will not rest until we hunt down every wraith. Too long have those beasts harassed us in Alari." He pointed at the severed heads, now swimming in a pool of viscous blood. "For those living in Kyansari who are *unaware*, these three dragged off citizens in a raid on the outskirts of the capital last night. My rangers are hunting for traces of any survivors."

Vesryn clenched his fists. "To the wraith, we will return tenfold the horrors they have tormented our people with. Those of us at Centarya will not rest until we wipe the scourge clean from our world. This is my promise to you."

The chamber broke out in hesitant, scattered applause at the prince's words as people helped the collapsed nobles find their feet.

He's a fanatic, Serenna thought, convinced she felt anger radiating off him like heat from the sun.

The prince held up a hand with a command for silence. His fingers twitched as if agitated. "Now, on to the reason I assume many of our court members are in attendance." He paused, letting silence stretch. "No doubt everyone has seen the completion of Centarya's Coliseum at the Terminal during your tours. For the half-breeds unfamiliar with Alari's competitive tournaments, the capital holds war games each season. The most influential houses clamor to sponsor champions."

Serenna studied the change in the nobles' demeanor. A palpable hush exhaled from their side of the chambers. A feverish gleam sparkled in their eyes as they fastened their full attention on the prince, completely disregarding the wraith's decapitated heads on the floor.

Vesryn's jaw clenched, rendering his features sharper than a stiletto's blade. "We will have our own Essence Tournament held at Centarya's Coliseum."

Serenna scoffed at the announcement. *A tournament?* She wanted to laugh. *I thought we were here to prepare for war. Not provide...entertainment!* This was worse than being thrown at the wraith. This was a mockery of their purpose to protect these so-called nobles.

"Each magister and magus may sponsor one initiate as their champion in the dueling games," the prince said, pacing the length of the dais with the lethal grace of a panther. His heeled boots clicked on the marble, echoing in the silent hall. "At the end of every season, Centarya will host a weeklong competition for the Kyansari courts. It is up to each instructor to train their champions and prepare them for the tournament."

Vesryn sliced through the aristocrats' excited whispers as he turned to the gathered recruits, effectively dismissing the Kyansari attendants with his back. "Since Centarya is under my command, I'd like to use these council-mandated *games* to at least serve some purpose beyond providing entertainment and gambling."

Serenna's brows rose in disbelief. She nearly admired how Vesryn had no reservations about making his disdain obvious.

But she frowned, considering why he didn't share in their enthusiasm. The tournament did pale against the threat of the wraith and she wondered why the citizens didn't seem concerned with the monsters attacking their city. *Stars, those creatures were there last night.* Perhaps the wealthier elves were safe behind their estate walls.

"If you have ambitions beyond simply being fodder for the wraith," the prince said, "I suggest you consider finding a magus or magister to sponsor your participation in these games."

Crossing his arms, Vesryn drummed his fingers while he studied the gathered recruits. "I will permit those who rise to the upper ranks in the duels to select their position on the war front. Hopefully, this is enough incentive to master your powers and focus your attention on why we're *actually* here."

Irritation bristled up Serenna's spine. *That's hardly fair.* The elven-blooded from Alari were leagues ahead of those from the human realms in magic mastery. *Most of us haven't even sensed Essence yet.*

Those like Ayla had already been at Centarya for *years* and had manifested their powers. Combined, the magus and magisters numbered just a tenth of the recruits—severely limiting those selected to take part in the games.

Returning his attention to the nobles, Vesryn said, "In three months' time, we will distribute information to all noble houses detailing the first tournament's schedule." The prince extended his hands in a dramatic gesture that contrasted his expressionless face. "The council intends for these games to be even more exciting than the entertainment you're accustomed to in Alari."

Enthusiastic cheers erupted from the nobles. *I'm sure they can't wait to watch their half-breeds bleed for them.*

Vesryn allowed applause to flood the chambers, all while peering over the crowd. Serenna's stomach swooped when his gaze snagged on hers. *Stop being so star-blind. He's looking at everyone.*

Biting her lip, Serenna considered if her father would approve. If she dedicated herself to her studies, it was possible she'd be competitive enough to secure a championship under a magus. Surely, being one of the few to compete in the tournament would be an achievement and bring honor to the Vallende name.

The elven games were obviously important to the nobles, and the idea of *not* getting hacked to pieces by a wraith was preferable. Straightening, Serenna decided she would do what needed to be done in order to seize a better position than on the front lines.

Realizing how witless the thought was, she shook her head. *I haven't even manifested my powers yet.* Everyone of note from Alari was going to be scooped up by a magus as soon as they exited the hall.

Serenna considered asking Jassyn to be her trainer, but she suspected he wouldn't take part in the tournament—the magus' participation wasn't required.

Where is Jassyn anyway? Concern creased her forehead as she registered his absence among his gathered peers. *Is he still in the capital?* She desperately hoped he wasn't near the wraith attack.

Facing the recruits, Vesryn said, "This is a warning for our initiates." He paused, ensuring he had everyone's attention. "If you cannot handle the mental and physical rigors of the academy or if the magisters deem your abilities are dismal, we will return you to your realms in shame."

The prince picked at the threading of his stitched dragon as if untangling the strings were more interesting than the power he had to unravel their lives.

"We will cull the bottom five percent after four seasons and reassign you to unfavorable duties among the humans on the war front," he said. "This is to discourage any lapses in your resolve."

Vesryn scanned the gathered recruits, his piercing gaze skipping over everyone. "There is no way out of your responsibilities to your realms or your purpose in the coming fight. Remember that."

A hushed silence followed the prince when he stepped over the severed heads and stalked out of the Grand Hall.

Serenna's heart thudded in her ears, the only sound in the quiet chambers. *I won't be sent back to Allaenar and have the opportunity to study my magic ripped away.*

She could hardly believe that not even two weeks ago, her greatest desire was to secure a distinguished suitor backed by a powerful elven family. Those aspirations seemed insignificant now.

A silly dream for a silly girl, she thought with self-conflagration. Waves of anxiety crashed over her as she accepted her life's reality and her role in the upcoming war.

This is real. No pressure.

CHAPTER 17

SERENNA

Later that week in the Infirmary, Serenna separated strips of linen for bandages. Jassyn had arrived at Centarya earlier in the day and had sent a message informing her she could begin aiding him that afternoon.

She arrived to discover Jassyn mending an initiate with a rather gruesome shattered leg. A soft red glow emanated from a corner of the healing wing, where he pulled up a chair to studiously channel his power.

While Serenna usually would have jumped at the opportunity to observe magic, her stomach wasn't quite ready to see the insides of a body slashed open for display. She preoccupied herself with other tasks in the meantime.

The hairs on Serenna's arms lifted, as if sensing some imminent threat. She froze in the middle of cutting another strip of cloth. A subtle tug, like the pull of a gentle current, flowed through her.

A deep voice, reeking of delight, rang out. "Oh, look who it is."

The doors slammed shut.

Serenna cringed when whipping her head to the entrance pinched a nerve in her neck. Her heart pitched, threatening to capsize in her chest, when she saw the prince.

"It's my absolute favorite half-breed cousin," Vesryn said, sauntering through the Infirmary as if he owned the place. Well, in a way, she supposed he did.

The prince was quite distracting in those black leathers that somehow highlighted every curve of muscle. Serenna couldn't pry her eyes from his magnificent form. The hours he spent in training with the other magus had molded him into a toned menace.

Not that she paid any attention to how much he sparred.

It was simply an uncanny coincidence that she wandered by the Combat Yard, clear across the island, in the evenings.

At the same hour every night.

Vesryn flung a forearm under Jassyn's nose, ignoring the moaning recruit below their hands. "Mend this."

Bile crept up Serenna's throat when she glimpsed bones sticking up in the bloody, mangled mess of the initiate's leg. She swallowed, *never* wanting to be on the receiving end of a spiked mace.

Jassyn served the prince a scowl. "We don't heal bruises. Those are your orders, are they not, Your *Highness*?" Jassyn knocked Vesryn's arm away. "I'm rather occupied unless you've completely missed that."

Serenna's mouth fell open as she stared, stunned by Jassyn's forcefulness. He swatted the prince as if he were a petulant child. *I didn't know Jassyn had defiance like that in his bones.*

Fully invested in the exchange, Serenna abandoned the bandages on the table, angling her chair toward them. Holding her breath, she waited for Vesryn's reaction.

Instead of an outburst like she expected, Vesryn released a delighted cackle and slapped Jassyn's shoulder with startling familiarity. Like they were friends.

The prince flopped on the clinic bed, blatantly ignoring both the bloody sheets and the inhabitant. He faced Jassyn with a wicked grin, flashing all of his perfect white teeth.

"I see living among humans hasn't softened you up." Vesryn hooked his ankle over a knee. "Don't you tire of that spear up your ass?"

The prince shifted his weight on the sagging bed. The recruit emitted a wail at the jostling. The prince rolled his eyes and jabbed a thumb at the initiate's writhing form behind him. "Can't you shut this oaf up with your *healies* or a grubby tuber?"

Jassyn bared his teeth and lunged forward.

Snatching Vesryn by his leathers, he hauled the prince off the bed. Pushing Vesryn in Serenna's direction, Jassyn said, "Bother the aides if you need a bandage."

The crimson light returned as Jassyn settled back into his chair. He ignored Vesryn and continued mending the recruit without a second glance at the prince.

From her vantage at the table, Serenna gaped at the entire exchange. Her spine hit the back of the chair as she stiffened, realizing she was the only aide around.

And directly in the prince's line of sight.

Vesryn straightened his tunic with a yank and paused, raking his attention over her. Rolling a loose thread from the stitching of his dragon in between his fingers, he tilted his head. Curiosity smoldered in his eyes as one corner of his mouth lifted.

Serenna hurriedly averted her gaze and reabsorbed herself in splitting the linens. Through the roar of blood pounding in her ears, she heard the prince's footsteps approaching, as unavoidable now as an arrow streaking toward her.

Vesryn shoved his arm in front of her face.

The smallest bruise, no bigger than a thumbprint, colored his skin.

Serenna emitted a choking noise that was almost a laugh while attempting to gauge his sincerity. *Is he seriously insisting on having that healed?* Perhaps this was her chance to inspect those corded muscles she had *not* been ogling all week. As if drawn by a strange gravity, her hands snaked out to touch him.

Serenna met his eyes. The prince didn't appear to be jesting. His emerald gaze blazed into hers, utterly disarming her.

Thinking better of it, Serenna withdrew, clearing a nervous flutter in her throat. "What am I supposed to do for that?"

"Heal it, you harpy," Vesryn clipped.

Serenna reared back and blinked. *Harpy?* After a tick of hesitation, she admitted, "I can't."

"Why not?" The prince's question was harsh. Like a command.

Serenna's frustration simmered, both at herself for not being able to heal something so simple and for being on the receiving end of his ire. This wasn't how she'd imagined their interactions.

"I haven't manifested mending yet." She wasn't about to admit she hadn't sensed *any* magic.

"Then why are you taking up space in the Infirmary?" Vesryn demanded, still holding his arm out expectantly.

Serenna released a huff, exasperated by the way he towered over her. She rose from her chair. Which did nothing helpful but put her level with his shoulders. She concealed a wince when her muscles protested in a hundred different ways from the previous two weeks of conditioning.

She gave the prince her best dismissive sniff, ready to defend herself. "I'm Magus Jassyn's aide."

"You're not a very useful one."

"That doesn't require healing, and you know it," she snapped, annoyance rendering her mindless.

A muscle in Vesryn's jaw flexed. Serenna's heart leaped into her throat, realizing she'd irritated him.

A moment too late, she heard the lack of respect in her tone. She was speaking to the *commander* of the academy, *and* the royal prince, no matter how absurd he was acting.

Drawing herself up, Serenna braced herself. Perhaps it was a feeble attempt at maintaining some shred of dignity while forced to look up at him.

Vesryn's lip curled into a sneer while silence suspended between them, as tangible and sharp as the blades at his belt.

Tucking his outstretched arm to his chest, he snapped his hand into a fist. Streaks of shadows erupted from his palm.

Serenna convulsed when every muscle contracted. Night warped around her like ribbons of fog. She emitted a surprised gasp as she went rigid, losing control of her body. Frozen as solidly as ice.

Panic seized her heart. *He's using magic on me!* Serenna's lungs pulled in a sharp breath as the feeling of being confined pressed against her chest. Her eyes darted to Jassyn's back, but he was healing the recruit. Gritting her teeth, she refused to call for help.

Serenna struggled against the ebony wisps constraining her, willing her body to move. The black tendrils of magic billowed around them, binding her too tightly to permit any motion.

Serenna's mind darted to the memory of Magus Kieryn backhanding her for speaking out of turn. *Is Vesryn going to do the same? He doesn't need to restrain me with magic to do that.*

Orbiting like a wolf, the prince's inspecting gaze prowled over her. Serenna was as defenseless in his power's grasp as she would be against him in combat. She inhaled an unsteady breath, unable to retreat.

Moving uncomfortably close, the prince crowded over her, completely ravaging her space.

Serenna ground her teeth at the invasion, anxiety battering at her ribs. Annoyance outweighed her fear when Vesryn peered into her face, like he was attempting to intimidate her with his proximity.

Radiating her displeasure, Serenna lifted her chin in indignation. She could move that much.

"Address me properly," Vesryn hissed, his arrogance steaming like water tossed onto coals.

Serenna blustered a scoff at the unspoken threat. "Or *what?*"

An inhale lodged in her throat when something she couldn't read smoked in his eyes like the magic coiling around them. The prince pushed her fortitude with silence.

Committed to her defiance now, Serenna refused to surrender to his gaze, denying him the satisfaction of capitulating. She'd already repelled the urge the last time he tried this ridiculous game of dominance. Resistance was all she had left.

Ignoring the fluttering in her stomach, she kept her eyes narrowed on his. "Release me," she ordered.

A shade of a smile tugged at the prince's mouth. "Release yourself." Vesryn cocked his head. "You have rending. Use your magic to counter the bind."

Serenna glared at the taunt in his tone. *Somehow he knows I don't have access to my power.*

Vesryn took an aggressive step closer, bumping into her shoulder.

He smirked when Serenna's nostrils flared. He opened his mouth, but what he was about to say, she didn't find out.

Having finished mending the shattered leg, Jassyn thankfully rushed to her rescue. Seemingly unconcerned with the shadows cascading around them, Jassyn wrenched Vesryn's arm and steered the prince a pace away from her.

A burst of red light flashed, erasing Vesryn's bruise.

The prince made a show of inspecting his forearm before dropping it at his side. The darkness dispersed when he released the shadowy hold on her.

Serenna loosened an exhale, resuming control of her body. *That was unpleasant.*

"Will you leave now?" Jassyn demanded more so than asked.

The mended recruit wisely slipped out of the Infirmary, leaving the three of them alone in the wing.

"Who would have thought we'd both end up here at your academy?" Vesryn draped an arm around Jassyn's shoulders, giving him a shake. "I'm thrilled about all this time we'll get to spend together."

"Right." Jassyn shoved Vesryn away with his nose wrinkled in displeasure.

Folding his arms, the prince stood straighter, roaming his attention over Jassyn. "I heard you finally made your way back from playing peasant, and I'm rather disappointed you haven't sought me out yet."

For every inch that Jassyn was taller than the prince, he somehow appeared to take up less space, like he was a tree without branches. Present, but not casting a shadow with its shrouding leaves.

"I've had better things to do," Jassyn said tonelessly.

Vesryn's mouth curved as his eyes volleyed to Serenna and then back to his cousin. "I see you wasted no time cozying up to *Princess* Vallende. And here I was, convinced you were determined to hold out much longer." The prince emitted a dark chuckle, his voice lowering sensuously. "I take it that this 'tutoring' you oversaw has her well informed of our…*open-minded* couplings in Alari?"

Serenna's brows flew up her face at what the prince insinuated.

Jassyn tensed beside her but met Vesryn's stare, his expression blank. She couldn't gauge if the prince's intent was to make them uncomfortable or if he had an indecent sense of humor.

Jassyn had been nothing but proper. If anything, the *prince* was the one acting uncouth.

"Which reminds me," Vesryn said, clicking his tongue. He circled the pair with his hands clasped behind his back. "How many elven females are you servicing now? I can never keep track. Is it three or four?" Noting Jassyn clenching his fists, Vesryn's satisfied snort echoed in the still room.

Stepping closer, the prince extended a finger and flicked Jassyn's curls away from his forehead. His words were vicious. "I heard Lady Farine just celebrated her seventh century." He poked at the exposed trillium tattoo. "Were you there *rollicking* with her?"

Jassyn flinched and retreated out of the prince's reach. Obviously hitting his mark, Vesryn's lips curved into a malicious grin.

Serenna blanched, contemplating what Vesryn meant. Something in the prince's words had obviously bothered Jassyn, but she had no idea what he was referring to, besides reaching unpleasant conclusions.

Jassyn shrinking back had her stomach roiling. *Why isn't he standing up for himself? He did earlier when the prince was being foolish.*

Silence suffocated the room, and a feeling of foreboding constricted the air like smog. If Jassyn wasn't able to do anything, then she would. *What will Vesryn do, paralyze me again?* A chill of unease fled down her spine. *Or he could lop my head off like he did with those wraith.* His twin glaives were absent today, but she assumed he didn't need weapons to behead a foe.

Serenna squared her shoulders, gathering her courage. She wouldn't stand by and accept this treatment. Someone this cruel to her friend was no prince to *her*. *Vesryn was the one who came here for no reason other than to poke fun at Jassyn!* If anyone deserved the prince's ire, it was her for talking back to him.

"Do you take such a perverted interest in everyone's couplings?" Serenna bristled, stepping toward the prince, her fury flaring like feathers rustling. "Are *conquests* some type of competition among the elves? Are you worried you're not winning?"

Vesryn's gaze swiveled to her. His eyes flashed, studying her.

Robbed of logic, Serenna didn't think—she had his attention now. Springing forward into the pocket of space between them, she shoved Vesryn's leathers to force him back.

He didn't budge.

She nearly shrieked in frustration and considered beating her fists against his chest, but trying to move him was like pushing against a boulder.

Vesryn's brows rose when he glanced at her palms. His attention flicked to Jassyn before hooking his gaze back on her.

Realizing her error, Serenna yanked her fingers away as if burned, balling them into fists at her side. Laying hands on the prince wasn't the best of her ideas. *Not that it even did anything but prove he's a brute.*

"It seems like you're the one jumping at the opportunity to be added to my...*conquests*," the prince said, arching a brow. "Is this you begging for the honor?"

"*Honor?*" Serenna laughed in shrill disbelief, holding her ground while her nails bit into her palms. "I'm not that desperate."

Continuing to berate them, Vesryn asked, "Have you met your grandmother yet? *Lady* Farine?" He cocked his head at her. "I wonder if the same...*appetites* run in the Vallende family. I have a feeling I'll find out."

"That's enough," Jassyn said quietly from behind her, but his voice emitted a heat like flames.

Serenna didn't have time to analyze Vesryn's statement before his hand whipped out, seizing her chin. The prince tilted her head up to peer into her eyes.

A gasp fled from her throat. Under his fingertips, a jolt, like a small current of lightning, zipped through her veins. Serenna's knees locked as the electrifying shock whirred through her body.

An inexplicable sensation warped her perception of the room until Vesryn was the only thing in focus. The prince gave an amused grunt before dropping his hand almost as soon as he touched her.

The moment was so fleeting, Serenna wasn't convinced it happened.

No, she could still feel the impression his fingers left on her face.

They stared at each other. One heartbeat stretched out before Serenna fully processed what had happened and how the prince had taken the liberty of handling her, subjecting her to more of his magic.

"Don't touch me," she fumed at him, disgust boiling her blood. His sheer entitlement threatened to ignite her temper.

Serenna blinked at the sudden violet light slashing through the air. Jassyn barged between them, breaking whatever spell Vesryn had put on her, encompassing them in a shield.

A vein in Jassyn's temple pulsed wildly as he faced the prince, planting his feet. Serenna had never seen Jassyn look threatening before, and her stomach churned with unease. She readied herself to react. Though she had no idea what she could do without magic.

"Serenna needs to finish her work, and I'm sure *you* have more pressing matters to attend to," Jassyn told Vesryn in a voice that sounded like it scraped across his clenched teeth.

Vesryn grinned, dragging a finger down Jassyn's shield. The ward parted under his touch like paper ripping. The prince patted his cousin's face through the gap in the barrier before peering around Jassyn's shoulder to fasten his gaze on her. "We'll be seeing each other again shortly."

Pivoting on his heel, Vesryn swaggered out of the Infirmary, drawing a belt knife, tossing the blade into the air and catching the leather hilt as he left.

Jassyn touched Serenna's shoulder in a wordless comfort while the surrounding shield dissipated. "Are you all right?"

"Scorching stars!" Serenna swore, giving herself a shake. "If Vesryn is here, then that means I have rending at the next bell."

The prince had only been on campus at night since the start of the term, presumably hunting wraith during the hours his class was supposed to meet. This would be their first session.

If the last few moments were any indication of their future interactions, Serenna had no interest in spending more time than necessary around someone so repulsive.

Jassyn squeezed her shoulder. "Be sure to lock your jaw."

She blinked up at him. "What?"

"If Vesryn uses rending on you in class, which I'm sure he will. If you clench your teeth, you won't bite your tongue in half."

Serenna swore again. For once, Jassyn didn't admonish her for her language.

CHAPTER 18

SERENNA

Rending was as terrible as Serenna had imagined.
No, on second thought, it was worse.
Stomping to the Rending Field, Serenna kicked at the immaculately trimmed grasses, sending tuffs of green flying in front of her boots. What she would give to conjure those fabled shamanic powers and channel an inferno to unleash her fury in every direction as a raging storm of fire.

No. Just at Vesryn.

Serenna spat his name as a curse in her head as if it were something distasteful to be forcibly expelled. The elven prince certainly was *not* how she imagined Alari's royalty. She wanted to smack that condescending grin right off his irritatingly attractive face. Vesryn's behavior shattered every fantasy she fabricated about the elves.

She couldn't think of any reasons why the prince would take such a twisted pleasure in Jassyn's discomfort. *They're family!* Not to mention Jassyn was perhaps the most compassionate and selfless person she knew.

Something protective inside of Serenna flared. Her hands trembled, imagining her fingers wringing around the prince's throat. Never mind Vesryn could wave his hand and snap her like a twig.

If her father wanted a tie to Vesryn so badly, then *he* could be the one crawling into the prince's bed. *Why should I care about my father's wishes? He didn't bother telling me I have a sister and stars know how many other siblings.*

Not being important enough hammered a painful spike into her chest. *He probably gave Ayla the same advice of getting closer to the prince.*

Well, she can have him! They'd be a perfect match!

The practice field came into view while Serenna grappled with her mind—attempting, and failing, to quell her turbulent thoughts and the sinking feeling in her gut. Situated beside the Infirmary, she knew the placement wasn't by accident. *What is the prince going to do to me?*

Glancing around at the other pale-faced recruits, Serenna hoped she didn't look as nervous. They'd likely heard horror stories from the gossiping magus about this controversial class. Presumably, rending had the potential to turn the tides of war with waves of bodily destruction. They'd never before taught the magic at Centarya.

Until Vesryn seized command.

She groaned when her eyes landed on Ayla and Mishryn's matching plaited hairstyles. Since Serenna shared no classes with Velinya, her friend wouldn't be present to offer any additional support.

In every class Serenna attended with her sister, Ayla made a point to highlight Serenna's ineptitudes and draw attention to the fact that she hadn't even sensed her magic.

We've only been in session a week. Jassyn said it took him years to manifest the full spectrum of his power.

Ayla was in the center of the Alari group, and, of course, they all appeared relaxed, with their judgmental noses in the air and sneers directed toward everyone else.

Rolling her eyes, Serenna watched them reverently greet Vesryn with their hands over their hearts as they approached his position in the field. She assumed the prince would give their realm preference—most of the other magisters and magus did.

Serenna ground her teeth when her gaze settled on the prince. Recalling Jassyn's instructions, she clenched her jaw even tighter. Vesryn stood planted in the center of the arena, still flipping that stupid dagger.

He must not have any magus, Serenna thought, since he was alone. *No surprise there. I'm sure no one wants to be around him.*

"Due to the sensitive nature of this class," Vesryn started without a greeting or preamble when the recruits assembled before him, "I have given the High Council my reassurances that we will only use rending in controlled environments."

He paced, stirring up dust in the ring. "If I hear of any instances of this magic being used outside of our designated instruction time, you will face severe consequences. Do I make myself clear?"

To add to his point, Vesryn paused, snatching the blade from the air to glare at everyone. Collectively, the recruits mumbled their acceptance.

"If you're found violating these explicit rules three times, I will expel you from the academy. I don't care what potential you have or what your family name is." Vesryn prowled again, focusing his attention back on the knife, like it was the most interesting thing in the world. "Be assured, I will *personally* see that your assignment will be to an unfavorable location on the war front." He arched his brow, as if a thought occurred to him. "Digging latrines, perhaps."

Serenna's eyes narrowed, suspicion invading her thoughts. *He seriously expects us to believe no one will receive preference? I have yet to see evidence of that.*

Returning to the center of the ring, Vesryn sheathed the dagger and held up a finger. "The punishment for the first infraction is a broken finger. Mending will be denied for three days. This should be minor enough to *remind* you to adhere to the rules."

With a raised second finger, he said, "The second infraction will result in shattering your dominant forearm with a five-day delay on healing."

Serenna's breath hitched. *I guess he's skipping straight to broken bones.*

With a raised third finger, Vesryn added, "If you still feel the need to set yourself above these rules, the final punishment will be rending before your expulsion. I assure you, you'll be a slavering idiot when your mind cracks from that torment."

The prince cocked his head, regarding everyone. "Is this clear?"

The hushed voices of the initiates hardly relayed their assent.

Judging from the bulging eyes of the surrounding recruits, it was clear Vesryn had effectively horrified the class.

A twinge of satisfaction slithered up Serenna's spine as those from Alari averted their gazes, appearing more subdued.

"Good," Vesryn said with a nod. Shadows materialized in a billowing cloud before coiling around his lifted arm as if the wind consolidated his power.

Serenna's hand reflexively went to her throat, recognizing the impairing magic he'd used on her not even an hour past. All eyes were pinned on the prince as his power rushed, swirling and gathering like a coalescing storm. Everything went still, like something stole the wind.

Vesryn curled the three raised fingers into a tight fist. A pressure pounded into Serenna's chest when a surge of darkness exploded from his hand. The midnight cloud swallowed the training field.

The world plunged into chaos.

The entire class crashed, writhing, to the ground with a collective howl.

A scream erupted from Serenna's throat, breaking through her locked jaw. Her muscles disintegrated when the shadows engulfed her. Panic poisoned her thoughts as her vision went black, drowning her in a cataclysmic wave of agony.

Serenna's awareness scattered like sparks bursting from the crackle of a burning log. Some dim part of her mind registered her body violently thrashing on the ground as if a seizing fit plagued her.

A surge of pain crushed her, boiling her from the inside out. Fire lanced with a thousand needles, searing through her veins. Her bones stretched to the point of breaking, twisting and slamming into the sand like they were trying to bury themselves in the earth.

She convulsed in the most unnatural ways, every separate muscle spasming and contracting in a different direction.

Serenna gasped, unable to draw in a complete breath, her ribs threatening to bend backward and burst from her chest.

Her mind unraveled. She didn't know how long she writhed uncontrollably. It felt like ages—a never-ending torment.

As suddenly as the flames of scorching pain appeared, they fled, unfurling like a wisp of smoke.

Curled up into a defensive ball, Serenna panted to catch her breath, choking on relief over the torture's end. She heard ragged gasping from her classmates, weeping, and more than one person retching.

She lay there, stunned, shaking uncontrollably as the minutes ticked by. Scalding flashes of pain lingered behind Serenna's eyes as the heaviness of her body tried to drag her into a safer place—one where she couldn't feel. Like a gull on the wind, she let herself drift.

Get up, a voice challenged. She twitched.

Serenna shook her head, clearing the haze of fog. Some instinctive part of her mind stirred, corralling her scattered thoughts in an attempt to reassert control of her faculties.

With a pained moan, she rolled over and pushed herself to her hands and knees. Her limbs trembled, straining to hold her weight. It took an effort to rein in her jagged breathing.

Swallowing the vestiges of panic, Serenna ran her tongue along the inside of her mouth. *Still in one piece.* She nearly wept in relief.

Get up!

Driving her hands in the sand, Serenna lurched to her feet in an unsteady motion. She swayed but didn't fall. Chest heaving from the effort, she stabilized herself and straightened. Back cracking, her muscles shook from the aftermath of the excruciating magic. With a quick glance around her, she saw that everyone else lay dazed and senseless on the ground.

Rubbing dirt off her face, Serenna blinked her vision into focus. When she lifted her eyes to the center of the ring, her head emptied of thought, devastated by the attention of the prince.

A flush scorched the tips of her ears, realizing that Vesryn's gaze was fastened on her. Serenna's face pinched into an automatic glower in response.

Vesryn tilted his head, his smirk morphing into a smile. Not a friendly smile, but rather one a delighted predator would deliver to their cornered prey.

He doesn't have any right to look so pleased!

A braid of terror and alarm strangled her when the prince raised his arm again, shadows lashing around.

Scorching stars! Serenna gritted her teeth while helplessly watching him curl his hand into another fist. She steeled herself, wanting to scream, knowing it wouldn't do any good as he slapped her with another wave of darkness.

Her legs crumbled to dust when the shadows devoured the training ring.

Serenna's body seized. She collapsed to the ground, dropping as boneless as a floating jelly tumbling in the sea. Her vision went black as her limbs and muscles contorted again in all the ways they shouldn't.

Clutching onto stubborn outrage through the flames of agony, Serenna clawed at her awareness, refusing to surrender to the darkness wrestling her into a nightmare of torment. She would *not* give Vesryn the satisfaction of fainting.

She had no concept of how long the rending lasted. It took her significantly longer to sway to her feet the second time the prince's magic subsided. Her throat burned with a whimper at the memory of the torrid pain while her lungs sucked in breaths as sharp as blades.

I'm going mad already, she thought, violently shoving away an annoying voice buzzing in her head.

Serenna's eyes darted toward the other recruits, worried she'd taken too long to recover. More than a few lay sprawled out, incapacitated by the successive wave of power. Others sobbed their misery, and an alarming number of initiates were now throwing up.

Why am I the only one standing?

Realizing her body wasn't broken and shredded like she thought it should be, Serenna's contempt fossilized into a tangible force, crystalizing like ice inside of her.

A rage blanketed Serenna's mind, shrouding her thoughts. Her fury didn't blind her completely. Rather, her wrath gave her a direction to aim her focus.

Vesryn, she snarled.

The prince was the one responsible for this feeling of helplessness, dispensing whatever torments he deemed fit. *I'm not going to roll over and accept this treatment. This isn't a lesson; this is torture!*

Time slowed to a warped distortion while he raised an arm again. Serenna frantically considered how to retaliate or deny his dark magic's consuming power.

No! Her silent scream tore through the confines of her mind. She refused to relinquish control of her body and be reduced to a worm wriggling on the ground.

At that moment, Serenna realized she *despised* the prince. For how he treated Jassyn, and for what he was doing to her. To all of them! They didn't even stand a chance of defending themselves against his magic.

I will not be controlled! Narrowing the focus of her disdain, she skewed Vesryn with her rage. Serenna's attention remained fused on the prince's growing shadows while his hand rose higher.

And then, spurred by wild desperation, something inside of her split and *shattered*. A hairline crack fissured in the abyss of her soul, like a chasm fracturing into a gaping hole rent in the earth.

Serenna gasped, her perception plunging into the expanse of that empty space. Delving. Tunneling. Searching for a locked piece of herself, suppressed into a slumber.

Do it.

The command reverberated through her body, rattling her bones.

Serenna's consciousness flew into a starless sky, drifting like a ship without an anchor. For the first time, her mind emptied completely. As she fell deeper into the darkening depths, an unfathomable expanse opened up before her.

And there it was.

The reservoir of her power. Her Well on the horizon, magic roiling like clouds brewing before a storm. She reached to trail phantom fingers on the churning waves. Stretching, straining, to grasp the magic. To fall into it.

Into oblivion.

She perceived…twin cords, one bright and one dim, silver threads twining like ivy, floating on the surface of her power like lily pads on a pond. Seizing both, she heaved the magic toward her.

Nothing happened.

Her Essence recoiled from her touch.

No!

Discarding the silver cords, Serenna lunged her awareness at the reservoir of her magic, fumbling, straining, diving into the night.

Essence crashed over her like a tidal wave, utterly consuming her. She didn't need to wrestle for control. The blackness of her Well exploded in a sea of stars, engulfing her in a torrential blaze of power.

Serenna's awareness flew back into her body, feet staggering backward in the sand. Shadows whirled around her. *Her* shadows.

Limbs shaking, Serenna's nerves erupted from the rush of energy. The power threatened to incinerate her if she failed to channel the mountain of magic.

In any direction.

Serenna's attention latched onto the prince's grin. *He's enjoying this! That monster.*

She thrummed with energy, a maelstrom ready to be unleashed. Darkness howled through her like a black wind. Tendrils of night spiraled around her as she gathered the whirlwind of power. A sliver of innate knowledge blossomed in her mind, impelling her, giving her a trail of insight to follow.

Serenna attacked with her magic. Shrieking, she let anger fuel her reaction, lashing out with a tossed hand, flailing, desperate to prevent another wave of rending as Vesryn began to form a fist.

From her palm, a sprig of midnight streamed toward the prince, sailing across the ring.

Vesryn's fingers twitched when her magic struck him.

The movement was so subtle, Serenna almost missed it. But his motion halted.

He dropped his arm.

Serenna's eyes flew back to his face. To his satisfied smirk.

Her outrage and the surrounding shadows of her power receded like a falling tide, replaced by a lightheaded intoxication. Her head spun and her vision swam.

With no warning, the flood of Essence abandoned her, guttering out. Serenna gasped at the sudden loss of the exhilarating magic.

Dizzy, she wobbled on her feet. The absence of its presence left her drained, like rivulets running their course and disappearing into a mire.

The prince's mouth curved into a disarming smile, which disturbed her more than anything else so far. Serenna bared her teeth, glaring back at him, detesting the way he evaluated her. As if he *knew* something about her and, even worse—was *proud* of her.

"That," Vesryn said, beginning to prowl around the ring again, "was two ten-second cycles of rending." The prince roved his attention over the recruits. The majority were on the ground, but a few were finding their unsteady feet.

Twenty total seconds? Serenna released an incredulous, maniacal laugh. Their torment had to have lasted longer than that. It felt like *years*.

"Blood rending, if you need a technical name," Vesryn said, frowning as he toed a fainted recruit in the ribs. "This stage of magic doesn't damage the body beyond what you do to it while you're thrashing about. The more advanced powers shatters your bones, flays your skin, pops your eyeballs, and disintegrates your flesh in an explosion of gore.

"Those of you who've soiled yourselves are dismissed," Vesryn clipped. "I don't want your stench lingering. If you swallowed your tongue, go see the menders."

Serenna glanced around, checking her trousers in a blind panic, but then sighed with relief. *At least I didn't do that.*

A handful of initiates dejectedly shambled out of the ring, while others left with bloody hands covering their mouths. Hardly anyone remained from the initial group. Serenna looked away, embarrassed for everyone else. *He couldn't have warned us?*

The prince walked among the scattered recruits, stepping over those still unconscious like they were piles of dung. Most flinched when he peered into their faces. Serenna felt a small seed of satisfaction germinate as Ayla and Mishryn stared at the ground. Both of their braids hung loose and disheveled—they hadn't had an easier time than her.

For whatever reason, the prince seemed to purposefully avoid her, not assessing her while he circled the class, making a show of intimidating everyone else. This only heightened Serenna's awareness of him. Like he was singling her out.

But by doing nothing. *No, I'm being ridiculous for trying to interpret his actions.*

Vesryn addressed the standing recruits after he finished his rounds. "Only one of you has snapped into your rending ability."

Air froze in Serenna's lungs. *Is he talking about me?*

"We will continue with these exercises until *everyone* has manifested their power." The prince shrugged his indifference after a round of gasps. "As unsavory as you might find this, rending is invaluable and may save your life once you develop and hone the skill."

A willowy Alari woman raised a timid hand. Vesryn nodded, giving her permission to speak. Everyone else shuffled away from her, obviously not wanting to be any closer to the range of his attention.

Serenna couldn't blame them.

"What's...what's snapping?" the woman stuttered, not meeting his eyes.

"Snapping is when you're *provoked* into your power." Vesryn flicked stray strands of hair out of his face. "With trauma or emotional manipulation."

He grinned. The bastard *grinned.*

"It's the fastest method we've found to propel half-breeds into abilities. Since we're short on time with the wraith stirring, I won't hesitate to exploit your...human emotions to push you into your power."

Anger singed Serenna's veins. A darkness shimmered in a corner of her mind, rending now calling to her. The excitement of finally sensing and using her magic was snuffed out faster than a doused candle. *Like he's so different from us.*

Judging from the stark terror on everyone's faces, nothing about this class would be enjoyable, especially since the prince admitted he would torture them into their power.

"That will be all for today." Vesryn swiveled and strode away, leaving everyone else in the ring. The remaining initiates lingered, paralyzed with dismay, glancing around in disbelief. The class hadn't lasted ten minutes.

Vesryn beckoned over his shoulder. "*Princess* Vallende, with me."

Serenna's eyes darted to Ayla before she registered the "princess" comment. Ayla took a step toward the prince before she paused, glaring at Serenna.

Chills scraped down Serenna's spine as her mind imagined all the terrible ways Vesryn would discipline her for striking out. A riptide of dread yanked her stomach to the ground.

She was going to throw up.

CHAPTER 19

JASSYN

Upon entering the greenhouse, Jassyn's knees buckled. He collapsed, propping himself against a glass wall.

The encounter with Vesryn stripped what remaining strength he had left. His cousin's appearance had only exacerbated the hammering in his head, threatening to split his skull like the blow of an axe. Vision blurring, the lush surroundings only seemed to beat in time with his pulse.

Overindulging in Stardust the previous three days at the Vallende estate had nearly incapacitated him, leaving him with a ruthless ache in his bones. The drug's lingering effects had Essence slipping through his fingers like a stream of water while he fumbled with healing that recruit's leg.

Hopefully, the residual dust doesn't interfere with regenerating tonight. A trickle of fear cascaded through Jassyn's thoughts that he'd have to wait a handful of days before the traces completely vacated his system.

Unsurprisingly, the prince revealed to Serenna what Jassyn's life entailed in Alari. His gut writhed with mortification, surrendering the air from his lungs in an unsteady exhale. Steepling his hands over his face, he swallowed the bitter taste of humiliation slithering up his throat.

He wasn't ready for her to judge him like everyone else in the realm. To observe the shift in her behavior toward him, whether it be in curiosity, sympathy, or revulsion, when she realized his *purpose*.

Jassyn tucked his knees to his chest. Wrapping his arms around his legs was a frail attempt to hold himself together even though all he wanted to do was fall apart.

He questioned why Serenna's opinion mattered to him until he relented and picked it apart. Awareness of the contracts wasn't what dictated her behavior toward him—she didn't view him as an extension of the council's will. *Not yet.*

For the first time, he'd experienced a sense of worth. For whatever reason, he mattered to someone beyond what value the realm assigned him. He'd spent his entire life attempting to amount to something beyond the price set on his bloodline.

Jassyn's chest tightened with resentment and resignation as his ears started to ring. Vesryn's interference threatened to manipulate Serenna's perception of him too. The elves had already ripped away his choices, his future, and whatever feeble relationships he crafted.

Jassyn's eyes unfocused on his boots until he blinked, sensing motion at the edge of his vision. Tendrils of the hanging vines crept across the ground, like they had an agenda of their own. The plants drew a sad smile to his face. He extended a hand toward the peculiar behavior.

He assumed the pull of Essence attracted them, but didn't have any evidence to prove the thought. Magic couldn't make anything grow—he'd already tried that.

The leafy vine coiled around his fingers, his skin tingling at the contact. A sliver of dread lodged in his chest loosened at the silent comfort. A pathetic, self-deprecating laugh bubbled up. *Wonderful, a plant is making me feel better.*

Jassyn wished he had the power to intervene in whatever Vesryn devised to unleash against Serenna in the Rending Field. He saw that familiar gleam in his cousin's eye. She was going to be a shiny novelty, an interesting challenge. Something else for the prince to break and discard when amusement ran its course.

His legs didn't have any remaining strength to wander to the ledge of the roof to observe the practice yard. He wanted to, but his entire body trembled from the effort of not completely shattering.

There was hardly anything he could do against his cousin's power anyway. *Oh sure, I'll wave a useless shield around just so Vesryn can slice through my magic as effortlessly as tearing a page out of a book.* Jassyn knew he was no match for the prince, even if he wanted to rise to Serenna's aid.

But he didn't believe the prince would irreparably harm her. Guilt still settled on his shoulders for leaving her to defend herself while he focused on mending the recruit.

But then again, Serenna had spent the entire time defiantly holding her own, even after his cousin had constricted her with his power.

I'm the one unable to muster the will to fend for myself.

In fact, Serenna had been the one to rescue *him* in the healing wing. Still bewildered, Jassyn couldn't fathom why she had defended him. Vesryn was as stunned as he was—someone had *dared* to lay hands on him.

Jassyn didn't miss the prince's tell, the slight twitching of his fingers. There was still some satisfaction to be had at witnessing his cousin's discomfort. Jassyn unapologetically burned Vesryn's incredulous look into his memory when Serenna charged at him with nothing but her bare fists.

Jassyn had no idea why Vesryn's attention had drifted to him as if *he* were supposed to offer an explanation or, better yet, *help* him out of the situation he'd snared himself in.

Frowning, Jassyn studied the vines as they slid across the ground and wound around his boots, realizing the prince had never once directed his dark magic toward him. Surely that was a coincidence. *Well, Vesryn knows he can torment me in other ways. He doesn't need Essence for that.*

Jassyn swallowed a thick feeling in his throat, and the vine tightened against his hand in response. The gravity of his remorse pressed on him for shoving away the one person who'd been reaching out. Serenna had extended an offer of friendship, plunging him into unfamiliar territory.

Everyone has a motive and demands. What are hers?

Disgusted with himself, Jassyn shook his head, dispelling the thought. He didn't believe that. And he knew she had no intentions of using him for personal gain. She wasn't like her sire or every other elf in Alari. Elashor's suggestion of bearing offspring for the prince to achieve status had left her appalled.

Jassyn closed his eyes and rested his head on his knees, breathing in the earthy air. He was beyond exhausted from the visit to Farine's estate and had only returned to Centarya that morning. His Well threatened to fizzle out, depleted of power.

The thought of lingering in Kyansari had panic threatening to stop his heart. He didn't want to spend a moment longer in the city than necessary. Utterly consumed with thoughts of fleeing the capital, he now regretted not seeking clandestine mending before departing.

Exhaling a deep breath, Jassyn relaxed the tension in his shoulders, releasing the hold on his magic, unraveling the mirages obscuring the evidence from the past few days. To conceal his shame, he'd selfishly siphoned Essence into maintaining illusions.

His chest hollowed for squandering his power. The other magus would need his assistance mending the recruits after Vesryn's class. But he didn't have the courage to return to the healing wing. *Not like this.* It wasn't as if there was enough Essence remaining in his Well to do anything useful before he could regenerate his dwindling power. *I'll need the stars' aid to regenerate tonight.*

Jassyn squeezed his eyes tight, attempting to forcibly expel the memories, wishing he could take the coward's way out and portal. Somewhere. Anywhere. He'd run away if he could, disappearing into the mortal realms.

What is wrong with me? Why can't I accept this is my life? Others have it so much worse; I saw the oppressed humans.

Most of Jassyn's acquaintances in the same circumstances—elven-blooded males bound to contracts—delighted in the attention and the benefits distributed to them. More than a few willingly sought extracurricular pairings to distribute their *services* to the realm, traveling from one estate to the next.

The gifts heaped on Jassyn just made him feel even more defiled. Like riches were any consolation for the transaction of using his body.

But Farine didn't care about producing offspring. Her contract with him wasn't about that. No, she wanted to exploit and degrade him because of who he was and the line he belonged to—the Raellyns. Farine inflicted pain and humiliation on him for his mother's transgression, that's what it came down to.

Jassyn doubted his family even paid attention to the Vallendes' retaliation; his servitude was their doing, and the hardships he endured were his own. He hadn't communicated with any of his blood besides Vesryn since he'd left the palace nearly fifty years prior. And his association with the prince certainly wasn't by choice.

What history lingered between the Vallendes and Raellyns families, Jassyn couldn't say. He assumed there was a grudge against his mother for being the one to secure his sire for coupling at the dawn of the elves and humans mingling. Back then, the council was cautious about startling the mortals with their differences in selecting multiple partners, so the realm restricted the first generation of pairings.

Aside from his sire hailing as a king from the northern realm, Jassyn knew little else besides that he was his only elven-blooded offspring. For whatever reason, the Vallendes and Raellyns fought over that human bloodline like they were vultures devouring a rotting carcass.

If I was raised in the human realms like Serenna, I would've been spared this fate. But thoughts like that are pointless.

Pride had Jassyn abstaining from Stardust beforehand—next time, he decided to black out *before* entering Farine's lair. He remembered nothing beyond the first encounter at the estate, where afterward he stole away and locked himself in a bathing chamber to inhale as much of the drug as he could.

He didn't need to bother bringing the supply he'd pilfered from Thalaesyn. There were individual vials of the glowing blue dust decorating every room like some demented party favor.

Jassyn's stomach turned over, recalling his last memory before everything went black. Of course, Elashor was there smirking at him from across the chambers over a glass of wine while someone healed his body so he could *perform* again.

What happened to him and what he couldn't remember, Jassyn didn't care to dwell on. *It doesn't matter.* Nothing mattered. He knew the memories would be horrific, judging from the revel he walked in on and the few moments he'd be forced to live with for the rest of his life.

Farine had assembled close to twenty nobles for the night of planned debauchery. And Jassyn's arrival had only commenced the events.

The vile crone took pleasure in watching carnal acts nearly as much as partaking. Being forced to service so many surely should have been beyond the scope of his contracts.

But no one cares.

Like an earthquake, Jassyn's body expelled a tremor at the memory. In her chamber of perverse horrors, Farine instructed him to stand there, unclothed on a pedestal, while the elves *marveled* at his anatomy and human complexion. Like they'd never laid eyes on an elven-blooded in the past century.

Or engaged in similar events.

Farine told him he should be flattered for being so desired and fetching a price so high—no other half-breed was as coveted as him. And then she promised she'd make him pay for it later.

From the furrows of nail marks down his chest and across his back, and the chunks of flesh missing from his neck, she was true to her word. Overpowering others gave the Vallendes a sense of superiority.

Shuddering with a heavy sigh, Jassyn clutched at the vines looping around him, taking a moment to breathe. In through his nose and out of his mouth. He grounded himself as the sun sank lower, feeling the textures of the leaves under his fingertips, inhaling the damp earth, and fighting to keep the darkness from caving in at the corners of his vision.

When Farine summoned him to her estate again, Jassyn feared he'd lose the will to live if he had to remember.

CHAPTER 20

SERENNA

He's going to punish me for retaliating.

Somehow, Serenna convinced her leaden legs to follow the prince out of the training ring. Her heart tripped over a beat when the unbound portion of Vesryn's topknot swung around his shoulders as he turned to face her. She halted a short distance away, in the shade of towering oaks.

"Was that your first time?" Vesryn asked.

Serenna's pulse fled, quickening under the attention of his gaze. *It's only because he's handsome,* she assured herself, recognizing she had no control over her body's absolutely uncalled-for responses. *He has no other redeeming qualities. Of that, I'm sure.*

The prince folded his arms and casually leaned against a tree, propping a foot behind him. Serenna had no idea how it was possible to *lean* with an air of arrogance, but he did.

"What?" she asked brainlessly, realizing he was waiting for her to respond.

"Was today the first time you touched your power?" Vesryn reached to tug at a low branch, plucking off a scattering of leaves.

Serenna squinted distrustfully at the prince's apparent patience, attempting to gauge what behavior she should expect from him.

Having witnessed an entire spectrum of his actions within the last hour, she couldn't predict what he might be capable of.

"Oh." She cleared her throat, swallowing her nervousness. "Yes."

"I can only assume it was your first time, since you obviously have no idea what you did." Vesryn's eyes lit up, glowing with self-satisfied amusement as he shredded the handful of plants. "I daresay this is a first for me as well."

Oblivious to what the prince found so humorous, Serenna combed through her sporadic memories of class. She irritably shoved a loose section from her braid behind her ear.

Words tumbled out of her mouth before she could still her tongue. "Why bother asking if you already know?"

Evidently, she'd asked the wrong question. The prince dismissed her comment while studying her, idly tugging at a thread from the stitching of his dragon sigil. "This was the first lesson I instructed. I managed to not only snap your rending ability into place, but I also was responsible for your first *touching* of Essence."

He arched a brow frustratingly high as if expecting a reaction. Serenna gaped at him. The way he said "touching" was beyond suggestive.

"I expect we'll have more firsts to look forward to." Vesryn's grin only widened as he watched the realization strike her.

Other firsts? Like what? Stubbornly ignoring his attempts at the inappropriate insinuations, Serenna scowled, biting out each word. "You didn't *teach* anything."

"Which is why I'm impressed," Vesryn said, running his hands across the overhanging branch. "I can feel your other abilities hovering under your skin. Your magic only needs to be drawn out by the appropriate emotions. You managed to shape rending the first time you *touched* it—which isn't an easy feat."

Serenna ripped her eyes away from the flash of flesh near his waist as his tunic pulled up while he was *rubbing* the bark above him.

"Stop saying it like that," Serenna snapped, putting her hands on her hips, more aggravated with herself now. "And don't patronize me."

Eyes narrowing, Vesryn crossed his arms as he stood to his full height.

Glancing around nervously, Serenna realized they were quite alone, as the training fields were now deserted before dinner. Well, except for the handful of recruits still fainted on the sand.

Serenna wasn't sure what the prince would do to her if she provoked him any further. She'd already pushed the boundaries of his tolerance and discovered how effortlessly he could reduce her to a writhing idiot.

Why am I being singled out? Because I was the only one to manifest my power? Even though she had no desire to stroke his ego, curiosity flickered, a part of her wanting to discover what she was capable of.

"What did I do exactly?" Serenna asked against her better judgment.

"Well, I felt a tingle of rending brush my fingertips." Vesryn held out a hand, surveying his nails. His raised brows somehow felt both encouraging and condescending. "With practice, you'll be able to accomplish so much more."

The prince rended nearly fifty recruits simultaneously, without even exerting himself, and she had barely *brushed* his fingers with her magic? Her insignificant power was laughable at this point.

Serenna shook her head. "I don't want to learn how to use that ability. No one deserves torment like that."

"The wraith do," Vesryn insisted, stalking forward to jab a finger at her. "They're mindless beasts. Would you like to be ripped apart while you're still alive, screaming as their fangs sink into your flesh? You'll be thanking me when rending saves your life... I expect you'll show your appreciation in more ways than one."

Serenna retreated a few steps to compensate for how he'd advanced. Which, by the curve of his mouth, he found entertaining. *He's toying with me!*

"You're so sure of yourself, aren't you?" she spat. The prince might be correct about the wraith, but she wouldn't admit it. Not now. "I'd rather use that power against you! Especially if you're going to behave like I *owe* you something." She pointed a finger back at him. "You didn't even do anything but torture me!"

"And were you harmed?" Vesryn asked, tilting his head. "You

needed to be angry enough to access your rending ability. You're welcome, by the way."

What? Serenna blinked at him. "But…but…that doesn't give you the right!" she protested.

Vesryn shrugged, smug satisfaction radiating from him in waves. "It worked, didn't it?"

His voice lowered sensuously, dark like his magic. "I'll keep in mind that, apparently, our foreplay in the Infirmary didn't have you warmed up enough to summon your power."

Serenna folded her arms and expelled her annoyance with a scoff, not in the mood to justify his unconventional methods or acknowledge his crass words. "This is all a game to you, isn't it? Let's poke at the *half-breeds'* emotions to see what they're capable of."

"Oh, I can do better than that, if it's games you desire." Vesryn circled halfway around her.

Serenna whirled to face him straight on, irritation soaring at his innuendoes and the way he herded her.

The leaves of the training yard's perimeter trees rustled behind her in a sudden breeze. Her eyes darted to the Infirmary, wishing Jassyn would appear.

No, I can handle this lout!

"I have other areas besides my hands I'd be more than willing to let you *brush* your magic against." Vesryn met her scowl with a grin as if daring her to say something. "If you're asking for extracurricular practice."

"Aren't you a little old for such juvenile humor?" Despite the embarrassed heat rushing to the points of her ears, Serenna served him her frostiest glare.

Breezing toward her, Vesryn surrounded her faster than a gale of wind. Serenna scrambled backward, every sense blaring in alarm. Her mind knew she'd never been close to real danger before.

Until now.

A surprised squeak fled from her throat when her back collided with a tree. Serenna's blood surged and her terror spiked when the prince planted his palms against the bark, caging her in. Every instinct told her to flee, her nerves alighting with a frenzied burst of energy, begging her to run.

Vesryn leaned down. Uncomfortably close to where she could count his dark eyelashes if she tried. Not that she *wanted* to ever be this close to him.

Serenna's stomach leaped, confused between deciding if fear was the appropriate response or if she liked the unexpected proximity. *No, he's just trying to intimidate me!* And the stars could scorch whatever magnetic pull she perceived emanating from him.

The prince lowered his mouth to hers and whispered, "Oh, I'm not going to stop while you keep giving me such a satisfying reaction with that delightful fury."

The heat from his words sent a shiver down her spine. Scents of crisp wind and leather invaded her senses. Serenna's heart flogged the inside of her ribs as if it wanted to pound out of her idiotic chest and into his.

Vesryn retrieved a loose strand of her hair. After rolling the locks between his fingers, seeming to study the color, he tucked it behind her ear. His fingers lingered, tracing her lobe, sparking a tingling current where he touched her skin.

Serenna inhaled a sharp hiss through her teeth at the sensation. She was beyond frustrated with herself for being stunned stupid by his barbaric strength. He was obviously getting some egotistical satisfaction while she let him overpower her.

What the bleeding stars am I doing? Was she going to stand there and *allow* the prince to stroke the points of her ears? Velinya had insisted the elves viewed the act as more intimate than fondling breasts! *I should have worn plated ear cuffs like Jassyn.*

She wanted to bask in the excitement of finally sensing Essence, not fend off the prince's improper advances. *He's just doing this to provoke me!*

Gathering her strength, Serenna furrowed her nails into the tree before she convinced herself she'd had enough of the prince's audacity.

She lunged, a *smack* of skin against skin sounding between them as she snatched his wrist, halting his wandering fingers.

"Don't touch me," she said in a level voice, glaring into his eyes. "I'm not telling you again."

Holding his gaze, Serenna ignored the electric surge of his power strobing beneath her fingertips. She recognized her own traitorous magic humming under her skin as if roused from the contact.

Vesryn's eyes widened almost imperceptibly and flicked to her hand clenched around his wrist.

Serenna flung his arm away before freezing like a startled deer, not daring to breathe while she waited for his backlash.

Vesryn straightened with a smirk. "So the harpy has a bite." He wiggled his fingers in front of her face. A challenge sparkled in his jade eyes, shining with arrogant glee. "You have no idea what you started, Princess."

He tapped the end of her nose.

Serenna spluttered an incoherent reply, too slow to smack his hand away.

Suddenly, the prince pivoted on a heel and strode off. Like he'd *won* whatever standoff they were engaged in or had lost interest in making her uncomfortable.

Vesryn left Serenna standing with her head spinning and her heartbeat thudding in her ears.

CHAPTER 21

SERENNA

Rooted in place, Serenna didn't move while Vesryn prowled away. Which, she grudgingly acknowledged, wasn't a bad view. *How does he walk in leathers that tight?* She idly picked embedded pieces of bark out of her palms, mesmerized by studying his backside. The loose portion of his hair swayed in time with his imperious stride as he disappeared into the Spire.

She gave herself a shake.

Stars scorch him! He's taunting and mocking me. That's all it is. He wants a reaction, and I'm the stargazer giving it to him. No matter how striking the prince looked in his rugged armor, it didn't change the fact that the more she learned about him, the less she liked him.

Serenna lingered at the edge of the training yard until her heartbeat slowed to a more reasonable pace. After regaining some measure of composure, she peeled away from the tree, appreciating the support it gave. Otherwise, she had no doubt her legs would've collapsed.

It was too early in the evening for the communal dinner in the mess hall, but there was always food available in a buffet-style arrangement. Serenna hurried toward the Spire's cafeteria.

She selected cured meats, cheeses, fruits, and breads at random, intending to take something to Jassyn, since he might mend recruits well into the evening after the prince's "class." Doubling back, she grabbed two slices of that sickeningly sweet chocolate cake he liked.

The Infirmary was less busy than expected when she shouldered her way through the entrance doors carrying the tray of food. Perhaps Vesryn had talked to her longer than she'd realized, and most of the initiates had already received healing. Serenna's mind was infected with a fog, the details of their conversation after class now hazy.

Except her heart accelerated when she spiraled back through the memories of him trapping her against the tree.

Stop it.

As a half-breed, Serenna knew she wasn't anything special. Vesryn's disdain for the initiates was obvious, considering how he delighted in manipulating their *human* emotions and *torturing* them. There were a thousand reasons she should stop thinking about the prince.

But is he really trying to make everyone angry on purpose in order to manifest their rending power?

Serenna thought no more of it, noting Jassyn's absence among the healers tending to the handful of recruits. Peeking into his office, she didn't find him there either.

Winding up the tall staircase in search of him, she wondered if he was tending to the plants. It took her a few moments of blinking away the setting sun's glare before she could squint to scan the rooftop.

Serenna frowned. Jassyn sat in the greenhouse, leaning against the glass. With worry prickling at her scalp, she balanced the platter of food on a hip to open the glass door.

When she saw him more clearly, shock loosened her grip. The tray of food crashed to the ground. Aghast, Serenna placed a hand over her mouth. Purple bruises and *bite* marks marred every surface of his neck. Trenches left by nails disappeared under his white leathers.

He looked ravaged by an animal.

"Are you okay?" Serenna asked, rushing to kneel beside him. She swept vines away to clear a space. "What happened?"

Jassyn didn't meet her eyes. "It's not as bad as it looks." Studying the plants twisted around his palms, he rubbed the leaves between his fingers. "I'm waiting until the stars are out so I can regenerate to… cover everything back up."

"Should I get a mender?" Serenna asked, knowing that self-healing wasn't possible. "A few magus are still in the wing."

Jassyn's skin was so inflamed and shredded that he had to be in pain. *This doesn't appear to have just happened… He must have concealed the wounds with illusions.*

Jassyn shook his head. "I don't want anyone to see me like this."

Serenna studied his injuries and placed what she hoped was a comforting hand on his arm. *This is too severe for any salves to work.* Judging from what she knew about him, Serenna doubted he was involved in a passionate tryst. Not that she wanted to make it her business.

His hesitation and shame hovered between them like smoke. *Surely a lover wouldn't do this kind of damage.* Serenna drew in an uneven breath, recalling exactly how Vesryn had taunted him.

"Was…was this against your will?"

Jassyn recoiled, pulling out of her grip. His voice cracked. "I think…I think I'd like to be alone now."

Serenna's heart shattered into a hundred pieces for him. "Who did this to you? Was it this Lady Farine?"

My grandmother? The thought of Jassyn enduring such obscenities against his wishes burned like acid in her stomach. The unwelcome savagery slashed into his skin ignited the fires to her fury.

This was a cruelty worse than what Vesryn had subjected the class to. This was an atrocity.

Jassyn's head dropped into his hands. "It…doesn't matter." His whole body trembled with an unsteady exhale.

"Jassyn," Serenna whispered, clutching his arms. "It matters to *me.*"

When his gaze lifted to hers, the despondency in his eyes evoked Serenna's anger in a thundering surge of power. Her Essence roared to existence, disbelief racing alongside her outrage that someone had forced him to experience such a horrific act.

The world came into a sharp focus. Serenna trembled with the force of her new magic. Life hummed around her. She could count the individual veins of the surrounding leaves. She sensed the living pulse of everything in the greenhouse. But her attention was on Jassyn.

Black shadows whipped like a billowing sail, enveloping them in a vortex of darkness. Serenna's wrath was strong enough to drown her in a wave of hatred. Her lungs yanked in air as she struggled to control the tide of her power. She wouldn't let anyone hurt him again.

Jassyn's eyes widened as Essence wrapped around them like a midnight veil. "I don't think rending is going to be of much help."

"Give me a minute with this Lady Farine," Serenna hissed, "and I'll do more than *brush* that elven bitch with my magic." The sinister power thrummed in time with her disgust. The shadows reeled her in, sucking her down a whirlpool of loathing.

"How do I mend you?" she asked, leaning forward to hover her fingers near his neck. Black tendrils coiled around her hands, writhing like vipers, poised to strike.

"It's not that easy," Jassyn said quietly, touching her wrist. "You need to access a different talent in your Well. You won't find healing with your contempt."

Serenna searched his face. "Vesryn snapped me into my magic. Can you do that?"

Scowling, Jassyn declined. "Snapping is a hazardous way to reach your abilities and instills some dependence on using those emotions to summon talents. Even if I knew how to make someone snap into mending, I wouldn't subject you to trauma."

"I don't care," Serenna protested. "You're hurt."

Jassyn shook his head. "I'll live."

He released her to grip the vines, like he was taking strength from the earth. The blanket of leaves sheltering his legs didn't seem to bother him.

The plants coiled around Serenna's boots. Not having time to wonder about the unusual behavior, her mind raced. She recalled how Vesryn said he would manipulate emotions to draw abilities forth. If the prince somehow knew her powers were close to manifesting, she should be able to access her other talents with a little encouragement.

Mending should be gentle and kind since it's the opposite of rending. Serenna dug down deep, struggling to bury her malice, the effort as difficult as upending a mountain with her fingertips. She forced herself to only think of helping Jassyn by stitching his wounds. The surrounding darkness withdrew like mist burned off by the sun when she shoved her rending magic away.

Serenna gently grazed the markings along his neck. She fought to navigate the correct path through the maze of her emotions. Closing her eyes, she descended into the embrace of Essence.

The strange silver cords wrapped around her Well drew Serenna's attention again. Not knowing anything about her manifested power, she hauled the strands toward her in a second attempt, but they slipped through her imagined fingers.

I'll have to ask Jassyn about that magic later. She tried something else.

Gripping shimmering Essence in a tight fist, Serenna searched for a different lair, picturing herself in a dark underground cavern, exploring for another ability.

Unformed magic swirled around her, glittering like a stream of stars. Harnessing raw power wasn't quite a talent, but it was a way to perceive and examine other life forces. Serenna had already learned menders used the skill to assess injuries before they began healing. Maintaining a shroud of unformed Essence was a common practice before directing an ability.

Letting intention steer her, Serenna sank into her memories to haul other emotions forth. Rifling through their shared moments, she dwelled on how she looked up to Jassyn, reminiscing about their first meeting—reliving her excitement of having him as a tutor.

Her thoughts drifted to Vaelyn's beach—remembering how unfair she thought her life was, conscripted to the academy. But Jassyn had been there, towing her away from the edge of despair. He patiently handled her outbursts, unprovoked into anger even when she erupted.

Serenna channeled feelings of his kindness into the expanse of her Well, delving deeper into her power. Jassyn was compassionate and concerned with the welfare of others—to a degree she didn't think she could ever achieve.

Reaching, grasping, Serenna molded and shaped the fondness she had for him into a tangible force. When rending snapped, hostility encased her in a husk of loathing.

Mending was the gentle opposite, like a moth emerging from a cocoon. A serene scarlet light flowered in her hands, illuminating them in a radiant glow.

Serenna's attention flew to the savage marks of ownership under her fingertips. Since Jassyn had depleted his Well, he couldn't demonstrate how to mold the magic. The magus had fabricated a handful of basic mending lattices during class, but she obviously hadn't practiced.

I should have watched him heal that leg earlier.

The fibers of power fanned out and settled on Jassyn like a scarlet web. He tensed while her fingers directed the crimson filaments of light. Serenna perceived more wounds concealed by his armor and wrestled down an emerging wave of rending that seemed determined to overwhelm her.

I can do this. Serenna shaped the magic into unrelenting steel and attacked the bruises and gashes with a vengeance, willing Jassyn's skin to knit and restore itself, setting his body back to its correct form. Tugging the mending threads into a knot of healing light, she reconnected the broken skin. Flesh rippled like a wave, stretching and shifting, lacing and twining together. For the bruising, she soothed the inflamed vessels and swelling, reversing the brutal damage.

Jassyn exhaled a wheeze as if her magic punched the air from his lungs. Startled, Serenna jumped and lost her concentration. Her Essence retreated to the corners of her mind.

"Did I hurt you?" she asked, wiping beads of sweat off her forehead. The effort of using her power had her catching her breath like she'd sprinted laps around the island.

Jassyn raised a trembling hand to his neck, prodding his skin. "No." He emitted a weak laugh. "It's been a while since I've received healing by one learning the craft—but you did well."

Serenna sat next to him, scooting back to lean against the wall. The vines had wiggled back to their hanging planters.

"Can I stay with you?" she asked. "To regenerate my power? I'll leave if you want me to." She didn't wish to abandon him on the rooftop, but she wanted to give him the choice. "But...I don't think you should be alone."

Jassyn nodded and closed his eyes.

The sun drifted lower, casting long shadows in the greenhouse. A heavy silence settled between them as they waited for the stars to shine. A flock of yellow finches chattered outside, roosting in trees for the evening. The birds were a mockery of freedom, having the luxury of flitting from place to place.

"If you ever want to talk," Serenna said, finding his hand to squeeze, "I'm here."

Jassyn winced when he swallowed. He stared off into the curated jungle before speaking, dragging a hand through his curls. "There are four elven females I'm required to couple with when they summon me."

A barb lodged itself in Serenna's heart at the unexpected admission. "Wh-what? Required?"

"Up to four times a year with each, as demanded in binding contracts dictated by the High Council..." Jassyn's voice trailed off as he sighed the confession like he had to strip the words from somewhere deep in his chest.

Serenna's shock morphed to dismay while she listened in growing horror to Jassyn dejectedly informing her of his forced servitude to the realm. How he was obligated to couple with those who secured a position on his contracts, and how he changed handlers every year if they no longer needed his *services*.

Jassyn wrapped his arms around his knees when Serenna asked if he could refuse. His eyes glazed over. "I'm too much of a coward to even consider going against the realm's demands. I've heard stories of those who...disappear if they defy the will of the council or the king. And I doubt they're simply banished."

Serenna shivered at the uncomfortable thought of the elves disposing of those who resisted their orders. For a race that came to the mortal shores enlightened, they had a backward way of treating their people—especially now she had this knowledge of Jassyn's contracts. *How can they do this to their own kin?*

Serenna sat in a bewildered silence, letting her thoughts drift. She didn't know how Jassyn found the strength to help others when the realm had treated him so terribly his whole life. *Maybe it would be better for the wraith to win this war.*

No, even considering Vesryn's cruelty and the vulgarity Jassyn was subject to, the elves didn't deserve death. Their people were misguided—struggling to survive. *Surely they'll put an end to the practice soon since the elven-blooded are bolstering their number. But still...Jassyn shouldn't be treated this way.*

Jassyn shoved the curls off his forehead. "The handlers are allowed to mark us. Wherever and however they deem fit. So everyone in the courts is aware of whom we belong to. It's a competition for some—securing those with a more favorable bloodline for their family and paying the highest price. I don't think this servitude has anything to do with the elves' survival anymore." Jassyn's voice dropped. "It's about control."

Serenna covered her mouth, horrified by the barbaric practice. And there were countless times that she'd badgered Jassyn about his tattoos. She'd even complimented them! The corners of her eyes stung. She couldn't look at the sigils.

"I'm so sorry," she whispered. "I didn't know."

Jassyn's despair caused a lump of agony to form in her throat. Serenna swiped away tears, wanting to comfort him, but she wasn't sure how. *Would he even want to be touched?*

Tentatively, she reached out to wrap an arm around his shoulder.

That was all it took for him to shatter, sagging against her and weeping into her embrace.

CHAPTER 22

LYKOR

The second time the bond ripped at his chest, Lykor combatted the urge to recklessly tear open a portal. Fangs elongating, his knuckles tightened on the lift's railing. The plates in his single gauntlet squealed, grinding steel against iron in his clenched fist.

The wind whipped at his ebony hair while he descended into the depths of the mountain, deeper into the wraith's stronghold. Shafts of sunlight streamed in from thousands of feet above, reflecting and bouncing off scores of mirrors suspended from the rockwork, lighting the cavern as brightly as the frozen surface.

Lykor scoffed in disbelief, knowing the desire was instinctive—the need to rush to the bond-holder's aid when the connection called. Over the previous weeks since the magic's inception, he'd ignored this hovering link between him and the unknown person. Now, in a moment of weakness, he searched for their location while the bond yanked on him like a fucking leash.

Lykor sensed their position, but they weren't in the southernmost area of the continent again like he expected. The pull came from somewhere closer. He wondered why they'd traveled to a different realm.

Unclasping the buckles binding the fur cloak across his shoulders,

Lykor left the glacial air behind. A lake of fire spewed molten rivers of magma at the base of the stronghold, providing heat for the vents and flames for the forges. Nothing survived on the tundra's surface—not anymore—but down here, at the root of the mountains, in this dormant volcano, life thrived.

While he folded his cloak to carry, Lykor discerned an inferno of hatred searing through the link. Even half a world away, he experienced the intensity of the bond-holder's emotions. He doubted the person on the other end was aware they were jerking on the connection.

PROBABLY FUCKING AROUND WITH THEIR MAGIC, Lykor thought.

He refused to embrace this intrusion linking them with tendrils of power. Lykor had no desire to dwell upon how long this vestige of a bond would hover between him and whichever figure he'd observed that stormy night on the shore. With a disgusted growl, he assumed the connection would last an eternity if they never met in the flesh to accept or reject the magic of the bond.

As if he wanted an aspect of Essence to shackle him to another.

We're both probably bonded to them, the other entity in Lykor's mind mused.

While fucking ridiculous, the quiet statement made Lykor stiffen, hackles rising like hearing a whisper in shadows. They rarely addressed each other directly. That is, until a few weeks ago when the other presence took an interest in the discovery of their bond-holder. Surely talking to the other in his head would grate at his focus—making his stability more difficult to maintain than it already was.

The other being had seldom risen to the surface of their thoughts during the past century they'd existed together, dwelling in the same mind. That fragment of himself had been content to lurk. To watch. To let Lykor serve as the host of their actions—the protector.

The other being was a shell of the elf he used to be. Weak. Pathetic. A coward not strong enough to survive. Lykor's consciousness sundered from the other to defend. Safeguard. Preserve.

Lykor's existence was the only reason they'd persisted—enduring torture as some fucked-up personal shield. The other never felt the need to emerge from the safety of his shelter.

Twenty years of indescribable torment in the elven dungeons would shatter anyone, let alone one on the cusp of maturity, unable to understand why he'd been targeted by those closest to him and ripped apart. The experimenting had fractured who he was, splintering his sanity like the Maelstrom had shredded the Aelfyns' galleons in the Cerulean Sea.

The other presence detached from their thoughts, avoiding Lykor's memories scraping their captivity. Conveniently, the nuisance left. Lykor had mastered how to influence the other being, pressuring him to retreat further into their mind.

Now reminded of his origin in the prisons, Lykor tugged off the gauntlet from his one accursed hand that had never changed back to its original shape. He inspected his claw. A wraith's limb. Then muttered to himself in annoyance upon noticing the trimmed talons.

The other presence never missed an opportunity to groom their appearance. It was like the other being made it a point to fuck around, controlling their body when Lykor's awareness slept. But as soon as Lykor's consciousness stirred in the mornings, the other retreated into the grottos of their mind. Or rather, he used to.

Lykor shoved the gauntlet onto his claw, sheathing the reminder of how the elves had diminished his body. He was now reduced. Wretched. Transformed.

But the sheer arrogance of the elves would be their downfall—Lykor would see to it. They'd left him rotting in the dungeons alongside the wraith, with a fraction of his former power.

A fresh wave of anger crashed over him at the thought of how the wraith had been harmed. Broken. Defiled. He'd bargained his compliance in the elves' research to spare his people from the same experimenting.

He loathed all elves and the taint they left on the world. Essence answered his anger, black tendrils of rending lashed around him, spurred by his wrath.

But there was one he hated above all the others. Lykor's thoughts twisted into compliance, cursed by the elves' magic. *Him* he would kill on sight. There was no escape from the coercion.

Tethered and defenseless with a lacerated mind, the elves embedded commands into Lykor's flesh, demanding his obedience. To kill *him*.

I'm not compelled to harm him, the quiet voice said.

YOU'RE IN NO POSITION TO TAKE OVER, Lykor snarled.

Rolling his shoulders and releasing his magic, Lykor expunged the nightmares of the past. He turned, leaning against the railing as the lift slowed its journey to the bottom of the chasm.

Glowing lichens and mosses illuminated the way to the lower levels of the underground keep. The fading sun reflected in the suspended mirrors. He studied the wraith going about their daily lives as evening neared.

How this ancient druid capital existed, hidden from all knowledge, was beyond him. Even after all this time, his people continued to discover concealed chambers in the depths below the earth. Lykor frequently wondered how decay hadn't overrun the fortress. Perhaps there was residual druidic magic he couldn't detect.

Everything about the keep was exotic, but equipped as if the former stewards had simply vanished. The druids left behind rugs, tapestries, weapons, and even armor to accommodate shifting into their dragon forms. It was almost as if this place waited for new masters, frozen in time.

Lykor stepped off the platform and pried a metal lever, sending the contraption sailing back to the surface for when the sentries changed shifts. Even decades later, astonishment nearly had him gaping as he watched the cables spin and gears grind on the druids' machines.

The elven culture had long since become stagnant, abandoning their interest in innovation. How far their race fell from their former glory. A time when the legends said they used to travel between the stars.

I doubt there was anything glorious about the Aelfyn, the other being muttered.

Even though he agreed, Lykor ignored the comment, not wanting to entertain a conversation or dwell anymore on the elves.

He wandered through the majestic caverns of the stronghold, intent on making his daily rounds and gathering reports. The winding stone streets, so at odds with the sharply gridded roads of Kyansari, made him feel like he was roaming aimlessly in circles around the keep's residence level.

Lykor's scalp prickled as he realized he'd never set foot in the capital beyond the dungeons—those weren't his memories.

Lykor focused on the task ahead of him. Now that the wraith had survived for decades after their escape from the prison, his people's safety was his purpose. The driving force propelling him forward. He would do everything in his power to ensure it. Someone had to protect them from the elves.

The remote location of the ancient stronghold had bought them time. The wraith had scraped a semblance of a life in the Hibernal Wastes. Not the existence they were accustomed to, but a small fraction of normalcy.

As normal as the wretched could get.

To everyone's surprise, a substantial number of offspring were born after they established themselves in the keep's safety. The wraithlings had shifted their focus away from simply surviving; his people now had something to live for—a future to prepare for. Their numbers had increased fivefold over the past eighty years of freedom.

Two thousand five hundred and twenty-one, the other recited, like Lykor had asked him to flap his numerical mouth. *With another wraithling due any day from Kal's clan.* In their mind, Lykor watched the other presence fold his arms, leaning against a fabricated doorframe to chuckle. *As you'd expect, there is some confusion about who the sire is, but—*

Lykor growled in annoyance and drove the commentary away, shoving him into a room.

He angled toward the forges to inspect the status of the smelting. The wraith's advantage against Essence. He'd driven the smiths relentlessly to craft golden weapons.

Lykor considered changing his route when he spotted a cluster of boisterous wraith from Kal's clan on a collision course with him. Of course, his captain's son, Fenn, led the pack, laughing alongside the other wraith before they warped closer to greet him.

IT'S LIKE FENN HAS AN EXTRA WRAITH ABILITY SPECIFI-CALLY FOR SENSING MY LOCATION, Lykor peevishly thought to himself. The lieutenant crossed paths with him more often than not.

Striding through the cluster of his younger warriors, Lykor warded off a persistent invitation from Fenn to join them at the Lagoon.

You could give them more of your time, you know, the other said, reemerging to apparently natter at Lykor incessantly.

WE ARE NOT GOING TO THE LAGOON, SO DON'T EVEN ASK. AND DON'T GIVE ME A FUCKING LECTURE ABOUT HOW IT'S NOT TECHNICALLY A LAGOON—I DIDN'T NAME THOSE HOT SPRINGS.

The other being pursed his lips. *It wouldn't kill you to get to know them. Fenn looks up to you, as do the others who were born here.*

HE SMILES TOO MUCH, Lykor grumbled as Kal's clan disappeared around a corner.

Maybe if you tried that next time, you'd scare them off faster.

Lykor dragged a hand down his face before flinching from another blast of unexpected emotion. He crushed his gauntlet into a fist. *DRACOVAE'S TITS!* This was the second time in the past hour the bond-holder had assaulted him through their connection. Wasn't his fucking head already full enough?

This tentative link put his people in danger. What was to stop the other person from seeking him out? It was a risk to assume they were inexperienced with their magic. A risk he wasn't willing to accept much longer.

Perhaps they didn't have the portaling ability, or they weren't strong enough in their power to sense the connection over this great of a distance. There were too many unknowns.

The night the link appeared, the other entity defiantly declared he wouldn't permit Lykor to kill their bond-holder. Uninterested in fighting a battle of wills or wrestling for control over their body, Lykor stayed his hand. Otherwise, he would've slaughtered those two on the beach to decimate the threat.

Apparently, you have an aura similar to someone else's if Essence linked you, the other jested. *Technically, the bond connects our Wells.*

FUCK OFF.

Lykor's chest heaved with fury that this connection plagued him. Trembling, he struggled to suppress his magic, which threatened to spiral out of control. He gathered his will and rammed steel bars around his thoughts to obscure his awareness of the bond-holder's emotions.

Until he realized he was grasping at nothing, like clutching smoke. The elves had thoroughly obliterated his capacity to form any mental barricades.

Lykor's fangs clenched in outrage at his mind's evisceration, drawing blood from his gums. The vulnerability had dread accumulating in his gut like toxic sludge in a bog.

Frustration exploding, Lykor pivoted and twisted, smashing his gauntlet against a wall. A spray of rocks clattered to the ground. He panted, drawing in jagged breaths.

A little dramatic, don't you think?

Snarling, Lykor yanked his fist out of the stone and departed the forges before he lost control and caused actual damage. The workshops, furnaces, and clang of metal shaping gold created a cacophony, pounding in time with the pulse in his temples and the wrath roaring in his ears.

He needed the privacy and solitude of his quarters to clear his head. If he couldn't keep a grip on his power, he didn't want to worry his people again.

Lykor hastened through the streets of the residential district. He assumed the druids had also previously dwelled in the rectangular buildings carved into the rock. Most of the clans were inside their homes for their evening meal as night approached, the sun's reflection fading from the mirrors.

Focusing his attention on ascending the stone stairs, Lykor contemplated their latest raids. The gold ore they recently stumbled on and secured from the Foothill Mines was invaluable. He'd instructed the smiths to shape arrows, daggers, and shackles—hoping to tether any elves they came into contact with if the realms continued stirring.

Even considering the elves had Essence, it wasn't like they'd bothered mastering their powers. Lykor was confident his people would have a fighting chance if the elves ever decided to hunt them down. The wraith wouldn't be defenseless—Lykor had ensured his people learned how to fight and use what abilities they did have.

Having lived the past eighty years in the most remote location in the known world, they all were unsure of Alari's current state. Lykor had hoped the elves would eventually die out from the druids' curse.

He'd intended to keep the wraith hidden, biding their time in safety. But the humans gathering in camps and the evidence of the half-elves on the southern realm's beaches suggested something was happening.

Reaching the top of his tower nestled on the side of a mountain, Lykor entered his chambers and blinked while his eyes adjusted to the failing light spilling in through the elongated windows. The sun ignited the frozen peaks on its descent below the frosty horizon.

He preferred living alone in the aerie apartments, not inclined to join a clan. Warding off his captain's irritating interest, Lykor placated Kal with assurances that dwelling away from the population was only to see the stars, having spent his entire existence in the dungeons deprived of the celestial light.

As he paced well into the evening, Lykor's thoughts ricocheted with worry that those with magic were increasing in number. Drawing to a halt in the center of his sitting room, he caught himself staring to the southeast again, in the direction of the bond's pull.

WHERE ARE THEY? Alari's borders felt likely, but surely their location wasn't as far as Kyansari. None of his people had been to the elven realm since they'd fled from the prison. The risk was too great. He wasn't inclined to go back. There were too many of his own dark memories in those forsaken lands.

The other in his mind was fiercely curious, urging him to seek their bond-holder. Lykor only debated the temptation if there was a way to exploit the connection to his benefit. But that meant he needed to meet them in the flesh to fully form the hovering link.

Perhaps he could capture and tether them, and then manipulate the bond between them to utilize their power for himself. He was desperate enough to resort to any advantage to protect the wraith.

Even binding himself to a stars-cursed elf. Or half elf. Whatever they were.

Lykor grudgingly gave in to the other's incessant urging, if only to shut him up. He had no intention of granting him control of their body.

Cloaking himself in shadows, Lykor twisted open a portal to the location where he last sensed the pull of magic. Stepping out to a darkened rooftop on the other side, he released his power. The gateway flickered out behind him.

Reaching into a pocket in his leather tunic, Lykor seized a golden tip from a crossbow bolt he kept on his person. Touching gold to skin masked the bond completely, just like it suppressed access to Essence. Whoever was bonded to him would be none the wiser of his proximity. When he got his bearings, he would untether himself to discover the holder.

Night engulfed wherever this location was. Lykor adjusted his vision as well as he could to see in the dark. Glancing around, he didn't perceive any activity.

The only structure on the empty roof was a lone greenhouse bursting with plant life. He wasn't in the capital; that much was obvious as he sifted through the other being's memories for any recognition. The other entity was silent, watching through Lykor's eyes.

Lykor gazed out as far as he could see. A disorienting gap at the horizon sliced into the sudden sharp edges of trees. It took a few confused moments for him to comprehend he was on a landmass in the sky.

Such a place hadn't existed when the other had lived in Kyansari. Lykor wandered to the railing and peered over the edge, spine tingling as he wondered what this place was.

A massive spire rose to the clouds, and buildings lay scattered across the grounds. Immense sand fields filled in the areas between the structures. A few of the yards contained what he assumed were soldiers locked in combat, even at this late hour.

Lykor sucked in a shocked breath, apprehension and disbelief clashing inside his skull as he deciphered what this location was.

There was no other explanation. After all this time, elves had established a military training ground.

The king had bred his magic-wielding army.

The elves were preparing to kill his people. The wraith.

Lykor shoved the golden bolt back into his pocket. Seized by uncontrolled fury, his wrath detonated in an explosive wave of anger. He didn't even notice the punch of force shattering glass or the spray of soil and plants ricocheting off his spiked armor.

WE WILL BRING THEM WAR.

CHAPTER 23

SERENNA

How is it already time for another rending class? Serenna wondered, regretfully leaving the Infirmary. Compared to her other courses, assisting Jassyn was by far her preferred method of learning more about magic. Under his guidance, she'd substantially refined her mending techniques.

Since she wasn't a magus, restricted from healing minor ailments, Jassyn had allowed her to mend scrapes and bruises. That was, after Serenna mentioned the loophole in Vesryn's "orders." The realization had elicited a little conspiratorial grin from her friend.

Neither of them worried that this skirted the prince's rules. If Vesryn ever voiced a complaint, Jassyn assured her he would insist she needed the experience to improve.

Jassyn's attitude toward her was shifting, like the protective walls around him were slowly eroding. A few evenings, he'd even invited her and Velinya to the Terminal to explore the growing town and to spend the balmy nights strolling the lakeshore. They'd collected hyacinths from the water's edge to help Nelya rebuild her collection.

The fact that someone had destroyed the greenhouse, apparently with a blast of force, appalled Serenna. *Why would anyone do such a thing? Is it because the research would benefit humans?*

They'd salvaged what plants they could, but the insurmountable loss weighed heavily on them. It had taken Nelya decades to accumulate such an assortment from all corners of the realms.

Surprisingly, Vesryn assured the magus that he'd punish the culprit if they were ever discovered.

I'm sure he just wants an excuse to rend someone.

Which brought Serenna back to the present just as the Rending Field came into view. *Why can't Vesryn find some wraith to terrorize instead of holding class?* Earlier in the week, the monsters had dragged off five citizens from Kyansari, leaving no remains behind. The prince had tracked down the handful of offending wraith.

At least he didn't bring us their heads this time.

Since manifesting rending two weeks prior, Serenna was one of the few Vesryn hadn't abused with his dark magic during their classes, which now, unfortunately, met every day. He hadn't singled her out again either.

His relative disinterest brought her a sliver of relief—if she could consider being the target of his wolfish gaze to be indifference.

I'm sure he's not done with me yet. The thought of another encounter with him twisted her anticipation and agitation together in what she could only interpret as dread tying her middle into a knot.

"I was hoping to run into you," a velvety voice chimed when Serenna entered the practice field.

"I'm not in the mood," Serenna said, glancing between Ayla and Mishryn, who led their entourage in the same direction.

Facing Ayla in their combat class was humiliating enough. Serenna hardly needed a daily reminder of her dismal progress. She was well aware of her pathetic attempts to master the fundamentals of balance and strength training—she had the sore muscles and bruises to prove it.

Mouth tightening, Ayla stopped in her tracks, obviously peeved by Serenna's attempted dismissal. "You will respect your betters!"

Rolling her eyes, Serenna didn't slow her brisk pace.

A slash of violet light arced in front of her, solidifying to form an impenetrable wall. Slamming into the shield's web, Serenna toppled backward, crashing to the ground with a painful jolt clattering up her spine.

The tips of her ears fanned with the flames of embarrassment. Serenna scrambled back onto her feet to the snickers of the Alari recruits.

"I have a matter to discuss with you," Ayla said, nonchalantly tapping a finger to her ruby lips.

With a swell of loathing, Serenna pivoted to confront her sister, her pulse thrashing in her temples. Digging her boots into the sand, she anchored herself to the ground. Tension rolled through her. She balled her hands into fists to prevent her limbs from shaking.

Serenna clenched her jaw. "And what is so pressing?" she bit out.

"Have you received permission to leave campus for the Summer Lunar Solstice?" Ayla asked, picking at one of her lacquered nails, giving her fingers more attention than she afforded Serenna. "I saw our sire yesterday." Her lips curved somewhere in between a vicious sneer and a scathing smile when Serenna stiffened. Ayla tilted her head. "Did you?"

Serenna's stomach dropped to her feet. *He didn't even see me when he was on campus?*

Uninterested in Serenna's response, Ayla continued, "He'll be escorting me to court for the royal ball and presenting *me* to the noble families during the solstice."

Serenna was familiar with the celebrations in the southern realm when the moons eclipsed each other on the longest and shortest days of the year, but the elven traditions were foreign to her. The Summer Lunar Solstice was still two months away, occurring near the Essence Tournament.

The last time Serenna saw her father was when he introduced her to the prince. An empty feeling spread in her chest as her annoyance cooled to dejection. *He's taking Ayla to court instead of me.*

Noting Serenna's dismay, Alya emitted a delighted laugh. "Oh, you were unaware? I suppose if our sire didn't tell you, then that must mean you're not…*invited.*"

She flashed Serenna a vain grin, somehow even making that look beautiful, despite the maliciousness in her words. Serenna's stunned silence only seemed to evoke more condescension.

"The Summer Lunar Solstice is the most celebrated event in the elven realm. Since I doubt you're familiar." Ayla brought her flame-colored braid forward to stroke the gathered hair. "Only the most influential families receive invitations to King Galaeryn's palace."

"I'm sure you'll have a lovely time," Serenna said, forging cool steel into her voice, hoping she didn't reveal her crippled feelings.

Turning to retreat, Serenna swallowed the bitter jealousy blocking her throat. She refused to give Ayla the satisfaction of knowing how effortlessly the news had knifed into her heart.

What's her issue with me? She already has the greatest strength and control of Essence on campus. What more does she want? It was only fitting that their father would present his most prized offspring to the nobles. *It's not like I've done anything significant to earn his approval.*

How foolish she was for assuming she could ever amount to something—not when there was someone like Ayla to compete with. No matter how hard she tried, Serenna would never be accepted or belong in their realm. The elves were going to dispatch her to the front lines. She'd be nothing more than another body to throw at the wraith.

This time, when magic pulsated behind her, Serenna didn't ram into a shield. Instead, a force similar to a violent slap of solid wind launched her forward into the air.

She sailed like a hurled, wingless bird.

Throwing her hands out to catch her fall, Serenna crashed to the ground ten paces ahead. Skidding to a halt, sand shredded her palms. The impact drove the breath from her lungs as her chest collided with the earth. Her cheek stung, scraped by the coarse grit of the yard.

A chorus of laughter reached her ringing ears through the stirred cloud of dust. Serenna's vision blurred as she blinked back humiliated tears. Her entire body shook from disbelief at her incompetence, helplessly knowing Ayla wasn't going to stop.

Serenna swallowed the emotions thickening in her throat. *I am not going to cry.* Pushing herself off the ground, she wiped the dust from her face before balling her scratched hands into trembling fists. Regaining her feet, she spun to confront Ayla. Her irritation only reinforced her. She'd had enough.

"I wasn't done speaking to you," Ayla said with false sweetness, resting a hand on her hip. "I didn't give you permission to leave."

"I don't need your permission," Serenna snapped, her indignation cracking like the lash of a whip.

She angled herself toward Ayla as the cluster of Alari recruits backed up their mistress. *All I ever did was try to compliment this stars-cursed woman.* Not caring if she lost what laughable nonexistent control she had in this rapidly deteriorating confrontation, Serenna abandoned all efforts of wrestling her smoldering frustration into submission.

Her evolving anger instantly funneled her magic straight into her marrow. The world sharpened when Essence barreled through her. Serenna wrapped rending in a tight grip, the energy crackling through her with a steady hum, beating in time with her furious heartbeat.

Ayla already used shielding and force against me, I don't have any other defense. A thick veil of black clouds rippled around her as she gathered her power.

Ayla's disbelieving laugh tinkled across the training yard. She disinterestedly surveyed Serenna. Though, her unperturbed gaze lingered on the climbing shadows. A pulse of energy like the pressure of rumbling thunder converged and vibrated through the surrounding air while Ayla prepared her next wave of magic.

"You think that *you*, someone who might as well be more human than elf, is *my* better?" Ayla asked, streams of Essence glittering around her in a halo.

"Let's find out," Serenna said, rising to the challenge.

Their eyes locked and her sister's manicured brows shot up in surprise. *Apparently, she's forgotten we both have mortal blood in our veins.* The differences between them were so negligible, it was laughable.

Well, one of us grew up in Alari—which apparently makes all the difference.

Serenna didn't think—her anger consumed her, making her brash. Extending a hand, midnight tendrils of magic twined around her arms like curls of smoke. Like she'd observed from Vesryn numerous times, she crushed her fingers into a fist.

Channeling the flow of her power, rending streaked straight toward Ayla's chest. The shadows consumed her sister like a tumbling avalanche. A satisfying shriek ripped from Ayla's throat when she toppled to the ground.

Pouring the entire force of her annoyance and contempt into the attack, Serenna directed waves of searing torment into Ayla's spasming form.

Her skin prickled as she recognized the weighty charge of magic surrounding the rest of the Alari initiates. Unformed Essence shimmered and whirled around them.

Serenna accessed the reservoir of her power and wrenched her entire Well toward her, letting the ravenous pull devour her. It was as if the floodgates of a dam opened, releasing the wrath of a raging river.

Turning, Serenna gritted her teeth and planted her feet in the sand to brace herself. With a sweeping gesture of her other hand, she included the rest of the Alari initiates in her onslaught before they disabled her first, smothering them with a storm of rending.

Everyone collapsed, contorting on the ground to join Ayla in uncontrolled writhing.

Serenna clutched two fistfuls of darkness. Cyclones of twisting shadows connected her to the screaming recruits. The rampaging magic buffeted her like a squall, distorting the air. Her body vibrated as the torrent of Essence blazed through her. Chest heaving from the effort, she clenched her power with all of her strength, never before having channeled the full extent of her power.

A vision unfolded in Serenna's mind, showing her how to divide the bundles of rending.

Serenna split the currents of magic into two.

And separated those channels into four.

And then repeatedly divided Essence, creating separate streams of magic to each of the eighteen recruits. Drowning in her outrage, she didn't dwell on where the knowledge came from.

A shard of awareness fragmented Serenna's focus, diverting her attention away from the screaming initiates. Her magic spun around them while they flailed on the ground, trussed to pain.

Scuffed boots appeared at the edge of her vision, the boundary where the grass met the sand of the field. Serenna's knees locked in surprise.

Arms folded across the dragon on his leathers, Vesryn stood as an impassive observer. He arched a brow, glancing at the shrieking initiates and then back to her.

Serenna's breath lodged in her throat, trapped by the shock of seeing him. The hold she had on her power fizzled out faster than a doused flame. She staggered when Essence abandoned her, gulping in a breath at the loss.

Dismissively stepping over the recruits strewn across the field, Vesryn didn't halt his approach until he loomed over her.

Serenna straightened and scowled at the shade he cast, effectively obscuring her view of everything else. Despite the faltering of her heart, she lifted her chin.

"Not bad," Vesryn commented, turning to study the Alari initiates as they lurched to their feet before pinning his gaze back to her. "But your concentration and stamina have room for improvement."

The prince allowed the moment to lengthen while he considered her. Serenna didn't flinch from the intensity of his viridian stare.

The side of his mouth twitched, drawing her attention to a flash of a dimple before he lowered his head to whisper in her ear. "If you're still looking for that extracurricular practice, I happen to be well versed in absolutely tantalizing exercises you might find useful in improving your...*endurance*."

Before Serenna could voice a retort, Vesryn's power flared. She tensed when a crimson tendril of Essence unfurled to stroke her cheek. Tingling as it suggestively glided up and down across her skin.

Heat scorched her cheeks as the prince's mouth quirked. How was it possible for him to sensuously graze her with magic?

Serenna rediscovered her backbone. "I have no doubt about it," she seethed, well aware he wanted to make her squirm. "I've heard more than I care to. Your *reputation* doesn't impress me."

Vesryn clicked his tongue. "And I suppose you believe everything you hear." He extinguished his power. "How predictable."

He brushed past her, clipping her shoulder.

Serenna vented a disbelieving scoff when she righted herself from stumbling. The gesture had the wild semblance of an adolescent challenge.

She had half a mind to lasso *him* with her rending magic while he strolled away in that haughty way of his. In those ridiculous leather pants emphasizing every muscle in the back sides of his legs. She didn't know how it was possible someone could look so lithe but also appear coiled as if they could spring in any direction.

Serenna glanced around and noticed that everyone had been staring at their interaction. At least Vesryn's towering form blocked their view of him *caressing* her with magic.

Wait.

Her hand flew to her cheek. Streaks of blood and grit came away on her fingertips, but she touched smooth skin that lacked any sting. She stared at him, uncomprehending. Her awareness hooked on her restored palms. *He mended me?*

Serenna ground her teeth. She wasn't sure what game the prince had just initiated, but she would have to figure it out. *I'm not letting my guard down around that lout!*

Following the recruits to the center of the Rending Field, Serenna kept half of her attention on Ayla's group as they shambled to take their spots facing Vesryn. They shot daggered looks in her direction, but Serenna knew they wouldn't retaliate in front of the prince. With a vengeful glint in her eye, Mishryn appeared more furious than Ayla, baring her teeth.

Serenna rolled her eyes, brushing off their threats, and allowed an exhilarating rush to breeze through her. She'd shaped her power into something useful and protected herself; she didn't know splitting magic was possible. *Maybe Ayla will think twice before confronting me again.*

But could I control two abilities at once? Well, she had to manifest other talents for that. Rending and mending didn't exactly work in tandem, and healing needed delicate focus. *Healing two people at once wouldn't be feasible.*

Vesryn's raised voice addressing the class severed Serenna's thoughts. "One of you blatantly disregarded the regulations we all agreed to at the beginning of the term."

He paused dramatically, obviously drawing out the spectacle, taking his time to survey the recruits.

Oh stars. Anxiety slithered in Serenna's stomach while her eyes darted around the ring. Overwhelmed by the intensity of the confrontation, she didn't even recall the restrictions the prince had put into place. *Surely he doesn't mean—*

"*Princess* Vallende." Vesryn gestured for her to join him in the middle of the yard.

Ignoring the unfolding terror inflicting a stutter in her heart, Serenna's nostrils flared with annoyance at the way he'd twisted her title into a joke.

With everyone's attention glued on her, it took longer than she thought possible to close the distance to the prince. Serenna might as well have been wading through tar instead of walking across sand. Her skin pebbled as the entire class watched in anticipatory silence.

"First infraction," Vesryn stated, holding out an expectant hand.

Serenna's nails bit into her palms. She silently declined. *I only defended myself!*

Vesryn's mouth thinned when she balked. He pitched his voice low, his words not drifting beyond them. "I distinctly remember you demanding I keep my hands to myself. So, now, it's your turn to come to me."

Serenna's vexation overshadowed her fear with this forced participation. She battled the prince's stare with equal intensity, irritated that he expected her to be grateful for not laying a hand on her. As if he wasn't about to shatter her finger.

"Right," she said tonelessly. "How gallant of you."

Vesryn nodded toward his outstretched palm like the gesture was supposed to be silent encouragement. Heartbeats passed before Serenna slumped in defeat. She was only prolonging the inevitable.

Lifting her hand as if it were the heaviest weight in the world, she paused halfway when a smug smile tugged at a corner of the prince's mouth.

She spoke before thinking. "You won nothing, so I suggest you wipe that satisfied look off your face."

Vesryn's expression darkened, eyes flaring with a dangerous flame that sent her heart thundering.

"And I suggest you address me with proper regard," he hissed back. "'Prince' or 'Commander' will do. I'd hate to make two examples out of you because of your insolence."

"Then maybe you should do something to actually earn my respect," she snapped.

A muscle in Vesryn's jaw ticked. Serenna shut her mouth, biting her cheek. *I went too far. But he's utterly infuriating!* As meekly as she could manage, she mumbled a pathetic, "Commander."

"Oh, very good, *Princess*." Vesryn drawled out the word, the sarcasm as scathing as his tone. "Your decorum astounds me. Now, are we going to stand here all fucking day or get this over with?" His fingers twitched in what could only be irritation.

Serenna tossed her braid over a shoulder before viciously shoving her hand into his. A current raced up her arm when their skin met, unnerving her even further. She had no idea why he felt the need to shock her into submission.

But she fumed in silence, holding her tongue while her treacherous magic practically summoned itself, pelting against the prince's palm. Like her power *called* to him.

Vesryn's gaze bored into hers as he gripped her hand almost to the point of discomfort. His rending shadows spiraled and whipped around them, nearing the intensity of a typhoon.

Angling his head, the prince asked, "Any regrets?"

Serenna clenched her teeth. "No."

Her attention sharpened to a honed edge when his thumb swiped over the back of her hand. She exerted all of her willpower to refrain from yanking her fingers out of his. "I am *not* apologizing for defending myself."

One side of Vesryn's mouth curled. That's all it took for her stupid heart to fling itself against her ribs.

"Good." Something gleamed in the prince's eyes. "You would disappoint me if you did."

Serenna sniffed dismissively. "I don't need your approval."

Vesryn's lips tightened before his magic pulsated and entombed them in a veil of midnight, obscuring them from observers. Globes of soft illumination spun to light the pocket of darkness.

This is utterly unnecessary.

Serenna squeezed her eyes shut to ignore the distracting way his warrior-size hand engulfed hers. The roughness of his calluses only made his grasp seem stronger. More primal, as her skin prickled against his. Her perception narrowed further, and her awareness existed entirely in the warm space where their skin touched. *How would it feel if he—*

Stop it. Serenna forcefully redirected the obnoxious trail of her thoughts. Her stomach clenched as she wondered if her finger breaking would be worse than her whole body being on the receiving end of rending.

"Look at me," Vesryn commanded.

Serenna hated how her eyes obediently flew open before her mind had even processed the demand. She struck him with a glare. "Are you intentionally dragging this out, *Commander?*"

Vesryn tugged her close. "Fight for me."

Stumbling after her pulled arm, Serenna pushed a hand against his chest to create more space between them. She blinked up at him while his penetrating stare dismantled her irritation.

"Fight what?"

"As my champion for the Essence Tournament." Vesryn's gaze examined her in a manner that was oddly serious and alarmingly hopeful.

Serenna let out a breathless, disbelieving laugh as a hundred thoughts flew through her head like a flock of pigeons scattering from a roof.

He has to be joking. Every initiate from Alari had a greater mastery over Essence than she did. Even a magus wouldn't be interested in putting in the effort to train someone like her.

"*Your* champion?" Serenna backed away as far as she could while he kept a hold of her hand. "Why?"

"Think about it." Vesryn's fingers tightened around her trembling palm. His forehead creased before his face returned to a stony stare. "And relax," he said, his gaze softening under dark lashes. "This won't hurt *you*."

"What do you—"

Vesryn flinched.

Multiple *cracks* sounded. Serenna's attention soared to her hand, still a prisoner in his. She gasped in horror.

Her index finger drooped like a wilted flower. Each of her three joints jutted out in contorted, crooked angles.

Suddenly, the shadows concealing them vanished like smoke on the wind. Serenna blinked against the abrupt light.

Releasing her palm as if it were a hot coal, Vesryn strode around her to address the rest of the class.

Serenna tried to make sense of the prince's request and the complete absence of pain in her obviously shattered finger. Several thoughts warred for her attention as she stared at him, shocked and baffled, analyzing the past few minutes, struggling to comprehend his intentions.

First, he healed me. Then, he asked me to be his champion. And for some reason, I didn't feel my finger breaking. What is he playing at?

Serenna noticed everyone who hadn't manifested their power screaming as they writhed on the ground. *I guess today's lesson is starting.* She almost swore the rending on the Alari initiates lasted longer than with anyone else. But, of course, that was preposterous.

Upon dismissing the class, which Serenna couldn't even recall the details of, Vesryn called, "Princess Vallende, a moment."

Serenna's pulse gave a startled jump. *What now? Why won't he leave me alone?*

Ayla glancing their way didn't even provide Serenna with any satisfaction, as she recalled what happened the last time the prince had singled her out.

Vesryn glared at the initiates brave enough to look in their direction. When shadows reared behind him like a threatening wave, everyone scurried off.

"Let me see it," Vesryn commanded, extending a hand when she approached him in the center of the ring.

Serenna's stomach pitched like an overturned boat when she glanced at her crooked finger, jutting out at a disturbing angle.

"What did you do?" she asked, studying her hand. "Why didn't I feel anything?"

Vesryn's fingers twitched, almost impatiently. "Give me your hand. I'm not in the habit of asking twice."

Serenna jammed her hair behind an ear. *Of course he refuses to answer me.* "Tell me what you did," she demanded, shifting her weight to fold her arms. She deliberately planted herself a handful of paces away from him.

Vesryn's jaw tightened. Serenna assumed he was accustomed to getting what he wanted.

"Would you let me see it?" he bit out, annoyed now, a flame of irritation flickering in his eyes.

"Why?" Serenna knew she was being reckless at this point. But the prince made the mistake of allowing her to trample over the line of defiance and didn't punish her for acting out, so she pushed even further. "Will you throw a royal tantrum if I don't?"

"If I have to." Vesryn's strides devoured the distance between them. He stalked toward her in a slightly terrifying way, boots kicking up puffs of dust in the ring.

He's not going to intimidate me with this threatening warrior performance! Serenna's defiance might've had more strength if her stomach didn't slam into her spine. She quickly thought better of opposing him further.

Serenna clenched her teeth. "Fine." She shoved her hand at the prince before he had a chance to do anything else.

Vesryn had the nerve to give her an amused grunt before snatching her extended palm.

"Why do you do that?" Serenna asked, the muscles in her arm spasming from a tingle of power.

She attempted to wrestle out of his grip. Vesryn only held on tighter the more she struggled. Breaking out of his unrelenting grasp was pointless, so she grudgingly gave up with an irritated huff.

"I'm not doing anything." Vesryn's brow furrowed while he evaluated her finger, turning her hand over to inspect the shattered joints.

"Well, what do you call that shock of power then?"

"It's your magic."

"Why would—"

"Shut up. I need to concentrate for this." A pressure thrummed, unformed Essence surrounding them like a starry heat wave.

"It happens to me too," Vesryn admitted.

Serenna gaped when a soft red light sprang between their hands. Tendrils of mending laced around her broken finger, numbness enveloping her joints.

"I thought you didn't permit healing for three days." Stunned, Serenna stared at her crooked finger. She frowned. The rather sloppy lattice of magic would've offended Jassyn, agitating him enough to drive *both* of his hands through his curls.

"Is this even considered…mending?" she asked.

Vesryn rolled his eyes and released her hand. "I set the bones and dispersed the swelling. I can't manage anything beyond that, but you won't perceive the break. You can have it straightened next week."

Serenna's brows rose, shocked that he'd admitted to a deficiency in skill. She nearly thanked him before she recalled *he* was the one who'd fractured her finger. Even if she broke the rules. And she wouldn't hesitate to defend herself again.

"Why?" She blinked questioningly at him. Not understanding his motivation only steered her thoughts into an endless loop of uncertainty.

Vesryn shrugged. "I didn't want to feel it."

"Feel it?" She waved her hand in between them. "It's *my* finger."

The prince crossed his arms, studying her. "You have no idea, do you?"

Serenna settled on mirroring his stance. She glared back at him, not having any inkling of what he was referring to. "Please enlighten me. *Commander.*"

"Come with me." Vesryn pivoted, prowling toward the perimeter of trees at the edge of the Rending Field.

Serenna had half a mind to dismiss him and walk in the opposite direction.

The prince motioned over his shoulder for her to follow. Serenna's nerves grated at his expectant attitude and dismissal of her questions. Expelling an exasperated sigh, she hurried to catch up to his long, ground-eating strides. Her curiosity replaced the only grain of common sense she possessed.

"And where are you taking me exactly?" she asked when she caught up.

"We're going somewhere to practice your magic. I want to see what you're capable of."

"Is there something wrong with the training fields?"

Serenna glanced around nervously when Vesryn steered them deeper into the grove of pines. The fanned branches interlocked to form a cage against the falling sun. A layer of needles muffled their footsteps. The silence and dusk casting lengthy shadows only heightened Serenna's increasing anxious thoughts as the trees leaned in around her. *No one would even know we're here.*

"I'm not going to hurt you." Vesryn looked at her sideways, like he could sense her unease. His teeth flashed as he unsheathed his belt knife. "Much."

"Is that supposed to reassure me?" Serenna stopped in her tracks, skidding on the fallen pine needles, too uncomfortable to keep following.

"We're portaling off campus." Vesryn faced her and flipped his blade. "I don't exactly need gossip spreading that I left with a recruit, now, do I? The magic I'm going to show you isn't for everyone. The last thing I want to do is supervise every bumbling idiot wielding it."

Flip, flip, flip. The steel whistled as it cut through the air. *How does he make something like a knife irksome?*

Serenna tossed her hands. "And you're choosing me for this extracurricular activity because…?"

"You managed significant control of rending on more than one target," Vesryn said, approaching her. "I was even impressed when you split your magic into different directions after only being shown once. I'm curious how far we can stretch your anger and if your abilities are capable of reaching the limits of our power."

Serenna's jaw dropped. "That was *you*? You showed me how to divide my magic?" Her voice rose in pitch. "And then…and then you *punished* me?"

"You'd already sealed your fate before I arrived." Vesryn snatched the knife out of the air. "And *I* absorbed the pain of your punishment." He leaned forward to curl a finger under her chin. "A little *gratitude* would be welcome."

Serenna's pulse hummed in her ears. She certainly had no interest in guessing what *gratitude* he expected of her.

"Why did you?" she asked, pulling away, eyes tightening with suspicion like she could find the answer by searching his unreadable face.

"Clearly, you don't appreciate my benevolent intentions." Vesryn sheathed his dagger and aggressively tied half of his hair in a topknot, securing it with a leather strap he pulled out of a pocket. "Don't worry, *Princess*, it won't happen again." He turned and walked deeper into the thicket of trees.

I'm not following him alone into this creepy forest.

Serenna spun on her heel, intending to leave, when a sudden *yank* radiated from her chest. She whirled around. *What was that?* She felt the pull again and staggered in Vesryn's direction.

If this lout thinks he can bully me—

I'm running out of patience, Vesryn's voice echoed in her mind.

Serenna's blood chilled at the intrusion, his thoughts skimming across hers. She put the pieces together. *That was* him *taunting me on the first day of class, telling me to get up!*

Even though she didn't have the telepathy talent herself—Velinya and Jassyn did—Serenna knew that communication could travel in either direction while the person with the ability maintained the link. She could only assume Vesryn kept a grip on her mind.

Get out of my head! she seethed.

Serenna took a long, steadying breath. The invisible line pulled at her again, like an anchor dragging on a line. She stumbled forward.

Fine. Relenting, she followed the prince. She'd already unwittingly entertained him enough to make it this far, but she still distrusted him. Though she was mildly interested in their destination since he wanted no observers.

I do not *want to spend any more time in his presence,* she assured herself. *I simply want to learn more about my magic.*

Vesryn waited in a dim glade, tapping his fingers on his thighs with an open gateway beside him.

"I don't understand why you're taking such an interest in my abilities," Serenna said, folding her arms.

Vesryn's brows rose. "Do you actually think you're *ready* for the tournament? I have two months to prepare you, and it's obvious you need all the training you can get."

Serenna scoffed at his assumption. "I never agreed to participate."

Vesryn jabbed a commanding finger at the rift.

Serenna shot him a glare, flicking her hair over her shoulder. She swept into the dark embrace of the portal, leaving Centarya behind her.

CHAPTER 24

SERENNA

On the other side of the gateway, Serenna stepped into a rolling sea of grasses waving across a valley. Distant snowcapped mountains framed the expansive prairie. The sun angled behind the peaks, shrouding the untamed vale in a soft golden twilight.

The portal faded after Vesryn appeared, drawing her attention away from the unfamiliar landscape.

"Where are we?" Serenna asked, running her fingers over the knee-high grassy tuffs, gazing out to the distant summits. A gurgling stream flowed with the mountain's runoff in the cradle of the vale.

"We're in the outskirts of the western realm." Vesryn's magic sparked, igniting around him. "The Hibernal Wastes are over that pass." He pointed toward the setting sun.

Serenna trailed behind the prince through the meadow. He extended a hand to cast out tendrils of raw power like a cloud of shimmering fog. Since manifesting Essence, she could see the evidence of someone holding their magic. *Not that a warning would even be helpful against him.*

"Why choose me as your champion?" she asked, watching Vesryn send sheets of Essence out like he was searching for something.

"Believe it or not, I think it's possible you may possess a scrap of potential." Swells of glimmering power blanketed the swaying grasses.

Serenna scowled at his back. "Are you always this condescending?"

"Are you always this irritating?" The prince rounded on her, sending the loose portion of his silvery hair flying around his shoulders like a mantle.

Serenna opened her mouth, but he interrupted. "That was rhetorical, you harpy. I had no interest in training a champion for the tournament until that entertaining performance you pulled off today. You've shown such an improvement with your control since the first time you *stroked* my fingers." He shrugged. "I didn't realize a half-breed could manipulate that amount of power by channeling an emotional response."

Serenna glared and crossed her arms. She wasn't obligated to tolerate his rude remarks about their differences. "I'm not going to be your champion if that's how it's going to be."

Vesryn cocked his head to the side. "Why not?"

"Why are you assuming I actually *want* to train with you? Just because you're the *prince*?" Exasperation had her grinding her teeth. "You're a prick."

Vesryn snorted, wandering away and effectively ignoring her protest. He continued to send out wispy sheets of unformed magic over the rippling prairie. "I guarantee every other recruit would fight to have the opportunity."

"Then hold another tournament for your salivating *half-breeds*. Have those bootlickers battle for the honor if you need someone to *stroke* your ego." Serenna didn't realize how aggravating conversing with his back would be. "Take me back."

Vesryn turned with a smirk. "No."

Serenna stared at him. "What don't you understand?" She called out to him as he strode through the valley. "I want nothing to do with you."

A sharp, high-pitched scream echoed in front of them under Vesryn's curtain of power. Serenna froze, peering out into the meadow toward the shrieks.

The prince's fingers curled. Two rabbits flowed toward him, struggling and kicking against blue-tinted bindings she recognized as force.

Confusion compounding, Serenna's brows rose, studying the flailing creatures twisting in the air. "Are you taking back a pet?"

"Not quite." Vines of darkness lashed around the prince. "Rending kills as effortlessly as it constricts a body or inflicts pain."

The blood drained from Serenna's face. "Please tell me you're not going to torture them."

Vesryn rolled his eyes. "I'm not going to torture them."

Two things happened at once. Arcs of violet light branched in front of them, expanding to form a shield.

And then one rabbit *exploded*. There was no other way to explain it.

Gore and blood sprayed across the barrier like water spouting from a well. The ward flashed where the rabbit's insides slammed against the shield.

Serenna covered her mouth, stifling a shriek. Bile rose in her throat as she swallowed a wave of nausea. She gagged as a string of bloody entrails *thumped* to the ground in front of the barrier. Ignoring the sick feeling roiling in her gut was a losing battle. Her vision pulsed white. Grabbing her knees, Serenna bent over and emptied her stomach.

Insides writhing like a tangle of snakes, Serenna gulped in fortifying breaths before straightening. She panted to catch her breath, wiping her mouth with the back of a hand. She stared at Vesryn in horror, uncomprehending of why he would do such a thing.

The prince's eyes were on her, like he was bored waiting for her to finish throwing up. With a flick of his wrist, the shield disappeared. Tendrils of force collected the fur and guts of the eviscerated creature. He deposited the carnage into a gory pile under the remaining rabbit still struggling in the air.

"What the bleeding stars are you doing?" Serenna shrieked. "What is wrong with you? Do you get off on rending defenseless animals?"

Her panic climbed into her throat, her head becoming weightless. For an entirely different reason, Serenna's stomach clenched at the realization she was just as powerless as the rabbits. She was alone, in the middle of nowhere, with a crazed elf for company. Clutching her waist, Serenna's entire body shook as she lurched from a wave of dizziness.

"Calm down." Vesryn grabbed her arm to steady her. "They won't be going to waste." He nodded to the remaining rabbit wriggling in the air. "Your turn."

Serenna's gaze darted between him and the suspended creature. She was seriously questioning his sanity.

"You're mad," she said, struggling to pull away.

Vesryn's fingers tightened. He gestured curtly at the screaming rabbit. "Summon your power."

"No," Serenna said, even though her erratic magic was flinging itself against her skin like it was trying to reach the prince's fingertips. Baring her teeth, she ignored her stirring power. "Find someone else who has the same sick, twisted idea of fun as you. Take. Me. Back."

Vesryn released her. "Look. You need to master your abilities. You can't exactly practice turning your peers inside out. For obvious reasons." He scrubbed a hand across his face, like she was testing his patience. "And I'm not taking you wraith hunting until you have more control over your power." Vesryn thrust out a finger. "So focus your magic on the rabbit."

Serenna blinked. She certainly had no intention of joining him on a wraith hunt. *What gave him that idea?*

"No," she said again, her breath now coming in quick bursts. "I *won't* use rending like that. I can't explode other initiates during the tournament, so I don't see the point. I'm not interested in learning how to kill."

Serenna flinched when she sensed Vesryn's patience snapping like a branch crashing from a tree.

The prince savagely seized her leathers, hauling her to her toes. "You will," he snarled in her face. "Why else do you think you're here? This isn't about the fucking tournament. The wraith won't hesitate to slaughter you—it's either you or them."

Vesryn gave her a shake, rattling her clenched teeth. "You're going to learn how to defend yourself with your power." His unrelenting eyes pierced into hers, drilling in his point. "Refusal is not an option for you, *Princess*."

A gust of dark wind blew through Serenna, furious at Vesryn for pressuring her to tear apart this helpless animal. *Well, I'll strangle him with the guts if he's not giving me another option!*

"Fine, *Commander*."

"Summon. Your. Power," Vesryn hissed through his teeth, biting each word off. He pushed her away.

Serenna tripped, feet tangling in the grasses. She shot him a scowl before trudging a few paces ahead, just to get away from him. She couldn't think of a way out of the situation. *Why did I follow him through the portal?*

The rabbit kicked feebly in the air. Its nose quivered, dark eyes darting around wildly.

Fury igniting, Serenna submerged herself in the fountain of her magic. Her power sprang to life in her outstretched fingers, simmering as unformed Essence. Twisting the windstorm of her anger, she lashed her wrath into a raging tempest. Vesryn's presence made summoning her outrage effortless. Black tendrils curled around her hands when her powers soared to her call.

Vesryn spoke behind her. "You need to harness and channel your intent to kill to maximize your rending ability."

Serenna ignored the prince. She wanted to fling her power at *him*, but she knew her pathetic magic would have no more effect than a nettle sting. The thought fueled her anger even further. She silently apologized to the creature.

Her Essence contorted, evolving into something darker, more sinister, than blood rending. The midnight whirlwind of power crackled with frenzied energy. A vortex of shadows soared from her fingertips when she released the volley of magic.

An explosion of blood, fur, and innards erupted from where the rabbit's body hovered. Warm liquid and chunks of gore splattered Serenna's face, streaking across her uniform. With a strangled cry, she tossed up her hands, attempting to ward off the outburst of carnage.

Serenna only had a moment to process the aftermath of her power's destruction before she gagged and vomited whatever little was left in her stomach.

Vesryn dashed forward and dragged her away as she spilled her guts on the ground. "Stop! You'll spoil it." Casting his power, the prince gathered the insides of the rabbit. He organized the remains into another pile.

Serenna wiped her mouth with the back of her hand, only to realize she'd smeared more blood over her face. Crouching over with her hands on her knees, she hurried to spit, but ended up dry heaving against the metallic taste on her tongue. The need to extricate herself from her vile actions outweighed any sense of embarrassment.

"Here." Vesryn directed a hovering orb of liquid near her with tendrils of force. "It's water from the stream over there." He gestured behind him. "I guess I was incorrect to assume your stomach was as strong as your will."

"Oh, go get scorched by a star," Serenna snapped at the backhanded compliment before reaching out to dip her hands into the hovering globe. She glared at the prince, taking note he didn't have a drop of blood on him.

Splashing handfuls of water over her face, Serenna swallowed the bitter taste in her mouth. "You better have a reason for not including me in your ward."

Vesryn's face was a mask of false innocence. "I already took care of you once." He shrugged. "I suppose I thought you might return the favor, but you left me having to take care of myself."

Serenna's mouth hinged open with a protest about not having manifested shielding, but she froze and stopped scrubbing the blood off of her cheeks when another piercing screech split the air.

Spinning to the noise with a refusal on her lips about participating in any more sanguine theatrics, she stood paralyzed instead when her eyes landed on an enormous creature *flying* straight at them.

Serenna gasped, ready to bolt in the opposite direction from death-on-wings. Vesryn must have sensed her intent to run. His arm whipped out, snatching the back of her tunic. He prevented her escape like he was restraining a disobedient hound by the scruff of the neck.

"Don't move," he commanded.

"How is it possible that everything with you only increases in stupidity?" she shrieked.

This day was by far the worst she'd had since the night of her conscription. Serenna squirmed in his grip, struggling to free herself. Vesryn didn't seem concerned about the monster streaking toward them. *But he's not exactly a shining example of sanity.*

A *whoosh* vibrated through the valley with every stroke of its wings, colliding with the thunder booming inside of her chest. Outlined by the fading twilight, the obsidian creature appeared to be at least twice the size of a horse as it drew closer. The feathered head, neck, and wings joined a scaled reptilian body, ending in a finned tail.

Eyes round in disbelief, Serenna held her breath as the lizard-bird cut through the air.

The creature lowered its four tucked-in legs. The earth shook when it landed on the ground with a heavy *thud*. It ambled closer to them, its gait similar to a gallop, but its body wriggled like a reptile slinking away. Emitting a screech, it tossed its eagle head from side to side like a horse frolicking.

A tingle in Serenna's fingertips drew her attention to the way she forcefully clutched Vesryn's arm. Like she was depending on *him* for protection.

Recoiling, she asked, "What…what is it?"

Vesryn didn't release her tunic. "He's a dracovae. Bred from an ancient line the Aelfyn brought to the mortal shores."

The prince extended his other hand as if to touch the approaching beast.

"What are you doing?" Serenna asked, her voice strangled by fear. Shaking her head, she tried backing away, eyeing the giant beak that looked as if it could swallow her whole.

The prince hushed her when the creature slowed from a run to a trot, taloned feet beating against the earth, sending tremors up her legs.

Vesryn's hand ran up and down the length of her back. Serenna tensed. *Is he trying to calm me?* There was nothing comforting about his pathetic attempt at putting her at ease. *Why isn't he worried about this beast?*

Serenna's breath caught as the dracovae approached. He inspected them with intelligent, white-irised eyes, tilting his head from side to side. His dark pupils pinned rapidly when he reached his hooked bill to touch Vesryn's palm, like he was excited to see the prince.

Vesryn stepped away from her to caress the creature's beak. "This is Naru."

When the prince left her side, Serenna suddenly felt more vulnerable, anxiety plowing her stomach. *Why am I wanting his help? He's the one who put me in this situation in the first place!*

The dracovae released an odd series of trilling chirps, closing his eyes when Vesryn stroked the black feathers around his face with a disturbing fondness. Naru leaned into the prince's touch with a chuffing grunt and a chorus of clacks. With a rumbling sigh, his exhale stirred Vesryn's hair. Naru's plumes flared when the prince vigorously ruffled a hand under the feathers to scratch the corner of his cheek.

"Hold out your hand," Vesryn said, shifting and planting his feet to brace himself against Naru's angled weight.

Apparently, his idiotic ideas continue. "Are you mad? That Naru *thing* could snap me in half." Even Vesryn's height didn't put him up to the dracovae's feathered chest!

"Would you just trust me?"

"You're kidding, right?"

Serenna kept her eyes fixed on the dracovae, attempting to predict the beast's next move regardless of how docile it seemed. *At least we won't be exploding this Naru creature, since Vesryn seems attached to it.* She didn't know the prince was capable of such feelings, and apparently the beast reciprocated them.

Serenna bit her lip, studying the apparent regard between them as her nerves settled like a quiet dusting of snow. *Surely Vesryn didn't bring me all this way just to be Naru's snack.*

Swallowing her unease, Serenna stretched out a trembling arm.

Something warm and slimy plopped into her lifted hand. She pulled her eyes away from watching the dracovae. And nearly gagged when she saw that the prince had used his power to place bloody pieces of the rended rabbit into her waiting palm.

She took an unsteady breath and pursed her lips into a thin, disapproving line. Vesryn arched a brow at her questioning look.

The dracovae's eyes snapped open. Naru latched his pearly gaze onto Serenna's palm, shifting his head from side to side, analyzing what she held. Serenna frantically looked between Vesryn and Naru, the dracovae seeming to have changed his mind, eyeing her like his next meal.

"Rabbits are too small and quick for dracovae to hunt." Vesryn gave his beast a pat. "But Naru is especially partial to their hearts. I promised him I'd bring him some on my next visit."

Serenna's mouth fell open. The prince grinned at her while she gaped at him, speechless. "So you're telling me all of this exploding rabbits was to prepare him a…a *treat*?"

"Well, he could rip the rabbits apart on his own, but I wanted you to use your power." Vesryn stepped back and flapped a hand in Naru's direction. "Don't keep him waiting."

Serenna shook her head in disbelief. Lifting her arm, she presented the bloody bits to the dracovae. Liquid from the organs pooled in her palm, dripping through her fingers. She steered her thoughts away from what she held and focused on the beast.

Naru's pupils constricted and expanded repeatedly. He shifted his attention between her and the rabbit's heart, eyes shining with a mysterious intelligence while considering her.

Serenna sucked in a breath when he stepped forward on a clawed foot and stretched his beak to her shaking palm. *Please don't eat my hand.*

The dracovae inched his razor-sharp bill toward her and picked up the offered gore with such precision that he didn't even graze her skin. Serenna finally exhaled, reassured any potential danger had passed when the creature swallowed.

She jumped when Naru pranced around her on his peculiar raptor-taloned feet to inspect the remaining piles. Vesryn chuckled to himself, a strange affection shining in his eyes.

Movement in the valley grabbed Serenna's attention. The first splash of stars twinkled above the darkening prairie. She squinted across the vale, seeing a fuzzy patch of white come into focus. "Is that another dracovae?"

Vesryn followed her gaze. The smile slipped from his face. "That's Naru's mate, Trella. She keeps her distance."

Naru, collecting the fragments of the rabbits in his bill, bounded off on all fours toward Trella. The muscles in his scaled legs coiled and sprang as his wings flapped. Flying low to the ground, his talons trailed in the grasses. He landed at the edge of the valley, bowing and bobbing his head to offer his mate a portion of his prizes.

"That's...oddly sweet," Serenna commented, watching Naru attempt to feed Trella pieces of meat. Apparently she could feed herself because she headbutted Naru out of the way. Serenna smiled, immediately liking her.

"Are they yours?" she asked, rinsing the last of the blood from her hands in the hovering globe of water.

"Naru tolerates me and will often come when I call him." Vesryn watched them with a distant look in his eyes. "He permits me to ride him when we go scouting for wraith."

Skeptical, Serenna asked, "You *ride* him? As in *fly*?"

She shook the water droplets from her fingers. The thought of perching on top of the towering beast's back had her questioning his sanity again. It had taken all of her determination to simply offer a *hand*.

Like Essence-infused emeralds, Vesryn's eyes glowed from the vestiges of twilight. "Do you want to see the rangers' flight of dracovae?" he asked, his grin reblooming across his face.

Serenna's heart stumbled as she met his gaze before shifting her attention to a portal opening.

Captivated by intrigue, she stepped through the rift to discover where this bizarre training session of his would lead her next.

CHAPTER 25

SERENNA

On the other side of the portal, Serenna glanced around, observing they were inside a massive stable. But the barn didn't have the scent of dusty horses, earthen grains, or sweet hay. Instead, there was a distinct dry and powdery smell, like leather baking in the sun. Blanching, her stomach rolled as she registered a metallic tang lingering in the air that she could only assume was blood.

Stunned, Serenna watched the buzzing activity as Vesryn strode down the barn. More than half of the workers present were elven-blooded. She warily followed the prince as he led them down an expansive dirt-packed hallway large enough to accommodate at least twenty horse-drawn carts side by side.

Illumination bathed the massive building in light. The peaked roof reached higher than Vaelyn's castle walls. Stalls lined each side of the corridor.

Several dracovae hung their eagle heads over the open top portion of the doors, leaning forward to inspect them with a cacophony of chattering beak clacks and chuffing grunts. While Naru's feathers and scales had been black, the creatures staring at them came in a multitude of colors—whites, browns, grays, and mottled patterns.

Stable hands bustled with a purpose—mucking out straw bedding, filing talons on the dracovae's clawed feet, and flaring Essence to haul deer, cow, and goat carcasses into the stalls.

Vesryn angled straight toward an ebony-skinned, silver-haired warrior wearing leather armor, the material overlapping with black scales, exactly like his. Except…Serenna studied the sigil. The woman had a dracovae stitched on the front instead of the prince's dragon.

Clapping the sturdy woman jovially on the shoulder, the prince relieved her of a feed bucket. He introduced "Princess Vallende" to Zaeryn, flight captain of the rangers, his second-in-command.

Serenna blinked, momentarily astonished that an elven-blooded was in such a high position. *But why would the elves bother themselves with working in a barn? For that matter, why is the prince here?*

Vesryn took off, waving for Serenna to follow, apparently assisting with evening chores. "We keep all the dracovae in the stables and adjoining paddocks," he said when she reached his side. "The rangers fly on them during patrols to hunt any leads we have on the wraith."

"But not Naru and Trella?" Serenna asked as two riders trotted down the hallway on a pair of brown dracovae. Vibrations from the ground rattled through her legs. One beast tossed its head and snapped at its companion in a seemingly playful manner.

"Trella…became unruly when her rider died." Vesryn's knuckles turned white on the pail's handle. "And keeping them confined didn't sit well with me." He gave a bitter laugh. "I figured they'd be happier together in the wilds if Trella wasn't willing to accept another rider."

Serenna's heart was *not* melting from the warmth he directed at the creatures. The prince's attitude toward the dracovae and the elven-blooded in the stables was so inconsistent with his usual sneers and patronizing behavior. She wasn't sure what to make of it.

Serenna stepped around a mound of straw in the hallway. A dracovae stretched over its stall door. Snatching a beakful of the substrate, it flung the dried grasses into the air with an excited screech.

"But Naru still comes when you call him?" Serenna asked. Thinking back, Vesryn's dracovae had seemed to appear out of nowhere in the valley. "How do you do that?"

"If he's within a few miles, I can touch his mind telepathically with pictures and concepts he can comprehend." Vesryn smirked at her. "He'll arrive every time—especially if I send images of the incentives."

"That's not funny," Serenna fired back, shooting him a scowl. "You could've explained what we were doing instead of leading me to believe we were exploding rabbits for your personal amusement." She crossed her arms. "And I still wouldn't have wanted to."

Vesryn shoved the bucket he carried into her hands. "I doubt you would've been able to draw forth enough rending power to kill if you weren't angry."

Serenna ground her teeth upon seeing the bloody innards of some unfortunate animal, nose wrinkling in disgust. She thrust the pail back, but the prince only danced out of the way.

"Does annoyance summon any abilities?" Serenna snapped.

"Not 'annoyance,' but I have other *exercises* in mind to draw forth your remaining talents," he said with frustrating smugness.

Serenna pursed her lips. "So, I always have to be furious to rend?" She readjusted the bucket's handle on her arm, not appreciating that he'd intentionally provoked her. "That should be easy if you're around."

"Not necessarily." Vesryn ignored the jab and picked up a white feather off the ground. "You half-breeds just need to channel emotions the first handful of times to access your power. With enough practice, you'll be able to wield your magic regardless of how you feel."

Serenna readied a retort about her *half-breed* differences, but didn't voice it as she grew distracted by the curious way everyone in the stables interacted with the prince. The elven-blooded going about their duties drew Vesryn's attention the further they walked into the barn. She gaped as the rangers addressed him with reverence, their faces lighting up as if they were pleased to see him.

Vesryn took up so much space with his own gravity; everyone seemed to be drawn to him, like planets falling into orbit around the sun. Regardless of whether they were a warrior or a worker shoveling dung, the prince greeted everyone by name with either a slap on the back or a clasp of the hand.

Serenna struggled to absorb and process how Vesryn was a

different person among the rangers. It was obvious he had their respect.

Why does he treat us so harshly at Centarya then? His methods are a little unconventional.

"We have nearly eighty dracovae in our flight," Vesryn carried on once the flurry of people had passed. He steered them toward a specific stall. "The past few decades have brought numerous hatchlings. We're hoping to expand our ranks as the fledglings mature."

"Are the stables for breeding more?" Serenna asked.

"This place is more than that, thanks to the wraith." Vesryn peered through a window-like slat, since neither of them was tall enough to look over the open portion of the stall door. Beaming, he glanced over his shoulder, motioning her closer with an urgent wave. "The rangers are now an elite force of Essence wielders and weapons masters. There may not be many of us, but we all share the same goal: to hunt the wraith and expunge them from our lands."

"And aside from your duties at the academy, you also…command the rangers," Serenna concluded. Vesryn snatched the bucket from her and leaned over, placing it through the window. *Are we really having a casual conversation?*

The prince grabbed her arm and hauled her forward until she could see the inside of the stall. Serenna released an undignified noise somewhere between a gasp and a squeal when she saw three cat-size dracovae hatchlings. Their scales appeared smooth like fish skin. Downy feathers decorated their heads, giving them a fluffy appearance.

The bucket's carnage drew forth excited flaps and chirps. Her heart gave a squeeze despite the messy way the creatures were gulping the gory innards from the pail.

Two adults lay curled up, napping in the bedding. One peeked an eye at them and rose, ruffling its feathers and scales in a rattling clatter. Vesryn backed away to give the beast space to lean over the open portion of the door.

"I established the rangers, but previously, the dracovae were my brother's project." He stroked the gray plumage of the parent. It closed its eyes, emitting delighted trilling clacks at the attention.

"My...interests at the time lay elsewhere." The prince caressed the beast while he spoke, like he found something interesting in the plumes. "But since his death and the emergence of the wraith, I've taken over. Training warriors to hunt those monsters in his memory." The dracovae's contented exhale breezed through their hair. "They... they took everything from me."

Serenna stared at the hatchlings, now coiling under the other parent's wings. Her chest tightened, feeling more than a little overwhelmed that the prince was sharing this much with her. Jassyn had told her Vesryn never spoke of his brother and she was unsure what the appropriate response would be. *I'm sorry* seemed an inadequate reply to recognize such loss.

Something in the prince's unfocused gaze had Serenna feeling like his thoughts were realms away. She studied the way he absorbed himself in stroking the beast. Like if he stopped touching the gray feathers that moored him to the moment, he'd fall apart. Understanding his vendetta against the wraith stirred an unexpected respect for him.

"Trella was your brother's dracovae, wasn't she?" Serenna asked quietly, stepping next to the prince to join him at the stall. Lifting a hand more confidently this time, she stroked the creature's neck.

Vesryn tensed. He halted with a feather in between his fingers, but resumed petting the beast with a nod.

Serenna swallowed a heavy feeling of sadness. She could almost sense the sorrow radiating from him as her throat cinched tight. Before comprehending what she was doing, she reached out to touch his arm.

And then jerked her hand away when that strange current dashed through her skin. *He said he wasn't doing anything to me, so why is my magic reacting to him?*

Glancing around the stables to find something else to talk about instead of letting the awkward moment linger, Serenna asked, "Why show me all of this?"

Vesryn glanced at her and then down the barn. "Joining the rangers is competitive, but our ranks could use someone with your rending potential if you can stomach being around me to develop your magic." He scratched the dracovae's beak, his nails sounding like they scraped against stone. "If you become my champion and start winning duels, I don't see why you couldn't choose to join their number."

Like a lock opening, something clicked in Serenna's mind—she'd figured him out. Understanding Vesryn's interest in her power was easier to comprehend if he was looking to add her alleged rending abilities to his command.

Folding her arms, she asked, "And manipulating me with adorable hatchlings is your way of ensuring I consider it, right?"

"Is it working?" Vesryn asked, flashing his teeth. "If what we do isn't enough incentive to master your power, then I'm not sure what else would be."

The dracovae peeked an eye at her and flicked its rubbery tongue to lick the dried blood flecked across the front of her uniform. Serenna resisted the urge to shy away.

She contemplated if the prince's training could prepare her enough to win duels against the Alari initiates. A few months hardly seemed like a sufficient amount of time. Lacking confidence in her abilities, Serenna had no doubt in his.

Jassyn already said he wouldn't participate as a trainer; otherwise, I'd rather enter as his champion. I can't imagine what other exercises Vesryn has in store. I'm not rending any rabbits again.

"Did you choose me because you really think I have potential, or is there some other reason?" Serenna asked with as much dignity as she could while the dracovae cleaned her tunic. "My father said I have to earn my place in the elven realm, but I feel like the only thing I've managed to earn is punishment for rending."

"And I suppose your sire's advice about *earning* your status includes fucking me?"

Serenna stiffened, a flush of embarrassment racing up her neck.

Vesryn laughed. A startling, booming sound that echoed to the vaulted ceiling. The dracovae tossed its head with an answering ear-splitting screech, making her wince.

"You're not the first progeny Elashor has paraded by me. Trust me, I'm flattered." Vesryn snorted. He gave the beast a final pat, turning his attention toward her with a quizzical frown. "Honestly, I'm actually a little concerned about his persistence."

Serenna's stomach turned, but the prince's words weren't a shock. The last thing she wanted to do was bear offspring to simply gain rank in the realm. Instead of bedding prominent elves, like her father desired, she thought about what she could make of her own future. *Being sent to the front lines to fight the wraith isn't what I had in mind, though.*

"If I'm going to consider being your champion, then I don't want you to call me a half-breed," she said. Vesryn blinked, which only spurred her on. "Serenna is sufficient, since apparently you're unable to use my title without mocking me."

Shaking loose fringes of hair out of his eyes, the prince studied her with an unreadable look.

His silence only prompted her to fountain more words. "And I want you to stop harassing Jassyn."

There was no way Jassyn would approve of her decision to become the prince's champion, but she could at least try to prevent his maltreatment.

Vesryn's mouth twitched with amusement.

Serenna's hands tightened at her sides. Keeping her anger over the prince's behavior toward Jassyn repressed for so long only made her disgust simmer now. She wondered if Vesryn chose to ignore the devastating effects of the contracts or if he simply used those *obligations* to tear his cousin apart.

"What do you find so humorous?" she questioned. The dracovae stamped its taloned foot at the bite in her words before retreating back into the stall.

Serenna took an assertive step closer and craned her neck to glare at the prince. Indignation boiled under her skin like a screaming kettle. Uncontrolled shadows sprang to life and whipped around her while she trembled.

"You're going to stop tormenting him with those vile contracts." Emboldened, she drove a finger into the dragon on his chest. "Or I'm not even entertaining this tournament or ranger business." She punctuated the last word with a jab.

Vesryn's brows rose at her command before his eyes pinned on her whirling power. Serenna didn't flinch from his eviscerating gaze, but she pulled her hand back when she thought she'd made her point.

Sensing his magic ignite, Serenna braced herself. Digging her nails into her palms, she waited for him to put her in her place.

Instead, Vesryn's power shimmered, as bright as the ocean's surface reflecting in the sun. Raising a hand, he sent a thread of Essence to coil around one of hers, light twining with night.

As if curious, the prince tilted his head and asked, "What's Jassyn to you?"

"Does it matter?" Serenna bit back, ripping her winding shadows away from the touch of his magic. "There shouldn't have to be a bargain for you to be decent."

Vesryn extinguished his power and squared his stance. His gaze roamed across her face, examining her. She couldn't decide if the weight of his attention intrigued her or made her uncomfortable.

"Is there anything else?" he asked, folding his arms, his fingers tapping.

Serenna released a breathy scoff. *Is he even taking me seriously?* If this was his way of negotiating with her, she didn't have a list of demands ready.

With a steadying breath, Serenna released her magic. "I just want to know *why*. Why select me? Every other recruit from your realm already handles their powers in ways I can't even imagine."

"I chose you because you're a fighter. You may lack control, but you have rage." Vesryn glanced around before leaning toward her and lowered his voice. "I can teach you how to *handle* your magic, Princess."

"My title is irrelevant." Serenna retreated a step, vexed by his continued insinuations. "I don't feel like a *princess* when I'm stuck here with everyone else."

The resurrected sting of the past seared through her chest. Her mother had discarded her from court without a second thought.

"What?" Serenna asked when the prince's brows drew tight.

Vesryn stepped forward to hover over her. "And what is it you want? To return to a life where you're only a pretty princess confined in a castle?"

Pretty? She didn't mean to falter, but he'd caught her off guard. His gaze dove deeper into hers. The tension pulsed between them, neither of them looking away.

"I don't have the choice to go back," Serenna finally said, blinking to break the intensity of his stare.

"Do you think you'd be content choosing that life?" Vesryn seized her arm, steering her from the center of the barn to let a dracovae and its rider pass. "Would you want to live without magic, not even knowing the extent of what you're truly capable of?"

"I don't know." Serenna extracted herself from his grasp. "I have no say or the luxury of deciding for myself. Because I'm forced to fight in *your* war."

Vesryn tugged at the threading on his sigil like she was thoroughly exasperating him with her arguments. "Duty may have brought you to Centarya, but you're in control of your own destiny."

The prince's words were kindling to her temper, stoking her aggravation. "That's easy for you to say. You're the prince, and the realm's will doesn't apply to you." Serenna flung an arm at the stables. "You get to play with dracovae hatchlings if you want to. The elves didn't give *me* a choice in my future."

Vesryn scoffed, his stare predatory like the surrounding beasts. "You're ignorant if you think I'm not subject to the realm's will just like you."

Serenna rolled her eyes. The prince had the freedom to do whatever he wanted. She couldn't leave Centarya without permission or an escort. She wasn't even permitted to venture beyond the Terminal—something he conveniently disregarded.

"Fine," Vesryn growled. Muttering to himself, he opened a portal.

Serenna eyed one of the buckets containing innards and considered throwing it at him before he disappeared.

Stalking after the prince through the gateway, the roar of the ocean overran Serenna's senses. Her boots scraped against rocky ground. Spinning around, she oriented herself in the inky, starlit surroundings.

A cliff. She was on a precipice overlooking the sea. The light from the waning moons glimmered off of the gentle waves lapping against the shore. Her hand flew to her mouth, stifling a gasp of surprise. Across the waters, Vaelyn's castle overlooked the crescent bay.

Serenna whirled toward Vesryn, who wandered to the edge of the bluff. She didn't expect to see her home anytime soon.

"What are we doing here?"

Vesryn peered over the ledge to the sea below. "You wanted the choice, so now you have it." He straightened and swept his gaze over her.

Serenna stared at the castle. Torches flickered through the windows against the deepening night. The sconces held flames, not the steady illumination she was becoming accustomed to. An emptiness opened like a chasm inside of her. *Why doesn't this feel like home?*

"You can't decide to release me from my duty at Centarya." Heart drumming in her chest, Serenna swallowed but lost the forcefulness of her voice. "Can you?"

She doubted her mother would even permit her return, considering she was the one who'd sent her to the academy.

Vesryn shrugged, as if it made no difference to him. "Why couldn't I?" The warm breeze tugged at strands of his hair. "Since you seem to think I have so many *privileges*, I'll give you the same option." He tipped his chin toward the castle. "You can go."

Serenna's breathing quickened while she weighed her options, trying to decide if she wanted to return. She didn't have an answer. Vesryn's offer of freedom left her with a sense of confusion and apprehension.

The prince was right; she wouldn't be content within the stone walls, tethered again. *I wasn't happy here before. Why would I be now?* But if her time at Centarya among Alari's elven-blooded was any indication of how the elves would treat her, she'd never belong in Kyansari either.

I can't abandon Jassyn to the horrors he has to face or desert Velinya in the coming war.

The familiar scents of the salty waters lingered on the wind. Serenna studied the horizon, the starry seam between the sky and the sea. This choice was too sudden. She needed more time to think.

"You've been here before?" she asked, diverting the prince's attention and hopefully buying time before he wanted her answer.

"Once." Vesryn brushed breeze-blown strands of hair away from his face. "Over a month ago."

Serenna counted back the weeks. "I would have remembered seeing you at court."

Vesryn's eyes widened slightly, which only made her flush. *Well, it's not my fault he stands out.*

"I…" Vesryn paused. To Serenna's disbelief, the prince hesitated and shifted his attention to the castle. "I only opened a gateway on this cliff. I didn't go anywhere else."

Frowning, she glanced around. "Why would you bother coming here?"

The gravel crunched under Vesryn's boots. He approached her with deliberate steps, like he was intentionally measuring each foot forward. Stomach leaping automatically in anticipation, Serenna steeled herself but didn't retreat from his advance. For once, there wasn't anything intimidating about his stride.

Lifting a hand, Vesryn cautiously reached out as if tentatively probing, exploring what her breaking point would be before she pulled back. "If you want to stay at Centarya, there's another reason I think you should train with me. It has nothing to do with the tournament."

The prince's steady gaze captured hers. He was so close she could see the stars reflecting in his eyes. Serenna tensed when his knuckles brushed the bare skin of her arm. She trembled when the current rushed through her veins, her magic rising in response.

"We're intertwined," he said, his fingers warm, unfolding against her. "I felt your presence appear in my mind the night I portaled here. I'm assuming it was because you were untethered for the first time."

Serenna inhaled a serrated breath when he gently trailed his hand up her arm, sending comets of magic shooting under her skin.

"I know you feel it too," he whispered in a voice as soft as dreams. "This power when we touch."

The heat from Vesryn's body warmed the edge of her senses. The space between them was too tight, their rising chests nearly colliding with every shared breath.

With her pulse hammering in her ears, feeling as if her heart threatened to careen her off the cliff, Serenna asked, "What does it mean? Why does my magic respond this way to you?" Her voice was breathless and light, hesitant to admit the effect he had on her. "My power doesn't react when anyone else with magic touches me."

Vesryn's fingers abruptly halted their journey dancing across her skin. He dropped his hand, and his wrist twitched as if annoyance struck his joints. He stepped away.

The world tilted back into place when the magnetic pull of the prince's presence slackened, leaving Serenna dizzy and standing on shards of the broken moment. *Did I say something wrong?* "I didn't mean—"

Vesryn interrupted her in a gruff voice. "It's a bond."

"A bond?" Serenna repeated. Like that was supposed to explain something.

"Our..." He grasped at the air as if he were trying to gather the right words. "Essence has the ability to form a connection with another person, linking our Wells, binding us together."

Serenna blinked. Her disbelief clamored with her shock. "You... you created a magical connection with me? What does that mean? *Why?*" She couldn't even begin to sift through her feelings about the intrusion. "You never asked." Her outrage flared, and she took a step toward him. To do what, she had no idea. "What gave you the—"

"I did nothing." Vesryn grabbed the hand she was getting ready to shove against his chest.

Like that worked so well to move him the first time. A muscle in his jaw strained as if *his* irritation was *her* fault.

"Sometimes the magic forms automatically. Like in our case. You don't have to accept the bond," he said in a chiding tone, releasing her. "I didn't want this *distraction*, I assure you."

"If neither of us want it, then why does it exist?"

Serenna recalled how his rough fingers had grabbed her chin in the Infirmary, the first time she'd felt the electric current flow through her, unaware of what it was. Once she'd manifested Essence, her power seemed to respond to his touch.

"What's lingering between us is a fraction of what an accepted bond is capable of. Both parties have to consent for the connection to fully develop." Vesryn held up his fingers, inspecting his nails. "The little zap is our magic straining to intertwine, but our power will never be able to merge completely if we both don't agree to the link."

Why do I have a bond with the prince? Serenna looked at her hands as if the magic under her skin contained the answer. He was significantly more powerful than her, an arch elf, not to mention a pure-blood, and nearly two centuries older than her. *Not that he acts like it.*

"Why would our power...do that?" she asked.

"Elves can form bonds intentionally, but it's an archaic practice. Hardly anyone does it anymore, even though there are advantages to consolidating power." Vesryn rubbed his forehead as if her questions aggravated him. "As to why the magic forms on its own, I think it's simply a remnant of our past. It's rare, but not unheard of. The entire Aelfyn race used to be bonded—or so legends say."

Serenna gave an involuntary shudder at the thought, unwilling to dwell on what being bonded to everyone would be like. The connection with the prince had already scrambled her thoughts, and she hardly knew what it meant.

"Are you going to reject the bond then?" she asked, since the connection was a *distraction*. "Or have you already? Do we both have to do it?"

Vesryn tossed his hands in the air. "I doubt you're even capable of managing that much because you haven't manifested all of your abilities yet."

Serenna didn't miss him failing to answer her questions, so she tried something else. "Then what happens until I come into my power?"

"The bond will hover as an annoyance until you learn how to dispel it." Vesryn kicked a rock over the edge of the cliff. "Nothing more."

Serenna chewed her lip while she analyzed the pieces of information he'd provided her. The link must be why she thought she could sense his presence and emotions—it wasn't an eerie attunement because of his...masculine elven magnetism. *He acts like he has a familiarity with bonds.*

"Do you have a bond with someone else?" she asked.

Vesryn's eyes unfocused into the distance over the waves. He squared his shoulders and opened a portal. Serenna didn't think he was going to break the silence.

"Not anymore." Pivoting on his heel, he strode toward the gateway.

"Wait!" Rushing to him, Serenna seized his arm before he walked through. The desperation in her voice made her falter. *Did he reject that one too?* Vesryn glanced at her hand but didn't shrug her off. "You're leaving me here?"

"This is your chance to make your own decision. Stay if you want to be a princess locked behind your stone walls." Vesryn pried her fingers off his arm but wrapped his palm around hers before tucking her hand against his chest. "Or come with me and learn about your magic. If you'll trust me, I can use what's between us to teach you how to focus and channel your power."

Serenna swallowed hard, her mind racing, but any response evaded her. The prince was asking for more than she thought she could give.

Vesryn's hand tightened around hers. "I brought you to the rangers because I wanted to show you something important to me and prove you can determine your own destiny in our realm. Maybe you'll figure out what you actually want."

Releasing her, Vesryn retreated to his portal. Before Serenna could react, he vanished through the rift.

He doesn't get to tell me a sad story about his brother, tease me with information about the rangers, the bond, and this champion business and then just leave. Before the air closed behind his scuffed boots, Serenna dashed through the gateway.

Back at the glade in Centarya, Vesryn spun toward her with a triumphant smirk on his face and a gleam of victory sparkling in his eyes. Somehow, probably through the bond, he'd *known* what she was going to choose, and he wasn't planning on letting her live it down.

Fine, you insufferable prince. You win this round.

Serenna flicked her hair over her shoulder, taking all the time in the world, like she didn't just scurry after him like a loon.

"When do we start?"

CHAPTER 26

LYKOR

"Don't kill the humans," Lykor growled as a reminder. Upon their arrival, the handful of shepherds fled to their village.

Despite the risk of spreading hysteria, he didn't want to extinguish lives needlessly. The elves wouldn't do anything about his warriors appearing in the eastern realm, anyway. It wasn't like they would lower themselves to bother with the suffering of mortals.

The wraith flowed in a stream, fanning out in squad formations away from his rift. As the only one with any magic, Lykor frequently supervised their raids. He didn't join them through the portal every time, but he had a special interest in today's plundering.

Drawing on the other's memories in their mind, Lykor knew where to find the elves' resources. Each mortal realm channeled specific goods into Alari. The west harvested lumber, and the south mined ores and cured fish from the sea. The north grew crops and farmed livestock for food. The east fabricated textiles in their foundries and herded various animals for their fibers to be spun into materials.

Lykor had carefully stockpiled such things over the years. But this excursion wasn't about preparing for battle or delivering provisions to his people.

Their population in the Frostvault Keep had grown to the point that it had become an operation to provide for themselves—even considering he portaled his people daily across the realms. The glacial land was unforgiving and unsustainable for so many.

By raiding the supply lines into Alari, Lykor discovered the humans were totally defenseless and unprepared to form any resistance. It created a low risk and effective way of gathering provisions. He wondered if the elves would ever protect "their" goods from the wraith's continued looting.

Seemingly content, the humans funneled all of their resources to Alari. But what would happen if the mortal's slumbering powers ever stirred and they decided to stand against their oppressors? Perhaps that was the awakening the world needed to dislodge the elves' grip on the land.

Not everyone in Alari was blind to the oppression the Aelyfn had initiated a millennium ago. But no one dared oppose King Galaeryn and his growing power. Stars, how many discussions had he and—

Lykor snarled at the other entity's memory resurfacing, his thoughts skimming dangerously close to chaos by dwelling on whom he was compelled to kill. Leather armor creaked as he rolled his shoulders.

Lykor banished the whispering demands of the tyrannical coercion twisting his mind. He clenched his gauntlet into a fist, the grinding metal grounding him to the countryside.

Losing focus now was not an option for him. Not while they were out on a raid, away from the safety of their fortress. He doubted the humans would fight back, but the wraith couldn't afford to take unnecessary chances before he was ready to strike the floating isle.

The wind from the plains ripped his raven hair, striking his face like vipers. Lykor hastily restrained the irritating mass into a coiled knot at the base of his skull.

Shaving everything off wasn't an option. Oh no, the other presence had gone ballistic when Lykor raised a knife with the intention of severing the aggravating locks.

Recently, the other had the nerve to paralyze Lykor's hands into fists for an entire day until Lykor relented and *convinced* him that he wouldn't cut his fucking hair.

But it was hardly the only topic they disagreed on. Listening to the other being bitching about appearances wasn't worth his time.

Ever since Lykor discovered the elves' military island, the other had been alarmingly more restless in their mind. Anxious. Troubled.

The other presence was uneasy about taking the offensive. But Lykor exerted control over their faculties with an iron fist, refusing to allow the other presence to intervene and fuck up his plans.

I'LL DO WHAT MUST BE DONE TO PROTECT THE WRAITH.

Lykor studied the warriors while they formed a loose perimeter around the open, rolling pastures. His seasoned soldiers were level-headed, but he included nearly fifty of the younger wraith. He watched for any signs of overeagerness, lest he needed to restrain the adolescents with his power.

Again.

Some of those born in the newer generations took to calling themselves "reavers." They were going to be a problem if Lykor didn't give them an outlet—one that didn't harm the mortals. The first—and last—time they'd "accidentally" killed humans, Lykor ripped out the offenders' fangs and talons.

That made everyone else think twice. Still…some of the hotheaded "reavers" were a little too enthusiastic when they practiced with the druids' gold-firing crossbows.

THEY'LL HAVE THE CHANCE TO PROVE THEMSELVES SOON ENOUGH.

The wraith wouldn't have been aggressive. But the elves changed that. His people were all next to fucking useless surviving in the wilds when they fled the prison. A handful of them had prior skills, but most of them had been idle nobles. It was a wonder their surviving group had such diverse former professions.

A nagging thought had him thinking of the future. The wraith would need to relocate if they couldn't eradicate the impending threat of the elves' military in training—especially if the elves used the human population to seek them out.

BUT WHERE?

There wasn't a single place in their world where Lykor felt he could keep his people safe. Perhaps Mara would decipher more of the druids' secrets in their library and give them a direction.

King Galaeryn was unfolding something—Lykor had no doubts about that. They'd heard whispers of the monarch's plans while in the prisons. The wraith had been the catalyst for the king amassing power.

Kal and Fenn strolled through the portal after the small army, drawing Lykor out of his contemplation. Fenn flashed Lykor an excited, fanged grin before loping down the grassy hill, warping to catch up with the rest of the band.

Lykor's captain raised his pierced brows upon taking in the surroundings, seemingly unconcerned with the persistent breeze tearing at his multitude of braids.

"Don't you think this whole venture is a tad…frivolous?" Kal asked, hefting his crossbow over a shoulder.

Kal's presence had Lykor's muscles spasming involuntarily. He recalled his captain's crucial involvement in aiding their escape from the dungeons.

It had taken Lykor nearly twenty years to work up the nerve to have Kal extract the tethers from his flesh, accepting he might die in the removal process—or from infection after.

Lykor cracked his back, reliving how Kal and Mara had excavated the embedded golden stakes the king skewered along the length of his spine. He didn't care to remember how Kal had kept him conscious long enough to open a portal so they all could flee—the agony of the metal ripping away from his bones had nearly killed him.

If Kal weren't so competent, Lykor wouldn't include him in any of the scouting missions, but he was one of the few with any notable military training. Still… keeping him so close sent his captain the wrong message.

Or rather, Kal insisted on reading into an irritating situation that had nothing to do with Lykor.

"The goats will give the wraithlings a task to tend to," Lykor muttered, unsure why he deigned to defend his reason for the raid. "Everyone contributes."

"Yeah, but…" Kal's attention shifted to Halaema's countryside. He holstered his crossbow in the strap on his back. "Can you even rightly call these fuzzy creatures *goats*?"

As if measuring, Kal held up his clawed hands. "These goats look smaller than the vulpintera," he said, casting Lykor a red-eyed glare. "And I think you've already indulged the wraithlings quite enough by letting them keep that colony of nightmares in the caverns. Stars, those flying foxes are a nuisance. I fucking hate those things. Last week, one of them—"

"Kal," Lykor growled under his breath as a warning to shut the fuck up.

"I'm just saying, where will we keep these…pocket goats?" he asked, tossing his hands in the air. "What good are they going to be? Since *everyone* contributes. I can't imagine you'll let us slaughter them for stew once you distribute them as pets."

Lykor snarled in annoyance at the questioning and strode down the grassy hill to join his warriors. Taller than the elves, the wraith appeared distorted, like their skeletons had stretched—forever gaunt, even if they weren't starving in the wilds anymore.

Weaving a wall of shields, Lykor halted a section of the herd so the wraith could retrieve the goats without warping all over the pastures and scattering the flock further. He could sacrifice some of his magic to accelerate rounding up the creatures.

Kal's incessant jabbering buzzed around him, more maddening than a relentless cloud of mosquitoes. His captain would ramble all day if Lykor gave him so much as a grunt of acknowledgment. Or breathed in his fucking direction.

Evidently, twenty years in a dungeon couldn't exterminate such an aggravating habit.

Unfortunately.

"What are you going to do with these pocket goats? Milk them and make cheese?" Kal kept pace with him, clicking his clawed nails in front of Lykor's face like a crab closing its pincers. "I can't imagine they'll appreciate their teats being stroked by our talons."

As if reminded, Kal extended a fang. He scraped the underside of said talon with a sharp canine, a habit that sent the other presence in Lykor's mind flying into a spluttering protest.

"The kitchen staff mean well," Kal persisted. "But they fuck up enough food, and I've already shit my guts out more times than I can count by trying their experiments. Do you remember the first time they tried to prepare those glowing mushrooms?"

Lykor's hand jerked in a half-hearted attempt from the other presence wrenching control of their body, intending to seize Kal's finger and drag it out of his mouth. Lykor balled his gauntlet into a fist and ignored them both.

"Next, we'll have to locate resources to feed these pocket goats," Kal said, rolling whatever he dislodged from his claw in between his fingers before flicking it away. "Are you going to stockpile hay now? Sure, might as well convert the cavern gardens into a pasture while we're at it because these woolies won't survive outside of the keep—no matter how furry they are. I guarantee that."

Finally taking a breath, Kal stationed himself as a sentry beside him, idly chewing at one of his lower lip rings. "I'm just trying to be practical," he muttered.

Lykor tensed when his captain suddenly grabbed his shoulder.

"This trip is rash and unnecessary," Kal said. "You're pushing yourself beyond any sane means preparing for this assault. Mara and I have reservations about—"

Lykor whipped his gauntleted claw up and seized Kal by the throat. His chest heaved with his irritation. *HOW IS THIS PRATTLING FOOL THE WRAITH'S BEST MILITARY MIND?*

The stars had already cursed him enough. Why did they have to banish him with the former captain of the princes' guard?

"Shut. The. Fuck. Up," Lykor snarled. "I don't care about these *reservations*. We're taking the fight to them. I won't hesitate to put someone else in your position who will stand by my decision." His lip curled into a sneer. "Your son perhaps."

"My *job* is to question you," Kal growled, but he didn't struggle to free himself from Lykor's grip. "Let me talk to *him*. There's no way he agrees with this."

"I'm not *him*!" Lykor raged, baring his fangs. "You've had a century to reconcile with this change. It's past time you do."

The overfamiliarity still grated on Lykor like a desert's blasting sand. Kal refused to accept him as a different individual and only saw the *other* being. Lykor couldn't care less about the history they'd shared before the dungeons—it wasn't his past.

Despite the soul-shattering torture Lykor had repeatedly endured and all he'd sacrificed, no one would blink an eye if he faded away into nothingness, permitting the other presence to permanently emerge.

If he willingly allowed the other being to control their body, Lykor feared he would drift away. A leaf on a breeze. Forgotten. Irrelevant. No longer needed. So he asserted his domination relentlessly, like a wolf clamping its jaws around a hare, refusing to release his hold.

"You *are* him," Kal argued, his canines elongating. "He's in there. But you don't let him out." His taloned hand wrapped around Lykor's gauntlet, almost pleading.

Lykor disregarded the protests, increasing the pressure around his captain's throat. Half of Kal's personality was quarreling with him anyway.

HE DOESN'T SEE ME. HE NEVER HAS. MAYBE I SHOULD DISAPPEAR, IF THAT'S WHAT THEY ALL FUCKING WANT.

"And you think *he* still loves you?" Lykor hissed, words dripping like venom, hoping the poison stung. "He doesn't. Do you hear *him* correcting me?" Kal still flinched at the false and callous undercut. "You have a clan and offspring. Worry about them. I grow weary of this unending fixation."

Lykor flung him to the ground.

Kal warped, disappearing in a cloud of shadows before he fell. Rematerializing back in front of him, Kal stumbled to right himself.

"You're still the same elf," Kal pressed. "Somewhere in there." He thrust his crossbow holster back into place over his shoulder. "Regardless of the imprisonment we endured, what I feel for you hasn't changed. Why do you insist on pushing everyone away, *Lykor?*"

Lykor split the air with a portal back to their keep's cavern gardens. He pointed toward the herd. "Get me forty of those fucking pocket goats."

Kal took an aggressive step toward him. "You could have a place with us, *your* people, with *me*, but you lock yourself away, alone in your tower. Why—"

Lykor bared his fangs and punched a burst of force into Kal's chest, sending him sprawling again.

"NOW!" he barked with finality.

Why do you treat him like that? the other presence asked.

FUCK YOU, Lykor fired back, pivoting away from Kal. *AND FUCK HIM TOO.* In their mind, Lykor watched the other entity rolling his eyes. *I CANNOT FATHOM WHAT YOU SAW IN HIM.*

But Lykor wasn't blind. Despite being a wraith, Kal possessed attractive features he could appreciate—sharp cheekbones, a sinewy form, honed points to his ears. Even if they were riddled with rings.

But that hardly meant Lykor wanted to be in his captain's presence a moment longer than he needed to be. There was only so much he could tolerate, forever cast in a shadow of who the other presence used to be. Kal saw who he wanted to see. And it wasn't Lykor.

THE ELVES WOULD HAVE DONE US ALL A FAVOR BY TAKING KAL'S TONGUE, Lykor snarled.

How can you jest about that? The other presence bristled, glaring at him. *He's an honorable male. And he's not wrong. This raid is an unnecessary risk. Don't get me started on this war you want to wage. I won't let you—*

Lykor wrestled the voice into the furthest depths of his mind. Crushing it. Smothering it.

Watching the warriors herding the flock toward his portal, Lykor begrudgingly contemplated if Kal was right. Perhaps he was being fucking stupid on this raid. But the wraithlings loved those flying vulpintera, and he thought they'd like caring for the goats. They deserved the normalcy children should have growing up. He tried to give them that.

Lykor would sacrifice his life to buy his people another day of safety—pay whatever price to provide them with enough time to gather their strength and flee if the elves were going to hunt them in force. He needed to stop the king before it came to that. Eliminate the threat.

He was doing his best to prepare the wraith for sustaining themselves and surviving without his power, knowing he wouldn't be around forever.

His people would endure—their wraithlings could have a future in a better world. Previously, Lykor thought it would be as simple as waiting for the elves to die out, but that wouldn't happen if they continued to breed with the humans.

A whirlwind of shadows unfolded in front of him. Lykor's gauntlet snapped into a fist, ready to smash Kal's face if his captain insisted on opening his mouth again.

Instead, it was Fenn who materialized with a bewildered-looking goat tucked into his arms.

"I saved the best one for you, Lykor," he said, grinning. The lieutenant shoved the furry animal at him. "Look." He tapped one of the goat's legs. "He has one silver hoof, just like the color of your gauntlet."

The shroud of Lykor's dark mood slipped, the permanent scowl ridged between his brows sloughing away as he took the animal.

Fenn warped away, back to the portal.

Lykor studied the creature as it bleated up at him with dark, helpless eyes. Careful to use his elven hand and not his clawed gauntlet, Lykor scratched the underside of its fuzzy chin, unaware of the sad smile he wore. The goat blinked before relaxing, leaning into his fingers.

What he was doing with these pocket goats…it had nothing to do with the war he was preparing the wraith for.

This was about leaving something behind.

Something untainted by the darkness eviscerating his sanity or the compulsive magic butchering what was left of his mind.

CHAPTER 27

SERENNA

This had better be important.

Storming up the stairs of the Spire, Serenna fumed that the prince had *yanked* her through the bond, hauling her out of sleep. *He only brought me back to campus a few hours ago—it's hardly dawn!*

She'd tried rolling over and ignoring him, but the persistent pulling nearly dragged her out of bed. Cursing a litany, each step triggered a more colorful swear word than the last as Serenna ascended the tower.

If Vesryn presumed she'd be amenable to training this early in the morning, then he'd have to find someone else to torment as his champion.

Serenna's violent thoughts multiplied when her spine spasmed involuntary. Another tug lurched through the link, like the prince reeled her in on a line.

Can't the stars-cursed bastard tell I'm on the way?

The connection between them was obvious now, appearing as two silver threads floating in her Well. Serenna didn't know if she could send any signals through the nexus, but she clenched her fingers anyway, imagining throttling the prince for rushing her morning routine.

One of the cords connecting them seemed faint. *That must be the bridge to link our Essence if the bond is ever fully formed.*

Unfamiliar with the upper levels of the Spire, Serenna followed the general direction of Vesryn's proximity, assuming he might be in his office.

"Just go to the top floor," she muttered.

She hoped Vesryn had to climb these scorching stairs every day. Multiple times. There had to be a few hundred. *Knowing him, I'm sure he portals.*

Fire seared her lungs and burned through her thighs, but the ascent was easier than the first time she climbed the tower with her father.

Straightening her bodice, Serenna panted, catching her breath, finally at the top. Vesryn's intimidating guards stood stationed in front of a door in the empty hallway. The stoic warriors didn't acknowledge her approach. Shifting her weight, Serenna waited for them to permit her entry.

They remained motionless.

Serenna cleared her throat, but they continued to ignore her, staring ahead. Unsettled, she gathered her courage and barged between them to open the door herself. They made no efforts to hinder her, but they didn't aid her either. *I'm not surprised the prince keeps such rude company.*

This chamber wasn't his office.

She found herself in Vesryn's living quarters, which were fit for royalty. Exquisite leather furniture and tables in dark complementary tones decorated the room. Gaping, Serenna studied the rows of books lining mahogany shelves, ruthlessly organized by spine color.

An array of richly woven tapestries depicting mountains similar to the dracovae's valley covered the white walls. Tasteful diaphanous curtains permitted the bright glow of the morning sun, outlining the arched windows overlooking the academy's grounds.

Angling her thoughts toward the bond, Serenna sensed Vesryn's presence nearby and wandered around his apartments. She peeked into a room, discovering his sleeping chambers. A massive four-poster bed draped in heavy curtains dominated most of the space. A sea of pillows blanketed the expanse of the mattress—more than would be comfortable.

Unable to resist the temptation, she ventured farther in and peered into a walk-in closet brimming with black uniforms. In fact, she didn't see any variance at all. *Is that all he wears?* Apparently, he only had a single pair of those rugged boots, because there weren't any others present.

Even more curious than his singular style of clothing was an array of feathers arranged on one of his dressers, fanned out in shades from whites to blacks. They were as long as her forearm. On a thoughtless whim, she grabbed them, suspecting they were Trella's and Naru's.

Carrying the feathers, Serenna strayed back to the sitting room and stepped out onto the balcony to appreciate the blushing colors of the sunrise. She rarely roused before the day dawned.

The waters cascaded down from the portal above the Spire, flowing past as a roaring waterfall. Idly stroking the plumes, she marveled at the breathtaking view the building's peak offered.

But her heart strained with a heavy weight as she studied the luxuriousness of Vesryn's apartments. There weren't any personal effects or evidence of his life within the confines of his rooms. His only possessions were his leathers, weapons, and a handful of feathers.

Am I any different?

A door banged open.

Jumping, Serenna whirled around. Vesryn stalked into his chambers, joining her on the balcony. Her attention darted over him, from the sharp tips of his ears to the toes of his scuffed boots.

He wore scaled leathers with shoulder pads and vambraces along with two short glaives peeking over his back. An intricate braid running down the center of his scalp protruded like a ridged crest.

Serenna froze, realizing how intimidating he looked in full armor. Vesryn tilted his head, eyes locking on the feathers in her hand. He must've registered that she'd ventured into his sleeping chambers, but spared her the embarrassment by not mentioning it.

"Did you get lost?" he drawled.

Serenna ignored his question. "Why am I here?"

"I wanted to determine how good your recall is when summoned."

The prince swiped a dislodged strand of silvery hair away from his forehead.

"Seriously?" Serenna balled a hand around the feathers and braced her fists on her hips, ready to expel her irritation, which was rising like the morning sun. "I climbed all those scorching stairs for your *entertainment*? I could have slept another hour!"

Turning, Vesryn dismissed her complaint. He motioned over his shoulder for her to follow.

Serenna seethed at his back. She shifted her awareness toward the bond, considering if she could jerk him around in the same manner. Gritting her teeth, she threw her will at the connecting leash, wrenching the hovering cords as viciously as she could.

Vesryn stumbled through the open adjoining door. He rounded on her, his eyes threatening retaliation with his glare. Serenna's foul mood lightened significantly by annoying him.

Whisking past him into his adjacent office, Serenna asked, "Does your bonded *pet* get breakfast at least?"

The prince gestured to an arrangement on an end table. It appeared his servants had brought a morning feast to his chambers. She didn't envy them for having to carry everything up the stairs.

"If you'd be more comfortable eating at my feet, I can put a plate on the floor," he said flippantly.

Serenna awkwardly placed the feathers on a corner of his desk, pretending like he wasn't watching her every move. She folded her arms with a dismissive sniff. "I'd rather starve than eat your table scraps."

Vesryn grunted. "I haven't touched it. Hunting wraith is best done on an empty stomach."

He did appear to be preparing for battle. Strewn across his desk were dozens of daggers in varying shapes and sizes, organized in precise lines according to length.

But the prince's sole hobby of tracking wraith hardly justified why he forced her to ascend the Spire like a trained hound.

Since Vesryn failed to satisfactorily answer her earlier question of why he'd summoned her, Serenna glanced around his study attempting to determine the reason. She recalled their first meeting in the same room. A thought struck her as her attention latched onto a familiar closed cabinet.

She asked, "Is the Heart of Stars still here?"

"It's back in the palace's treasury." Vesryn's forehead furrowed. "Why?"

"I was just thinking about when I was here before. Does it—" Serenna nearly inquired if the artifact spoke to everyone, but stopped herself. *Wouldn't he think I'm mad if I told him I heard a voice?*

"What is it exactly?" she asked instead. "Besides a relic?"

Vesryn picked up a knife from his desk. The sunlight glinted off of the steel. "It's a piece of glass that glows with our abilities, I guess."

Pursing her lips, Serenna assumed he was making fun of her words before the Heart unveiled her talents. "It doesn't have any other...powers?"

Vesryn paused his thumbing of the sharp edge of the blade to study her with a raised brow. "What are you asking?"

"Does it speak to you?" Serenna suppressed a cringe for voicing something so absurd. *Why did I even say anything?* But she recalled the guttural voice unfurling in her mind and knew she'd said too much to backtrack now.

Vesryn went still, his attention focusing on her like a predator stalking prey. A shiver fled down her spine while he took his time scrutinizing her. "The Heart...spoke to you?"

"I...I don't know anymore. Maybe I was mistaken." The tips of Serenna's ears heated. "I'd discovered magic existed a few days prior, and I left Vaelyn that same morning, and then my father brought me up here so suddenly..."

She was rambling and barely stopped herself from bringing up her father's suggestion about getting *closer* to the prince. No need to remind Vesryn of *that*. Swallowing her embarrassment, Serenna took a stabilizing breath. "But I probably just imagined whatever I thought I heard."

"I remember you startling through the bond," Vesryn commented, sheathing the knife at his hip. "What did it say?"

He studied her, but she didn't sense he doubted her. *So, it wasn't him manipulating me telepathically, like Jassyn mused.*

Emboldened by his belief, Serenna's words cascaded like a falling cataract. "It…it said whelps stole its magic. Maybe elemental magic? It wanted the Hearts returned—the voice, that is. It said there were five Hearts keeping it bound. And it called me a hatchling or something like that. I think."

Flushing further, Serenna looked away, mortified she'd brought up the memory. And to the prince! *He's going to think I'm ridiculous.*

Sunlight gleamed in Vesryn's vibrant eyes, reflecting curiosity as he searched her. Analyzing. "I don't have an answer as to what the relic is beyond its use in determining abilities."

The prince traced his lower lip with a thumb before he frowned. His mouth parted as he paused before he spoke. "I heard a theory once of what it might've been used for…a long time ago. Perhaps I can retrieve it the next time I'm at the palace if you wanted to…hold it again?"

Serenna cleared her throat and readjusted her hair over her shoulder. She tried to shrug off her discomfort. "Um…sure." Changing the subject, she asked, "So why are you hunting wraith this early?"

The prince stared at her for a moment before picking up another dagger. "Elashor stationed sentries in the more populous human areas since the wraith are now targeting the mortal realms. The sentinels portal to the capital and alert the council of any nefarious activity."

His fingers flexed, the blade shaking in his white-knuckled grip. "They reported that four wraith slaughtered an entire village of shepherds in Halaema." Vesryn's jaw clenched before he continued. "Those monsters are growing too bold, now butchering livestock and humans for sport. The council sent a missive this morning detailing where the creatures were last sighted. I'm leaving to track them down."

Four wraith murdered an entire village? Serenna's gut twisted with apprehension over learning the wraith were expanding their reach of terror. *When will the council have us meet them in force?*

"Anyway," Vesryn said, loosening his shoulders, "I doubt I'll be gone long, but I wanted to give you your stipend."

"Stipend?"

Flipping the dagger into the air on his way to a wall of cabinets, Vesryn twisted his arm behind his back with little attention to sheath the blade in the bandolier strapped along his spine. Serenna rolled her eyes at the display, even though the cut edges of his muscles did look quite impressive through the gaps in his vambraces. *Does he really need eight knives?*

She didn't realize there was a shield until one flared when Vesryn's magic pulsed. Dispelling the ward with the wave of a hand, he swung a door open to retrieve a tear-shaped vial. A white light glimmered through the crystal.

The prince extended the container toward her. "I would be a horrible trainer if I failed to fund my champion now, wouldn't I?"

Serenna frowned and grabbed the offered vial, turning over the shining bottle in her palm. "And you're paying me with…an illumination light?"

"It's not just some bauble filled with illumination."

Serenna squinted at the vial, still confused.

Vesryn clicked his tongue as if a thought occurred to him. "Oh right, I suppose you might not know. In Alari, we use magic for bartering." He nodded at the container. "That vial holds Essence potent enough to restore your Well."

Vesryn closed the cabinet. A violet ward flashed when he wove another shield to lock the remaining bottles inside. "Surely you've learned of the concept in your illumination classes?"

Shame heated Serenna's face as she realized the prince must think her ignorant due to her origins in the human realms.

Trying to recover, she recited what she *did* know. "Everyone with a drop of elf blood has the illumination ability. You can intentionally withdraw Essence from your Well—either a fraction or all of it—and dispense your magic to another, restoring their reserves."

"Right." Vesryn returned to his desk. "And instead of directly transferring your power, you can infuse your Essence into containers. The more potent the magic within, the more value it has."

Serenna's lip curled in disgust when the prince spat on a whetstone.

"For your weekly stipend, I drew out an estimate to cover any fun you want to have at the Terminal, but not enough for you to go rogue and buy out a tavern."

"But how is Essence worth anything?" she asked, finding the view outside the windows more preferable than watching the revolting way the prince sharpened a dagger. "Everyone can meditate and replenish their Well."

Depending on how much power she used throughout the day, she didn't regenerate every night if her Well was mostly full. *I'll have to this evening, between Ayla attacking me yesterday and Vesryn making me rend that rabbit.*

"You're assuming all elves bother with regenerating." He sighed, turning the saliva-smothered blade over. "Instead of honing their power, most citizens pour their resources into indulgences—using Essence to craft Stardust instead of doing anything useful with their magic." Vesryn scoffed and sheathed the knife in the remaining empty scabbard on his chest. "Once the destructive cycle starts, it's nearly impossible to replenish power with a mind addled from that drug—that's why bottled Essence has value."

Sufficiently—well, probably excessively—armed, Vesryn absorbed himself in rearranging the stack of feathers methodically from shades of blacks to whites.

"Laziness and inaction are perhaps the biggest problems in our society. At least among the arch elves and those with a higher percentage of abilities. The half-bree…" The prince trailed off, blinking at a black plume in his hand.

Serenna reared back in surprise, eyes snapping to his face. *I guess he did take my requests seriously.*

"It's different with the elven-blooded, but it's not like they have a choice," Vesryn said.

Serenna studied the vial, processing his admission and correction. "So this is your power?" she asked, assuming it was.

"Yes, but don't get sentimental about it." He stroked a feather. "Just because it's my magic doesn't mean it's worth more than anyone else's."

"I'm shocked you feel that way," Serenna said, not really believing him this time. "But how would I use it to restore my reserves? I haven't manifested illumination yet."

Lifting a hand to his chest, Vesryn extracted an orb of radiant luminescence. It appeared different than a simple illumination light. The globe was brighter, pulsing with streaks of silver, like stars streaming across the sky. He approached her with the sparkling Essence hovering above his palm.

"You can either absorb it on your own or I can infuse it for you," he said.

Serenna sensed him setting a trap, judging by the silent humor rippling through the bond.

Vesryn tilted his head. "Whichever way you prefer to be filled."

Serenna refrained from giving him an exasperated look, ignoring his comment. "Won't you need all of your Essence to hunt wraith today?" Surely he'd want all of his available power, despite being a lethal whirlwind with his glaives.

"As touching as your concern is, I have plenty at my disposal—it's only a sliver of power from my Well. "

"I see you wake up radiantly arrogant." Serenna stifled an additional remark, biting the inside of her cheek instead. He was being uncharacteristically civil. Sort of. But she didn't make any move to accept the light blazing between them.

Vesryn raised his brows. Whether in question or asking permission, she wasn't sure. Decisiveness echoed through the bond, and his jaw flexed as if in determination.

Reaching out, he gripped one of her shoulders, holding her in place, like he thought she would retreat. Serenna didn't flinch, but stilled, watching him warily.

Vesryn plunged the light into her chest.

Serenna gasped at the intoxicating charge of energy. Her body buzzed as if electrified from the ground up. The exposed skin above her uniform *glowed* like she'd swallowed a burning coal. The light fractured and dissipated inside of her, briefly flooding the veins in her chest with glowing streaks before fizzling out. Magic sizzled through her nerves, burrowing into her Well, replenishing and invigorating her power as if fed by an underground spring.

"If you don't use any Essence today, you can skip regenerating tonight." Vesryn's slanted grin stirred an ember of warmth in her heart.

Serenna's attention drifted to his fingers lingering on her shoulder. She lifted her eyes, and their gazes collided. Her fingers tightened around the vial, her stomach dashing with a surge of anxiety for reasons she couldn't comprehend.

Vesryn's hand twitched, his thumb skimming her neck. The caress kindled a shudder underneath her skin as the familiar current raced through her veins, waking her power.

A rising heat emanating from somewhere in her chest clashed with the bond's magic. The sensations spiraled around her body in a frightening but mesmerizing way.

Serenna cleared the flighty nerves from her throat and diverted her awareness away from the prince's gaze, which lingered distractedly on her lips. Her blood lurched in every direction, the pressure of his attention weakening her spine.

"So...happy hunting?" she said to stave off the tension of the moment.

One side of Vesryn's mouth tilted, the dimple deepening in his cheek. Like he knew how to direct her focus right back to it.

"Something like that," he said with what felt like a deliberate brush of his fingers down her arm as his hand slipped off her shoulder.

Snatching the feathers from his desk, he shoved them at her. "Keep them."

Serenna steadied the tremor in her hand before retrieving the offered gift. She stared at the black and white plumes and couldn't help but think he'd shared something important with her. Holding her breath, Serenna hoped that the coiled knot of her feelings wasn't bleeding through the bond.

Vesryn cleared his throat. "Don't you have somewhere to be?"

Serenna blinked, the spell snapping. That was all she needed to surface from whatever flowing undercurrent she'd invented between them.

"Yes, *anywhere* else, I think." She spun around to let herself out of his office.

Right before turning the handle, she faltered at the door. Serenna tried to decipher her concern. She twisted back toward the prince, her lips parting, but no words emerged while she watched him open a portal. Vesryn glanced in her direction.

Be careful? Is that stupid to tell him?

"You're not going alone, are you?" she asked.

"I'll be fine."

"But—"

He vanished.

Leaning against the door as the portal faded, Serenna chewed on a nail while the fluttering in her heart settled. She tunneled her focus through the bond while staring at the vial of Essence. She hardly perceived Vesryn's presence in her mind, and couldn't identify his location, as he seemed to be both in the east and the west. He had thoroughly jumbled her thoughts.

Stars, does he have this effect on everyone?

CHAPTER 28

JASSYN

Jassyn's eyes bulged. "What is this?"

He flipped Serenna's hand over to inspect the disfigurement from every angle. After her aiding hour, they stood alone in the healing wing. The evening shuffled in after they finished mending the surprisingly few injuries from the final combat class of the day.

It was nearly time for the dinner bell, leaving the Infirmary deserted. Jassyn wanted to grab something to eat before he had to leave for Kyansari, unsure when his next meal would be.

No, I'm not thinking about that right now. Draping a shroud of darkness to muffle those thoughts, he brutally focused on what was in front of him, clutching at his magic so his wavering power wouldn't flee.

The persistent thundering in his skull had other ideas for his attention, each heartbeat drawing his awareness back to his impending *duty* barreling toward him like the rainstorm outside. Judging from the way his head pulsed, he could tell it was approaching the time when he normally consumed Stardust to wind down for the day.

Casting out a thread of Essence to assess Serenna's mangled finger, Jassyn determined the fragmented bones had calcified. If Vesryn pulverized her joints mere days ago, the injury should still be inflamed. *Did another recruit try healing it?*

Shaking Serenna's hand in her face, Jassyn asked in utter disbelief, "Who botched this up?"

"Vesryn *mended* it. Well, to the best of his abilities. If you can even call it that," Serenna said with what was decidedly a giggle, her eyes dancing with mirth. "You would've had a fit if you had to witness his jumbled attempt at a healing lattice. It was more chaotic than when I manifested my ability."

"Why in the bleeding stars would he try?" Jassyn rolled his shoulders to dislodge his frustration. "I thought he forbade mending anyway."

His cousin had never bothered honing his rehabilitating magic, so this bungled excuse for healing wasn't a surprise. *It's not a useful ability if it only helps someone else.*

"Vesryn set the bones and took away the swelling." Serenna shrugged. "But you can heal it now because three days have passed."

Not sharing in her humor, or appreciating this alarming familiarity with the prince, Jassyn released her hand and the hold on his power. Irritation had him driving his hands through his curls. "How did he break it?"

Stroking her finger idly, Serenna said, "With rending, of course."

Jassyn stared at her, suspicious of why she wasn't taking her punishment more seriously. Or why she'd disregarded the rules to even warrant such a sentence.

He'd heard the wildfire rumors of how Serenna had incapacitated nearly half of her class before Vesryn showed up. Handling that amount of power when she'd manifested her ability was an impressive feat.

That was, it would've been with any other magic besides rending.

"Well, Vesryn will have to break it again before I can heal..." Jassyn shook his head, gesturing at her hand. "Whatever you want to call what he did to *mend* it."

"What?" Serenna's gaze jerked back to her finger before meeting his stare. "Why?"

Releasing an exasperated sigh, Jassyn began closing the windows before the rain arrived. "Who knows if this was Vesryn's idea of yet another twisted joke, but by setting the break in your joints, all he accomplished was making the damage permanent. Like if you never had the fractures healed and time ran its course."

He tugged the curtains, shutting the blinds for the evening. "Had he not *intervened*, you would have been uncomfortable for three days, but the injury would've been recent enough to rectify."

"Can't *you* re-break and mend it?" Serenna asked, chewing her lip. "I don't think Vesryn intended to cause any harm. He seemed sincere about healing it." Her mouth opened as if she was on the verge of saying something more, but stopped.

Jassyn frowned, unable to fathom what his cousin was up to. "Breaking bones isn't one of my talents. Vesryn needs to shatter the joints again in the same way. Your body believes this is the form of your finger now."

Serenna scoffed. "I'll…deal with it later."

Fabricating new illumination lights to fill the wall sconces, he asked, "I heard a confrontation with Ayla is why you used rending?"

Serenna didn't meet his eyes while she fidgeted with the laces of her bodice. "I tried to ignore her, but she was star-bent on escalating whatever issue she has with me."

"You threaten her position in the realm." Jassyn's glowing orbs cast a gray color that mirrored his gloomy mood. "I know it's not your fault you share the same sire, but I'm concerned your retaliation will only provoke her further."

Serenna gave a dry laugh. "What threat could *I* possibly pose to her?" Nose wrinkling, she stripped a clinic bed soiled with blood. "Ayla is stronger than me since she has more abilities *and* she has a powerful family in Alari's courts." She ripped off the sheet. "Not to mention, she has the most developed control of her magic on campus. And don't forget she has our father's favor too." Serenna threw the bedding into a hamper.

"You're lucky, then," Jassyn muttered, mostly to himself. Setting a reassuring hand on Serenna's shoulder when she finished aggressively dismantling the bed, he gave her a squeeze. "Don't give her the power to frustrate you."

"How am I supposed to do that?" She tossed her hands in the air. "Let her continue flinging me all across campus? It's humiliating."

"I understand, but rending isn't the answer." Jassyn's heart tightened in response to the treatment she endured. He was no stranger to the feeling of being powerless, completely at the mercy of others. "If you keep this up, you'll be expelled. I actually agree with Vesryn's restrictions on the magic, even though the punishments are excessive. What if your power ran wild and you hurt someone?"

"It's all I'm capable of!" Serenna protested, stepping away. "What would you have me do?" She folded her arms, displeasure swirling in her eyes. "Accept whatever treatment the elves deem fit? Like *you* do?"

Jassyn tensed, sucking in a shocked breath that sliced down his throat. "That's not fair," he breathed. "I don't have a choice."

"Then explain why you allow Vesryn and half the magus to trample all over you. You have a *choice* about that." She pointed an accusing finger at him. "Vesryn *respected* me for defending myself. He asked me to be his champion because of it."

So that's his plan. Dazzling her with attention like he knows she's been craving it her whole life.

"Do you think becoming the prince's champion makes you *special*? It doesn't." Overcome with disbelief, he erupted with a barbed laugh. "Earning Vesryn's *favor* isn't something to be proud of. I've known him for decades, and you've only been here a handful of weeks. You know nothing about him," Jassyn said, contempt controlling his voice. "Don't come weeping to me when he hurts you. Because I've already warned you—you'll find no sympathy from me."

Serenna's eyes went round in shock but then tightened with indignation. Silence frosted the air. He knew any further words spoken in anger would shatter the sheet of ice forming between them.

Jassyn's pulse flogged the inside of his skull as he anticipated the moment. Wind howled in the gathering storm. A charge coalesced in the atmosphere, dropping the pressure, but neither of them reacted when lightning fractured through the gaps in the curtains.

"You're too scared to actually stand up for yourself," Serenna said, inclining her chin. "Maybe if you actually had the nerve to be assertive for once in your life, the elves wouldn't treat you like a whore."

Jassyn flinched, his heart dropping to his stomach. It hadn't taken long for her to throw his servitude back in his face after he confided in her, exposing his vulnerabilities. Only one night with the prince, and she already acted like him. *I don't need to tolerate this.*

Pivoting on a heel, he retreated to his office.

"Jassyn, wait. I'm sorry." Serenna rushed to him and clutched his arm. "I didn't mean that."

He couldn't hear anything beyond the roar in his ears. "Do you actually *think* you're ever going to be equal to the elves? You're not." Jassyn's voice came out as a scathing whisper. "I don't know what illusion you're living in, but you're nothing to them."

"I'm not accepting that." Serenna squeezed his arm. Her innocent blue eyes, the Vallende eyes that made him want to cower, misted as she blinked back tears. "And you shouldn't either."

Jassyn stared at her, debating whether he should say more. He knew he should've kept his thoughts to himself, but he was already volatile, cut open and bleeding. Retaliating to hurt her back, the rancor in his voice cracked like ice chipping when he finally broke through the silence.

"Your sire only feigns interest in you because of your breeding potential. He cares nothing for you beyond how you can extend his line." Jassyn's throat trembled from clenching his jaw so fiercely against the sharp sting of bitterness.

The color leached from Serenna's face. Hating himself for every word, Jassyn couldn't stop.

"Elashor didn't bring me to Vaelyn to *tutor* you. He brought me to impregnate you. But I refused," he hissed. "So please excuse me if my *defiance* doesn't live up to your expectations. I'm broken, and all I have left to fight with are the fucking pieces."

He ripped his arm out of her hand. "We're done here," he said, storming off to his office. "I have *whoring* to do."

Serenna pleaded to his back. "Jassyn, I'm sorry."

The crashing sound of him slamming his office door reverberated through the empty Infirmary and blocked any attempts at a further apology.

CHAPTER 29

SERENNA

Trembling with disbelief, Serenna stared at Jassyn's closed door. Self-hate crippled her, shredding her from the inside out. *Why did I say that to him?* She couldn't undo the damage of those heartless words. Her savagery drove him to the point of retaliation, meeting her blow for blow. It wasn't like him to lash out.

Denial tried to beat through Serenna's chest. Jassyn's words cut deep, but everything her father had orchestrated made sense—Jassyn being from a powerful line, his role as her tutor, and her swift introduction to the prince. The reality stung, but she knew her friend had told the truth.

Serenna's own silent suspicions sprouted from her father's comments, but it felt like a slap to hear them voiced. Anguish cracked her chest open, unleashing frustration and anger—at herself, for thinking her father cared and for ruthlessly pushing Jassyn until he broke.

What kind of monster am I to torment him about his contracts?

She gently knocked at Jassyn's office door for one last attempt at an apology, but only an oppressive silence answered.

Departing the Infirmary with a heavy heart, Serenna followed Centarya's central stream, wandering to an edge of campus. The storm traveled past without dispensing any rain, leaving behind a blustery breeze and flashes of lightning webbing across the sky.

Using stepping stones to cross the rippling creek, Serenna navigated to a rocky perch overlooking a waterfall. Crumbling on a boulder in the middle of the brook, she folded her legs to her chest. While clouds shielded the sun's descent, she detachedly watched the water cascading off the island.

Eyes burning, Serenna clutched her knees, unable to restrain the sorrowful emotions. Her self-loathing and remorse warred together in an eruption of grief. Tears welled, blurring her vision as she pressed a hand over her mouth to stifle a sob. Succumbing to her regret, she dropped her head in her hands to weep. Her crooked finger jutted out, an ugly reminder of her own cruelty.

Serenna knew she only struck out because she was upset about being helpless in the elven realm. Unleashing her anger on someone more vulnerable than her accomplished nothing beyond spreading more pain.

Heart aching, she rested her head on her knees, waiting for the torrent of tears to subside.

Serenna remained at the edge of the island until the stars kindled, shining through breaks in the clouds. The quiet sky offered no comfort while she wrung the misery from her soul.

A boot landed with a *thud* beside her.

Serenna jumped from the shock ripping through her chest. Vesryn's approach was silent compared to her calamitous thoughts and the bubbling stream. Consumed by her distress, she hadn't registered the prince's vicinity through the bond.

Serenna's heart thrashed in mute horror, barricading the breath in her lungs when Vesryn folded himself next to her on the boulder. There was hardly enough room on the rock to comfortably accommodate someone of his size, so she scooted toward the water's edge.

Vesryn's proximity invaded her senses with an eerie tingle. Her heightened awareness latched onto the nonexistent space between them. *What is he doing here?*

Pulling her knees tighter to her chest, Serenna swallowed, her breathing sounding too loud in her ears. Out of the corner of her eye, she studied the prince, doing her best to act like she was ignoring him. As if she could ignore the warm heat of his body radiating into hers through the pressure against her thigh.

Vesryn sprawled back, hooking his ankles and leaning on his palms, effectively taking up most of the limited space. Like the sun evaporating dew, the impact of his presence ebbed the flow of her tears. Serenna hastily wiped the dampness off her cheeks.

Was he flying today? The powdery reptilian smell of the dracovae wafted around them in the fleeting breeze. Vesryn idly picked at the boulder to dislodge a flake of a stone before dropping the loose gravel into the water with a *plop*.

The prince was the last person Serenna wanted to witness her crying, having already embarrassed herself enough in his presence. She would've preferred Ayla, Mishryn, and every other Alari initiate watching her wallow in misery instead of *Vesryn*. That he was seeing her so vulnerable sent a fresh flood of anxiety churning through her middle.

He broke the silence first. "Do you want to talk about it?"

Serenna's thoughts fragmented like a smashed pane of glass. *Is that why he's here?* She didn't know if she should laugh. "No," she hurriedly said, realizing he must've sensed her distress. She strained to hear past the thundering of her heart. *Why would he even care to ask?*

Vesryn shrugged, his shoulder muscles constricting with the motion before his attention drifted upward. Splashes of stars glittered in the sea of darkness, the horizon now devoid of clouds. Through their link, Serenna sensed the prince relax into shallow meditation.

His aura hummed. The enormous pressure of his power weighed on her like the ocean's squeeze during a dive. *Stars, how strong is he?* Essence whirled and coalesced around him while she felt his mind reaching a quiet regenerative state.

His magic shifted like a flock of starlings racing the wind, changing course with the drafts of air. The Essence at his disposal was a physical force—warping, shimmering, and crackling with palpable energy.

Serenna's erratic pulse showed no signs of slowing with Vesryn lounging next to her in such an ordinary manner—apparently comfortable enough to restore his magic beside her. She could admit his flustering presence would distract her from meditating.

But why would he be anxious like I am? It's obvious I'm being absurd. He just wants me to come into my power so I can sever this link between us. He did say the bond is an annoyance.

Serenna's thoughts wandered to Jassyn's repeated warning about the prince. *But Vesryn has the rangers' respect. He keeps the realms safe by hunting the wraith.* Her heart dropped. *But he also torments Jassyn with his servitude.*

And I'm no better.

Vesryn's magic stilled, like the calm after a storm. The splash of the stream was the only noise rushing past in its never-ending flow off the island. Wisps of spray from the water striking the rocks left a fine layer of mist lingering in the air. The tension from Serenna's shoulders slowly slackened while they sat in silence.

"Do you wonder why it's easier to regenerate our power under the stars?" Vesryn asked suddenly.

His eyes flickered with a flame of contemplation while he studied the sky. The light from the moons, one a waxing crescent, the other nearly full, set his unbound hair alight with a silver fire.

Serenna frowned. *Obviously, the stars are always present, even if we can't see them during the day.* "I assumed it was because of the elves' connection to the cosmos. I thought we just needed to reach a meditative state to replenish our power, but regenerating under the stars makes the practice easier."

"For some, it's possible to restore Essence at any time, but it's significantly quicker to regenerate when the stars aren't veiled. That galaxy there…" Vesryn leaned toward her and pointed above the horizon. Serenna's stomach lurched when his shoulder bumped hers. "The cluster with the blue stars in the middle and the surrounding spirals? I think that's the Aelfyn homeworld."

Serenna released an unbidden laugh but noted Vesryn's serious demeanor while he studied the sky. "You're joking, right?" The prince turned to meet her gaze, his eyes bright with the light of the universe blooming above them. "I know the elves *believe* they originated from the stars, but aren't those legends to make sense of their beginnings?" *I doubt they'd admit they came from the same place as humans.* "What makes you think that specific cluster of stars is their...homeworld?"

"Don't you feel the energy radiating from that galaxy? Doesn't it make you want to imagine there's something more up there?" Vesryn extended his hand as if trying to touch the astral light to harvest the gems from the blanket of sky. "Try focusing on those stars sometime when you're regenerating. I think you'll perceive a difference when restoring your power."

That doesn't explain how the Aelfyn came from the stars. Serenna didn't have an inkling about the truth of their origins, and she doubted the elves did either.

Vesryn's magic flared, curling around them, like a warm ocean breeze gliding across skin. A small light, mirroring the blue galaxy, hovered above his palm. The hanging light cast a cobalt hue across his features.

"So you think our power is drawn from a source somewhere in the galaxies?" Serenna asked, watching the glowing orb twinkle above his fingers.

"It makes sense, doesn't it?" Vesryn asked, studying her, like he was searching for something.

"Are you a scholar on top of everything else too?" she asked, not knowing what answer he wanted.

"Do I look like a scholar?" With a chuckle, the prince extended his forearms, flexing in a way that had Serenna rolling her eyes.

Lacing her hands around her knees certainly was *not* to restrain herself from running her fingers along the presented corded muscles.

"Nosing through books was my brother's specialty," Vesryn said with a sad smile, his eyes reflecting the memories of his past. "Even so, he was probably still a more formidable swordsman than me—at least back then. Though, I suppose he trained as much as he did so he had an excuse to spend more time around our captain." The prince shook his head and gave a snort. "Anyway, Aesar believed our race was removed from the origins of our magic for too long—perhaps a reason why Essence has started to fade."

Serenna studied the sky with an uncomfortable weight settling against her chest as the prince confided in her. The conversation seemed important to him, even though she couldn't guess why he shared more about his brother.

Vesryn turned pensive, staring out across the horizon, his eyes becoming as distant as the stars. "All we know for certain is that Aelfyn history began over five thousand years ago. What little else we know is hardly more than stories, passed down from the remnants of their people who crashed on the mortal shores."

"Do the legends say why the Aelfyn never tried sailing back across the Cerulean Sea? Couldn't they portal?" Serenna asked.

"The Maelstrom was to blame, and I think it's more than a storm." Vesryn split the illumination into dozens of glittering jewels that floated around them like hummingbirds. "I can't explain it. I've flown near the tempest on Naru, and the energy it emits is like nothing I've ever sensed before." He traced his lower lip in thought. "Someone may have created the storm—maybe the druids. The only explanation is that the Maelstrom's purpose was to prevent the Aelfyn from crossing the ocean. But to keep them on which side of the world is anyone's guess."

Before Serenna could ask more about the druids, Vesryn waved a hand. A rift opened above them. "And as for not portaling back..." Tiny white discs danced through the air, drifting to settle on their hair and shoulders.

She gasped, excitedly catching the fluffy flakes before they melted into her skin. "Is this *snow*?"

Vesryn extended his palm, and with a tangible *pull* of force, snowflakes mounded in his hand like a pile of sand. The prince flashed her a grin, sending her stomach fluttering. "Portals have limitations based on how strong the user is in the ability. From Centarya, some initiates can only create rifts to the Terminal below."

With a significant look at the gateway dispensing snowflakes, Serenna asked, "And I'm assuming *you* can open one anywhere?"

Vesryn raised his brows before tapping her nose in his aggravating way. "I think you're flattering me, Princess." He chuckled, fending off her defensive swipe. "You have to be familiar with both locations and have enough strength in your power to bridge the distance." He balled the snow in his hands before tossing the frosty globe to her.

Vesryn settled back, reclining on the boulder. "I can open a rift anywhere in the four realms from Kyansari, but only because the capital is centrally located. If I want to travel any farther, I have to portal jump—breaking up the journey into separate trips with multiple gateways."

Her fingers chilling, Serenna squeezed the snowball, letting the broken flakes drift through her hands. "So, the Aelfyn couldn't portal back because the ocean is so vast," she said.

"Most likely." Vesryn released his power and the rift above them faded. "Perhaps someday we'll find a way to travel to the other side of the world and discover if the ancient Aelfyn left anything behind."

"Discovering their origins would probably be important to the pure-bloods," Serenna mumbled.

Vesryn tilted his head.

"I mean..." She glanced away, finding the stream easier to look at. "I can't imagine the elves believe the elven-blooded also have a claim to the stars along with your Aelfyn ancestors." Serenna's throat constricted and she swallowed to stave off any reemerging tears. Strength fled from her voice. "Not while we share human blood."

She leaped up, searching to find another rock to jump to and escape. "Nevermind. That's stupid to voice."

Serenna's stomach jolted when Vesryn snatched her hand, his calluses scraping against her skin. He dragged her back to sit on the boulder.

"I don't think we're so different," he said as something strange dimmed in his eyes, his expression nearly softening to pity. "The bond linked our magic, after all."

Jassyn's warning circulated through Serenna's thoughts, her senses urging her to be wary. The prince hadn't exactly treated Jassyn as an equal. Focusing on the bridge between them, Serenna perceived no dishonesty. Vesryn felt...as melancholy as she did.

"I don't know if a relation to our Aelfyn ancestors is anything to be proud of," he said when she didn't respond.

Serenna shifted to get more comfortable and tried to pull her hand away, but Vesryn didn't let go. "But you—"

He gave her fingers a squeeze. "I said I was curious about what was out there, not that I wanted to be like them."

Serenna stared at their entwined hands before blinking up at him when he spoke.

"In my mother's library, my brother and I stumbled on an ancient text disclosing the Aelfyns' folly—the cause of their downfall. Instead of coexisting with other magics, our ancestors harvested dragons for their elemental power…or tried to."

Serenna stiffened, not daring to breathe when Vesryn brushed the back of her hand with his thumb. She assumed he didn't realize what he was doing.

"History has conveniently forgotten the rest, but I imagine the Aelfyn were to blame for starting the Great War." He shook his head. "Their pursuit of gathering power brought more than the end to the dragons—the magic of the druids and shamans also went extinct."

This must be what Jassyn remembered hearing in the palace. But why was their magic lost? The prince was unexpectedly giving credit to the human's folklore, too. *What other hidden knowledge is in his head?* Jassyn had already told her the extent of what he knew. If she didn't press too aggressively, perhaps she could uncover the truth in time.

"Your sigil." Serenna nodded at his uniform. "Is that why you wear a dragon instead of a dracovae like your rangers?"

Vesryn glanced at his armor and released her hand to tug at one of the frayed threads. For being royalty, the prince didn't maintain impeccable clothing like she'd expect. *He could certainly learn a thing or two from Jassyn.*

"The dragon was more so to piss my sire off." Vesryn emitted a humorless grunt. "I hoped to remind him of the Aelfyns' destruction in their search for a greater power—not that he pays any mind to anything I do beyond keeping a precise tally of my failures."

Vesryn's mouth twisted when the thread snapped, as if disappointed the strings broke free. *Well, what does he expect with the constant fiddling?*

With a drawn-out sigh, he said, "Really, it was a tough decision. I spent three years deciding between a dragon or two mating dracovae, but I thought the dragon would chafe at him more."

Serenna burst into a fit of laughter. She slapped a hand over her mouth to stifle it, not wanting to ruin the moment. The inappropriateness only made her suppress more giggles at the notion. Vesryn's lips twitched, restraining a smile.

"If you're entertained by the idea," Vesryn said, his eyes gleaming with mischief, "I can commission your tournament uniform to illustrate two copulating dracovae. It is a…*fascinating* sight."

"No, please," Serenna said with a laugh bubbling up. "I'd rather have the dragon. With no graphic details revealing its gender," she hastily added, feeling the need to specify. Serenna snorted when the visual formed.

Vesryn's brows shot up to his hairline at the sound she made, and he failed to contain his laugh this time. The booming vibration resonated through her chest. "Princess, I think your decorum is eroding the longer you're away from the civility of the human courts."

Struggling to rein in her humor, Serenna automatically smiled back. All she could focus on was the way her heart stumbled like it had joined the waterfall launching off the island. She hooked a stray lock of hair behind her ear, trying to avoid thinking about how she could get used to hearing the prince's rich laugh.

Flustered by his amusement, Serenna cleared her throat. "I'm not convinced you're the best influence in terms of propriety."

"I try not to be." Vesryn's teeth flashed again before he directed his attention to trailing his fingers in the stream.

Serenna watched the prince more openly this time, appreciating his profile, her involuntary smile lingering. From the sharp points of his ears to the cutting angles of his jaw to his piercing emerald gaze to —

The right side of his mouth quirked.

Oh stars, he has a sense of what I'm thinking through the bond. Beyond mortified, Serenna buried her face in her palms when Vesryn chuckled. His warm laugh only sent heat spiraling down her spine.

"Please tell me you can't read my mind," she pleaded.

Vesryn's amusement spiked. She risked a glance. He knew exactly what effect he had on her, judging by the cunning look reflecting alongside the starlight in his eyes.

Serenna considered jumping off the island.

"Don't worry," he said, drawing her hands away from her face. "Even with a telepathic link or a fully developed bond, your thoughts are your own unless you send them with direct intention."

Serenna's voice was strangled. "Then why did you give me that look like you knew what I was thinking?"

A shiver danced under her skin when Vesryn circled a finger up her arm.

"As I'm sure you've noticed," he said, "we can perceive each other. Even though this connection isn't nearly on the same level of...*intimacy* as an accepted bond."

Serenna swallowed when his evergreen eyes focused on her mouth. Vesryn's fingertips traveled up to her shoulder. He twirled a strand of her hair. She went totally still.

"For instance," he said, smirking, "you seem to receive no small amount of pleasure when you look at me, and I can feel how—"

Serenna cut him off with a strangled protest, shoving his arm away. "Okay, you win, you lout." She hoped the cover of darkness concealed the fire fanning her cheeks while he laughed.

"Do you want to get out of here?" he asked.

Serenna's stomach swooped. "What?" Not for the first time this evening, his question disarmed her.

Vesryn's leathers creaked when he rose. He reached down with an assisting hand. *How uncharacteristically chivalrous of him.* Serenna contemplated the gesture until he arched a brow, challenging. She clasped his fingers, prepared for his touch to send her magic speeding under her skin.

Vesryn released her as she stood. Leading, he navigated over the boulders of the stream.

"Why did you come out here?" Serenna ventured to ask, jumping to an adjacent rock to follow.

Vesryn glanced back at her as he entered a grove of birch trees. "Your misery annoyed me."

She released a breathless scoff. *There it is.* The familiar barb wrapped in the kindness he feigned. Whatever moment she thought they shared disintegrated, like the snowflakes he brought through the portal.

"Excuse me?" she asked, ducking under a branch. "I think I'm entitled to my emotions. Shouldn't there be a way to block out the other person through the bond? If sensing what I feel is so *annoying*?"

"Don't worry, I have a diversion planned to take your mind off of things." Vesryn glanced over his shoulder. "And besides, we need to begin training for the tournament."

Serenna couldn't decide if she wanted to find out what he regarded as a distraction. All she envisioned was counting how many rabbits he'd make her turn inside out this time.

Vesryn seized her hand. Green light flashed before a portal swallowed Serenna in a pocket of darkness.

CHAPTER 30

JASSYN

Jassyn stumbled to the chair behind his desk before he collapsed, his malice evaporating like a puff of steam. Tunneling his fingers through his hair, he stifled a defeated sob. The twinge of pain from yanking his curls stranded him to the present moment. He'd overreacted.

Significantly.

Guilt ravaged him, its razor talons slashing through his chest. Somehow, he had at least refrained from informing Serenna of Elashor's proposition to dissolve his contracts if they produced offspring together. He wasn't sure why he didn't want her to know. Perhaps he worried she would offer. And he refused to succumb to the general's manipulation by using her.

But every other admission was only to wound her in return—a wretched attempt at getting his power back in the most destructive way.

He knew Serenna's fiery attitude wasn't a character flaw—it was her backbone. And he belittled her for that, for having the courage to stand up for herself.

She was right. He was the one who was weak.

Jassyn flinched when a quiet knock sounded on the door, but he didn't have the nerve to answer, assuming it was her. Not until he composed himself and thought through an apology. Staring at the wavy grains in his desk, Jassyn held his breath, listening to his heartbeat until he heard footsteps retreating.

His arms propping his head shook while apprehension flogged his thoughts. Serenna's scathing comment couldn't have come at a worse time. Fear, transforming into shadows, edged at the corners of Jassyn's vision. He had to leave within the hour to attend the summons of Lady Farine.

Again.

At the rate Farine was going, she would exhaust her contractual allotments for the year before the summer, but what would stop her from demanding more? Jassyn scrubbed his hands over his face, swallowing a congealing panic.

He envisioned the worst—Elashor forcibly dragging him away from Centarya to present him to his mother in tethers. Unease over this not-so-improbable reality burned a hole from his mind straight down to his chest.

On unsteady legs, Jassyn rose from his desk, hoping enough time had passed for Serenna to leave the Infirmary. He wasn't ready to face her yet if she'd lingered. Not with his *obligations* looming over him like a noxious smog, plaguing his thoughts. And if he delayed any longer, he wouldn't be able to gather the strength to leave.

How many of his free days had he wasted in bed, unable to rise, blanketed by a fog of existential dread? *I don't have a purpose beyond fulfilling contracts. Not anymore.*

In a moment of clarity, Magister Thalaesyn had confided in Jassyn that he didn't believe there was a cure for elven sterility. The magister was losing hope, along with everyone else. Jassyn didn't know if it mattered. He had a feeling the council wouldn't release him, regardless.

But if he failed to attend to Farine when summoned, he couldn't imagine what would happen. Far too many people vanished with no explanation if they went against the council's wishes. *Does Vesryn hunt offenders like he does the wraith?*

Jassyn considered finding out. The brief freedom would be worth whatever punishment the council sent his way. *Maybe all of this would be over, then.*

After Farine, his cousin was the second-to-last person he wanted to think about. Jassyn couldn't say he was surprised Vesryn had claimed Serenna as his champion. Especially after her apparent proclivity for rending. *She can make her own decisions, but I hope she knows what she's doing.*

As his final ritual before leaving the Infirmary, Jassyn checked in on Magister Thalaesyn, who typically was in a stupor by the twilight hours. He wasn't helping himself to more Stardust this time—he already had an adequate supply.

When the opportunity presented itself, Jassyn took a few minutes to study the coercion on his mentor's mind and to ensure Thalaesyn was situated for the night. The magister spent more evenings on his couch than at his residence in the Spire.

Jassyn believed he was gaining a better understanding of the restrictive magic. He wondered if their relationship was stable enough to inquire if Thalaesyn was aware of the coercion. Even as a pure-blooded arch elf, the magister had always treated him with courtesy and respect.

Something was driving his mentor into a downward spiral of madness, and Jassyn wanted to help alleviate his distress.

What secrets did the king lock in Thalaesyn's mind?

Jassyn launched inquiries to his peers pertaining to the compulsive magic, asking offhand questions, but few elven-blooded were familiar with King Galaeryn's power. He found that no one else at Centarya was subjected to it.

Nelya informed him their mentor's rapid deterioration had begun when the council dictated Centarya's priority be a military operation. At the time, Jassyn was already assigned to Vaelyn.

Does his distraught behavior have to do with the threat of the wraith? Thalaesyn's banishment to Centarya occurred when the academy opened—not long after the creatures emerged. But the details around why the magister had fallen from the king's graces were kept quiet.

Jassyn doubted he could replicate the telepathic power the king had placed on Thalaesyn. Not that he had any desire to exert such control over another person.

But it should be possible to untangle the magic—Elashor unraveled the coercion on me. Perhaps I could loosen the magical bindings. Somehow.

Jassyn didn't know how the magister managed to instruct classes, demonstrate mending techniques, and regenerate his power, but Thalaesyn apparently found a balance consuming Stardust so his functionality wasn't completely impaired.

Regrettably, Jassyn started using a pinch of the drug in the evenings to encourage sleep when his breathing exercises failed to settle him. His mind drifted with worry that he was starting to look forward to that release every night. *It's not a dependence—it's a liberation.*

More often than not, the anticipation of feeling numb and letting everything go was the only thought keeping him afloat. That he had a tiny box of glowing blue powder in his chambers was his lifeline against the oppressive burden of a meaningless existence threatening to drown him.

Tonight would be different, though. He doubted losing consciousness was safe, but he didn't want to remember whatever the next few days would bring. It was a risk he accepted. He would do anything in his power to forget what happened at Farine's.

Placing a hand on the Infirmary doors, a wave of panic locked Jassyn's joints, plunging his mind into a sinkhole of despair. It was hard to breathe, the pressure in his chest increasing until he thought his ribs would crack under the strain.

Squeezing his eyes shut, Jassyn leaned his head against the door, unwilling to leave the safety of the clinic. Allowing a stray tear to fall, Jassyn tucked his anxiety away before distress permanently shackled his feet to the floor.

It's fine. You won't have to remember. Get it together. Shoving a hand through his hair, not even bothering to calm himself with steadying breaths, Jassyn yanked the doors open to walk back to the magus' quarters.

At his apartments, he packed a few sets of clothing. Like he was taking a trip. *A nightmarish sabbatical to look forward to.* He assumed Farine had outfits planned for him. His dread of the evening was tangible, dismay pooling in his stomach from the futility of it all.

Like a stone tossed across a pond's surface, Jassyn's eyes skipped over the package lying open on his table. He didn't possess the mental capacity to process the meaning of the *delightful* surprise Vesryn had left at his door.

At the same time, Jassyn was unable to resist the impulse to run his fingers over the garments. He'd never encountered a material so soft —even finer than silk.

He'd deciphered from Vesryn's nearly illegible blocky lettering that the apparel was *sleepwear*, of all things—spun from goat hair. Jassyn hadn't decided if the garment's intended meaning mocked his servitude. *I'm sure it's a slight.*

The prince disclosed this new "cazhmare"—spelled incorrectly, Jassyn realized after some research—was going to increase significantly in value because the wraith slaughtered shepherds and livestock. Vesryn thought he would enjoy the luxurious material, since he knew Jassyn liked "exquisite" things.

Like Vesryn knows anything about me.

Overwhelmed and at a complete loss as to what to do with the clothing, Jassyn left the package where it was. Too many components of the gift disconcerted him. *What in the stars possessed Vesryn to give me an item like this? Is he that insensitive or simply daft?*

Jassyn refused to consider his cousin as *thoughtful*. Like the prince found a bizarre crossroads between an indulgence for him to enjoy while exacting retribution against the wraith.

A wave of shame crashed over him. Jassyn recoiled from admiring the clothing as if burned. *How many humans went hungry or died bringing things like this to Alari?* He deserved the situation the council forced him into if he found pleasure in the goods the mortals suffered for.

Forgoing dinner, Jassyn took a portal from Centarya to Kyansari and then from the capital's traveling platform to Farine's estate. The

Vallendes were wealthy enough to employ their own staff of portal attendants. Not that they needed others to spin a rift, considering they were all arch elves. *But why exert yourself if someone else could do it instead?*

Situated on a significant plateau, the mansion crouched on the mountainside overlooking Kyansari and the Sapphire Basin. The glass spires of the capital reached up into the sky, the city glittering with light against the night. The height of the manor wasn't so great that it had him sweating.

Other reasons overshadowed that.

Under different circumstances, the view would have been stunning.

If genuine beauty could exist in a place so horrific.

Jassyn willed some steel into his spine, adjusting the pack on his shoulders as he entered the courtyard. Lightning darted through the gray clouds enveloping Kyansari. His hair stood on end, the danger from the skies as palpable as the horrors waiting within the estate. If given the choice, he'd stand in the middle of the storm instead of entering Farine's lair.

Fishing the box of Stardust from his trouser pocket, Jassyn opened the container and studied the glowing blue powder. His deliverance. The guards stationed around the manicured gardens ignored him.

Jassyn decided he wouldn't make the same gut-twisting mistake as his last visit—he planned on obliterating his mind *before* entering those ghastly doors.

Fingers tightening until they shook, he silently begged his body to take over. The thunder in the sky roared in time with the pulse in his ears. Strikes of lightning blinded him, searing afterimages behind his eyelids.

Opening his senses and a channel to Essence, Jassyn inhaled the powder, infusing himself with the Stardust's magic. Eyes watering, nose burning like he breathed in pepper, Jassyn didn't stop drawing the substance into his body.

Darkness shrouded his mind like a comforting cloud. Jassyn's anxious thoughts dissolved while his dread evaporated. His blinks became slow and drawn out, along with his heartbeats. As his consciousness drifted away, so did his worries.

With his awareness drowning in a sea of black, Jassyn never recalled the lightning he momentarily clenched in his fists.

CHAPTER 31

SERENNA

A screech tore through Serenna's throat on the other side of the portal. Her stomach plummeted as she teetered on the edge of the world. Vesryn's fingers curled around hers, stopping her from tumbling off a cliff.

Serenna's senses reoriented when her surroundings tilted back on their axis. She stood at the crest of a thundering waterfall that cascaded down to an immense body of water hundreds of feet below.

The lake sprawled out before her, stretching farther than she could see. Like gems glittering in the sun, the starry sky dispersed pinpricks of light above her. A fine mist swirled in the air as the river roared over the brink of the boulders, curving down in a jumbled torrent to greet the basin below.

Serenna clutched her chest as if she could haul on the reins of her cantering heart. "Do you always portal so close to the edge?" she asked over the clamor of the falls, her voice pitched an octave too high.

"Only to elicit a reaction," Vesryn said with a grin, tugging on her hand to lead her away from the brink. "And you did not disappoint. If we didn't share this connection, I wouldn't have realized how… dramatic human emotions could be."

"I'm more elf than human," Serenna muttered, unsuccessfully

attempting to reclaim her arm. "My feelings are hardly different from yours."

Examining the valley below from the vantage of the rocky plateau, she assumed they'd portaled to the Cerulean Basin. No other lake was nearly as expansive—on maps at least. A range of jagged snow-covered mountains framed the landscape, the silhouette of the peaks highlighted by the moons.

"It's nothing to be embarrassed by." Vesryn followed the bend of the river away from the waterfall. "I happen to think that trait of your personality is endearing."

Flushing because the prince had a personal window into her emotions, Serenna distracted herself by asking, "What are we doing up here?"

Vesryn released her hand as he seized his power. "I'm going to help you manifest force, since I assume it's only a matter of time before you retaliate with rending again." With a flick of his wrist, he cast a handful of silver orbs whirling, illuminating the surrounding space. "As entertaining as that was."

Serenna's brows jumped in surprise. "You remember which powers I have?"

He has a point. Probably. Force seemed like the next most useful ability—especially if Ayla continued to confront her.

Vesryn halted midstride, scandalization drawing his face into a frown. "I was there." He resumed walking away from the stream. "Since you're using emotions as a crutch to summon your abilities, force should be easy for you."

Along the shoreline, the eddies flowing around the boulders were less violent as the river split off into numerous channels. Smooth black pebbles scraped under her boots as Vesryn led them down a tranquil inlet.

Serenna poked at a light hovering next to her as she kept pace with the prince. Her fingers slipped through the magic. Igniting her own illumination would be useful so she didn't have to rely on Velinya to keep their chambers alight.

Unsure which feelings she needed to draw forth, Serenna reflected how she felt when she manifested rending and mending. Velinya used force to maneuver objects in their quarters by pushing or pulling on them—using the pressure of the earth or the mass of the items to move them through space.

"Force seems as if it's all about intention and determination," Serenna said.

"True. But there's another comparable feeling I think you'll find more…enjoyable to evoke in order to manifest your ability." Vesryn's eyes were bright in the moons' light.

Facing the water with the wave of a hand, he sent hundreds of stones sailing into the stream, as if demonstrating the talent. The gravel splashed, sending out rippling waves that lapped onto the bank.

Serenna's boot tapped on the pebbled shore while she waited, expecting the prince to say more. He was clearly withholding something, judging from that spreading smirk.

Suddenly, a pressure shoved her forward, like the magic Ayla used to launch her into the air. Losing her balance, Serenna stumbled, hands shooting out to brace her fall.

Vesryn blurred, dashing incredibly fast in front of her. Serenna clutched his waiting arms, catching herself before she crashed to the ground. He helped steady her with a wickedly feral grin.

"What was that for?" she demanded.

Vesryn's hands clamped around her like twin manacles of steel when she tried pulling back. Suspicion knotted in her gut.

Serenna's heart burst and disintegrated, battering the inside of her chest, as the prince's fingers bracketed her chin, tilting her face to meet his eyes.

"Read my emotions," he said, his evergreen stare penetrating her in the most uncomfortable way.

Heat rose in Serenna's cheeks at their proximity, but she couldn't look away, trapped in his gaze.

Unblinking, Vesryn sieved feelings through the bond, like sifting shells from sand. Pushing feelings at her intentionally, gently, like his fingertips stroking her face and arm, building static where they touched.

Serenna's eyes widened when phantom threads caressed her mind. Stiffening at the sensation, she inhaled a sharp and shallow breath.

Those certainly weren't *her* feelings. Blood skipping in response, her pulse scattered in every direction like an exploding star when a perceptible featherlight graze brushed down her neck.

"What…" Serenna cleared her throat. "What is that?" Her voice was weightless and breathy. Unrecognizable.

Releasing her chin, Vesryn whispered in her ear, "You tell me." His hands slid to her waist. She couldn't ignore the sweep of his thumb caressing the dip of her hip.

"I think"—Vesryn's fingers tightened around her middle—"you can call this"—he leaned closer and sent another rush of emotions through the bond—"desire."

The prince angled back to meet her eyes. Serenna's heart slammed against the inside of her chest, crawling up the rungs of her rib cage to perch in her throat.

She attempted a scowl. "You're out of your mind. I have no *desire* to manifest my power like that."

Vesryn's fingers constricted into an unyielding grip, like he heard her breathing the lie when she tried backing away again.

A tendril of longing brushed the corners of Serenna's thoughts like a current of wispy clouds floating down her cheek. When the invisible touch thumbed across her lips, her mouth instinctively parted.

A twist of tension lingered between them, but Vesryn's eyes never left hers. Ripples of lust, like gentle waves gliding over a sandy shore, flowed through the bond. Serenna's hands reflexively tensed on the prince's forearms as she forgot how to breathe.

"Stop it," she whispered in frail protest, if only to maintain a shred of her dignity. *He can't possibly be feeling this way.*

"I will." A smile crept across Vesryn's face before he lowered his mouth to hover over her neck. "If you can convince me you actually mean it."

Resolve splintering, Serenna shivered from the warmth in his words grazing her skin. *Bright stars.* The feelings the prince projected through their connection threatened to fling her toward insanity.

She gasped in surprise when Vesryn tangled a hand in her hair, cradling the back of her head. He caught the lobe of her ear with his teeth and tugged.

Serenna slammed her palms into his chest to shove him away, but all the strength drained out of her arms. Stars exploded behind her eyes when his mouth grazed the sensitive point of her ear. She fisted his leathers before her knees melted, shifting closer to him instead.

"Vesryn," she whispered with a vacated breath, unsure if it was a curse or a plea—if she wanted him to go further or stop.

As if hearing his name sparked a response, the prince released a sound somewhere between a growl and a groan, threatening to shatter any resistance she thought she had left. His lips skimmed against her neck, fanning flames that collected like coals low in her belly.

I can't let this continue. But Serenna's thoughts grew foggy, not making sense.

The prince's voice was a dark rasp in her ear. "Summon your power."

Serenna breathlessly laughed at the ridiculous order, her chest bumping into his. There was no way she could do anything with her magic—her power was busy enough slithering under her skin, flinging itself against her veins in an effort to reach him.

Vesryn's mouth traveled over her neck to the edge of her jaw, searing kisses along her throat like a riverbank flooding with flames of passion, setting her ablaze. His lips were a whisper, sweeping the soft skin at the curve of her shoulder.

Serenna burrowed her hands into the prince's hair. She slid the silky starlight strands through her fingers, pulling him closer.

Vesryn began untying the laces of her bodice, panting in time with her while he continued planting heated kisses across her neck.

Serenna blinked. He was undoing her ties with alarming speed, near frantic, unweaving and ripping the straps out of the loops.

I can't even undress this fast! She refused to let him have this much control. *How did he pull my chemise so low?*

Snatching his wrists, Serenna halted the prince's impressive progress. He reared back from her, glancing at their hands. His gaze lingered hungrily on her heaving chest until she spoke.

"You don't get to touch any more of me until you kiss me first."

Vesryn's eyes narrowed on hers before his nostrils flared. Serenna sensed a whiff of irritation and a gust of desire breeze through the bond.

Her heart bolted when the prince's mouth hovered over hers. Taunting. "Summon your power, then."

Serenna's thoughts dispersed like a shoal of scattered fish. Feeling reckless, she went to grab his face. The only thing she could think about was wrestling his lips to hers.

Only…he moved faster. The prince's iron grip clasped her forearms, keeping her hands in place. Serenna struggled against him.

Control gave way to chaos. An animalistic urge solidified, clawing at her mind. She flailed against him, overcome by a wild madness fueled by lust.

Vesryn breathed out a teasing laugh in front of her mouth. Serenna battled him to devour that sound. But reaching him was impossible. *Why won't he let me move? Isn't he feeling the same?*

"Use feelings of desire…" the prince said in a husky tone. "Summon force. If you can manage that…" He trailed off with the suggestion of more.

Serenna released a rough exhale of frustration while her breath sawed at her lungs. Through the bond, her kindling emotions mirrored his and ignited, consuming every other thought. Fire flooded her veins and burned against their connection.

Her magic flickered and then blazed into existence, invigorated by the challenge. Unformed Essence surrounded them, galloping in a spinning gale.

Trembling with frantic energy, Serenna corralled her erratic thoughts. She angled and steered her intentions toward the desire hovering between them. She plunged into the Well of her power, searching for her talent.

As if sensing what she needed, Vesryn reeled her in and sent a tide of passion sailing through the bond to guide her magic.

Serenna gasped and went rigid when his lips brushed her neck again in the softest caress. Her skin pebbled, every nerve combusting with the flames of desire. She dug her nails into his arms, releasing a whimper when his teeth scraped and captured the whirlwind of her heartbeat pulsing against her throat.

She gave in.

The prince's efforts against her neck doubled when she released a moan, as if her reaction spurred him. He trailed frenzied kisses across her skin, threatening to destroy her when his pants turned as desperate as her own.

There.

Launched by desire, force rushed into Serenna with a violent collision. Muscles trembling, her body thrummed with her power's raging energy. She didn't even care about summoning her magic anymore. What the prince was doing against her neck was more intoxicating than swimming in the sea of Essence.

I want him...

Vesryn erupted into wild laughter.

Jolted, Serenna blinked, her awareness flying back into focus. A crazed glint shone in his eyes, at odds with the ruddiness in his cheeks. At her dazed look, Vesryn burst into another cackling convulsion.

With a wheeze, he said, "Stars, I had to push you to the brink, didn't I?"

"Wh-*what?*" Serenna's disbanded thoughts staggered back in confusion. The insane lust threatening to consume her unraveled like thread on a dropped spool. The lingering vestiges of the heady emotion drifted away.

"*That* was a delightfully entertaining turn of events," Vesryn said, laughing as he released her.

Serenna gaped at him. *I don't understand.* The hold she had on her power flickered. She savagely snatched her magic in a tight fist. A fountain of Essence converged around her. She didn't think she could hang on to it.

He's laughing at me? Her mind pieced together the last few minutes—she'd been moments away from completely ravishing him. If he hadn't held her back, she would've forced herself on him like a mindless beast.

But now...now she realized his entire performance was a ploy to get her worked up enough to manifest her ability.

He used my emotions against *me?*

The magic racing through her veins bordered on the cusp of agony, a tight pressure building under her skin. Serenna's power pulsed within her embrace, Essence flaring around her as it threatened to spiral out of control. She didn't know what to do with the surge of power. The only thing she could think of was hurling her magic away in one violent release.

She shoved a hand forward and aimed everything at the prince.

Blue light blasted away from her palm. Serenna's magic streaked towards Vesryn like a ballistic arrow. The punch of force collided with the prince, whipping him off of his feet. He landed a few paces back with a crash on the ground, rolling over in a cackling fit.

Serenna didn't find the events as humorous as he did. *Did he assault me with his vile thoughts just to...arouse me?* Her skin crawled at the memory of his mouth against her. And she had *liked* it.

The thought drowned her in fury, the swell more violent than water gushing through a broken dam. Essence transforming, darkness sprang to life in a billowing storm cloud.

Vesryn pushed himself off of the ground and brushed the dirt off his leathers, chuckling.

"How dare you!" Serenna shrieked, stalking up to him. Her magic lashed around her, midnight shadows striking. "Is manipulating my emotions a *game* to you?"

Vesryn's eyes tracked her approach, obviously reading her intentions.

She didn't care. Serenna swung her arm with all her weight behind it to deliver a biting slap across his face.

He didn't stop her.

The blow landed with a *crack*, whipping his head to the side.

Serenna grabbed her stinging fingers. Her scathing scowl gave away the shame flushing through her, rooted in molten indignation.

"You bleached-haired bastard!"

With a wince, Vesryn rubbed his cheek, which was blooming a red streak in the shape of her hand. "I know, I know. I deserved that."

He suddenly grinned at her, not put off by her anger. Another lance of *his* desire speared through her chest.

Serenna's body seized. Her voice came out strangled and shrill. "Stop it!"

She stifled the sensation radiating from him. *How did I let myself fall into his trap? Feelings aren't facts. None of it was real.*

Vesryn kept a straight face when he asked, "Do you want your kiss now?"

Serenna bared her teeth.

She threw out a hand. A black tide exploded from her fingers, engulfing the prince in shadows.

CHAPTER 32

JASSYN

Jassyn twitched awake with a start. Sunlight streamed in through sheer curtains, rustling in the breeze flowing through the open windows. He tried to swallow, feeling so parched he feared his tongue had shriveled to dust. His head pounded like a flight of stampeding dracovae. Blinking at his surroundings, Jassyn oriented himself and rubbed his eyes.

He was alone at least.

Surprisingly.

This is a first. He assumed he must've satisfied Farine to earn such a *privilege*. Relief sluiced through him, like a cleansing rain. For once, he didn't wake up in a sea of unclothed strangers.

Jassyn sank deeper into the downy mattress while he stirred. The massive four-poster bed swallowed him. Similar to the palace, Farine furnished her estate in shades of white and silver. The drapes, wooden furniture, and tapestries canopied him like a snowdrift. *A little accent color would be nice.*

Aware he was distracting himself by forcing his mind to take an inventory of his surroundings, Jassyn squeezed his eyes shut. His stomach clenched with dread, wary of the events about to overflow into his mind.

Hesitantly, he thought back to when he'd portaled to the estate.

Except...

There was nothing.

Only the lightning branching across the sky when he arrived in the courtyard and then...darkness.

Blessed oblivion.

Blowing out a breath, the frozen feeling in his chest thawed like ice melting in a pond. *I did it.*

The door to the room swung open.

Flinching, Jassyn yanked the covers up to his chin.

But only a servant entered with a tray of steaming food. His stomach rumbled at the temptation, suddenly ravenous with a near dizzying hunger. Unwilling to guess how many times Farine had him healed throughout the night, Jassyn knew more than mending exacted a toll on his body.

"Lady Farine expects you to attend to her before the dinner bell," the elven-blooded woman said.

Bile snaked up his throat. *Of course she does.*

"What time is it?" Jassyn asked, averting his eyes to stare at the ceiling. Why couldn't Farine at least dress her staff appropriately? *Does everything about this place have to be so perverse?* The sheer fabric of the maid's outfit left nothing to the imagination.

"It's near midday. Our lady is most satisfied with your performance and is granting you a few hours to refresh. I'll return to assist with your bath—"

"No need," Jassyn interrupted. "I can ready myself."

The maid lingered at the edge of his vision while he waited for her to leave. "Lady Farine has selected your evening wear and has provided a gift for your enjoyment," she said, arranging attire on a dressing mannequin and placing a tiny, jeweled box on the table.

How generous.

Jassyn waved a hand, letting her know he'd heard. *I'm glad Farine remembered to feed her prized pet.* Or rather, he had *earned* a meal. Uninterested in dwelling on what he'd done to receive such an honor, Jassyn wondered if his mistress would force him to eat dinner out of her palm again. *That thought isn't any better.*

When the door clicked shut, Jassyn sat up with a groan, pushing his back against the headboard for support, each individual muscle screaming in a different way. Healing such discomforts would've been too much to ask. Besides, Farine would want to see the depravity painted on him, treating his body like her personal canvas.

Trailing his fingers over his neck, Jassyn assessed what damage she had wrought. *At least I didn't wake up in a collar again.*

He decided to seek mending in Kyansari for the superficial injuries before he returned to Centarya, rather than attempting to hide the wounds with an illusion he didn't have the strength to maintain. He didn't want to ask Serenna to heal him. It was bad enough that she could draw conclusions about what happened to him.

Guilt blurred his vision as his thoughts turned over memories of their fight before he left. *I'll try to make it right when I return. Only two more nights.*

Shoving off the plush covers, Jassyn swung his feet over the side of the bed in search of undergarments. *If there are any.*

His eyes popped.

Scorching stars! Farine had pierced his—

Jassyn gagged at the sight of the rings and studded jewelry glittering with Essence. He ripped the blanket over his lap as if hiding the decorations would make them disappear. *Why would... No, I don't want to know.*

At least someone had healed *those* punctures for him. Farine wouldn't tolerate anything that would hinder his performance.

Jassyn collapsed back into the bed, drawing his hands over his face, no longer interested in eating. Hopelessness turned over his stomach instead. Focusing on his breath, he wrestled every thought into counting the risings of his chest.

After a hundred cycles, Jassyn reluctantly acknowledged he should leave the jewelry. He was certain Farine would only pierce him again if he removed the gems. *Or worse. It's not like this body belongs to me anyway. So what does one more claim of ownership matter? It's a wonder the council even allows me to live at Centarya.* The brief illusion of freedom at the academy was laughable when he had to spend every waking moment strangled by dread.

Why not keep me locked away as a personal breeding appendage? Why bother with four slots on the contracts and limiting the handlers to four couplings a year? I should just ask to stay as one of Farine's companions while I'm at it. I would be more useful here anyway than wasting my time searching for a cure that doesn't even exist.

The food had cooled by the time Jassyn convinced himself to move. Defeated, he dropped into a seat at the table, not bothering to dress. He downed the pitcher of water and ate mechanically, not even tasting the roasted swan or sauteed mushrooms. Anywhere else, the exotic meal would have been a delicacy, but his motions were mindless, a feeble attempt to not dwell on what he couldn't remember or what was to come.

Intrigue kept sliding Jassyn's eyes to the delicate box. He assumed what its contents were. Hand trembling in anticipation, no longer able to resist the urge, he flipped the latch and swung the top open.

Crimson powder shimmered up at him. He wasn't familiar with this strain of Stardust. Jassyn could only assume the drug would enhance his *performance.* As long as it stole his awareness, he didn't care.

Regenerating and channeling magic was becoming a struggle, but he could manage. It wasn't like he consumed an exorbitant amount of the dust at Centarya. Just enough to take the edge off and keep his trepidation at bay.

In bleak spirits, but feeling slightly more alive after the meal, Jassyn glanced around the room, wondering how he'd gotten there. Rising, he inspected the clothing Farine had chosen.

It was an exquisite three-piece suit, striking in color. Deep purples were the rarest and most expensive dyes imported from Allaenar's coast. Jassyn's fingers traveled over the garment. He scoffed. Of course, it was crafted from the same cashmere fabric Vesryn had gifted him.

The coverings were unexpectedly decent, like they were attending a ball. An emerging weight of nausea almost made him vomit. He hoped he wouldn't have to go anywhere with Farine wrapped around his arm. How many would she make him service tonight?

It doesn't matter. I won't remember anyway.

Meandering through the chambers in search of the bath, Jassyn opened a door to discover a study. Detailed maps of the four mortal realms covered each of the expansive walls. Frowning but cautiously curious, he ventured farther into the office. Easels draped with sheets of paper bordered the perimeter of the room.

Jassyn wandered to a stand and studied the parchment, which was covered in writing rather than paint. The words appeared to be family names. *Human* names arranged in trees. *That makes no sense.*

Did these chambers belong to Elashor's sire? Fynlas Kovaer had disappeared in a wraith attack when Jassyn was young. Fynlas was an archivist, and Elashor always kept that fact about his sire quiet, as if being related to a historian embarrassed him. The general opted to take his mother's name, despite Fynlas being a confidant to King Galaeryn.

And we're all aware of how close Elashor is to the king.

Fynlas had been one of Farine's…companions who lived at her estate, but she obviously never bound herself exclusively to anyone. Jassyn knew of at least two females and three males who maintained a permanent residence in the manor. But it still baffled him that Farine had dabbled with a scholar.

Jassyn looped around the room until he came to the northern realm, his sire's homeland. A breath snared like a tangled briar in his chest while he studied one of the family trees. A lone circled name jumped out at him. Jassyn ran his fingers over the letters, disbelieving, as if touching the words would offer an explanation.

It was his. *Is this…my human line?*

Jassyn swallowed a disgusted feeling, jerking his attention away from the scores of names below his, written in a different hand. He'd never attempted to discover the offspring he sired even though he assumed a few were at Centarya.

Why would an elf trace my mortal lineage? How had Fynlas tracked it? His ancestral tree covered thirty-two generations, spanning all the way back to the apparent arrival of the Aelfyn, judging from the years. Jassyn studied the chart, thoughts wavering like a mirage.

What does it mean? Frantic, he dashed to the other easels in the room and scrutinized the genealogies, paying attention to the names close to the bottom of the sheets. He recognized more than half.

The circled names belonged to those forced into servitude to the realm, bound with breeding contracts like him. He struggled to grasp why these specific human families had been traced throughout the years. His mother's line was why the elves wanted him, not his mortal sire's.

Jassyn wobbled on his feet, the blood draining from his head. *Was I produced...intentionally? Along with these other people?*

This research must be the reason for Elashor's obsession with him bedding Serenna, but he didn't see her name among those listed. Why would it matter if they joined their human lines? The elves cared nothing for mortals beyond their usefulness in providing resources. Or so he thought.

Jassyn desperately leafed through a stack of books on the desk. Farine must have wanted him to discover this. She wouldn't have put him next door to the room with this information otherwise. *Is she playing another perverse mind-control game?* It would be like her to find a sick new way to assert her dominance over him—she had already grown bored subduing him with her magic.

Rifling through a tome, Jassyn paused and flipped back the page. His gaze landed on an image depicting a five-pointed star. The ink was so faded, it was difficult for him to decipher. An illustration accompanied each point to the shape. Elements.

Fire. Water. Earth. Wind. Lightning.

Shamans.

Fynlas traced the ancestry of human lines possessing the ancient power. And somehow the elves had curated them, binding those lines to the realm, breeding more offspring.

Whirling around, Jassyn scanned the scattered research. *Elemental powers don't exist. Not anymore.* The magic had gone extinct, suffering the same fate as the druids and dragons. *Surely we would've seen evidence by now if humans could manipulate such power.*

After disturbing the books, Jassyn noticed the top of another family tree buried on the desk. Retrieving the paper, he blinked upon reading the name at the bottom. The blood in his veins chilled like an arctic wind howled through him.

It was Serenna's.

CHAPTER 33

SERENNA

Serenna and Velinya lounged on the grassy lawn in front of their dormitory, basking in the sunshine during their free day of the week. They waited for Magus Nelya to escort a trip to the Terminal. Serenna was eager to spend more time exploring the budding town.

A soft breeze whispered through the trees, rustling the leaves and swaying the flowered vines. Opening a hand-size gateway between them, Velinya practiced portaling. The other end of her rift unfolded a few feet higher in the sky.

Using stubborn determination instead of *desire*, Serenna summoned her newly manifested ability. She swirled blue tendrils of force around a white flower hanging in a nearby willow tree.

Encompassing the plant with a pocket of Essence, she plucked it off the swinging vine. With her fingers twirling—which wasn't necessary but helped channel her focus—she pulled the threads of magic to prod the blossom toward Velinya's fabricated portals.

But Serenna struggled to manipulate her power. Her concentration continuously flickered, her Essence actively fleeing. The flower dropped through Velinya's gateway and tumbled away on a breeze.

Serenna sighed, knowing her distracted thoughts were to blame for her wavering control. Her heart fell, thinking about Jassyn facing those horrors in the capital—remembering the hurtful things she'd said to him before he left. He wouldn't be returning until sometime in the evening.

That, and her *lesson* with Vesryn. Serenna clenched her teeth, furious with herself for allowing the prince to manipulate her to the brink of carnal insanity. Now, every time she drew forth force, she had to stifle memories of exactly *how* he'd pried that power out.

Desire emotions don't have to be sensual.

When Vesryn had portaled her back to Centarya three nights before, Velinya hounded her on why she'd returned so late into the evening. After an extensive interrogation, Velinya remained thoroughly unconvinced there *wasn't* anything going on between Serenna and the prince.

Serenna finally relented, admitting to training as his champion. Ignoring Velinya's appraising look at the blatant evidence on her neck, Serenna couldn't bring herself to mention what had transpired beyond manifesting her force talent. Regardless, her friend promised to keep the details of their "training" to herself.

Vesryn must have perceived the molten river of her anger and surprisingly had enough sense to let her cool off. Serenna had thrown the entire supply of her power against him in a blind rage.

Of course, the bastard found it thoroughly entertaining as he effortlessly fended off her assaults with shielding, *taunting* her to the point where she had channeled her magic until she'd completely drained her Well.

Serenna wasn't ready to face the prince yet, or examine why he'd elicited such a passionate response from her. It was embarrassing enough that her emotions were on display for him. *Jassyn warned me about Vesryn's reputation; his obscene behavior shouldn't surprise me.*

"I'm starting portal rotations this week," Velinya said, chattering away.

With a slight flash of guilt for not paying attention to whatever campus gossip Velinya had been spreading the past few minutes, Serenna refocused on her friend. She found it difficult to care about who was coupling with whom when there were bigger problems, like

Jassyn's forced servitude and the wraith targeting those in the mortal realms.

"I'll be traveling to various locations with the magus to learn common waypoints so I can assist with transporting people to and from Centarya," Velinya said, twining a golden curl around her fingertips.

"You'll have to give me lessons when I manifest," Serenna said. She wasn't scheduled for portaling class until the summer, but she suspected Vesryn had his own ideas for the timeline of her education.

Serenna could only guess what *exercises* he had planned to ensure her a head start. Especially considering trust and yearning were emotions the magus elicited to draw forth portaling. Serenna nearly buried her face in her palms as she realized how close *yearning* came to *desire*.

A senseless, idiotic curiosity gripped her while she considered what methods Vesryn might employ to extract her remaining abilities. Heat rose to the tips of her ears—she could almost feel his teeth tugging on her skin again. *Stars, I doubt I could focus on my power if he—*

Serenna ruthlessly throttled those thoughts. Nails digging into her palms, she remembered Vesryn laughing at her after she'd melted into his arms.

The feelings he projected mean nothing, she told herself for the hundredth time. *All he's doing is exploiting this bond to manipulate my emotions. He's probably only "training" me for his own entertainment, and getting some demented enjoyment for his efforts.*

Velinya sighed with a faraway look past her rift. "I just love how romantic portals are."

Yanked out of her inappropriate thoughts, Serenna paused, hovering another flower above their heads. She glanced toward her friend skeptically. *"Romantic?"*

"Apparently, you can weave a portal to a place you've never been before," Velinya said, opening and closing another set of gateways, positioned farther apart in the sky this time.

Serenna released her power and rolled over onto her stomach to face her friend, resting her chin in her palms. "I thought you had to be familiar with both locations to open a rift?"

"If you share a bond with someone, you can travel to wherever the other person is, or get close to the location if you're strong enough—even if you've never been there before. So you'll always be able to find each other." Velinya sighed, thoroughly romanticizing the idea. "I hope to create that type of connection with someone."

Serenna suppressed a shiver. That must've been how Vesryn had traveled to her in Vaelyn when he'd sensed their link.

"But what if you can't portal? Like Jassyn?" Serenna asked. "Not everyone has the ability."

Velinya frowned. "Well, I guess it doesn't work, but you can still perceive the direction of the other person."

Serenna was aware of that; she typically felt Vesryn traveling from Centarya to stars knew where. Just this morning, he'd disappeared from the island, but she didn't have any idea where he was beyond somewhere to the far west. *Probably hunting wraith.*

Still, she perceived the shadow of his presence lurking in the corner of her mind. Sometimes, she thought he was in two places at once, but perhaps she wasn't strong enough to sense his changing location if he flew rapidly through the skies on Naru.

"You'd really want to create a bond with someone?" Serenna asked. "I heard it's not a common practice anymore."

"We were on the topic in class, and some of the magus believe combining power might offer advantages in war. A few have even bonded intentionally to put the theory to the test," Velinya said, corralling the mass of honey-colored curls into a tail at the top of her head. "Wouldn't a magical connection with someone be exciting? The bond certainly doesn't have to lead to anything *romantic*, but the link can develop into something deeper than kinship." She tossed the gathered hair over her shoulder.

Serenna hadn't shared the details of her connection to the prince with anyone. It was only a matter of time until she learned enough about her magic to reject the bond, as Vesryn intended. *It'll hover as an annoyance*, he'd said.

Serenna wasn't interested in dwelling on why her stomach dropped at the thought. *Neither of us asked for it,* she reminded herself.

It wasn't like there were any *advantages* for them without the connection being fully formed.

"Oh, Nelya's here!" Velinya said, disbanding Serenna's thoughts. Both women rose to join the group of initiates gathered around their residence hall.

On their way to the Portal Platform, the recruits engaged in excited gossip about the Essence Tournament. Lately, every conversation strayed toward activity at the coliseum. The academy buzzed with frenzied energy like a hive of honeybees at any mention of the games. The magisters and magus had already selected notable initiates as their champions. To no one's surprise, nearly all contestants came from Alari, but that didn't prevent enthusiasm from spreading.

Like most of the mending magus and researchers, Nelya declined to participate in the tournament as a trainer. "I think our time is better spent elsewhere than on this…*entertainment*," she said when asked.

A trip through a portal transported the group to the Terminal below. Once there, they were free to wander as long as they agreed to take a gateway back to Centarya before the rising of the second moon.

Velinya and Serenna began their afternoon of exploration, meandering down the gridded cobblestone streets. The town was unrecognizable from the last time Serenna had passed through a handful of weeks ago with Jassyn.

White limestone shops dotted the major avenues. The upper levels of the tapered buildings contained apartments for the shop owners and other permanent residents of the growing city.

Elven-blooded vendors flocked to the open-air market to display their wares. Their canvas tents rippled in the breeze like clothes on a line.

"What do you think I can get for Jassyn?" Serenna asked after sharing with Velinya that she owed their friend an apology. "Maybe a set of those plated ear cuffs he favors?"

They found a jewelry vendor, and Velinya helped her select a silver pair. The delicate metal whorls twisted into a decorative leaf at the point. Serenna knew the gift didn't absolve her behavior, but she hoped Jassyn would appreciate the gesture.

Velinya let out a squeal and grabbed Serenna's arm. Serenna glanced up from settling the payment with the elven-blooded merchant. The vendor collected about a quarter of the Essence from the vial Vesryn had provided as her stipend, transferring the orb of light into another bottle.

Elashor strode toward them dressed in casual wear, still imposing as if he were in the capital's snowy armor. He wore a crimson brocade jacket open to reveal a white-laced tunic tucked into dark breeches. His shiny boots flashed in the sunlight with every step forward on the street.

Serenna went rigid, the hairs lifting on her arms. She swallowed a sharp feeling, recalling Jassyn's admission on why her father had actually brought him to Vaelyn as her tutor. She doubted he would bring it up anyway, considering she hadn't heard from him since he *exhibited* her to the prince the day he'd dumped her off at the academy.

He had time to speak to Ayla and to invite her to the Lunar Solstice. Jealousy morphed into disappointment and burned in her chest like dry kindling. *I don't need to be his favorite,* she admitted, *but it would be nice to feel like I matter.*

But Velinya's reaction had Serenna rolling her eyes. "Please tell me you don't *fancy* my father."

"I definitely fancy your father." Velinya straightened her hair and went so far as to loosen the laces of her bodice. "You're probably not the person I should tell where I'd let him chisel me with that jaw. I can't decide if I prefer the points of his ears or the width of his shoulders."

Serenna gaped at her friend as a disturbed feeling scratched at her skull. "Maybe if you keep staring like a stargazer, you'll figure it out," Serenna snapped as he approached, trying to erase the unsettling images Velinya had planted in her head.

"I'm glad I ran into you," Elashor said.

Serenna crossed her arms as he rewarded Velinya's efforts with an appraising look, spending an indecent amount of time fixated on the expanse of cleavage her friend had just exposed.

He lazily returned his attention to her. "The magus at Centarya said you were taking advantage of the Terminal today. Come walk with me."

Serenna handed Velinya the remainder of her stipend, telling her to spend it. She was amazed her friend even noticed, as she was thoroughly preening under Elashor's leer.

"Will you be around?" Serenna asked, tempted to snap her fingers in front of Velinya's face. She was about ready to shove her friend down the street before any *chiseling* took place in the middle of the market.

Velinya nodded, her attention on giving Elashor a coy smile. "I'll join everyone else at the winery."

"How are your studies?" Elashor asked as they started walking side by side down the gridded street, passing the vendors.

"I've manifested half of my abilities," Serenna said hesitantly. With the void in her heart, she wasn't sure how to pretend everything was fine.

"That's excellent news." She flinched when he squeezed her shoulder. "What about combat training?"

Serenna winced and directed her gaze to the end of the alley toward the shimmering waters of the Cyan Mere. "I was assigned to basic conditioning to start, but the magus advanced me to fundamentals last week."

"I wish we would've had more time to prepare you, but the decision to send you to Centarya occurred faster than I expected." A weapon merchant's tent caught Elashor's eye. He drifted over to browse the jeweled daggers displayed on a table.

"Word reached me that you've been the only initiate to violate Prince Vesryn's stipulation on rending?" Elashor thumbed a blade with an unreadable look. "He spent a fair amount of time assuring the council he could maintain order among the recruits. It's embarrassing that my daughter cannot heed her prince's commands."

Shock had Serenna dropping her jaw. She stared at her father, his words wrapping around her head like a gnarled rope. Unconsciously, she concealed her mangled hand behind her back. *Vesryn hardly seemed concerned. Surely he didn't say anything.* A multitude of thoughts warred in her mind. *Ayla must have told him.* Serenna refused to accept her father's chastisement and met him with a flurry of objections.

"Did these rumors mention *why* I violated Vesryn's rules? Your *other* daughter has done nothing but harass me the entire time I've been at the academy." Serenna fought the losing battle of keeping the hurt out of her tone. "So kind of you to inform me I had more siblings."

Frustration and sadness made her chest tighten with rejection. *I'm never going to be important enough to him.*

Elashor regarded her with an aggravatingly level look before leaving the vendor's tent. His lengthy stride forced Serenna to hasten her pace to catch up.

She wasn't sure why she followed. Perhaps there was a pathetic part of her still hoping she could earn his approval. He remained silent as they passed a group of recruits walking in the opposite direction.

"So, you're on a first-name basis with the prince?" he asked, keeping his attention focused ahead.

Serenna gave a breathless scoff. *Of course, he's ignoring everything I said about Ayla.* Obviously, the only important matter to him was her progress weaseling into Vesryn's bed. Which was the *last* thing on her mind. Uninterested in what he thought, Serenna decided to keep her "affiliation" with the prince to herself.

Elashor swiveled to hook her with an uncomfortable stare when she failed to provide an answer. "I see you're still embracing your human modesty. I'll permit it for now, so long as your *familiarity* with the prince increases. As for my lineage, I assumed Jassyn would have filled any gaps in your knowledge, given that his only concern was your education."

Serenna ground her teeth. She wouldn't blame Jassyn for her father's behavior or lack of involvement.

"I happen to think some matters are beyond Jassyn's responsibilities," she bit out.

Elashor grunted, steering them out of the market street to the edge of a pier. Gentle waves from the Cyan Mere brushed against the shoreline. Serenna watched an eagle plunge into the lake after a fish.

Her voice dropped to a whisper, but she had to know. "I saw what your mother did to him. Are you aware of what she forces Jassyn to do? It's…it's not right."

Elashor expelled a snort, making her stiffen. A sneer twisted his features into something sharper. Disdain. "Jassyn does his duty as a half-breed should."

Serenna's stomach roiled. *The elves already treat us as lesser. Can't we at least have control over our own bodies?*

Assembling all of her courage, she asked, "Is there any way you can convince the council to release Jassyn from his contracts?"

Elashor chuckled like her request was preposterous. He turned to face her. "Jassyn could have *released* himself. I've already offered him a resolution to his obligations, but I'm assuming he's told you nothing about our arrangement."

Serenna tensed, an icy wariness frosting her veins. "What arrangement?"

"I informed Jassyn I would see to the dissolution of his existing contracts with only one condition." Elashor leaned against the railing, utterly at ease. "All that half-breed has to do is provide me with an offspring." His piercing eyes hooked on her in a raptorial fashion, like the talons of the bird clutching the struggling fish above the lake. "One offspring. With you."

Serenna staggered back as if he'd struck her. "What?" Flames leaped to singe her cheeks despite the absence of a physical blow. "Why?"

Elashor shrugged but didn't answer her question. "He's either too stupid or full of pride—I haven't decided which."

Breathing became difficult. Serenna's ribs constricted to the point of discomfort. *He has that much control over Jassyn's fate?* She clutched the pier's railing for support before her knees could collapse under the weight of his conditions. Her mind raced, spinning in violent circles. *He tried to orchestrate Jassyn and me to…?*

But why didn't Jassyn mention that my father offered him a way out of his contracts? Serenna saw the destructive effect the duties had on him. And yet Jassyn had never coerced her into it. He even pushed her away as soon as she showed interest when they met.

He's too honorable. Far more than the male in front of her.

An angry fissure cracked inside of her. What gave her father—or *any* elf—the right to treat the elven-blooded in such a way? They had stripped him of all reasonable choices and subjected Jassyn to injustice his whole life.

"If Jassyn is important to you, it shouldn't be too much to ask," Elashor said, his voice edged in steel. "He has the modesty of a human, so you two have something in common. But I'm sure with a little convincing, you could change his mind." His knuckles tightened around the railing. The wood creaked under his grip. "You should have been providing my line with heirs by now, but nothing has gone the way I intended for you." His voice dropped to a mutter. "At least I secured your sister an acceptable match."

Serenna's eyes shifted under his penetrating gaze. Her father's desires for her future made her uncomfortable. She stared into the distance, watching Centarya's waterfall cascade into the center of the lake.

Serenna's heart splintered, knowing he cared nothing for her beyond her breeding potential, like Jassyn had said. Elashor's treatment of her indicated that he wrapped any approval in sharp edges. Serenna swallowed to dislodge the lead weight sinking in her throat.

She knew neither she nor Jassyn would choose to have offspring together. But Jassyn had already shielded her by continuing to suffer instead of taking the presented way to freedom. *Isn't it time I do something for him?*

Serenna clenched her teeth to prevent her voice from shaking. "If I do this, you will see that the council releases Jassyn from his contracts? *Permanently?*"

Elashor nodded. Serenna looked away, blinking back tears. She didn't want to show him any weakness. He would only use any shortcomings against her.

CHAPTER 34

SERENNA

Serenna spent the twilight hour flinging knives at a wooden practice target. Hurtling her frustration in the Combat Yard was more appealing than running laps around the island. She whipped herself into a frenzy after seeing her *sire* earlier in the day.

She wanted nothing to do with Elashor or his terrible demands, but couldn't see how else to help release Jassyn from his contracts. Nausea brewed in her gut and fermented into a sick tang of disgust for her friend's situation and the demeaning way the realm treated the elven-blooded.

Knowing Jassyn had refused Elashor's offer of freedom had her heart sinking into a mire. Jassyn had spared her from sharing in his fate, shielding her from the horrors he lived through by denying Elashor.

But if he'll let me help him, I will. He doesn't have to go through this alone. Not anymore.

"You've been angry lately," a low voice said behind her.

The steel hilt in Serenna's palm trembled before she sniffed, taking a step forward to ready herself for another throw. *I'm not in the mood to deal with him, either.*

"What an astute observation, Commander," she replied tartly, keeping her back to him. "Was that your own clever deduction, or did you have to read the bond to reach that obvious conclusion?"

With a violent catapult of her arm, Serenna released the blade. The weapon sailed end over end across the yard. The dagger crashed, skidding on the ground, not even striking close to the target. Just like all the others scattered in the sand.

"Dracovae's tits!" Vesryn swore.

Serenna frowned, mouthing the unfamiliar curse. *Dracovae's what?* She gripped another knife. *But dracovae don't—*

Vesryn's footsteps hammered against the earth. Serenna glanced over her shoulder as he stalked toward her.

"Which magus taught you this grip? Is *that* how they're instructing you?" Vesryn grabbed her hand and rearranged her fingers. "These are throwing knives, and they're weighted in the front, see?" He trailed a finger along the edge of the blade. "The load makes them more accurate than other daggers, but you have to hold them differently."

Baffled, Serenna blinked up at him while he hovered around her like an agitated mother hen. "Your feet need to anchor your weight to the ground"—he kicked back one of her boots—"so you can keep your balance."

The prince seized her right hip and twisted. Serenna released a squawk of protest when Vesryn pulled and shifted the angle of her shoulders. Reaching down, he turned her legs and pointed. "Your knees will follow where your feet point."

Obviously.

Vesryn backed up a pace with a self-satisfied air unfurling around him.

"Try that," he said, nodding to himself in approval.

Serenna refrained from explaining she hadn't learned knife-throwing. She wasn't *practicing*—this exercise was about releasing her anger.

And he's thoroughly undoing all my efforts! Serenna flipped her braid over a shoulder, rankled by his intervention.

"Don't lock your knees," the prince said behind her.

Grinding her teeth at Vesryn's instruction, Serenna loosened her limbs before whipping her arm, letting the knife fly. It *thunked* as it struck the wood. For the first time. She expelled a huff of annoyance.

The prince's baritone chuckle reverberated through her chest, striking a chord that strummed up her spine. Silently fuming, Serenna wished it were possible to conceal her reactions through the bond.

Her voice was accusing. "Don't you have something better to do?"

Serenna marched the handful of steps toward the target to retrieve the strewn blades. Vesryn kept pace with her. She glanced to the opposite side of the ring, where the magus and recruits engaged in extracurricular combat. "Shouldn't you be sparring at this hour?"

Vesryn glanced at her sideways. "I'm touched you know my schedule."

Serenna shot him a scowl.

The illumination hovering above the yard reflected the amusement in his jade eyes. He tucked stray hair from his half knot behind a pointed ear.

Serenna's hand jerked at the memory of those silver strands slipping through her fingertips. Her attention hooked on the tilt of his lips, remembering how his mouth had burned against her skin.

Serenna ripped her gaze away, upbraiding her mind for admiring his features.

"I wanted to ask what has you so worked up." Vesryn retrieved one of the dispersed daggers on the ground. "I doubt it's the throwing knives, despite how spectacularly you've missed the target." He flipped the blade into the air and caught it.

Serenna let his comment bounce off her. "Why do you care?" With a yank, she ripped the lone knife buried in the wood free. "Have you returned to entertain yourself at my expense or are you here to manipulate my emotions further?"

She stopped there, but really wanted to ask what everything had meant so her heart could stop spiraling in a loop of uncertainty.

Am I the only one imagining this friction between us? Or is it just the bond?

"Did I…do something?" Vesryn asked carefully. Too casually.

Serenna faced him with a disbelieving scoff. She hated how concerned his eyes looked in the fading light.

His attention flickered to her fists, clutching the knife at her side, before he offered the remaining collected weapons to her, hilt first. Serenna had half a mind to rip the daggers out of his hand to slice his fingers.

"Don't play stupid with me," she snapped. "Did you forget how you *toyed* with my emotions like I was some puppet? Or is that typical behavior I should expect from you during *training*?"

She didn't have the patience tonight to engage in the game of asking him a hundred questions only to receive deflections.

Vesryn faltered, his jaw working silently. A flush singed the tips of his ears. Serenna stared. *Surely the* prince *isn't blushing.*

His eyes darted across her face. "I didn't intend for everything to go so far."

"Well, what did you intend, then?" Serenna pushed, not falling into the intensity of his stare.

The prince must have extrapolated that she would've allowed his charade to continue if he hadn't jolted her out of the moment with his laughter. But apparently they made a silent mutual decision to pointedly ignore that piece of information.

"You found my reaction *hilarious.*" Serenna snatched the knives out of his grip. Vesryn's hand jerked back before the steel could bite into his flesh. "I don't appreciate you using the bond against me."

"I…" Regret rolled down their connection like raindrops running off glass. Vesryn swallowed, his gaze drifting away from hers. He apparently needed to unravel a loose thread on his uniform's dragon. "I won't do it again."

Serenna narrowed her eyes, gauging his sincerity. *That's not an apology.*

"I didn't know you would… I've never used a bond in that way before." The prince hesitantly met her stare as he rubbed the back of his neck. "Elves don't display such raw emotions, and yours are so close to the surface. I thought it would be easy to bring your power forth if you had a little encouragement."

"Well, it worked," Serenna spat.

Vesryn defensively held up his hands, as if warding her off. "I'll admit I got carried away and swept up by what you were feeling."

"Don't you dare blame your filthy behavior on me," Serenna seethed, shaking a knife at him. "I hope you're pleased with your experiment on my *human* emotions."

Stalking back across the ring to reposition herself, she decided she was quite finished being embarrassed by that evening.

Vesryn's thought brushed her mind, softer than a feather's caress gliding across her cheek. *I like your human emotions.*

The daggers fell out of Serenna's hand and clattered against each other in the sand. She tried convincing herself she'd imagined the prince's words while retrieving the blades.

Unable to voice a response, she asked through Vesryn's telepathic link. *Why?*

It's like seeing a kaleidoscope of colors when I've been living in black and white. Letting the human side of you feel is nothing to be ashamed of. I'm sorry I used that against you.

Serenna swallowed several complicated emotions threatening to constrict her throat. Her vision swam while she stared at the daggers shaking in her fingers. *If I cry in front of him again, I'll die.*

She'd spent her entire life embarrassed by her human heritage and how it had drawn a line between her and the elves. Her time at Centarya only made her realize the elves would never accept her because of it. But the prince—of all people—*liked* that about her?

She glanced in Vesryn's direction to find his gaze already locked on her. Serenna's heart fluttered against her chest from his attention.

"May I?" he asked, extending a hand.

She cleared her throat before dropping the cluster of knives into his waiting palm.

Vesryn's eyes pinned on her mangled finger. "Why haven't you had that mended?"

Serenna crossed her arms to hide her hand. "You made the disfigurement permanent by trying to *mend* it." She scuffed the sand with her boot. "It needs to be broken again before Jassyn can heal it properly."

"Oh." Vesryn's brows pinched together. "That wasn't my intention." With a roll of his shoulders, he positioned himself to throw a blade.

"Well, let me know when you want to have it healed, and I can absorb the pain for you."

Serenna's heart skipped before burrowing uncomfortably in her chest. Vesryn's eyes flitting to hers had Serenna pursing her lips. *No. He doesn't get to pretend like he suddenly cares.*

After flipping a knife in the air, Vesryn hefted the weapon in his palm as if weighing its potential. Nearly faster than she could track, the prince fluidly whipped one blade after the other. Serenna's eyes never left him. Judging from the rhythmic thudding against the wood, every dagger met its mark. She glanced at the target.

The handles quivered in the center, of course.

Instead of trekking across the yard to retrieve the knives, Vesryn lifted a hand and curled his fingers. The daggers loosened from the board, flowing back on the wings of windless magic to present themselves to Serenna.

"Show-off," she muttered, plucking the blades out of the air.

"You could also use force to bring them to you," Vesryn said.

Serenna's cheeks burned. "I don't think I'm ready to fling knives around with my power yet." Thoughts of that evening flashed through her mind, spiraling into heated images she couldn't banish. "And I know I can't summon *desire* on a whim as easily as you can."

The words came out like a rebuke even though Serenna sensed her talent ready, hovering under her skin as she thought about the prince's mouth roaming over her neck again in the most tantalizing way.

She ground her teeth, assuming Vesryn was aware of her feelings, but he wisely smoothed his features into a mask of innocence. "Once you manifest your ability, you can evoke your power without using your emotions."

Serenna sensed a remnant flicker of longing darting from him, as if *he* was one tortured by the lingering memories. Or were they hers bouncing back through their connection?

Whatever.

She faced the target to push him out of her view. "I see."

The prince wandered to the edge of her vision. "I don't get the feeling you're angry with me. In the same way at least." Vesryn tilted his head, his sharp eyes considering her. Peering deeper. "So, what's bothering you? Does it have to do with why you were upset a few nights ago?"

"I don't want to talk about it." Serenna flung a knife. *Why won't he let it go?*

"Why not?"

Her nostrils flared with irritation at his persistence.

Serenna threw the remaining blades to the ground and rounded on the prince. "Fine. Since you *need* to know. It's my sire. It's the elves. It's this insane obsession your kind has with breeding by *requiring* elven-blooded to procreate against their will."

The tide now released, Serenna unleashed a torrent of her irate condemnation. "I don't want to be told who I'm supposed to couple with. Shouldn't that be *my* choice? My sire is pressuring others to reproduce with me. It's disgusting."

Serenna hated how her voice rose to a shrill pitch as she lost control of her emotions. She wished she could be collected like the elves, not overwhelmed by the feelings threatening to burst from the surface of her skin.

With folded arms, Vesryn studied her, wearing an unreadable look, but he didn't interrupt. Taking a deep breath, Serenna steadied herself and reeled her ire in.

"I don't want to be used by him," she added more calmly. "And I don't want my friends to be used by him either." Dismay had Serenna shaking her head. Her voice weakened to a whisper. "But I'm powerless."

"Elashor is still trying to bind your line with Jassyn's, isn't he?" Vesryn asked.

Apparently, I'm the only one who didn't know. Serenna's lip quivered. She blinked back frustrated tears. With a nod, she looked away to the other end of the yard.

Her voice broke under the emotional strain. "Can you…can you do anything for Jassyn?" If Elashor could, surely the prince had more influence.

A muscle in Vesryn's jaw constricted before he answered. "Our sires have worked together for centuries. If I interfere with Elashor's plans, he'll make my position on the High Council…unpleasant."

Serenna threw her hands out in agitation. "Unpleasant? That's the worst thing that could happen to you? Your comfortable seat on the High Council might become *unpleasant*?"

She scoffed and took a step closer to him. "Unbelievable. Do you even care how *unpleasant* life is for Jassyn? He's in Kyansari against his will right now!" Serenna flung her arm in the capital's direction as if including the city in her accusations. "Jassyn is your family, or does that mean nothing since he's a *half-breed*?" Angry tears sprung back into her eyes. "Do you not see how we're treated?"

Vesryn's voice dropped, not rising to meet hers. "The elven race survives because of those contracts."

His impassiveness only stoked her infuriation. *Why would I think he cares? Because* I *do?*

Serenna's nails dug into her palms. "And our consent is irrelevant?"

"I didn't say that," Vesryn said, a growl creeping into his words.

"Your indifference does."

Unable to halt the avalanche, Serenna's anger rolled like a landslide tumbling down a cliff. "The elven-bloodeds' numbers rival that of the pure-bloods. The contracts aren't about survival. Not anymore. It's about making half-breeds inferior."

Vesryn unfolded his arms, straightening to his full height. "I can hardly solve every problem the realm has. I've had my own to worry about."

Something inside of Serenna ripped free from a cage. Her Essence flared, whipping a cyclone of shadows around her. She was clearly far from the control over her abilities Vesryn had described; anger still called her power.

"*You* have problems?" Serenna screeched. She laughed wildly in disbelief. "You've had Jassyn's whole life to help him, but you *choose* to torment him instead. I don't know why I bother saying anything. It's obvious we're only good for increasing the population and fighting your war."

The rising moons cast a haunting glow on Vesryn's towering form, his cutting-jaw outlined in the light.

"Do you think I'm oblivious to how much I've fucked up? Add it to the list," he snarled, clenching his fists.

Serenna backed away, feeling the heat of his anger radiating off of him like an exploding star. His outburst was unexpected. She glanced across the yard, but everyone sparring was too far off to notice their argument.

"That doesn't mean you get to ignore everything going on," she protested vehemently.

Vesryn bared his teeth. "I've ignored nothing. I've dedicated my entire fucking life to hunting the wraith and protecting our people."

Our people. He always included her when talking about the elves. *It doesn't matter.* Not when the realm divided them so effectively.

"And yet you never stopped to think *your* people might need protection from more than the wraith? You elves are monsters too."

Serenna's chest heaved. She battled against the power boiling in her veins, straining to keep the darkness at bay. She plunged the verbal blade as deep as she knew how. "Your brother is *dead*. Killing more of those creatures won't ever bring him back."

Vesryn went dangerously still. He didn't breathe. The muscles in his hewn jaw trembled from the force of him clenching his teeth. The prince's eyes hardened into steel and sliced into hers. His anger scorched her like a furnace through the bond, the heat of his emotions surpassing her own.

Serenna gasped. She had no warning. An eruption of midnight streaked out from the prince. He raised a fist, shackling her in shadows.

She'd gone too far. She knew it. But she was ready to be on the receiving end of his fury. Even if it meant he was going to hurt her— she just wanted him to feel *something* about the injustice. Her words undoubtedly warranted a punishment.

Vesryn gathered his power in a violent rush. But he wavered. His arm shook from how tightly he gripped his fist. Serenna had never seen his face so cold, so frigid with a glacial rage.

"Why don't you care?" she shrieked at him.

Vesryn's magic gusted around her like a fog of darkness. Like Jassyn, she'd shoved him off a precipice, and now he faced her with bared fangs and sharpened talons. She could sense she'd hurt him.

"We're nothing alike, and I don't know why this stars-cursed bond linked us," she spat while he hesitated. "What if I was in Jassyn's situation, forced to breed like an animal? Or are you so good at ignoring the living that it wouldn't matter if elves were using me instead?"

Assuming their connection meant something made her a fool. It was all in her head. His face remained frozen, white with anger, as Serenna continued her tirade.

"Well, you know what? Maybe I'll do what my sire wants. He *agreed* to have Jassyn released from his contracts. That's more than I should expect from you."

Serenna spoke so fast, she could hardly breathe, honing each of her words with scathing contempt. She didn't even struggle in her bindings. She let her magic go. Her Essence was nothing compared to his anyway.

"All I have to do is to be a good little half-breed and fuck Jassyn to produce an offspring. Isn't that what you elves—"

Vesryn's power exploded.

CHAPTER 35

SERENNA

Magic blurred faster than Serenna could blink. Vesryn's eyes burned with wrath, a comet blazing across the sky.

The prince's power blasted a punch of pressure through the yard, like a thunderclap smashing through the atmosphere. The field erupted with the strength of an earthquake, force power hurling the ground into the air.

With a shriek, Serenna staggered, released from Vesryn's bindings. Her hands flew to protect her face. Fear slashed down her spine, latching her breath to the inside of her chest.

A violet shield slammed around her, sheltering her.

Vesryn's magic lashed in all directions. A tempest of rending billowed, roiling like a storm, extinguishing the stars. Shadows writhed, like a thousand whips cracking. His Essence blazed brighter than the sun, the only light in the pocket of midnight. His power spiraled uncontrollably like a gusting hurricane.

The prince's rampage poured into the surrounding air, ripping apart and reordering the world. The full weight of his magic fountained, a geyser discharging.

Serenna heard alarmed cries from the magus as Vesryn thrashed the training yard into a tornado of sand with force.

The wooden targets splintered and ricocheted against each other. Perimeter trees exploded.

The throwing knives on the ground shot out like ballistic arrows away from the ring.

Serenna's knees trembled, threatening to crumble under her weight as she helplessly watched through the violet shield. Unknowingly, she had seized her power, clutching it with all her might. As if her Essence could do anything to protect her against the prince.

He was terrifying.

She sensed something within Vesryn fissure and crack, his emotions snapping, spinning free. Angling her perception toward him, she felt more than an ocean of rage warring in the tempest of his thoughts.

Vesryn was barely balanced on the edge of control. His arms shook, hands extended, muscles tense; his face twisted into an animalistic snarl.

When she reached out to examine his feelings further, he sundered her awareness of him. As effectively as severing a limb.

Serenna recoiled at the solid barricade. *He cut me off?* She could sense his presence, but he shielded his emotions. *He can block the bond?*

Her awareness battered at the foreign barrier between them, no longer able to anticipate what he might do. She'd crossed a line she shouldn't have by throwing his brother's death in his face.

The world howled around them. Serenna couldn't move, fearing he'd disintegrate her with the darkness lashing about. *Will this shield hold? Did he do that?*

She didn't know how much time passed while Vesryn generated an Essence-fueled storm, splitting the air. His magic eventually flickered and then sputtered as if his fury had run its course.

Panting and drawing in ragged breaths, his wild eyes met hers.

Vesryn went rigid, blinking rapidly, his awareness refocusing. Serenna had no idea what he was feeling, but she watched shock shift his features as he stared at her.

Serenna swallowed, waiting for the dust to settle before she dared to move. When she released her magic, the encircling shield disappeared. Her eyes darted around the empty yard. Everyone else had fled the prince's frenzied expulsion of power.

She took a steadying breath. Another. *I need to get out of here.* Locking her jaw, Serenna spun on her heel, fleeing toward her residence hall.

Vesryn dashed to her side, slicing through the space between them. He snatched her arm.

Skidding to a halt, Serenna struggled in his grasp. "What are you doing? Let go!"

"No." Vesryn's voice carried the weight of a command. "We're going to talk."

Serenna's skin chilled, unease clashing inside her head. She couldn't sense his intentions.

"We have nothing more to speak about." She was in no mood to continue her verbal dueling with the prince. "I'm. *Done.*"

"I don't *care*," Vesryn growled, flinging the accusatory words back at her.

Serenna flinched. She tried freeing herself again.

He didn't release her.

Serenna's spine snapped straight, anger grinding her teeth together. *What is he going to do with me?* Fear raced through her veins, shooting to her head in a rush.

"Let. Go."

A muscle ticked in the prince's jaw. He held her eyes for a prolonged breath. A long silence stretched between them, lengthening like a shadow.

Serenna jumped when the hum of Vesryn's magic pelted her again. He'd opened a portal. She glanced between him and the rift.

"I am *not* going anywhere with you," she hissed with more confidence than she felt, knowing he had the power to do whatever he wanted with her. She wasn't sure where he would take her, but she didn't want to be alone with him when he just raged uncontrollably.

Vesryn's voice scraped against her, like shale sliding down a ridge. "You're walking through that portal, or I'm dragging you with me."

"That's not a choice!"

He tugged on her arm.

Serenna went wild, rabid with fright, an animal trapped. The toe of her boot connected with his shin.

He didn't react.

Instead of pulling away, she surged forward, sending a fist flying straight toward his middle. Vesryn's other hand whipped, halting the blow. She might as well have run into a brick wall. He bared his teeth while she wordlessly screamed at him.

She flailed, pointlessly trying to regain possession of her limbs. It was all she could do. Neither her strength nor power were enough to take on the prince, but she wouldn't surrender without a fight.

Serenna screeched when Vesryn ripped her legs out from under her. The world flipped over. Her chest collided against a surface as hard as granite, air flying out of her lungs. With a strangled gasp, she labored to reorient herself.

He tossed me over his shoulder?

She kicked her feet and beat against his back with her fists. "Put me down, you big bastard!"

Trapping her legs against his chest, Vesryn barged through the portal. He dumped her on the other side like she was a sack of grain. Serenna's boots tangled in the long grasses before she righted herself.

She bolted toward the gateway, shrieking in frustration when it vanished.

Brushing past her, Vesryn walked a few paces and slumped to the ground. Globes of illumination hovered, casting a dim light around them, but his eyes were blank.

Searching for another escape, Serenna swept her gaze over the surroundings. Her chest heaved, fury sawing at her lungs at the sudden abduction.

The moons slid between the gaps in the mountainous peaks, highlighting the valley with their pale light. She recognized the silhouette of the vale where Vesryn had introduced her to the dracovae, a place she knew was important to him.

I guess it was easier to just toss me through a portal instead of saying where we were going.

Folding her arms defensively, Serenna shot the prince a glower. But he didn't look at her, running his hand through the grass, obviously dejected now. She still had no idea if he would erupt again.

Veiled in shadow, Vesryn's eyes unfocused out into the distance. "Look, I..." His fingers tapped anxiously on a knee. "I just want to talk."

Serenna hitched her bodice straight and twisted away from him. *We've said enough tonight.*

She froze when a sinking feeling of regret drifted from him, sailing through her. Serenna expected to sense anger, not grief.

Like a bee questing for pollen, she tentatively reached out with her awareness and grazed their connection, since he'd dropped whatever barrier he'd made against the bond.

A deep sorrow shrouded her—more sorrow than she'd ever experienced. His anguish eclipsed her ire.

"Please," he whispered. There was something pained in his voice.

A breath abandoned her as his plea shredded her indignation. Serenna recognized his sincerity, uncomprehending that he carried such painful emotions. It was the only reason she relented and folded herself on the ground beside him.

Time trickled by, slow like dew dripping from leaves. Serenna sat stiffly, listening to her heartbeat. Waiting. *Did I make him feel this way with my cruel words?*

Vesryn didn't meet her eyes, but he inhaled an unsteady breath. Serenna sensed him wrestle between grief and anger before offering her his hand. Hesitantly, but with a hint of desperation.

His words were sharp. "I won't stand by while Elashor manipulates you. He can't do anything to release Jassyn from his contracts. That would require unanimous support from the council." The prince scoffed and shook his head. "That'll never happen."

A fracture cleaved Serenna's heart. *I should've known.*

Vesryn's offered fingers twitched. "But I might be able to help. Just...don't do anything rash until you give me the chance to try."

Startled, Serenna blinked up at him. *Why would he care if I went forward with my sire's wishes?* Silence coated the space between them.

Her thoughts spun, pulling her breaths in shallow and quick. *He's serious?* She suspiciously studied his extended palm.

Hurt from her rejection flickered through the bond like a guttering flame. Vesryn balled his hand into a fist, withdrawing.

Serenna caught his retreating arm. "Thank you."

Shoulders relaxing, Vesryn twined their fingers with startling intensity. Her magic settled, almost with a contented hum, in the shelter of his rough palm.

Serenna's pulse thudded in her ears, deafening against the stillness of stars and the droning chirp of crickets. Guilt pooled in her heart, as it always did when she struck out callously.

I didn't want this to happen. I was just so angry that he didn't seem to care about Jassyn.

Again, she found herself needing to apologize, but knew it wouldn't heal the wound she'd ripped open. "I'm sorry about what I said. About your brother. I would have deserved—"

A muscle jumped in Vesryn's jaw, and a spark of fury echoed through the bond. Serenna shrank back.

"That's not the entire reason I was upset." Vesryn's fingers tightened around hers. "The only person who cared for me the way you care about Jassyn is gone." His voice dropped as he stared off at the snowy mountain peaks reflecting dim starlight. "But I'm the only one to blame—for everything. I lost more than Aesar and my mother the night the wraith attacked." His thumb stroked the back of her hand. "I lost the bond I shared with him. And the loss left me empty. I never figured out how to move past it."

Serenna's breath caught as her chest coiled with remorse. They hadn't discussed his former bond. She'd assumed he had refused that connection too. She felt his heart fold and collapse under the weight of his buried sorrow.

She had intentionally tried to harm him by viciously reminding him of his brother's death. *I didn't think I could cause him so much pain.* Squeezing his hand, Serenna hoped her regret bridged the chasm between them.

Vesryn's fingers trembled in hers. "I let grief consume me, and maybe I hurt those around me so I wouldn't be the only person suffering." His voice became heavy, carrying despair. "But maybe…maybe it's time to move on and become the elf Aesar would have been proud to call his brother. One who wouldn't fail him again."

Serenna swallowed, realizing death had robbed him of more than his brother. *I can't fill such an empty space.*

The prince's anguish cracked her chest open like a crevice in the earth. Serenna's heart fell into it, tumbling down every cliff. She didn't have any words.

Releasing her, Vesryn gouged his hands through his hair and blew out a breath, staring up at the ocean of stars.

Serenna leaned over and threw her arms around him. She started crying, feeling the weight of his pain. She understood. It was part of her now. And it hurt.

"I'm so sorry," she whispered against him.

Vesryn's arm tightened across her shoulders. "I would never harm you." He stroked her hair. "I'm sorry I frightened you, snapping you into another ability. I didn't mean to."

"I…" Serenna pulled back, sitting beside him. It took her a few moments to calm her breathing and dry her tears. She drew her knees to her chest and searched his face. "That was my shield, wasn't it?"

He nodded, his eyes swimming with regret, silver in the starlight.

She feared Vesryn's power, and hadn't expected him to react so strongly. But she never thought he would harm her—not mortally anyway. Her reaction to his outrage was instinctive protection—she knew his intentions weren't malicious.

Vesryn rose, opening a portal. "It's getting late, and I have business in the capital tonight." He reached a hand to help her up. She accepted, but he faltered, his brows pulling together. "Would you…want to resume your training tomorrow?"

Vesryn's fingers tensed around hers. He made no attempt to hide the flash of dread while he waited for her answer, like he expected her to decline.

A hint of a spark glimmered in Vesryn's eyes. Serenna sensed someone was seeing her—all of her—for the first time. The rage, the fear, and the ugliness. He didn't blink or look away. While he studied her with such intensity, she allowed herself to free-fall into the depths of his emerald gaze.

Serenna nodded, knowing a silent message passed between their clasped hands as if threads braided together in a first link of trust.

CHAPTER 36

LYKOR

Behind closed eyes, a weight shifted on Lykor's chest. Aiko, his vulpintera. Sleep had apparently claimed him at some point—he must've collapsed from exhaustion before the sun had set.

Lykor sensed his regenerated power. Shockingly, the other presence did something useful for once while controlling their body, restoring their drained Well.

Preparing for the attack against the elves, Lykor had been restless, training soldiers until he could hardly stand from the exertion. He portaled to his chambers after sending the wraith to three back-to-back locations earlier in the day. Harvesting timber. Hunting antelope. Collecting fish from their nets.

Lykor stroked Aiko, who typically curled up next to him. Expecting a purr when his fingers brushed her leathery wings and fluffy fur, he stilled.

Hair.

His hand clenched into a fist, encircling braids. His eyes flew open.

FOR FUCK'S SAKE.

Lykor shoved Kal away from him, clambering out of bed.

Fury igniting, a torrent of shadows burst around him. Lykor's chest quaked as his captain groggily blinked at him.

Lykor's awareness soared to the other being at the back of his skull. Of course, he slept as contentedly as a vulpintera coiled in the sun. *HE DID THIS ON PURPOSE.* Lykor nearly hauled the other entity out of sleep to berate him.

WAIT. I HAVE A BETTER IDEA.

He would take advantage of the silence. And the absence of interference.

Returning to full consciousness, Lykor fisted his eyes. He clutched his power, letting the shadows clash around him.

He perceived the bond-holder significantly closer in the east. Not at the elves' military base. Gallivanting across the fucking continent again.

Did they feel his presence yet? Lykor drew on knowledge of the bond's intricacies. The other presence had shared such a connection before his access to Essence was first manipulated—before Lykor emerged.

Now would be the time to investigate the layout and fortifications of the island if the bond-holder was away. He wanted to have his magic ready and untethered if he moved around the grounds.

"Put your fucking dick away," Lykor growled at Kal. As he shoved his legs through his trousers, he studied the windowless walls. And blew out an exasperated scoff.

Kal's chambers.

The second time this week.

His captain resided in extensive dwellings deep in the mountain. Lykor's skin crawled—the solid stone room gave him no perception of time.

This felt too much like the prison for his liking. The earth pressing in around him. Suffocating darkness. Deafening silence.

And Kal refusing to leave his side.

"What hour is it?" Lykor demanded.

Kal kept one eye on him while he rose, searching for his clothes. "We had dinner together not long ago. The sun can't be over four hours gone. We came back here after you regenerated and—"

"I don't give a dracovae's ass if you fucked each other sideways,"

Lykor snarled. "It wasn't *me*." The obvious fact he shouldn't have to voice. "You two are pathetic for holding on to the past."

His captain had his pick of males and females he could tumble with, even sired numerous offspring over the years. As the largest clan, Lykor lost count of how many were now in Kal's family group. But since the other entity had been more persistent these past few weeks in controlling their body while Lykor slept, he'd apparently felt the need to rekindle what Lykor assumed the dungeons had snuffed out.

Before Kal could interject, Lykor opened a portal to the roof he'd previously visited on the elves' floating island, hoping it wasn't vacant so he could rend something and expel his irritation.

"Hurry up," Lykor barked. "We're going to the elves' base for you to examine the fortifications."

Kal raised his brows as he shoved his rumpled tunic into his pants. "Right now? You're taking me with you? Do you want your armor or weapons? We can go to my armory and—"

Lykor bared his fangs and cut him off. "You would hate for me to repeat myself, *Captain*."

Kal's mouth thinned as he tugged on his boots. His eyes nervously darted at the rending shadows still roiling around him. Lashing, but not striking. A threat.

He kept silent. For once.

A fucking wonder.

"Cloak us," Lykor commanded before they trekked through the rift. He could cloak himself, but the trivial order would remind Kal of his subordinate position.

"I appreciate you not rending me again," Kal muttered, encompassing Lykor with his invisibility. The wraith could perceive each other through their concealment, even if no one else could.

"There's still time," Lykor growled, stalking through the gateway. He seriously doubted it would be the last time he woke up in Kal's chambers.

On the other side, silence encompassed the empty rooftop. It appeared the elves had constructed a new greenhouse to replace the structure he'd blasted apart. Lykor's shoulders twitched, considering smashing this one too, but he thought better about causing an unnecessary commotion. Instead, he released the hold on his magic.

Kal's red eyes glowed, catching shards of moonlight—both had now risen in the wheeling of stars. As he glanced around, his pupils expanded to absorb the night.

Lykor's sight was shit in the dark, since he wasn't wholly wraith. He didn't have the illumination ability anymore either, so it made seeing in pitch black impossible.

"I heard about the bond forming between you and someone here. I'm assuming that's how you portaled to this island the first time?" Kal asked, the rift fading behind them. They walked to the edge of the roof, unseen in darkness.

"That is not your concern." Lykor swiped his disheveled hair with a talon, aggravation gnawing at him from the absence of his gauntlet to conceal the cursed claw. He had no interest in rifling through memories of the evening to discover where the other presence had stowed it. And of course, it was no surprise *he* had shared their secrets with Kal.

Drumming his fingers on the railing while Kal surveyed the grounds, Lykor studied a scattering of elves sparring, wondering how many of these mixed peoples the king had bred. Or half-elves. Whatever they were. But still…they appeared to have more skill than the general's so-called soldiers, who hardly left the comfort of the capital.

They were still nothing compared to how he and Kal had prepared the wraith.

"Well?" Lykor questioned, waiting for his captain's assessment, peeved he had to prompt him.

"Obviously, we'll rely on your portals to transport us here." Kal pointed to the bottom of the tallest structure, which jutted up from the center of the landmass. "If you open four at the base, we'll fan out in all directions and establish a perimeter around the isle. I'll work on the roster to divide the warriors into squadrons for training in battalions. I can't imagine the population here is over a thousand." Kal craned his head, inspecting the peak of the central building. "Do you think there's a roof up there? That location would offer you the best vantage."

"Why would I need a vantage?" Lykor asked irritably, cinching his shoulders to crack his spine.

"Surely you don't plan to take part in the fighting." Kal drew Lykor's attention by fiddling with one of his earrings.

"You'll be a target with your magic," Kal continued. "What happens if you're injured and can't portal if we're forced to retreat?"

It was an absurd concern. Lykor had been half dead when he'd portaled them out of the elven dungeons.

"Retreat isn't an option," Lykor snarled. "We're going to eliminate the threat."

Turning away, Lykor grumbled under his breath, knowing the logical course of action would be for him to manage the operation from a distance. His captain was an overprotective, driveling lackwit, but he was right.

"Do you think we can warp up there?" Kal asked, staring at the pinnacle of the towering building.

Lykor shrugged. "Try."

Kal hesitated, glancing from him to the peak.

"You'll halt my fall if I don't make it, right?"

Lykor crossed his arms.

"Right?" Kal pushed.

Lykor studied the top of the tower. Though not fully wraith anymore, he retained at least some of their useful abilities. Warping allowed him to travel short distances without portals, but he had to have an unobstructed path and a clear view of the place he wanted to go. He hadn't discovered if his fangs had the same paralytic qualities, having not made a habit of biting others, as some of the wraith were inclined to do in…intimate settings.

Looking sideways at his captain, Lykor considered testing his venom potency on Kal and abandoning him on the campus. *I COULD ALWAYS RETRIEVE HIM AFTER THE BATTLE.*

Lykor scoffed to himself. No, that would mean he would have to fuck around with the rosters in his Kal's absence. Organizing the warriors was the last thing he wanted to bother with.

Lykor channeled his awareness to the center of his chest, a pressure building near the point of pain. The air surrounding him distorted like a reflection thrown off water. Just as he would close a book, Lykor folded in on himself and warped to the top of the tower.

Rematerializing, his boots struck marble. He sucked in a sharp breath after the jump, blinking away the slight spin in his head while his body oriented to the new location.

The zenith offered views of the entire island. There were more buildings across the grounds than he'd previously thought. Drifting to the marble parapet, Lykor studied the island's sharp horizon. He considered the staggering amount of power it must've taken to send this landmass to the sky.

Lykor recloaked them in shadows when Kal appeared next to him. His captain's near midnight skin took on an ashy hue from the alarming elevation of their destination.

Kal grabbed the half-wall's railing and released a disbelieving laugh as he looked over the edge. "You wouldn't want to fall from this height."

Water rushed past them from a portal in the sky. Lykor shook his head at the waste of magic. How many years did the wraith survive on lichens and mushrooms, while the elves created such impractical luxuries?

"I want you to command the army from the ground," Lykor told Kal, roaming his gaze over the isle. He discerned no apparent sentries. The sheer arrogance was astounding and had him doubting arch elves were even present if this was a place for the king's creations.

Night would be the perfect time to stage an attack and play to the wraith's strengths. "Warp up to me to provide reports when it's feasible. If we can strike them out in one blow, I'll rest easier."

"When are you planning our move?"

"Soon," Lykor said, scraping his talons across the stone balcony.

Kal's attention shifted from watching the water flow from the sky and back to him. "Are you sure this is the course of action we should take? We would be killing these half-elf pawns who had nothing to do with our imprisonment." He grimaced. "We could start a war based on this hunch you have. It's possible what's happening on this island has nothing to do with us. As far as we know, the elves never bothered pursuing our people after we escaped."

Lykor's eyes narrowed on Kal chewing the ring centered in his lip. "What's going on here could be part of their plan to search for the slumbering elemental power," Kal continued, moving to twist a stud in his brow. "We have no idea. Have you discussed this with *him*? Do you really think Aesar would risk—"

Lykor's wrath exploded, violent like a volcanic eruption. He would punish the blatant disregard of his command to never invoke the fallen prince's name. Seizing Kal's throat, Lykor drove him to the brink of the roof.

As if summoned, Aesar stirred in the back of his mind.

"Am I hearing your objection?" Lykor snarled, bending his captain backward over the railing to the point of cracking his spine. "Would you like to reconsider your protest on the way to the ground when I toss you off of this fucking roof?"

Kal gritted his teeth, his elongating canines flashing in the moons' light as Lykor severed his access to air.

"Retract your fangs," Lykor growled, knowing they extended as an automatic response when aggressed. He always kept his lengthened to make a statement.

Kal snarled back at him, clawing at his hand, but didn't comply. Lykor refused to lose a game of dominance with his captain—he only played this one to be petty now, since Kal brought up Aesar.

Lykor's muscles seized. A jagged inhale speared his throat.

The bond-holder was back.

He sliced open a portal and pitched Kal through, abandoning the island until their assault.

CHAPTER 37

JASSYN

Closing yet another book yielding no significant information, Jassyn exhaled a sigh and palmed his eyes. His vision unfocused on a vining plant in his office. Setting his chin in his hand, he allowed his mind to wander.

It didn't surprise him there was an absence of documented research pertaining to coercion. *But that makes sense since the king is the only one who can manipulate telepathy to such an extent and exert that level of control over others.*

Jassyn shifted his leathers to scratch the skin on his shoulder that twinged from the thought. The monarch's heightened abilities only reinforced his status as the ruler of the realm.

But what he couldn't understand was why the magnitude of the king's power increased over time. *That's not how Essence works. Wells can be stretched to accommodate a greater depth of magic to draw from, but a larger reservoir doesn't augment magical strength or aptitude—strength is typically relative to the number of abilities we have.*

The king's aura was simply more powerful each instance Jassyn was in his presence. As few as those were. *I'll just have to add this to the list of unsolved mysteries.*

Upon returning to Centarya from his assignment in Vaelyn and discovering the compulsive magic on Magister Thalaesyn, Jassyn devoured every text referencing studies of telepathy and afflictions of the mind. Determined to find deeper connections between the two, he hoped the research would help him understand the effects of coercion on the psyche. Or aid him in uncovering ways to ease his mentor's deteriorating state.

And besides, he had more time to spend on pursuing new studies since the research on elven sterility was apparently a dead end. Losing the time spent in Nelya's greenhouse was another reason to chase other interests. *Not having the ability to portal makes me useless in regathering the myriad plants.*

Pointedly ignoring the slight tremor in his hands, Jassyn rubbed his temples to alleviate the persistent throbbing behind his eyes. Every beat of his heart sent blinding flashes of pressure barreling through the back of his skull.

What was in that crimson Stardust? The withdrawal from a single day of not consuming the drug crushed his head with the force of a tumbling boulder.

Already, his nerves were humming in anticipation of inhaling some of the blue variety as part of his nightly routine. He found it hard to focus on anything else, his thoughts yanked back to the stockpile he had in his chambers.

As if reminded of the previous days, Jassyn's eyes tripped over the lone book placed at the furthest corner of his desk. Upon his departure, Farine presented him with a tome from Fynlas's study, asserting he might find the contents *interesting*. When his four mandatory visits were concluded, Farine offered a proposition where she'd grant him another text if he returned when summoned.

Jassyn emitted a self-deprecating scoff. *She's manipulating me with knowledge, and I'm desperate enough to find out more.* Corrosive slime gurgled in his gut. He'd agreed to her terms. *It doesn't matter. I won't remember. Maybe I'll find something useful in those volumes.*

Judging from the extensive research Fynlas had left behind, there were more secrets for him to uncover about the humans' ancestries and shaman lines. *What is the council up to? Does Vesryn know?*

Shaking the unsettled feeling off his shoulders, Jassyn opened another book. The contents pertained to a study of an elf who had more than one sense of self and expressed more than ten distinct identities and personalities. *Intriguing. But not quite a step in the right direction for coercion.*

"Do you have a minute?"

Jassyn's head whipped up. His eyes pinned on his cousin, sauntering into his office. Barging into the space like he was welcome.

Jassyn clenched his teeth. "No," he gritted out, despite not having anything to do until his shift on the healing floor in a few hours.

The prince loomed over his desk in his aggravating way, immediately fiddling with his quills.

"Well." Vesryn shrugged, his armor creaking. He absently twirled a stylus through his fingers. "Make one." He flicked his wrist and closed Jassyn's door with a push of force.

Jassyn slammed the book shut. "What do you want?" he challenged, crossing his arms. He leaned forward on his elbows, scowling at his cousin's disgusting boots. *He better not be tracking filth all over the Infirmary.*

Vesryn took his time regarding the office. He gave a grunt that almost sounded amused as his eyes swept over portraits of snowy mountain sunsets and the countless plants arranged in elegant ceramic pots.

"You need to decorate my chambers." Vesryn's gaze lingered on Jassyn's sconces. "I can't coordinate the color of illumination like you can."

No wonder, since the most vibrant tone you wear is black.

"Is that all?" Jassyn asked, his voice icy enough to freeze a pond.

The prince's hovering was making Jassyn's cheek twinge in an overload of irritation. He certainly wouldn't invite Vesryn to sit in one of the empty chairs.

Fingers twitching, Vesryn's lips thinned. Jassyn noted the absence of his quill, assuming the prince squirreled it away somewhere in his leathers when he wasn't watching. Vesryn tossed an envelope sealed with his dragon sigil onto his desk.

Jassyn's gaze flicked to the parchment, feeling as if his cousin flung a slithering serpent between them. He pierced the prince with a sharpened stare in return, wondering what scheme Vesryn launched him into now.

Vesryn rolled his eyes and tapped the paper. "You'll want to *open* it," he drawled.

After counting three more slow, deliberate breaths—while maintaining his level look—Jassyn reached for the envelope and popped the wax seal.

Scanning the document, a shiver of dread wove down his spine. Jassyn's breathing became as disjointed as his thoughts, a rapid drawing of air that didn't fill his lungs. Glacial fury like he'd never experienced before crystallized the blood in his veins.

Jassyn crumbled the documents into his fist. "Do you think this is *funny?*" he questioned, his ears starting to ring.

Vesryn scratched his jaw before his brows drew together. "Um... no?" He frowned at the crinkled parchment quivering in Jassyn's trembling grip.

Jassyn rose from his seat. His limbs shook, expelling an echo of his outrage. Forcibly unclenching his hand, he let the document tumble to the floor.

Discarding it.

Bracing his knuckles on his desk, Jassyn leaned forward. He saw red, his vision igniting with a wild, incandescent rage. He had no desire to engage in whatever game the prince devised.

"So...*what* exactly?" Jassyn's chest heaved with disbelief. "I'm to service *you* now?"

Vesryn's eyes widened before the color drained from his face. He opened his mouth, but Jassyn shoved words between them first. His voice wavered with an unrecognizable hostility.

"You claimed *exclusive* rights to me."

Perhaps Serenna's statement about his submissiveness haunted him, or perhaps the remnants of that scarlet Stardust made him erratic. Either way, something reinforced him, snapping his composure like an oar breaking in half.

Uncalled, Jassyn's magic erupted. He couldn't remember the last time he'd lost control. It didn't matter—the Essence shimmering around him was useless. Just like everything else about him.

Jassyn lunged across his desk. Seizing Vesryn's leathers, he hauled his cousin toward him.

"What. Does. This. Mean?" Jassyn snarled, baring his teeth.

Vesryn blinked.

Once.

Twice.

The prince knocked his hands away, pulling back to straighten his tunic with a yank. "I can see how this might be confusing. I should have explained first."

Jassyn's fists clenched and unclenched at his sides. *He's gone too far this time.* He contemplated whipping out one of his concealed golden blades and stabbing his cousin, not caring if his action would give Vesryn the grand reaction he must be seeking. *I can't take this anymore.*

Panting out of his nose, Jassyn felt himself dragged into a chaotic spiral, caught in a riptide. "If this is your idea of a joke, it's unacceptable. Even for you. It's one thing to ridicule me about my service to the realm, but now requiring me to—"

"Just...let me explain," Vesryn practically pleaded, holding up his hands.

Jassyn faltered at the apparent sincerity. *No, this is his way of reeling me in. He's about to set the hook.*

"Then *explain.*" Jassyn released his magic. His skull threatened to burst if he didn't.

"A...loophole exists in the coupling contracts. Sort of." Vesryn pursed his lips. "Of course, it only benefits the ten council members. But there's a line written where each member can claim 'exclusive' rights to a...an elven-blooded male and have sole access to that bloodline."

Vesryn angled his head like a hawk to study the tome about shamans at the edge of the desk. When the prince reached out to trail his fingers along the cover, Jassyn snatched the book away.

"Fascinating." Jassyn shoved the volume on a shelf behind him. *I'm not a "half-breed" anymore? I'm flattered.* They glared at each other before Vesryn continued.

"Each council member reserves the 'right' to claim an elven-blooded once a century. Perks of the position, I suppose," Vesryn said sarcastically. "I'm the only one who hasn't exploited the...way around securing a spot on those contracts."

"Until now, you mean," Jassyn corrected, crossing his arms. "You're rambling."

Vesryn scoffed. "Stars, let me get to it. As you'd expect, greed spurred everyone else to secure a line before you were even born. We're a few solstices away from the next claiming cycle, and..." Vesryn trailed off, shaking his head. "Well, Elashor plans to *collect* you. He's been adamantly vocal about that your whole life and already implied he...*owned* you, I guess." Vesryn shrugged. "So I got to you first."

Nausea had Jassyn's stomach rolling like a wave. *This has to do with Fynlas's research. Elashor wants my line for a reason.*

Wobbling, Jassyn caught himself on his desk, unaware his fate had been balanced on so thin a precipice. Being summoned sixteen times in a year was torment enough, but to be bound permanently to the Vallende line and *always* at Farine's disposal, forced to service everyone of her choosing...? He would've jumped off the roof of the Spire first.

The council must've refrained from claiming additional elven-blooded for themselves so as not to rouse any suspicion. Ten elven-blooded selected every century was alarming, but it was a small enough number that word wouldn't spread. *I wonder if this is why some people simply disappear. Do they..."collect" them?*

Jassyn locked his knees to examine his cousin as his world slanted under his feet. "So...what's the catch? *You* own me now?" A darker thought crossed his mind like a cloud shadowing the sun. His voice lost strength, coming out as a whisper. "What are you going to make me do?"

Vesryn reared back. "Nothing. I'm not requiring anything of you."

Jassyn blinked. "Then—"

"Your life doesn't belong to the realm anymore. Do with it what you will." Vesryn gave a dismissive wave, like he didn't just reconstruct Jassyn's reality.

Jassyn dropped into his chair, his legs buckling. Bracing his elbows on the desk, he drew his fingers through his hair. His throat closed around the air lodged in his chest. Engulfed with a spectrum of overwhelming emotions, he didn't even know how to process the moment. He went numb, feeling as if he were treading on ice, threatening to shatter.

The prince extended a hand. An orb of illumination drifted from a hanging sconce to rest in his palm. "Asserting my claim over you was the only way I knew how to release you from the contracts. No one can bind you into servitude again. Not while I live anyway." Vesryn stared at the globe, changing the light from a daffodil tone to an ocean blue.

It's over? I'm...free from all of this?

"I just returned from hand-delivering the notice to your handlers," the prince said. "When I dissolved the other contracts, I wrote in an addendum barring those families from contacting you." Vesryn's gaze flicked to his. "They won't be bothering you again. If they do..." The prince's mouth quirked. He nodded to the crumpled parchment on the floor, eyes glittering. "You'll see I was rather explicit that they risk being turned inside out."

Jassyn stared at his cousin. "I don't understand. Why do this?" His mind raced around every possible explanation, revolving like a sunflower swiveling towards the sun. There was no reason. "What's in it for you if you're not going to use me?"

"It was past time to do something decent," Vesryn said, his voice softening. "I should've put a stop to this nonsense before it started. But...I didn't." He sent the light sailing back into the sconce and wandered over to a potted plant.

"Stars, you weren't even of age when that female who calls herself your mother drew up those first contracts." Vesryn shook his head and traced a spade-shaped leaf dangling from one of his vining plants. "I let it happen when I should've protected you instead. I just wanted to fix something for once. I..." The prince trailed off. "I'm sorry I failed you for so long."

Jassyn blinked back the tears threatening to spill from his eyes. He rearranged the quills Vesryn had disrupted, putting them in order to distract himself from the tight feeling in his throat.

Why now? Jassyn had spent his entire adolescence looking up to his cousin only to receive disappointment.

Perhaps this was Vesryn's way of rebalancing the scales. Jassyn couldn't think of a more significant gesture that would've improved his circumstances. *Has living with us at Centarya opened his eyes?*

Jassyn wasn't quite ready for one benevolent deed to erase eighty years of harassment, but the prince had chosen a side. *And he picked me over the realm?*

Jassyn leaned over to retrieve the wrinkled parchment and flattened the paper against his desk.

"Did you think this through?" he asked. "You're going to make enemies of the most powerful families. The Vallendes, specifically. Elashor has nearly as much influence as your sire."

"I'll handle any backlash." Vesryn's hand snapped closed around the vine. "And fuck Elashor," he said, pivoting to face him.

The prince clicked his tongue, clutching a now broken plant in his fist. The hammering in Jassyn's head had him rubbing his temples as he rapidly ran out of energy to deal with his cousin.

"Elashor manipulated Serenna into thinking she could free you from your contracts if she…if you two… Well, I'm sure you know." Vesryn tossed the fragmented vine on his desk. "I sensed her determination and how much your servitude upset her. She was going to offer to carry an offspring for you." He scoffed. "Well, for Elashor. And that helped get my head out of my ass."

Jassyn buried his face in his trembling palms. *She would've done that for me?* Aside from a distrust of the general, he'd refused to mention Elashor's proposition because he wasn't interested in dragging anyone else into the depths of his problems.

Wait. Jassyn's neck snapped up so he could study Vesryn. *How does he even know this?* His eyes narrowed on the prince. *He's up to something.* Standing so abruptly that his chair screeched, Jassyn wound around his desk and stalked toward the prince.

"What does Serenna have to do with anything?" he demanded.

Surprised jolted Jassyn when Vesryn retreated a step. Recovering, Jassyn closed the gap again. "If you so much as *think* about using her for your entertainment, it'll be the last thing you do," he said, driving a finger into Vesryn's chest. "I've heard stories of—"

Vesryn interrupted. "It's not like that."

Jassyn scoffed and crossed his arms, wildly unconvinced.

"What do you want me to say?" Vesryn protested, defensively tossing up his hands. "I'm not that person anymore. I've spent a century trying to atone for—" He blew out a rough exhale and stared at the ceiling. "I won't hurt her. We share a bond and—"

Jassyn's jaw went slack. "You convinced her to form a *bond* with you?" *Why in the bleeding stars would she bind herself to him?*

"No, the magic bridged us on its own. It's not even fully formed." Vesryn's face fell. "She…Serenna didn't tell you?"

The prince reached out as if to grab his shoulder, but Jassyn sidestepped to avoid his hand.

Vesryn formed a fist and dropped his arm to his side. "No harm will come to her, I promise."

Serenna's defensiveness over him makes sense now. How long has this been going on?

Jassyn squinted, roving his gaze over his cousin, analyzing his honesty. The prince stood stiffer than usual, as if trying to dominate him despite his shorter height. As usual. *Does he even realize he's doing it?*

"You know," Jassyn said, probing to see what reaction he'd get, "it doesn't matter how straight you stand, you'll never be taller."

Vesryn gaped before he bristled with a roll of his shoulders, relaxing his stance.

Jassyn smirked, his comment clearly catching the prince off guard. Maybe there was something fun about picking at people. His gut twisted like a nest of writhing snakes. *No, as much as he deserves it, I won't be like him.*

"I'll see you at the magus training in the morning." Vesryn pivoted on his heel and strolled to the door.

"Can I get rid of them?" Jassyn asked the prince's departing form, distress controlling his voice.

Vesryn turned toward him. "Get rid of what?"

Jassyn held a trembling hand to his forehead, grazing the ink. "The tattoos. Unless…unless you require your sigil instead?"

"There's no need to ask. It's your decision to make." Vesryn talked to the wall as he ran a finger across the frame of a painting. "You only belong to yourself now. I don't care what that document says."

Vesryn cleared his throat and jerked his head toward the door. "Serenna is here."

A soft knock sounded on the other side.

Vesryn let her in. Serenna's eyes widened when she glanced between them, presumably confused that they shared the same space. Vesryn murmured something to her and brushed his knuckles along her arm.

Jassyn grunted to himself, disbelieving. He'd heard rumors in the capital about the prince's engagement. *Does she know?* And here his cousin was, appearing like he had eyes for Serenna.

Serenna's ears flushed, her attention anchored on Vesryn. Whatever the prince said next had her subtle smile morphing into a scowl. She brushed past him, flicking her hair at him like a dracovae swishing its tail as Vesryn let himself out. *Well, maybe she can hold her own against him.*

Sticking his head back in the office, Vesryn said, "I wouldn't say no if you wanted to slap my dragon sigil on your left ass cheek."

Jassyn pointed. "Out!"

Vesryn grinned at him before closing the door behind him.

An amused question shone in Serenna's eyes before her attention focused on him.

They stared at each other.

Their argument earlier in the week seemed so trivial now with everything that had happened. And she'd been willing to go through with Elashor's plans to help him. That gesture outshone her cruel jabs, surely just words from the heat of their squabble.

Jassyn's feet were moving before his mind caught up. Serenna met him in the middle of the room. He enveloped her in a crushing hug as both of them apologized. They lingered in an embrace, the comfortable silence conveying their regrets.

"Thank you," Jassyn said. "Vesryn told me what you wanted to do for me and—"

"He *what?*" Serenna pulled back, untangling her arms from his. "We only talked about it last night. And it doesn't involve *him* at all. I—"

"My contracts don't exist anymore," Jassyn hurriedly said before she could further argue the issue. Pinching the bridge of his nose, he filled his lungs to the point of bursting. "Vesryn took it upon himself to"—he waved a dismissive hand at the disheveled paper—"clear the matter up."

A wrinkle formed in Serenna's brows. "He…he did? Already?"

Jassyn drifted back behind his desk and motioned for Serenna to sit across from him, providing her with the rough details of Vesryn's doings.

"Thank you for the part you played," he said. "But you don't owe him anything. Remember that."

Serenna flushed at the implications. She crossed her legs once settled into the chair. "There's nothing like that between us. I think he simply delights in tormenting me."

"I'm sure he does." Jassyn steepled his fingers under his chin. "He told me about your bond." Unable to restrain his curiosity, he asked, "Are you thinking of accepting it?"

"What? No." Serenna's shrill laugh almost seemed forced. "That's ridiculous. He's just waiting for me to learn more about my magic so we both can reject the connection."

Jassyn frowned. That wasn't his understanding of how the magic functioned.

Serenna absorbed herself with smoothing the leather on her trousers. "Could you tell me more about bonds? Or at least how to shield myself so he can't read my emotions? I felt him block himself off when he was upset, and I was wondering if I could do the same."

Her nails dug into the soft cedar wood of the chair's armrests. Jassyn's eyes bulged at the scratch marks in the wax coating. After noticing his attention, Serenna winced while uncoiling her fingers.

"I'm lacking in detailed knowledge about the connection, but I can teach you how to guard your mind, since I doubt it's been covered in your lessons yet." Jassyn rearranged the books on his desk, not remembering Vesryn meddling with the stack. "Anyone with magic is able to learn—like assessing body conditions with raw Essence before we mend."

Did he seriously arrange the tomes by color?

"From my understanding, barricading your emotions from a bond works the same way as blocking someone from forming an unwanted link with you telepathically—which can be done even if you don't have the ability." Jassyn arched a brow. "I imagine you might find this skill useful as well since Vesryn possesses telepathic habits like a deranged leech if he wants something."

Serenna muttered about how she was well aware of the prince's tendencies. She twirled her braid, apparently lost in thought. The flush creeping to the tips of her ears and the faraway look suggested she had something on her mind. Jassyn had a guess. She always wore her emotions painted on her face like the kohl liner she favored.

I hope she isn't developing feelings for Vesryn. That's only going to end poorly for her.

"You know…" Jassyn trailed off, running his fingers along the grainy whorls of his desk. *How to put it delicately?* "Vesryn is promised to someone, right?"

Startlement flashed across Serenna's features before she sniffed, like she was indifferent. She asked, a bit too casually, "Since when?"

"I just heard. On my last visit to the capital." Jassyn swallowed back a bitter taste crawling up his throat. "The prince's engagement will be officially announced at the king's Summer Lunar Solstice celebration."

Concern darkened Serenna's eyes as she searched for the answers in his. "Do you know with whom?" she whispered.

Stars, she won't like this. Jassyn ran his hand over his mouth, wanting to hold the answer in, uncertain if it would provoke an outburst.

"Your sister."

CHAPTER 38

SERENNA

The news Jassyn divulged ricocheted through Serenna's skull the entire week. *Ayla must hardly be able to take it, having to wait until the formal announcement to shove the engagement in my face.* Envious thoughts skittered across Serenna's mind before she squashed them.

Choosing an elven-blooded with significant abilities and the most prominent bloodlines made logical sense. Were she to stay in the human lands, Serenna imagined her mother would've paired her off in the same way with another realm's royalty.

But she picked incessantly at the wound. *I've never seen the prince and Ayla interact before.*

Serenna's heart tightened with a jealous feeling she'd been suppressing, unsure of what to do with the emotion. It was messy and complicated, bruising the rungs of her ribs. She buried the resentful feelings deep in a cavern in her chest.

Ayla had everything Serenna grew up wanting—a life in Alari, a strong relationship with their sire, and now... She pried her thoughts away from Vesryn.

I don't want to be with him anyway. Our association is purely educational with this champion business. He's simply doing his job and helping me manifest my power.

The bond was the only reason anything hovered between her and the prince; she was obviously transforming the link into something it wasn't. *And he doesn't want the connection anyway.*

Giving herself a shake, Serenna refused to examine her feelings any further. Her thoughts spinning in circles wouldn't help her move forward.

But why did Vesryn bother freeing Jassyn from his contracts after all this time? Was it really because I asked? She supposed the prince's agenda didn't matter. She was grateful for Jassyn's liberation from the realm.

Serenna brought her awareness back to the dull carrying-on of the magus instructing the illumination class.

You'd think illumination would be easy to master since everyone with elf blood has the ability. Like turning over garden soil in her mind, Serenna attempted to cultivate feelings of happiness or tranquility. But trying to pull forth emotions in that spectrum was a fruitless endeavor.

She sighed, knowing why.

Serenna spent her time watching the other recruits master their magic while she failed to manifest her own. She shifted her weight, growing bored standing around.

Glass windows in the Citadel spanned the length from floor to ceiling, admitting the late-morning sunshine amid a scattering of fluffy clouds. Initiates flared orbs of light or transferred a portion of their Well's stores back and forth.

To keep herself occupied, Serenna focused on adjusting her mental walls. Jassyn had instructed her to visualize a barrier between her thoughts and the surrounding environment.

They'd practiced throughout the week after her aiding hour. Jassyn would link them telepathically, and Serenna attempted to dislodge his hold on her mind. She couldn't toss him out of her awareness every time, but she at least learned the concept of barricading her emotions from the bond.

She pictured her thoughts like a castle surrounded by a solid wall. *Let's see if Vesryn can break through that.* As an afterthought, she added iron spikes to her barrier.

The imagined layer of separation relaxed hidden tension in Serenna's shoulders. During her next training session with the prince, she could at least attempt to keep her tangled feelings to herself.

As if prompted by her thoughts, Vesryn's immediate presence slammed into her awareness like a meteor smashing to the earth. Serenna's spine went rigid, a rope drawn taut.

She ground her teeth. *What now?*

Serenna had sensed the prince leaving the island earlier in the morning, which seemed to be his usual habit. *Apparently, he portaled back. If that lout thinks he can just yank—*

An alarm clanged in her head, vibrating through her like a violent strike of a gong.

Serenna gasped.

Flames of agony crashed through her bones in undulating waves, pain radiating through the bond. It knocked the air from her lungs. The sudden onslaught punched her to the ground.

Serenna's knees gave out as she collapsed, catching herself with her hands. A jagged inhale choked her, Vesryn's injuries stabbing through her ribs with every breath.

Everything faded. A ringing buzz muffled her ears. A torrent of searing anguish roared through their connection.

Serenna scrambled to her feet. Her panic, more consuming than a wildfire, blazed through her, scorching the inside of her chest.

Stars, he's hurt!

Deaf to the vocal protest a magus directed her way, Serenna fled, abandoning the classroom. Her frightened heartbeat pounded through the silence in her head. Flying down the stairs of the Citadel, she sprinted to the Spire.

I need Jassyn's help, she thought, barreling through the entrance doors. Her mind flailed to keep pace with her running feet.

No. I don't have time to waste trying to find him.

Vesryn's injuries were too severe for her to comprehend through the bond and…and his presence flickered in her awareness like a sputtering candle flame.

Serenna dodged and twisted around the cafeteria attendants arranging the mess hall for the lunch hour. Before she made it to the other side, a thought flew through her mind.

Snatching a servant, Serenna gulped in air in between her words. "Jassyn. Magus Jassyn at the Infirmary," she panted. "Find him. Send him to the prince's quarters."

The servant blinked in response as if Serenna had gone mad.

Serenna swallowed more air and shook her. "Tell him. Tell him it's urgent."

The attendant just gaped.

Serenna struck out in frustration. Ripping the tray of cured meats out of the staring woman's hands, she threw the arrangement against the wall. The surrounding servants went still as the smashing platter sent food flying.

"Now!" Serenna screamed. The cafeteria's doors slammed open with a howl of wind. "Get Magus Jassyn!" Shoving the servant forward, she shrieked, "Run!"

Spinning around, pleading to the stars that the woman would obey, Serenna dashed up the Spire's stairs.

Her terror drove her into a wild, desperate hysteria to reach the upper levels. Laboring from the infinite stars-cursed ascent, she didn't allow her feet to flag. Legs pumping, boots hammering the marbled steps, Serenna sprinted up two at a time.

What few servants she soared past during her climb, she gave the same panicked commands: find Jassyn and bring him to the Spire. *One of them has to reach him,* she assured herself.

Serenna sailed beyond Vesryn's office, sensing he was in his chambers. His usual stoic guards were absent.

She tore at the handle.

Locked. *Or shielded?*

With more frenzy than a pack of blood-lusting wolves ripping into a deer, Serenna rammed into the door and yanked at the latch. Screaming and beating the wooden barrier from the hallway, she battled to get inside.

"Vesryn!"

The extent of the prince's injuries flogged her now that she was closer. Blinding white-hot pain radiated from his chest, shoulder, and side. Serenna sobbed in frustration, blocked from reaching him.

Threads of clarity knotted together, tugging her mind into focus.

What am I doing?

In her hysteric rush to reach the upper levels, a wall of panic had shadowed her thoughts. Serenna grappled with her Well before primal instinct consumed her. Uprooting her Essence, she wrenched her magic, bending it to her will.

Unleashed, her power surged to life, shifting the world into focus. Determination propelled her. With more strength than she'd ever summoned before, Serenna blasted a swirling vortex of force against the door obstructing her way. The wood exploded in a spray of splinters across Vesryn's sitting room.

Blood.

Puddles of crimson footprints materialized from the center of his apartments. Serenna's apprehension spiked at the sight.

Vesryn's twin glaives lay scattered on the floor. Still sheathed in his shoulder scabbards. With a wordless cry, Serenna stumbled, chasing the trail of scarlet tracks into the bathing chamber.

The prince, one of the realm's most lethal warriors, a master of magic and combat, lay splayed on the tile. He'd propped himself against the vanity under the porcelain sink. The sight of him broken rendered Serenna momentarily stunned.

She panted, her lungs burning on air. As she clutched the doorframe for support, Serenna assessed the inconceivable.

A scarlet river streamed out like a tributary in all directions across the floor. A black arrow with a shaft half the size of her wrist jutted out from Vesryn's shoulder. Another protruded from under his ribs. He gripped a towel swimming in blood against the center of his chest.

Serenna rushed forward, slipping on the drenched tiles. She skidded and collapsed to her knees beside the prince. Sliced by a razored edge of dismay, she gasped. Vesryn's pain was sharp in her mind. Piercing. Like the arrows embedded in his flesh.

She lifted an unsteady hand to help apply pressure against the cloth covering his sternum. The fabric dripped ruby raindrops, failing to stem the tide of blood leaking through his armor's shredded dragon. The prince's skin was colorless and chilled, like he'd just dived into icy waters. Through the trembling wall of his chest, his rapid heartbeat strained to pulse under her fingertips.

Serenna's body shook uncontrollably from the alarm settling in. She couldn't comprehend the sight of him reduced to such a helpless state. Her panic made the bond blur; she wasn't sure how much of the shock was Vesryn's or her own. Just sensing the amount of pain he was in flayed her bit by bit.

The prince's eyes met hers. He blinked slowly, laboring to take shallow and rattling breaths. His muscles seized as violently as Serenna's hands shook.

"You're here," he choked out. One side of his mouth quivered as he attempted to give her a lopsided grin. "And I…I didn't even summon you…this time." The effort of the words sent him into a gurgling, coughing fit.

"I need to get a magus," Serenna whispered, grabbing a less saturated cloth to wipe the frothy blood bubbling down his chin. "This is beyond me."

She questioned whether any of the servants had relayed her frantic demands to retrieve Jassyn. *Why didn't I just get a mender myself after sensing Vesryn was hurt?*

"No." Vesryn reached out. The effort had him groaning through clenched teeth. Doubling over his wounds, he hooked her wrist in a frail grip. "Don't…leave."

"But I feel you dying!"

"Stay," he said before closing his eyes to lean his head back against the vanity for support. "Please."

The despair in his voice fractured Serenna's thoughts. Her heart faltered. Darkness loomed to shroud her vision. A fresh wave of panic had her lungs hauling in air faster than she could breathe.

Fear clogged her throat as sound swam from her ears.

She couldn't catch her breath.

She couldn't rein in her terror.

Vesryn's presence darted in and out through the bond. Serenna's attention hurtled back to the moment. *No!* Retreating from the futile attempt of stemming the spurting blood, she seized his face instead.

The prince's arms slid limply to the floor.

"Vesryn!" she shrieked, jerking him. "Vesryn!"

His head lolled to the side.

What am I supposed to do? I haven't healed anything life-threatening before! She couldn't let herself succumb to panic.

I need to try.

If she could stall the flow of blood from his chest...maybe it would buy him enough time. *Please, Jassyn. Hurry.*

"Stars scorch you! You're not dying!" In an effort to snap the prince out of his daze, Serenna delivered a sharp slap across his cheek.

Vesryn's head swung limply to the other side.

Serenna stretched her awareness to the bond's two silver cords mooring their souls together. Sending the entire force of her power racing along the magical bridge, she seized the bright link of Vesryn's fluttering aura. With one ruthless yank, she heaved the connection toward her with all of her strength.

Vesryn's body bucked. He gasped, eyes flying open. Folding over, a fresh wave of coughs and blood flowed from his throat.

When his breathing became less labored, Serenna assisted him to a sitting position, leaning into him, to offer support so he wouldn't topple over.

"Vesryn," she pleaded, cupping his face. "Stay with me." She stifled a sob as his glassy gaze locked with hers.

Serenna chewed her cheek, clamping down on the worries welling inside her. She repositioned herself on her knees, leaning over him.

I can do this. I have to do this.

Moving her hands to Vesryn's chest, she opened her senses, drawing on the entire channel of her power.

Healing light bloomed like a crimson fountain beneath her fingertips, encasing Vesryn in a dome, waiting for her direction. Serenna's eyes unfocused as she burrowed into his veins. She scattered streams of Essence through every vessel to evaluate the extent of his injuries.

The arrows bit brutally into his flesh. One pierced his shoulder, striking the bone. The other metal barb skewered itself in between his ribs, puncturing a lung. *That explains the bloody coughing.*

She hurriedly cast a healing wave over the arrow's head to prevent fluid from pooling further. *I'll mend that later.*

Every heartbeat ejected spurts of blood through the gaping hole in

Vesryn's chest. Three shattered ribs connecting to his sternum wreathed the outline of the angry chasm.

Thankfully, his heart was missed. Did he already tear out the arrow?

Serenna began healing the most pressing injury.

"You slapped me." Vesryn wheezed, a chuckle that turned into gurgling coughs. He gasped and sputtered, "Can you do it again?"

Ignoring what was most certainly incoherence from the massive blood loss, Serenna focused all of her attention on closing his wounds. Filaments of Essence spooled around the prince, gathering like strings in a web. She twisted the threads of magic and plaited her power to stitch the hollow in his chest.

Working cautiously but swiftly, she layered one fragment of healing at a time. Fusing and restoring. Knitting bones and reconnecting severed nerves, muscles, and vessels. Vesryn's skin merged in a grotesque mass of melting flesh under her fingertips.

The mending surpassed anything she'd previously attempted. Serenna winced. It showed. The healed skin was a scarred, unsightly, and puckered mess.

He can worry about being pretty later. At least his chest isn't hemorrhaging anymore.

Despite choking on blood, Vesryn laughed. "That slap," he gurgled through a chortle.

Desire pounced on her through the bond.

Serenna gasped.

Her power guttered, Vesryn's passion flitting up her spine. She jumped when he anchored a hand to the swell of her hip. He clutched her like a maniac sailing in a squall, taunting the furious tides of fate to tear him away.

The prince cackled. Hysterically. He then lowered his voice and commanded, "Slap me again."

Serenna scowled, her fingers itching to do just that. "I'll slap some sense into you."

Vesryn *giggled.* Which sent him spiraling into another eruption of coughing.

Serenna's concentration wavered when the prince's hunger for her lunged through the link to ensnare her in an embrace. Her heart leaped, forcing her to grapple with her power. Like clutching onto a lifeline, she mercilessly tightened her grip around the fleeing magic. *His mind must be thoroughly addled.*

Satisfied she'd patched the hole in Vesryn's chest adequately enough for the immediate future, Serenna sat back on her heels and wiped her bloody hands on a soiled piece of linen.

Ribbons of dazzling silver beams, as brilliant as starlight, burst and radiated from the prince. The magic arced, a breathtaking dance of Essence unlike anything she'd ever seen. Vesryn's power landed on her like dozens of shooting stars, perching on her skin as flecks of light.

Serenna reprimanded him. "Save your strength and focus on not dying." She had no idea how the prince could channel power in his current state. *He probably doesn't even know what he's doing. At least he didn't rend me by accident.*

Grabbing Vesryn's arm, Serenna regenerated the lake of blood he'd spilled on the floor. Aiding Jassyn had given her plenty of practice with that technique.

The weak and rapid pulse of the prince's heart became stronger. Steadier. Color washed back into his face.

Vesryn's eyes cleared and refocused. As if confused by the magic spun around them, he squinted at the glowing stars. He released the hold on his power. The lights faded from Serenna's skin as he emitted a rickety exhale.

"I didn't believe I'd see anything as beautiful as a display like that," he said, the right side of his mouth tugging fleetingly to flash his dimple. Serenna froze when he cupped her cheek. "That is, until I saw you."

Serenna's power fled. She gaped at him. His smirk blossomed into a distracting grin.

She sucked in a stabilizing breath. This wasn't the time for the prince's irrational frivolity. His condition was improving, but he still had to contend with serious injuries.

Serenna pulled out of his grasp and unsheathed one of his belt knives. *No short supply there.*

Vesryn arched a brow as she gripped the blade. "Are you going to undo all of that mending?"

"I need to remove the arrows."

Serenna chewed her lip, determining the most efficient way to work. The prince's position propped against the vanity wouldn't make it easy. She needed to get his armor off first to further assess the damage.

Well, there's really only one option.

Serenna swung a leg over Vesryn's hips to straddle him.

And only somewhat regretted the action when he immediately grabbed her thighs and inhaled a rattling hiss.

"Fuck," he gasped, throwing his head back, squeezing his eyes shut.

Vesryn's curse rolled through Serenna like a thunderclap. She smothered the pleasure flaming through her. The bond was rather inconvenient while she strained to focus on saving his life. She didn't have the skill to assemble a mental barricade *and* heal.

Taking care not to disturb the arrows, Serenna sliced the leather armor away from his chest.

The prince's exhale was more of a groan. "Scorching stars, you're going to be the death of me."

Serenna struggled to dismiss the not-so-unpleasant sensations radiating through their connection. The flames of desire she doused were determined to flicker to life. The perception of Vesryn's pain was a numb buzz compared to the passion boiling in his veins.

As soon as she peeled away the armor to bare his chest and expose the rooted arrows, his excitement vaulted through the bond. Vesryn's fingers tightened, cinching over her legs. Serenna gasped, catching herself with a hand shoved against his chest as he savagely ground his hips against hers.

"Stop it," Serenna hissed, a half-hearted protest. "You're distracting me."

She tossed the knife to the floor and sat back on his thighs, wrestling her springing emotions, battling to jumble with his.

Vesryn perked up. "I could go for a *distraction* myself right about now, but I fear my current state may hinder my performance."

Serenna flushed. *I'm in for it.*

He chuckled and squeezed her hips. Apparently more alert with her perched on his lap, Vesryn's mind no longer skirted the line of unconsciousness. His breathing still had an audible click from the fluid remaining in the pierced lung.

Serenna scrubbed the hair out of her face with the back of her hand while she considered which arrow to dislodge first. The shaft jutting from his shoulder wasn't as serious as the one harpooned in his side. A heavy coat of congealed blood surrounded both wounds.

I wish Jassyn was here to help. With her Well's stores of power waning, Serenna caged her worry that she wouldn't be able to finish mending. *At least the prince doesn't seem as close to death now.*

"I need to pull the arrows out," she said. "I don't think I can push them through. The barbs..." She trailed off. *Well, I'm sure he's aware it's going to hurt.*

Vesryn extended his palm. "Hand me a leather strip."

Serenna dropped a piece of the dismantled armor into his waiting palm. The prince raised it to his mouth but then paused, focusing his sea-glass gaze on her. "Before I faint, could you answer me something?"

She waited for another round of bloody coughing to pass.

"You're coming to the Lunar Solstice with me," he said through labored breaths.

Serenna blinked. *The royal ball where they're announcing his engagement? I thought I regenerated enough of his blood, but it obviously hasn't made it to his head yet.*

"It sounds like you're ordering me. How about you live through this first?"

Vesryn huffed in answer, but folded the material and clamped the leather between his teeth.

"I'll count to three and pull the arrow out." Serenna cleared her throat. "Okay?"

The prince closed his eyes and nodded his acceptance. His breath came fast through his nose in anticipation. Serenna glanced at his hands lodged on her hips, hoping he wouldn't perceive her intent.

She leaned away from the jutting arrow. Wrapping the quarrel in force like a snake corkscrewing around a branch, she coiled her power.

"One."

With a burst of magic, Serenna ripped the shaft out in one stroke. The arrow shot out of Vesryn's side in a fountain of blood. It soared across the room to clatter against a wall.

The prince lurched, nearly vaulting her off of his legs as he arched his back. Serenna shrieked through her teeth, feeling the excruciating blast of fire blistering his body.

A sound more animal than elf erupted from Vesryn's throat, his pained scream splitting the air. The leather strap in his mouth hardly muffled the noise. The piercing howl clawed down Serenna's spine as the prince's fingers raked furrows into her leathers.

His eyes flew open and found hers. Whimpering breaths escaped through his nose as he trembled like a breeze-blown leaf.

Serenna grabbed a fresh towel. "I'm sorry," she whispered, wiping the sweat from his brow. "The worst part is over. Hold on, I'll start mending."

Vesryn spat out the leather, swearing. Quite colorfully about more dracovae anatomy.

Regathering her power, Serenna pressed the cloth to his side to halt the renewed flow of spurting blood. The prince drew in another sharp inhale at the pressure.

Their gazes gravitated together like the inevitable pull the earth had on its moons. Serenna swallowed. She could drown in those sea-green depths. For one absurd moment, she thought about covering Vesryn's mouth with hers.

She stiffened, eyes going wide. *Does he realize I want him?*

Serenna's answer in that brief suspension of time was a flicker of comprehension. A blink. Surprise flashed across the prince's features, causing her heart to bolt.

Vesryn didn't hesitate.

His hands shot up in a blur. Ignoring the arrow in his shoulder, he seized the back of her neck and hauled her mouth to his.

Serenna abandoned the cloth and grabbed his face in return. Their lips didn't brush in a hesitant, testing way; Vesryn's mouth met hers with reckless abandon, fierce and crushing, like he was drowning and her lips were his only source of air. Tugging her hair, he angled her head for a deeper kiss.

Serenna's body ignited like they were two galaxies colliding. Her magic threatened to explode through her skin where they touched, electrifying her nerves, flooding her with energy.

She gasped, registering a renewed flare of pain. Vesryn brushed his tongue through her parted lips.

He consumed her, a flash flood flowing across desert sands, sweeping her away. His breath was as jagged as hers, sucking in air around their mouths meeting, crashing against each other like waves against the shore.

Serenna pressed into him, needing to close the space between them, craving more of him. Vesryn hissed against her mouth as she jostled the arrow in his shoulder.

His pain jolted sense into her.

Stars, I need to finish healing him, not shove my tongue down his throat.

Serenna tried pulling back, but Vesryn's grip on her tightened, moving his hands to cradle her face, tugging her closer. She could live forever in the space under his fingertips.

Someone coughed.

Her breath caught.

They froze. Serenna drew away, parting their mouths.

She stared at Vesryn as they panted, their noses nearly touching. Her fingers brushed over his cheeks, an automatic response, fidgeting under his attention. He gave her a crooked grin, his thumb swiping his blood off of her lips.

Vesryn's eyes wandered behind her. His mouth twisted, either from pain or in annoyance. Serenna sensed both. When the prince dropped his hands from her face, she turned.

Jassyn stood in the doorway, his chest heaving. His startled look quickly vanished as he irritably swiped stray curls out of his eyes.

"I see you already went through the trouble of...*resuscitating* the prince," Jassyn said to her. He glanced at the pool of blood, to Vesryn's bare chest, and then back to her. "Charming." Disapproval wrinkled his brows. "Am I still needed or...?"

"Yes," Serenna said quickly, a flush racing to the tips of her ears.

"No," Vesryn growled, like a dog possessive over a bone. His fingers clamped down on her hips.

Jassyn rolled his eyes, muttering to the stars to send him strength, but hurried over. Not bothering to skirt the blood, he kneeled beside them while Serenna swiveled off of Vesryn's lap.

She swatted the prince's hands when he wrestled to keep her in place. She certainly would *not* straddle him with Jassyn present. Scooting across the floor, Serenna rested against the vanity next to him.

"I hate to interrupt," Jassyn said as healing light sprang up and enveloped the prince in a ruby glow. "If you prefer bleeding out first, I'll return later."

Vesryn's dark chuckle was a rasp against sandpaper. "That wasn't how I pictured things finishing." His hand roamed and found hers, fingers tightening in a curling embrace.

Serenna's chest loosened, releasing her fear. For the first time, she breathed easily, relaxing as Jassyn took over the mending.

"*I'm* not going to mount you, so don't get any ideas," Jassyn informed Vesryn, shooting Serenna what she decided was a judgmental look when he touched the prince's side.

"It was the best position to remove his armor," she insisted. As Jassyn gave her another glance full of accusation, Serenna mumbled, "I only did it to heal him."

Vesryn shoved a bloody strand of hair out of his face. "Your timing is impeccable, cousin. You know how to ruin a moment."

"I'm glad you have your priorities in order," Jassyn snapped, flicking the prince's ear.

"She's the one who jumped on me," Vesryn protested, scowling and rubbing his skin. "I have to say I prefer the princess's bedside manners over yours, Magus *Killjoy*."

"You already told me I'm going straight to the Vallende estate if you die," Jassyn grumbled. "I assure you, the only reason I'm even here is because it benefits *me*."

Vesryn spat out a mouthful of blood before giving Jassyn a crimson-streaked grin. "Keep telling yourself that." He patted Jassyn's cheek. "Come a little closer, and we can have our own moment too."

Jassyn's lip curled, but he kept his hands fastened to the prince as he continued to heal. "Serenna, put that leather in his mouth. Before I'm tempted to throttle him."

Vesryn exhaled a rough laugh as his skin knitted back together smoothly. Unsurprisingly, Jassyn's skill surpassed her own—there wasn't even a scar on the prince's side.

"I think I'd prefer a slap over strangling," Vesryn said, shooting Serenna a smirk before returning his attention to his cousin. "But I'm open to experimenting if you want to find out. Why don't you—"

Vesryn's eyes popped when Jassyn crammed a scrap of armor in between his teeth. The prince spat the leather back at Jassyn's head. Which, Jassyn pointedly ignored by deflecting the barrage with a brief flare of a shield.

Serenna's awareness drifted as they squabbled. Her body trembled as the events caught up to her. *Can I take away his pain?*

She descended into the bond. Closing her eyes and focusing on all the sensations strung out between them, Serenna grazed the agonizing pulse radiating from the prince and...enveloped the angry haze with her presence, absorbing the fog into her.

Serenna convulsed, shrieking through her teeth. *Scorching stars, this is with only one wound remaining.*

"Don't, you harpy," Vesryn warned, turning to her. He gave her hand a squeeze that was much softer than his tone. "I know you're strong, but you might faint."

"You did it for me," Serenna whimpered, breathing through her nose. Her fingers shook around his.

She gritted her teeth, the force of her will fighting the darkness creeping into her vision. A weariness settled into her bones, making her want to sink to the floor. She fought to keep her eyes open while her body recovered from joining the prince on his near-death experience.

Serenna hated how Vesryn was right.

Her awareness slipped like grains of sand through her fingers as she clutched his suffering. The pain spiked and darkness enveloped her when Jassyn tore out the other arrow.

CHAPTER 39

SERENNA

Low, bickering voices reached Serenna's ears as her awareness stirred.

Jassyn sounded half strangled. "Do you *have* to do that at the table?"

"What?" Vesryn asked innocently.

"You know *what*. You're ill-mannered."

"You're the one reading while we're sharing a meal. Seems impolite, Magus *Manners*."

"We are not *sharing* a meal."

Serenna roused, peeking an eye toward the argument. Vesryn hunched forward on his elbows over the dining table, trimming his nails with a belt knife. Across from him, with three open books arranged around his plate, Jassyn sliced strips of lamb roast with straight-backed etiquette appropriate for a royal feast.

Serenna's stomach grumbled in protest at missing lunch. Her Well felt nearly as empty from the effort of mending the prince.

Vesryn straightened, likely sensing her restored consciousness. He rotated toward her, his mouth tilted in amusement. "Don't say I didn't warn you."

With a moan, Serenna slung her feet off of Vesryn's sitting room couch and onto the floor. "How are you feeling?" she asked, searching him. "Shouldn't you be resting?"

Instinctively, Serenna reached out through the bond. She expected the prince's injuries to assault her senses, the memory still sharp in her mind. A relieved sigh escaped when she perceived nothing but his apparent humor.

Vesryn leaned his chair on two legs and flipped his dagger. "I haven't been this invigorated in a century."

Considering their damp hair and clean appearance, it appeared both Vesryn and Jassyn had time to refresh. Jassyn's bare feet peeked out beneath black pants and bounced under the table. Curiously enough, they both wore matching loungewear of an unfamiliar shiny material. *I'm surprised Jassyn found anything in Vesryn's closet besides leathers.*

Serenna glanced at herself, aghast she still wore her blood-soaked uniform. Her eyes darted around Vesryn's sitting room, seeing no trace of the splintered door. The servants must've been busy, judging from the tidiness of the apartments. Serenna studied her spotless hands with a suspicious notion of who washed them.

"For the record," Vesryn said, pointing his knife at her, "I tried removing your clothes, but Jassyn wouldn't allow it."

Jassyn rolled his eyes and stabbed his fork with more force than necessary to spear a carrot. The utensil *pinged* against the silver plate.

"He felt the need to *chaperone* until you woke up," Vesryn continued. "I'll make sure he leaves something for you to eat if you want to get cleaned up first. There's loungewear for you in the bathing chambers."

Serenna appraised the small feast. The three of them would struggle to finish everything on their own.

Vesryn raised a hand. A biscuit from Jassyn's plate levitated and floated into his outstretched palm. The tendons in Jassyn's neck strained with the flashing of his eyes, like he was at his wit's end dealing with his cousin.

Serenna could tell Vesryn intentionally pushed Jassyn to hazardous heights, aiming to shove him off the cliffs of irritation.

Scanning the windows, the fading light signaled half the day had passed. Serenna tried to make sense of her lingering fear. Vesryn had almost *died* and now acted like he was thoroughly enjoying himself hosting dinner.

"If the *commander* hasn't acknowledged what you did yet, I will," Serenna said, rising and giving Jassyn's shoulder a squeeze. "Thank you for coming." Studying the prince cutting his nails, she sniffed and muttered, "And for staying."

Something had shifted between them since Vesryn had disbanded her friend's contracts. Jassyn's precarious tolerance was a testimony to that. Despite Vesryn goading Jassyn, Serenna sensed an undercurrent of protectiveness when she angled her thoughts toward the prince.

Vesryn has an odd way of showing he cares, but it's something. And she didn't blame Jassyn if he wasn't ready to forgive his cousin yet.

Earlier in the week, Jassyn had his tattoos erased with specialized mending in the capital. Serenna's heart still twisted knowing the lingering effects of his servitude would go deeper than skin.

She narrowed her eyes on Vesryn. "You're going to explain what happened after I get cleaned up."

Vesryn scowled when Jassyn shot him a smirk. *Two of us against the prince should even the odds.*

Serenna entered the bathing chambers, discovering them to be sparkling clean. As if Vesryn hadn't bled out half his lifeblood all over the tiles. Her attention wandered to the vanity where he'd almost perished. It all seemed like a fading dream now. *I really helped save him?*

Unweaving the laces of her bodice, Serenna peeled off the crusty uniform. With an apology to whoever had to clean the blood off the clothes, she deposited everything in the hamper to join Jassyn's and Vesryn's soiled leathers. She doubted the prince's would be salvageable.

After using Vesryn's rain ceiling—she was still adjusting to the elves' running water instead of soaking in a tub—Serenna helped herself to the prince's ivory-handled comb, brushing out the tangles, letting her hair hang loose down her back.

Her attention roamed to the tiles again. Unprompted, her heart spasmed in response, dredging up the memory of the prince's mouth all over hers, repeating it in her mind.

She hadn't processed the unexpected kiss either, but heavy regret settled in her chest like a pile of stones.

I shouldn't have done that. She was only going to make it more difficult for herself when she had to accept his betrothal to Ayla. *He had to be joking about the Solstice.*

Serenna collected herself with a steadying breath and put on a facade of nonchalance. She glided into the dining room as if she were attending a grand ball. In whatever ridiculous two-piece loungewear she wore. *This material is finer than silk!*

Vesryn's eyes tracked her with a predatory gleam, doubling her heart rate. Serenna brushed off his attention as much as she could, grateful for Jassyn's presence. When she spared a glance toward the prince, his mouth twisted into a mischievous grin.

Insufferable elf. She settled into a chair at the end of the table and distracted herself by piling her plate with slabs of lamb, roast vegetables, and buttered bread.

On her right, Jassyn released a flurry of curses. Pulling her attention away from the feast, Serenna saw the prince crouched with a foot up on the edge of his seat.

Vesryn bristled, his dagger hovering above his bare toes. He shot Jassyn a glare. "What now, Magus of Complaints?"

Jassyn looked pleadingly toward her for reinforcement. Too hungry to care, Serenna waved to show her indifference, slicing into the roast. *We all swam in Vesryn's blood. A few clipped nails won't hurt anything.*

Well, he really doesn't have to do it at the table.

Jassyn flung his fork to his plate. "You will *not* do that while I'm eating across from you." If he was abandoning the cherry pie, the prince obviously peeved him. "I'm drawing the line there."

"These are *my* chambers." Vesryn waved the blade around the room before hacking off the overgrown portion of his big toenail with a swipe of the knife.

Jassyn's knuckles cracked as he dug his fists into his eyes. As if he could push the unpleasant image of Vesryn's nail sailing through the air out of his mind.

"What happened today?" Serenna asked, wanting some answers.

Why is he so calm? Her heart hollowed out as she thought of how close Vesryn had come to dying. He would have if they didn't share an awareness of each other.

The prince hesitated over another toe before swinging his foot to the ground. He tossed the belt knife on the table. Jassyn's mouth pinched as he glared at the offending blade, but he picked up his fork and refocused on his dessert.

"Wraith," Vesryn said.

"But you fight wraith all the time," Jassyn commented.

"These wraith were different."

"Different?" Serenna asked. Her spine crawled with a shiver of fear. *Wraith hurt him?* "How?"

Vesryn ticked off reasons on a hand. "Well, for one, they were wearing a type of spiked, scaled armor. Normally they have on rags." With another finger, he said, "Two, they were in a large group. I never see more than a handful together. And three, these wraith weren't mindless beasts, solely focused on sinking their fangs into flesh. This band was organized, trained, and had weapons. Some were *gold-tipped* weapons."

Jassyn gave an incredulous grunt and helped himself to another piece of pie. "How do they know of tethering?"

Vesryn shrugged. "If that golden arrow didn't incapacitate me, I would've made quick work of them. It…it tore through my shield. The quarrel came from a contraption I've never seen before." He mimed what Serenna assumed was how to operate the weapon. "Like a miniature bow, but you crank it."

"You're lucky to be alive, then," Jassyn remarked. His eyes reflected the same fear constricting Serenna's bones. "Gold can…tear through our wards?"

Vesryn released a sigh but nodded. "It's…not a comforting thought. And before I could summon any power to spin a portal, I had to rip the shaft out of my chest—which wasn't the most pleasant experience I've ever had." Vesryn's hand slipped between the laces of his tunic, rubbing the scarred mess she'd made. "By the time I did, they were making quick work of turning me into a pincushion with those stars-cursed barbed arrows. At least those weren't gold too."

"Were you alone?" Serenna questioned, though she could guess the answer.

"I always hunt them alone." Vesryn picked at a fiber in the tablecloth.

"That's absurd." She gave a disbelieving scoff. "You have rangers—their job is to pursue the wraith. Why didn't they accompany you? You almost *died* today."

Vesryn's brow furrowed. He yanked a thread, sending a runner up the fabric. "But I *didn't*."

"That justifies nothing. How could you be so reckless?" Serenna's hand tightened around her fork. "You're not invincible. Or did the last few hours do nothing to dull your ego?"

"She has a point," Jassyn interrupted, eyes volleying between the pair of them. Likely knowing she would erupt, he cut off her verbal assault. "Why didn't you take warriors if there was a report of so many wraith?"

Vesryn's glower shifted to Jassyn. "I was flying through the northern realm by coincidence, letting Naru hunt a herd of elk. I saw nearly a hundred wraith raiding a cattle farm." Vesryn packed the empty platter in front of him with another helping of dinner. "Not wanting Naru to get close to such a large group, I portaled from the air—and I'm glad I decided not to land him. I thought I could handle it. I *would* have handled it if they were the mindless wraith I expected and didn't have gold."

Serenna pushed her food around on her plate, her appetite fleeing. *He thinks he can subdue a hundred wraith when a handful of those creatures slaughtered an entire village a few weeks ago?*

"Do you think this points to more than one group now?" Jassyn asked, frowning and thumbing his chin. "It would be alarming if they're advancing this quickly beyond the mindless beasts that attack the capital."

"I don't know." Vesryn gnawed at a fingernail that his dagger evidently didn't trim. "They've spread across all the realms now, it seems. We have yet to discover any stronghold."

"Are we going after them?" Serenna asked. And by "we," she was hoping for those with more combat experience than the initiates—like the rangers or her sire's soldiers. If the wraith nearly killed the prince, there wasn't any chance she would survive an encounter.

"I sent the location of the raid to the rangers, but those beasts are long gone by now." Vesryn held up a parchment. "I received word that the farmers are safe at least. I don't know why the wraith didn't slaughter the village for sport this time like they have in every other raid. The rangers are attempting to locate the wraith from the air, but somehow, those monsters seem to have disappeared. *With* a herd of cattle."

Vesryn grabbed his belt knife and sliced a sliver of meat off of a leg bone. Jassyn's fork hovered in front of his mouth. His eyes went wide, watching the prince in horrified disbelief.

"Bleeding stars!" Jassyn swore at him. "You just used that on your *feet!*"

Vesryn shrugged before biting the lamb straight off the dagger. Like a barbarian. He held Jassyn's gaze as he chewed, grinning villainously. The obscene way he licked the blade clean was oddly suggestive.

Returning a disgusted sneer, Jassyn forsook all attempts at eating. He thrust a book in front of his face to block out his view of the prince.

Serenna didn't think Vesryn was taking the situation seriously. "Why didn't you portal to the Infirmary?"

The prince's mouth quirked before he answered. "We all would've been disappointed if opening a gateway there severed Jassyn in half."

"So, what was your plan?" she demanded, slamming her fork on the table. "To shove a rag into that gaping hole in your chest while you bled out alone on the floor? Why didn't you reach out telepathically for help?"

"I was in shock," he protested.

"How often does this happen?" Serenna bored her stare into him, twisting in her irritation.

"It doesn't." Vesryn straightened his shoulders and turned his attention to his plate.

"It *did*."

Serenna assembled her mental barricades to wall herself off from the prince. *Might as well see if it works.* Vesryn's brainless insistence on these dangerous solitary adventures was causing her annoyance to rise like heat from a fire. With one final imagined *click*, Serenna locked the prison of her mind.

Vesryn's head snapped toward her. "I've been meaning to ask when you learned how to do that."

Serenna glared at him. "Since *you* didn't tell me about that aspect of the bond, I asked Jassyn."

"Do *not* drag me into this," Jassyn warned from behind his book.

"Fine," Vesryn said to her. He trailed a finger lazily along the steel of the dagger, holding her gaze. "We'll play later." He tilted his chin in a challenge. "We'll find out just how well you can keep those walls up."

Jassyn released a strangled cough as he turned a page.

Still scowling at the prince, Serenna lifted her goblet to her lips. More so to prevent herself from arguing further. Reasoning with him was as effective as sparring against a stone. Vesryn's eyes hooked on her broken finger, protruding away from the glass.

He frowned at it and nodded. "Do you want that mended?"

Not waiting for an answer, he swept his arm across the table, shoving the dinner dishes out of the way. He placed a waiting palm in the space between them.

"Right now?" Serenna glanced at Jassyn, assuming the prince was offering his cousin's skill.

Vesryn voiced the obvious fact. "We're all here."

Setting his book down, Jassyn berated Vesryn. "You really should learn how to heal."

"It never came up. Too busy killing wraith, you know?"

"Right. It would be asking too much to care about someone besides yourself. Since healing only helps others."

Vesryn feigned offense, putting his other hand over his heart. "You wound me, cousin."

Jassyn threw his hands in the air in exaggerated concession. "It just seems like a waste of an ability."

Serenna gaped at them, wondering how long they would carry on. She placed her palm into Vesryn's to refocus him. When he gave her a squeeze, she gripped the edge of her chair to fortify herself.

The prince's rending coiled around her finger. The shadows caressed her provocatively, brushing up and down her arm.

Stars help me.

Jassyn rubbed his brows as if warding off the headache his cousin was likely giving him. He shot Vesryn a withering look before hovering his hand over theirs, a red glow emanating from his fingertips.

Vesryn's magic pulsed. He flinched with a wince when the three joints in Serenna's finger *cracked*, shattering again. Jassyn made quick work of stitching the shards of her mangled bones back together.

Serenna released an exasperated sigh at the absence of pain. Vesryn flashed her a crooked smile when he released her hand, looking pleased with himself.

"As much as I would like to extend this lovely dinner party," Jassyn said, closing and collecting the books, "I'm going to get some rest. As should you, Your *Highness*." He gave Vesryn a pointed look before hitching the tomes onto his hip. "And I'm taking these with me."

"Thank you," Vesryn said quietly when Jassyn reached the door.

Jassyn drew to a halt. His eyes darted to the side, but he didn't acknowledge the prince beyond giving Vesryn a slight nod before letting himself out.

"Where are your guards?" Serenna asked, seeing the empty hallway. "It would have been helpful to have them locate a healer for me, but they weren't around."

Turquoise light fountained from Vesryn's hand when he extended his palm to the sitting room. "Do you mean *these* guards?" The two warriors materialized.

Serenna scoffed. "They're illusions?"

Vesryn shrugged. "Their presence makes everyone think twice about bothering me." When he released his power, the forms of the soldiers faded.

She wanted to shake him for his insistence on doing everything alone. He was going to get himself killed. *I can't believe he doesn't have guards!*

"I want you to promise me something," Serenna said before she could think better of it. She paused, considering him warily, not intending to come across so strongly.

Vesryn cocked his head and flipped his knife, but his eyes stayed on her. "You know, it's more entertaining when I can perceive what you're feeling."

I wouldn't have known we could barricade each other from the bond if he didn't do it first. Staring back at him, Serenna let silence blanket the room. Her mouth tightened. She hoped she looked halfway formidable, even though she wore this delicate sleepwear. *For all the good armor would do against him.*

"Okay, what?" he irritably asked, wiping the blade with the table-cloth when she didn't relent.

"I don't want you hunting the wraith alone." Serenna traced her healed finger. "Take someone with you—the rangers, some of the magus." She rolled her eyes and met his. "Bring Jassyn to mend you if you're so star-bent on getting hurt. Just…promise me you won't keep going by yourself."

Vesryn released a scoff. "I'm not agreeing to that."

Serenna slapped her palms on the table, causing the silverware to jump. Hiding behind her frustration was easier than admitting the pang of terror at the thought of losing him.

She argued more vehemently, her irritation igniting. "I *felt* you dying today. I don't want to go through that again."

Vesryn stared straight ahead, not meeting her gaze. A tic appeared in his jaw while his fingers tapped across his folded arms. Serenna didn't need their bond to recognize the marked increase in his agitation. But her patience was on the verge of collapsing too.

He's throwing a tantrum over this?

"Look at me when I'm speaking to you," Serenna snapped. She ground her teeth until he finally turned his attention toward her. "You're being selfish for not considering how this connection also affects me."

Vesryn tossed a hand up. "Then reject the bond. I'm not stopping you."

Serenna shot up, sending the chair skidding behind her. Their eyes clashed in a collision course, warring in their matched willfulness. He acted like it was easy, something she wouldn't have to think twice about. Maybe it was for him, but it wasn't for her. *Why don't I want to?*

Serenna brought up what had plagued her all week, crippling her with jealousy and confusion. "Why? So this connection doesn't impede your engagement?" Her question was feeble, not the verbal blow she wanted it to be.

Vesryn's nostrils flared, his annoyance coiling around her like smoke. Somewhere along the way, her mental barricade had tumbled down. The prince rose to face her, balling his hands into fists.

"Our bond has nothing to do with my impending *betrothal*," he snarled.

Serenna's heart dropped. *Of course it doesn't. But I hoped the link would be something more, like Velinya fantasized.* She had misinterpreted their connection, misread what she thought she felt from him. Biting the inside of her cheek, Serenna considered keeping silent, but the conversation had already started.

What if I'm foolish for putting my heart in the open, and he doesn't feel the same way? We'll still be connected until I learn how to dispel the magic, and I don't think I can live with the rejection.

Her voice fell. "Didn't I deserve to at least know?"

Serenna buried a feeling of disappointment before it could transform into anything else.

Vesryn took a predacious step closer until he towered over her, fury boiling in his jade eyes. She backed away. His words were low and scathing. "Do you actually think this engagement was *my* idea? That I *agreed* to it?"

Serenna faltered, another remark ready to roll off of her lips. But then the memory of him, broken on the floor, drifted to the surface of her thoughts. And tugged on a frayed thread in her heart. She blinked up at him, unraveling, understanding he had no say in the king's decision.

Hurt settled like a stone sinking in a pond that he'd still kept it from her, even if it was arranged.

"I hoped not," Serenna breathed, failing to smooth the tremble in her words.

The voiced admission, unexpectedly revealed, though Vesryn could probably read it anyway, weakened her knees. Serenna placed a hand on her chair for support and blinked back tears. Furious tears, frustrated tears, heartbroken tears. She didn't know. All the strength she thought she had leaked out of her bones.

Serenna swallowed the bitter taste of resentment, hoping she'd stifled the emotion before he could sense it. *Do I mean anything to you?*

She whispered, "Why did you kiss me?"

Vesryn's face turned unreadable.

Serenna extended a tendril of awareness toward him to grasp for any sign of his feelings. To feel *something*. But a solid wall blocked her, completely sealing her off.

So that's how it is. Her heart twisted. He shut her out. *I have my answer.*

The suffocating stillness became too much. The walls were caving in; she needed to leave his apartments before she was buried in despair.

Clearing her throat didn't prevent her voice from breaking. "I'm going to get some rest." She staggered to the door, her legs unsteady. "Good night, Commander."

"Serenna."

The prince's voice snared her like a noose. Serenna halted in her tracks, shock locking her limbs from hearing him say her name.

With a brittle movement, she turned. Vesryn's eyes searched hers with uncertainty and something akin to vulnerability.

"Whatever this is…" His voice trailed off. The muscles of his jaw strained. "It's more than a bond to me."

Serenna didn't breathe, her body flooding with numb disbelief. She blinked at him, stunned by the acknowledgment. The prince's statement hung between them, silent like the calm before a storm.

Vesryn relaxed his stance, lowering his walls to let her in. As if giving voice to the words he wasn't sure how to convey or the feelings he couldn't identify.

Serenna sensed a turbulence in his thoughts, a whirlwind of confusion and hesitation. They matched her own. But there was something else, fragile threads woven into all the chaos, hope twined with affection.

Her eyes widened when Vesryn unveiled emotions he must have kept tucked away. *He feels that way?*

"I thought you wanted me to learn enough about my magic to dissolve this connection," Serenna said, scanning his face.

Vesryn speared his hands through his hair and shook his head. He blew out a breath before he whispered, "I don't want what's between us to be something else I fuck up. Can we…take some time to figure everything out?"

Serenna's heart stumbled, tripping over itself. *So, for now, he doesn't want me to reject the bond? If whatever this is between us is more than a magical connection, what does that mean for his engagement? I can't harbor feelings for someone who's claimed by another—even if it is by duty.*

But maybe that was a worry for a different day.

"Okay," Serenna whispered back. Her teeth dug across her bottom lip while her heart coiled into a knot.

For now, it was enough.

CHAPTER 40

SERENNA

Serenna bolted awake. She blinked, unseeing, in her darkened room. The blackness of night lingered as sleep fogged her thoughts. A haunting silence pressed in around her while the steady thunder of her heart pounded like a drum in her ears.

Exhaustion dragged on her limbs from a grueling day in the Combat Yard, and she'd collapsed into bed hours before. Finally advancing beyond the basics of conditioning and developing balance, Serenna was learning how to spar with her fists and feet.

Like we'll actually be fighting the wraith hand to hand.

On top of that, she spent the evening also training her magic with Vesryn. The prince had distracted her enough by relentlessly demanding more of her power, not allowing her time to dwell on their conversation the prior day.

Serenna squeezed her eyes shut and rolled over with a protesting groan. She strained to hear if Velinya had returned from her portal shift, uncertain of how late it was.

I'm sure she'll spend her evening—probably early morning too—carousing at the Terminal. Serenna couldn't understand how her friend could function with so little rest.

Serenna's breath caught, cleaving to her lungs.

Bloodcurdling screams.

Her eyes flew open.

Leaping out of bed, she dashed to the window. Not bothering with the tassel pulls, she shoved her weight into hauling back the bulky curtains.

Chaos unfolded in her dormitory's courtyard. Serenna's attention ricocheted across the grounds as she strained to make sense of what she saw.

Disappearing and reappearing shadows surrounded a handful of initiates. Shrieking, recruits attempted to flee. Some fell. But they didn't rise.

Illumination cast light on haunting forms streaming into the entrance of her building. Invading.

Wraith.

The calamitous thought twisted through Serenna's mind, knotting her terror. Fear crept across the corners of her vision. Every pound of her hammering heart threatened to swallow her in darkness. Air tangled in her throat. She had to remind herself how to breathe.

How are they here?

Serenna's gaze darted around her room like she was a fish trapped in a tide pool, searching for a place to hide. The recesses of her mind went into a frenzy, weighing all of her options.

What do I do?

The cloud of her dismay turned even darker. *How can I possibly survive an attack?* Despite weeks of training, she felt wildly underprepared to rely on her power.

A breath hitched in her lungs.

Velinya.

Her friend had portal duty and was somewhere on the grounds if she wasn't at the Terminal. The thought of Velinya fighting off those beasts nearly drowned Serenna in despair.

Tunneling her awareness to the prince through the bond, the twin silver threads shone brightly in her mind. Lacking telepathy, Serenna had no way of communicating with Vesryn besides tugging on the connection.

He's awake. She sensed an ocean boiling with rage. *Why are both cords now bright?* She perceived—

The distraught screams echoing from the lower levels jarred Serenna's attention back to her rooms. She steeled her uncertain resolve, unwilling to be helpless, waiting for death.

Wasting precious time, she donned her leathers, quickly tying all the laces of her vest. Her hands shook, knowing the flimsy armor wouldn't be effective against the wraith's butchering claws.

Serenna snatched a knife from one of her sheaths and clutched the dagger in a white-knuckled grip. The weapon offered an insignificant shred of security.

By the time she'd entered the hallway, her floor had roused. A cluster of half-awake and scantily armed initiates flowed down the spiral staircase with her, illumination lighting the way. Together, they spilled to the lower levels, frightened pants cutting through the distant screams. More recruits joined their descent as they followed the noises of the commotion.

The hilt of Serenna's dagger slipped in her sweaty palm. Her mind spun. *How many wraith are here? Is the island already overwhelmed? What am I supposed to do? I can't kill a wraith, I hardly killed a rabbit! Were the magus roused? They've been training with Vesryn, so surely—*

A wave of darkness unfolded as she reached the landing on the ground floor. Before Serenna even considered seizing her power, a shadow materialized in front of her.

Screaming, she blindly slashed the blade with a startled reflex. A spray of warm liquid fountained over her arm. The motion was far from a calculated heroic move. Scraps of training fled her mind faster than a strike of lightning.

Taloned hands seized her throat and yanked her off her feet.

Serenna's knife clattered to the ground. Ablaze with panic, she clawed mindlessly at the fingers constricting her airway. Kicking and shrieking, she writhed in the monster's grip, straining to release the biting pressure.

White canines flashed. The wraith snarled, blowing a gust of repulsive heat into her face.

Serenna blinked. Red eyes lined with a smear of kohl met hers. Midnight blue skin stretched over sharp cheekbones—the face could've even been feminine. Rows of black braids collected into a long tail. Rings swung from eyebrows, lips, and ears.

Pointed ears.

Serenna recoiled at the startling familiarity.

Agony flared. Claws scratched across her flesh. She couldn't draw a breath. The wraith was going to pop her head off with no more effort than a child picking flowers.

Serenna's sight flashed, threatening to cocoon her in darkness as her vision blurred. Tears spilled from her eyes as the pressure constricted her throat like a vise.

Sound muffled to a ringing buzz. Blood trickled down the sides of her neck in warm rivulets. Against her will, Serenna's limbs relaxed, strength draining out. She released her grip on the skeletal hand strangling her.

Serenna fell into the quiet twilight of her mind. Drifting into the still area between her thoughts. Her alertness dimmed, like stars winking out.

Involuntarily, Serenna twitched in the final throes of holding on to consciousness. Slanting closed like shutters, her eyelids fluttered alongside her flickering awareness. Her lingering worries faded as if floating away on a gentle breeze.

A deafening roar blasted her mind.

Serenna's eyes flung open.

Her body tensed in the wraith's grasp, electrified at the barrage of frenzied orders.

Vesryn.

Bellowing, the prince assaulted her thoughts with more might than a raging bull. Serenna couldn't comprehend the onslaught of his hysteric urgings.

Dread collided with her through their connection. Finally, one coherent telepathic sending came through.

Fight, stars scorch you! he raged at her.

She was going to die. Strangled, writhing like a fish on the ground. Time slowed, and the world around her distorted like she plunged underwater.

SERENNA! Vesryn howled at her, violently yanking the bond. His frustration and hysteria pummeled her. *HOLD ON!*

Vesryn's panic mobbed her. The bolt of his shock severed her obscured thoughts. The prince extended phantom hands down the nexus linking them and *ripped* at her aura, launching Essence toward her.

The frail energy at Serenna's heart combusted, shooting her awareness solidly back into her mind.

Her instincts roused, flaring to life. Serenna's focus snapped back to the present. Her Well crashed into her, swallowing her in a tidal wave. The exhilarating sensation of her awakened magic nearly overwhelmed her until she instinctively absorbed the current of her power.

Serenna lifted her face to meet glowing red eyes. Flames scorched her nerves, steering her perception toward a single point.

The wraith bared its fangs as it squeezed her throat.

There was no hesitation. Vesryn's emotions engulfed hers. Serenna consumed the barrage of the prince's rabid feelings pouring into her mind.

Rage directed her reaction. She wasn't ready to die. *I haven't lived yet!*

She expelled the remaining air in her lungs in a strangled wheeze.

Her power unfurled like a flower opening to the sun. Shadows sprang around her as specters of vipers, lashing in the sand. A blanket of black clouds streaked toward the monster.

Serenna grimaced in concentration. Transforming her fear into daggers of fury, she threw the shock wave of rending at the beast. She snatched the pulse of the creature's tainted blood and *shredded* it.

The arm holding her exploded.

Dropping to the ground, Serenna stumbled. An eruption of gore and bone splattered her like a bubble bursting in a tar pit, disintegrating the creature.

Even though it had been a matter of moments, Serenna took her first real breath in what felt like an eternity. *I just killed a wraith.*

She scraped the black liquid from her face. Placing her hands on her knees, she drew in frantic inhalations, crippled by uncontrollable trembling.

The last few minutes caught up to her. Her legs shook. A malformed silence rang in her ears. *I almost died.*

Coupled with the stink of gore, Serenna dry heaved from the flood of emotions overwhelming her.

Another body smashed into her.

The impact of the wraith sent Serenna crashing to the ground in a tangle of limbs. A scream ripped from her throat as she floundered beneath the weight of the creature. Claws sliced into her arms as the monster wrestled to pin her down. Serenna thrashed wildly.

She shrieked when fangs lowered to her neck. Terrified and fumbling, her magic shot out in all directions with a violent blast of force.

The wraith smacked the ceiling, punched by her power. Serenna rolled out of the way before it fell.

It crashed back to the ground in a heap. She disintegrated the creature in another spray of black blood before either of them could rise to their feet.

Vesryn's presence lingered in her mind. Serenna didn't feel so alone, having his awareness grounding her. She sensed he was nearby, but focused on his own fight. She tapped into his rampage to fuel her own before she could succumb to terror.

Serenna registered other initiates locked in their own haphazard battles with shadowy opponents. Too many recruits lay torn open on the floor from injuries wrought by weapons and talons.

Strobing illumination flaring around the common room contributed to the mounting horror by displaying the carnage's extent. Tables and chairs had toppled over, shattered among the mangled bodies on the ground.

Serenna's eyes landed on the closest pair locked in a deadly dance. A petite woman flashed blinding lights at a wraith's face as she barely skirted away from its enraged lunges. Stalking toward the creature, Serenna balled an outstretched hand into a fist, lacerating the beast into another burst of gore.

A small cluster of recruits banded together. The woman continued to flash her orbs of illumination, stunning the remaining wraith and revealing other cloaked creatures by shattering their invisibility. Suddenly, the surroundings blazed with staggering brilliance as the other recruits realized light would reveal the hidden monsters.

Rending the wraiths' bodies into eruptions of blood and bones came faster now. As soon as Serenna left behind an exploding body, she moved on to another one. Stretching the limits of her power, demanding more. Ebony shadows coiled and danced around her, ready to strike their next prey.

Violet shields sprang up, surrounding their growing party. The wraith hurled themselves against the barriers, only to stagger back.

Some initiates made the fatal error of abandoning their magic to meet the colossal wraith with weapons. The creatures were the better fighters, cutting down those who met them in a clash of steel.

Serenna assumed these monsters wielding golden daggers, ripping through their wards, were the same wraith who'd attacked Vesryn a few days prior. *How could they have traveled across the realms so quickly?* A surge of anger consumed her as she remembered that they'd almost killed her prince.

She wanted revenge.

Targeting wraith after wraith, she sent fountains of gore shooting in all directions as their group gained traction toward the exit. The recruits pushed the creatures back, straining to reach the courtyard.

The common room was a living meat grinder. Serenna slipped in the warm pools of liquid, swallowing bile when her boots squished through materials she didn't wish to name. Black blood dripped from the tip of her nose.

Fighting in such close quarters was a death sentence. Illumination shone through the smashed entry doors. Keeping her eyes focused out of the building, Serenna looked past the bodies littering the ground.

Exhaustion flogged her; she had no concept of how much time had passed. She'd pushed herself far beyond any limits of endurance she thought she was capable of.

Stumbling and gasping, their band emerged from the residence hall. Wiping her face, Serenna studied the courtyard, seeing no more wraith in their vicinity.

Living wraith anyway.

Everyone's disbelieving gazes numbly evaluated the evidence of pandemonium strewn across campus. Wraith and elven-blooded alike littered the grounds.

A sensation of fingernails clawed through Serenna's perception, like a presence scratching her thoughts. Her attention whipped to the Spire's peak. A rush of contempt assaulted her mind while her eyes groped the darkness. She blinked, straining to make sense of the eerie feeling. It wasn't Vesryn.

But a thrum, an intensity of crashing powers echoing around the grounds, pulled Serenna's awareness away from the tower.

Her group followed the hum of Essence to the center of the island. The magisters and magus had joined the fight, drawing the attention of the horde of wraith. Their numbers were so few compared to the monsters mobbing them.

Waves of magic crackled in the air as the magus worked cohesively as one unit. The weapon masters hovered near the perimeter of their coordinated band, skewering any wraith within their blade's bite, protecting those focusing on wielding Essence. Force flung the creatures away in violent blasts or pulled them toward the reach of a weapon.

Gold-tipped arrows flew from the wraith, slamming through the protective violet shields, claiming lives.

Serenna frantically scanned for Jassyn among the magus, but the activity was too chaotic. *He should be towering over everyone—easy to spot. Are the menders somewhere else?*

Serenna turned away from the battle, sensing the prince's presence before her searching eyes found him. A terrible white flame of wrath burned through the bond, but Vesryn's focus didn't waver. Dressed in scaled battle armor, he fought alone near the base of the Spire. More wraith surrounded him than had invaded her residence hall.

The prince was an army all on his own. A living weapon. His magic flew in a cyclone of power. His twin glaives flashed in a blinding blur as he swept forward, a whirlwind tearing through the ranks of wraith.

His hair shone silver in the moonlight, hastily tied back in a knot on top of his head. The loose edges flew around him like a curtain in the breeze.

Fighting with more destructive energy than all the recruits and magus combined, each of Vesryn's strokes blended into his next step in a lethal dance. Even alone, the prince didn't give ground, blocking the wraith's jabs with his glaives. Portals opened to swallow the few gold-tipped arrows streaking toward him.

It was obvious Vesryn had held back in the training ring. Now unleashed, he was a master of havoc and destruction, gliding with flawless grace. His blades hacked and slashed with a symphony of metal clangs, meeting wraith daring to come within the reach of his ravenous steel. The biting glaives cast fountains of black blood splattering in every direction.

Flashes of illumination erupted, blinding the creatures. Creating rifts, the prince blasted bodies through. He spun duplicate illusions of himself to disorient their attacks. Wraith exploded left and right if he wasn't cutting them down with his whirling blades.

He's weaving so many abilities at once. Vesryn's skill as a warrior was utterly devastating—he was a celestial prince of death.

Why isn't he fighting with the rest of the magus?

Serenna knew she didn't have the talent to join him, and the last thing she wanted to do was to distract him.

Instead, within the safety of her band, she began picking off the wraith at the edge of the group swarming the prince. Casting out threads of rending, she targeted the creatures' necks—the magic's destruction had the same deadly result as obliterating their entire forms. Coiling her magic's shadows around the wraith like a snare, Serenna separated heads from bodies with a *yank*.

Disbelief clashed through her skull, realizing everyone fighting the wraith was from Centarya. The creatures crawled everywhere, outnumbering them. *Has anyone alerted the capital? Is the army coming to our aid?*

Chest heaving from exhaustion, Serenna staggered with a gasp at the abrupt emptiness.

A startled breath froze in her chest. One heartbeat, her power was there; the next, it was gone.

Engrossed in helping the prince, she failed to notice her Essence dwindling. A sense of suffocating dread threatened to smother the air in her lungs. A chill scraped over her skin.

Her Well was drained of magic.

She was powerless.

CHAPTER 41

LYKOR

Lykor paced the darkened rooftop of the central structure. Restless. Monitoring the events unfolding below. Back and forth, boots striking stone.

His warriors had invaded the buildings with minimal resistance. This deep in the black of night, few were out on the grounds.

He grunted, his body spasming, folding in half.

Aesar clashed with him with the force of a battering ram. The other had never attempted seizing control to this extent before. As soon as Lykor assembled his warriors for the attack, Aesar went into a ballistic frenzy.

This is wrong! Aesar screamed at him. *Those here aren't our enemies.*

THE WRAITH WILL PREVAIL OR THE ELVES WILL. THERE IS NO MIDDLE GROUND BETWEEN US, Lykor snarled back.

He smothered the voice, shoving Aesar into a dark recess in their mind. Stifling him.

Lykor couldn't join the fight, even if he wanted to. Not like this. Waging war over control of their body. If the fallen prince seized power, his intervention would compromise everything.

A shadow materialized on the roof with him.

"Report!" Lykor barked, taking his agitation out on Kal. He

clenched his fists so his fucking arms didn't flap like a sail in the wind with Aesar's attempt at wrenching away control.

"Our force is through the portals," Kal said, adjusting his mace over his shoulder. "The perimeter around the island is secured. The squadrons are fanning out and combing through the buildings."

Lykor released the magic that held the four rifts open. He was unwilling to risk the chance of elves traveling through to reach their sanctuary.

"Do you want prisoners?" Kal asked.

Twisting on his heel, Lykor stalked toward his captain. "No. This is the last time I'm repeating myself," he snarled. "To the death. Kill. Them. All." Shoving his chest, Lykor sent Kal staggering. "Report back in a quarter hour."

Kal hesitated, shifting his eyes. "Killing our own doesn't sit right with me."

Lykor trembled, an explosive wrath blazing through his veins. "We are not *elves*," he raged. "Not anymore."

He stalked up to Kal, jabbing his armor again to force him back. "Or did you forget how they twisted us, transformed us, and tortured us to steal our magic? I haven't!"

"But those here had nothing to do with that," Kal protested. "The same thing could be happening to them for all we know." Kal searched his eyes, chewing on a lip ring. "I...I want to talk to Aesar."

Lykor's chest heaved with his irritation. He couldn't disregard Aesar's presence anymore if he was this insistent on being active in their mind. Kal's defiance only seemed to augment Aesar's influence.

Shadows blasted in all directions, answering Lykor's uncontrollable fury. Like lightning striking from storm clouds, his magic discharged toward his captain.

Lykor snarled when Aesar seized their magic, halting their power's advance. Rending restricted, Lykor slammed his fist into Kal's face instead.

A satisfying *crunch* of cartilage splintered against his knuckles before Kal crashed to the ground. He was lucky Lykor didn't drive his gauntlet through the back of his fucking skull.

"Get back down there before I rip your fangs out!" Lykor barked, hauling Kal up by his braids.

Kal wiped the blood streaming from his nose, not meeting Lykor's glare. He grabbed his mace, warping away without a word.

Lykor wouldn't allow the wraith to leave the island until they were the only ones left standing. They would eliminate this half-elf army.

A chill scraped under his skin. Aesar slammed against the surface of his awareness. The fallen prince threatened to break through. Like someone pounding under thin ice.

These people are not the enemy. You know this. Stop this attack before it's too late, Aesar pleaded.

I'M GIVING THE ORDERS!

Lykor's gauntlet screeched as he clenched the parapet's railing. The familiar squeal of metal failed to soothe him.

And what about the bond-holder? You can't mean to finish them too.

Lykor stretched his awareness to the one connected to him by magic. A shackle. Their bond-holder was somewhere on the south side of the island. Awake and terrified. He hadn't decided what to do about that inconvenience yet, but perhaps the wraith would take care of the problem for him.

A force punched him in the gut. Lykor doubled over with a strangled exhale, clutching the railing for support. A vise squeezed his chest, wrenching away control of his lungs.

He couldn't breathe.

Aesar viciously charged him, assaulting his mind. *Stop this madness!*

Lykor wouldn't concede to this sniveling shrew. They brawled in a tangle of wills. Their body seized and thrashed as they collided in their awareness, grappling for dominance.

Blinking, Lykor found himself on his side. Curled up and taking in whooping gusts of air. But he prevailed.

I hope we die, Aesar said bitterly, a muted buzz in his head. An insignificant fly. Pushing himself off the ground, Lykor swatted him away.

Fighting to draw in a breath, Lykor staggered back to the edge of the roof to resume his watch. Half of their force had disappeared into the buildings. The others engaged with a band of half-elves. The vibrations of Essence pounding through the air rattled him to his core.

His eyes snagged on one aura blazing near the base of the tower. Putting up resistance. Their pathetic attempt wouldn't last long against the might of the wraith.

Lykor squinted, adjusting his eyes to peer through the darkness. A single form radiated magic, surrounded by scores of his wraith. Surely one elf couldn't push them all back.

He stilled, blood running cold like ice crystalizing on a pond.

Fire writhed and simmered in his veins upon recognizing the familiar twin glaives flashing in the dim starlight. They were his weapons.

No. They were Aesar's.

Lykor's mind went numb, lacerated by talons.

His spine flinched.

A ripple of dark power billowed through him. A command twisted by magic.

Midnight coiled around him, a surge readying to strike.

To obliterate.

DESTROY HIM.

The weight of the coercion was just as deadly as when King Galaeryn implanted the instruction in his mind decades ago. Lykor lost control to the power.

"Vesryn," he whispered, the name tearing through the compulsion's magic.

But it wasn't Lykor controlling the words.

His fangs retracted with a *click*. Unbidden.

NO!

A force dragged Lykor's awareness into a black corner. The agony of not heeding the coercion threatened to sunder his mind.

Lykor clawed at Aesar, refusing to be caged.

RELEASE ME!

Night enveloped Lykor's consciousness amid his furious howls, extinguishing his awareness. Muting his control.

Darkness consumed him.

CHAPTER 42

AESAR

Arched over the railing, Aesar gasped, drawing in jagged breaths. He'd never usurped Lykor, content to live in captivity's shelter. Now, regret rolled through him for being so weak, permitting Lykor absolute domination in protecting them while he cowered.

Seeing Vesryn, knowing the parasitic coercion on Lykor's mind required his twin's death, had Aesar distraught with terror. The gut-wrenching thought of witnessing them slaughter his brother through Lykor's eyes—or die trying—spurred Aesar to a final act of desperation. It was a sheer phenomenon that he'd subdued Lykor once the compulsive magic activated.

I have to hold on.

Trembling, Aesar clung to the banister, grasping onto shards of control, knowing his dominance wouldn't last long. Containing Lykor indefinitely would be impossible. Aesar was aware he'd be overpowered soon, stashed away, forced to watch events unfold. An invisible bystander.

Lykor was like a hurricane of wrath, impossible to contain, driven by a feral desire to protect the wraith, intending to exterminate every elf. Restraining Lykor's volatile rage and ravenous retribution was as futile as barring the moons from rising.

How did it come to this? Will we ever be free from the king's darkness rotting inside of us?

Aesar focused on the ground, the sounds of chaos and battle echoing up to the roof. He released a whimper, laying eyes on his brother for the first time in a century. Surrounded by a swarm of wraith. Those he'd sought to protect—those drained of Essence whom Lykor shielded from the same experimenting by willingly participating in the king's torture.

But bringing the wraith here, endangering innocents on both sides isn't the way.

Vesryn drove the band back, away from the central building. Single-handedly. Too many wraith fell. *I have to stop this.*

Overcome with emotion, Aesar's knees crumbled under the gravity of the loss. He collapsed, catching himself on his hands, fighting to catch his breath.

His heart ached, wanting to go to Vesryn. To explain everything. *Would he even recognize me now halfway through the transformation?* But it was too late for him. Long ago, he'd accepted that any attempts at reaching out to his brother would be fruitless.

If they got close, Lykor would kill Vesryn before Aesar could speak. The king had seen to that, should Vesryn have accidentally wandered into their prison all those years ago and uncovered their sire's plans. There was no escaping from the king's tyranny.

Perhaps the stars shone on him for the first time since they'd cursed him, granting him this one final chance to balance the scales.

Lykor shielded me, taking the full impact of the coercion. I'm the only one who can end this and put a stop to the king's demands.

Aesar's chest trembled with the resurgence of grief. But Lykor stirred. A beast lying in wait, commanded to kill. He had to make a decision.

Kal warped beside him.

The creased lines of worry on Kal's forehead relaxed, recognition flickering across his features when Aesar rose from his knees to face him.

"These elves are putting up more of a resistance than Lykor predicted," he reported. "Even with our numbers...I'm not sure we'll be able to stand against their magic without taking catastrophic losses."

Kal hesitated, his jaw swiveling from side to side. His broken nose made Aesar wince. He'd pulled that punch as much as he could.

"You saw him, didn't you?" Kal asked.

Nodding, Aesar swiped at a stray tear, knowing Kal intentionally avoided mentioning Vesryn's name so as not to trigger an outburst—his own thoughts were dangerous enough, but he had Lykor subdued.

For now.

"Our soldiers can't keep fighting him." Kal's talons tightened on the handle of his blood-soaked mace. Ruby drops splashed on the marble. His voice fell. "What are your orders?"

Aesar heard the unspoken concern. Kal had been just as loyal to Vesryn as the captain of their guard—he didn't want to face the prince.

Aesar's attention hooked on the weapon. He'd already tried ending his life when he became aware of Lykor's intentions—before he even realized his twin would be among the number here.

His attempts had been in vain, even when he thought Lykor was unconscious in sleep. Somehow, Lykor always knew, seizing control to prevent any harm.

Aesar met Kal's eyes. Searching. Pleading.

Kal retreated a step, but his words were an order. "Don't you think about asking that again."

Flinching, his gauntlet formed a fist. Lykor battered at his shackles, snarling incoherently, fighting to break free.

Aesar's mind spun like the Maelstrom. He considered the best course of action. The only course of action. He had to act quickly before Lykor emerged—he couldn't let that happen. Never again.

Aesar rested a hand on his captain's shoulder, his most dedicated companion, despite the torments Kal endured from the other half of his mind. Regret battered Aesar's chest for the time stolen from them, their relationship not even unfurled when they were thrown in the prisons. But Kal never left his side, even after Lykor appeared and tried to drive him away. *I thought things could be different for us now...*

"Sound the retreat," Aesar said. "You need to leave before we lose any more lives. I'll fabricate portals where we traveled in." He pulled away, his voice dropping to a whisper. "I'm sorry for this mistake."

Kal's eyes widened. "And what about you?"

"I'll protect our people." Aesar's fangs protracted, Lykor cracking through with a snarl. "Hurry," he said, gritting his teeth, then retracting them. "Before it's too late."

Kal hesitated.

"Go!"

Kal's chin trembled, knowing what Aesar intended, but he would see to his duty. He always did.

Kal seized his hand. "Come back to us. I can't lose you again. Not after getting you back."

Aesar's fingers tightened around Kal's in a fresh wave of grief.

A farewell.

Kal warped below, leaving Aesar alone with Lykor and the coercion's madness.

The retreat sounded.

Aesar's heart ruptured when he pulled his eyes away from one last glimpse of his brother. He peered over the wall, watching the rivers of wraith converge. Extending a hand, he wove portals back to their keep. Most of his people would make it out safely. He hoped it was enough.

How many innocents had died on this island because he allowed Lykor governance over their actions? The king was the enemy. Not those below. They both knew that.

This was a waste of life. I should have tried harder to prevent this tragedy. But fear of the past had Aesar content permitting Lykor's reign.

Lykor thrashed, scraping at the prison, frenzied to enforce the coercion's demands.

Aesar clutched his magic for as long as he could, to the final moments before he thought Lykor would emerge. He bought time for as many as possible, begging the stars to forgive him for those he had to abandon.

A storm brewed in their mind; the struggle between keeping

Essence out of Lykor's grasp and keeping him tombed was beyond Aesar's skill.

Releasing his power, Aesar gathered his strength, channeling all of his efforts into binding Lykor, shoving him into the furthest cavern in their awareness. His whole body tensed, anticipating what he needed to do.

His boots scraped against stone as he climbed the parapet, pulling himself up on the verge of the guardrail. He balanced on the ledge, considering the ground hundreds of feet below. As he worked up the courage, the wind whistled, snagging his hair. Minutes ticked by as he listened to the snarling in his head.

Aesar swallowed the ever-present residue of fear and closed his eyes. If Lykor's folly forced his people to flee the Frostvault Keep, Kal would take the wraith to safety. Not everything was lost.

At least we did something right and escaped those dungeons.

Lykor slashed at him, bludgeoning his influence against the confinement. *BECAUSE OF ME!*

Aesar inhaled deeply and held his breath. He could do this. He *needed* to before he faltered further. This was his only chance.

How many times had he jumped from Trella, soaring through the skies? With Vesryn laughing wildly beside him? The thought tugged a weak smile through a broken sob.

This way was the best for everyone. Lykor had already wreaked enough havoc. Aesar would permit no more.

Squeezing his eyes shut, tears streamed down his face.

On his exhale, Aesar stepped forward.

His stomach plummeted as he fell.

The wind howled in Aesar's ears as he plunged into darkness.

CHAPTER 43

SERENNA

As the wraith fled through portals, Serenna also ran. Her clothing stuck to her skin, dried blood flaking as she forced her legs to move. Her knees screamed with the effort of keeping herself upright. She'd never been so exhausted, so drained.

In the distance, she registered Vesryn bellowing for prisoners. Not all the monsters would escape. The magus were making quick work of collecting the stragglers who failed to flee through the rifts.

Why did they leave when they had the advantage? She hadn't noticed any wavering in their onslaught—one moment, they were attacking, and the next, they were retreating, seemingly without reason.

Serenna tried to process the implications of someone who possessed magic working with those beasts. But she had more pressing matters on her mind.

She staggered, focusing on one thought as she worriedly scoured the grounds.

I need to find Velinya and Jassyn.

Serenna anxiously surveyed everyone she passed on her flight to the Portal Platform. *Velinya might've been forced to take a stand with the magus there if she's not at the Terminal; maybe I'll discover Jassyn mending someone along the way.* She searched everyone's haggard faces but didn't see either of her friends.

"Jassyn!"

Dodging, weaving, and stumbling over bodies, Serenna refused to glance at the ground. Her heart pummeled her ribs, flogging her chest with panic. *They're all right. I just have to find them. The wraith are gone. It's over.*

"Velinya!"

Soft gray dawn crept into the courtyard. Serenna's eyes landed on the traveling grounds, littered with elven-blooded and wraith alike. *So much death.*

Then she saw unmistakable honey-colored curls.

A body face down.

No!

Serenna drank lungfuls of air, apprehension shooting down her spine.

Releasing an incoherent cry, she stumbled forward. *Please, stars,* she begged the silent sky.

Serenna landed on her knees, the jolt from hitting the ground a distant pain. With a sob, she turned her friend over.

Talons had ripped Velinya's leathers into tatters. Serenna's heart stilled as she took in Velinya's mangled body leaking blood. She didn't even know where to begin putting pressure to halt the flow. Not wanting to release another tide of her depleting life force, she left the golden dagger lodged in her friend's shoulder.

Serenna looked around frantically for help. *What am I supposed to do with no magic?*

Dazed, Velinya blinked sluggishly at the sky.

Jassyn. Jassyn can heal her. He can... He could...

Serenna started screaming for Jassyn, the words ripping from her throat. She cradled her friend, hoping someone would hear. Her vision pulsed, compressing around the edges, distorting everything surrounding her except for Velinya's lacerated form.

Serenna gasped, her chest caving in on her heart. Breathing was hard. How could feeling this much pain be possible? She wanted to collapse from the world pressing in against her.

Shock shook her limbs, rattling her bones. Velinya wasn't stirring.

There was no flicker of comprehension, no smile, no breathless laugh, no gossip ready to spill from her lips.

There was just blood. A ruined body.

No, no, no. This isn't happening.

With a heartbroken cry, Serenna plunged into her empty Well. Sorrow and anger fueled her descent to where her Essence should be waiting. She clawed at the void, ready to sever a part of her soul, anything to sacrifice a scrap of power.

Even if it shattered her completely.

"JASSYN!"

Serenna drowned in tears, chest wracking in fearful sobs. Her heart fractured into splinters, bursting and cleaving from the inside out. Anguish smothered her when Velinya's pulse slowed even further with a flutter.

Serenna's vision pulsed, white streaks flashing in front of her eyes. She sucked in a breath, straining to stretch the chasm. Between her desperate cries, she battled to rip power from herself to heal her friend's body.

Shrieking in agony, Serenna sensed her mind splitting from the onslaught of her attempts to grasp for more magic. Nothing was there—a vacant expanse like a starless sky.

Stop. Vesryn's command jerked her to a halt.

Where is Jassyn? Is he alive? I need Jassyn, Serenna pleaded through his telepathic link. *A mender. Essence. Anything. Please.*

A trickle.

A trickle of power rippled in her Well, sent through the bond.

I need more! she shrieked at him, not knowing such a thing was possible.

Vesryn's presence shrouded her like a protective shield, but he remained silent for moments until he sent a thought back. *Jassyn is on his way. Serenna, I—*

The telepathic link dissipated. She's sensed Vesryn exhausting the remnants of his Essence with the scant amount he provided her. It wasn't enough to form healing threads to stitch Velinya's wounds.

But Jassyn is alive. He's alive. And he's okay. He's coming to help. I just need to hold on to Velinya until then.

Serenna grabbed that small fistful of magic and plunged her power into Velinya's body. She sent out tendrils of unformed Essence, reaching, delving, searching for her friend's life force.

She just had to clutch Velinya's light until Jassyn arrived.

Serenna clung to her friend as if holding on to her would keep a tie to her soul. She cinched traces of Essence around Velinya's flickering aura.

"Hang on, Jassyn is coming," she assured her. "I'm not letting go."

CHAPTER 44

JASSYN

A fist snatched Jassyn's mind, hauling his consciousness out of sleep. With a gasp, he jolted upright in bed.
Get up, Vesryn said.
Images of a horrific battlefield flashed through the telepathic link. Disoriented, like he was spinning from the sky, Jassyn wrestled his cousin out of his thoughts.

Jassyn seized his pounding temples, attempting to suppress the agonizing throb. He fell back into his pillow as a wave of dizziness bashed him over the head with the force of a club. His body spasmed when Vesryn ensnared him in another telepathic link.

Serenna needs you. Go to the Portal Platform.

Jassyn toppled to the floor, clutching onto a thread of awareness. The weight of Vesryn's command burned through his mind until he acknowledged it. The prince dissolved the connection.

Pushing himself up, Jassyn stumbled to his closet to drag on his armor. A cold sweat drenched his nightclothes. *The wraith assaulted Centarya? I slept through the attack?*

No...that wasn't correct. He was in a drug-addled stupor. The only reason he roused was because Vesryn had *yanked* him into awareness.

But I was so careful.

He'd discovered the right amount of Stardust to help him sleep—a dreamless slumber that didn't have him blacking out as soon as he inhaled the drug. He would wake relatively refreshed in the morning.

The tremor afflicting his hands was nothing to be concerned about.

Regenerating in the evenings had become a battle. *But I'm handling it.* Jassyn assumed the side effects would go away once the dust was out of his system.

If he could stop indulging.

After Vesryn freed him from his contracts a week prior, he'd abstained from fouling himself with the drug. For a few days. He'd stifled his urges, attempting to separate himself from the reliance he'd developed.

But Jassyn relapsed, the temptation too great, knowing he could escape from the memories still haunting him.

None of that matters now. I need to get out there and help.

The magus hall was silent when he left his chambers. Everyone else had gone to the fight. Vesryn had shown him the survivors gathered near the south end of the island, where they had corralled the remaining wraith.

Jassyn spiraled into a whirlwind of doubt that he wouldn't be able to access his power. *I've never had sleep interrupted after consuming the drug.* His awareness of Essence was hazy, like he was peering through murky water.

Focusing his blurred vision on a single point, Jassyn stifled dread while he raced to the Portal Platform. His footfalls faltered as he surveyed the butchery when he passed the Infirmary.

Nothing stirred, not even a breeze. His gut clenched when his eyes darted over the still bodies coated in red and black blood.

And where was *he* this whole time? Useless and sleeping when he should have been helping. Mending those who were hurt.

I failed them.

Swallowing against the burning in his throat, Jassyn abandoned those he couldn't save.

He caught movement in the misty morning at the edge of his vision. Skidding to a halt, Jassyn's jaw dropped as he looked up.

Someone plummeted from the roof of the Spire.

The air was quiet and heavy with Jassyn's apprehension, his unsteady breathing deafening in his ears. He watched the figure fall from the sky—his own nightmare coming to life.

They weren't shielding. They weren't portaling. *Were they pushed off a balcony? Are there still wraith in the building? Vesryn had shown those monsters fleeing.*

Jassyn didn't even realize he'd started sprinting. He opened his senses as he ran. If he could grab his power, he could shield the tumbling person to lessen the blow of their fall.

Stomach twisting, he dove deeper into his mind. His chest tightened, threatening to bind him with panic. His magic was there; he could sense his Well lying in wait. Stretching further, he strained to draw Essence toward him.

He ran into a blockade.

He couldn't do it.

The Stardust had locked his power away.

Near the front of the building, Jassyn collapsed, his knees smacking the ground. He hopelessly watched the body descend to the earth. Redoubling his efforts, he squeezed his eyes shut, convulsing in wracking waves from the strain of reaching for his Well.

His limbs shuddered as he clawed at his magic. With a savage push into himself, he burrowed his awareness to where he knew his power was sealed away, charging at the barrier obstructing his Essence.

Nothing happened.

Horror solidified in his chest. Once the person struck the ground, there wouldn't be anything left to mend. He was going to watch someone die because he couldn't access his power. Because he'd been incapable of stopping himself from obliterating his mind with Stardust. He wanted to weep a river for his failings.

Jassyn flinched.

Something in the earth shifted beneath his knees. The wind sprang to life, stirring and curling, like the air had a breath of its own.

A pulse.

Jassyn gasped, his heart beating in time with the world around him. The clarity of his surroundings came into a sharp focus, like a fog had been burned away from his eyes.

His attention whipped back to the tumbling body—he didn't think.

Jassyn slammed his palm to the earth and seized the vibration under him. It was a tap, a rivulet in a tributary. Twisting his fingers into the grasses, fingernails scraping dirt, he delved deeper, searching for the foreign sensation.

He just needed to reach it.

Jassyn went rigid, the power blasting into him like the slap of a typhoon. *What in—*

Running out of time, Jassyn hoisted the unfamiliar magic stirring beneath the surface.

The earth obeyed, bending to his will.

The ground under the falling body erupted with a spray of soil. Roots shot up, streaking toward the sky.

Jassyn gaped, unable to comprehend what he was seeing. *I'm hallucinating from the dust. Essence doesn't control nature.*

Tendrils wrapped around the person, halting their descent. Mere feet from death, the vines cocooned them in a protective shell.

Jassyn's hands shook. He stared at the cradle of plants. Swallowing hard, he unclenched his fingers. As soon as he released the soil, the shoots went limp.

The body hit the earth with a *thud.*

Scorching stars!

Jassyn shambled to his feet and dashed toward the person he'd saved, ignoring the fact that the ground had erupted at his command. *Later. I'll dwell on this later.*

He frowned at the foreign armor before studying the man's still face. Elven-blooded, judging from the dark hair and sharp ears.

This isn't a warrior from the capital. Did Vesryn assign new guards? It would be like him to outfit his staff with intimidating gauntlets and spiked leathers.

Kneeling, Jassyn found the man to be alive, but…feverish? The soldier's skin burned.

Clearing his mind, Jassyn reached for his power—the Essence he was used to. If this warrior were injured, he could try to do something useful. Vesryn would've said if Serenna were hurt, so he could afford the minor delay to help someone else.

After a few agonizing moments, Jassyn's magic flickered like kindling flaring to life. His breath came in rapid bursts from the strain, scratching his throat. A line of sweat trickled down his brow. He swiped it away with his arm.

The warrior's brows furrowed over his shuttered eyes. He emitted a spine-chilling roar, back arching, boots scraping against the loose earth before convulsing in a seizing fit.

"Easy." Jassyn pushed the man's shoulders to the grass before he hurt himself flailing. The warrior contorted in haunting ways a body shouldn't bend, as if pulled in every direction.

Eyes unfocusing, Jassyn cast out tendrils of Essence to assess the soldier. The man stilled as magic coiled around him. Tunneling into the channels of the warrior's being, Jassyn mended what minor injuries there were.

The center of his back was a twisted mass of muscle, old injuries that were never properly healed. Jassyn didn't have time to wonder about the soldier's history or why he didn't have those wounds mended. *At least he didn't break his spine from the fall.*

Stardust had Jassyn's awareness scattered like stones in a rockslide as he quickly healed, fretting that his Essence would dart away. So frantic to save at least one person, Jassyn didn't realize he'd started unraveling a tangle of telepathic power when his magic brushed the soldier's mind.

Jassyn blinked. Shock had him gasping as if he'd plunged into frigid water, coming up for a breath of air.

Essence abandoned him.

He's compelled too? Stars, how many has the king—

The warrior's eyes snapped open, pinning on Jassyn's face hovering above his. A heartbeat stretched while they regarded each other. Jassyn's eyes widened as their gazes locked.

Red eyes.

Wraith.

Jassyn reared back, heart vaulting into his throat. Releasing the creature's shoulders, he scurried backward on his hands, digging in the heels of his boots for traction.

Panic made him flounder as he blundered, reestablishing the hold on his magic, hectically braiding his power into a shield—he had no magic to destroy the creature with.

Regaining control, Jassyn enveloped himself with a violet ward as he retreated.

Essence slipped through his fingers. His hold on his magic fizzled like sparks falling on damp logs.

His shield vanished.

The wraith lunged. Impossibly fast. A blur.

A clawed metal gauntlet seized him by the throat. The breath punched out of Jassyn's lungs when the creature slammed his back against the earth.

Choking, chest sawing in terror, Jassyn ripped at the steel plates restricting his air.

The wraith bared his teeth. Jassyn's heart stopped when fangs elongated. This was the end. Death snarled in his face, ready to rip out his throat.

Jassyn twitched helplessly, imagining the canines sinking into his flesh, shredding his skin. He breathed rapidly through his nose like he was a rabbit tangled in a trap.

With no warning, a cage of darkness exploded around them, rending lashing about.

Wraith don't have Essence!

Jassyn snatched one of his daggers, only now recalling he had concealed blades in his armor. He shoved the golden knife against his captor's throat.

The entombing magic snuffed out like a candle.

Crimson eyes narrowed on him.

Leaning closer to his face, the creature's raven hair spilled over the spiked shoulder pads. The wraith growled, the primitive warning chilling Jassyn to the marrow.

Steel creaked as the creature's fist tightened. The skin under Jassyn's neck split with a streak of pain under the metal's sharp bite. Jassyn bared his teeth, digging in his knife, drawing a sliver of black blood in return.

He could free himself by slicing the wraith's throat. Nothing was stopping him—he had enough leverage.

But something stayed his hand. Stupidity, perhaps. Stardust, most likely, swimming in his veins. *I can't even bring myself to kill this creature to save myself.* Jassyn's pulse droned in his ears while time froze, neither of them moving.

A bitter laugh escaped his throat at the absurdity of it all. It was ironic that the only being he'd saved was the enemy.

But why isn't he finishing me off? And why doesn't he look like the other wraith?

The wraith's eyes widened when another chuckle bubbled up. The confused look only made Jassyn laugh harder, wheezing at the emptiness in his lungs. When was the last time he had found humor in anything?

No, nothing is funny. My head is just floating in the scorching clouds.

Seemingly unconcerned by the knife scoring into his flesh, the wraith's gaze darted to the Spire, to the sundered earth, and then back to him.

Jassyn silenced his addlebrained mirth as the wraith scrutinized him, dark brows furrowing over scarlet eyes. The warrior searched his face with an intelligent intensity that had Jassyn reconsidering everything he knew about the creatures.

Does he realize I stopped his fall? Is that why he isn't tearing me to shreds? The knife quivered in Jassyn's hand as the wraith's heartbeat drummed against the edge of the blade.

The cold steel around Jassyn's throat loosened enough for him to suck in a full breath. Tears pricked his eyes as he gasped, air rushing into his lungs.

The wraith released him with a grunt. He plucked the knife from Jassyn's numb fingers with as much ceremony as a bird picking a berry from a bush. Thumbing the dagger, the creature leaned back on his heels, impassively studying him.

Whipping out another blade, Jassyn sat up. The gold weapon quivered between them.

The hairs on his arms lifted when the wraith arched a brow. The gesture was familiar, eerie—he couldn't place it. He couldn't rightly even think of the wraith as a *creature* now that it wasn't snarling in his face like an animal.

His first assessment had been right—this being was elf-like. Somehow.

A portal opened. Jassyn gaped at the warrior and the rift. *This must be how their army arrived. But how did he create a portal to the island?*

"We're even," the wraith muttered. He frowned as he studied the decorative hilt on Jassyn's knife before trailing a finger across the leaves and vines. Rising, he tucked the blade behind his belt, apparently claiming it as his own.

He speaks too? This can't be real. Jassyn ignored the broken ground where his vines had sprung to catch the wraith's fall, not believing that either.

"*Even?*" Scrambling to his feet, Jassyn couldn't help but scoff at the claim, the Stardust obviously rendering him witless. "I saved you, and all you did was not kill me."

With a wordless growl, the wraith turned, stalking toward the portal.

Maybe that's his point.

"Was it the king?" Jassyn hurriedly asked, eager for any information. *Why would he be compelled? It makes no sense.* "Did the king coerce you?"

The wraith pivoted and rounded on him with a snarl, the first light of dawn flashing on his fangs. A breath of fear anchored in Jassyn's throat.

With a flick of his wrist, Jassyn made his blade disappear into his leathers, not wanting to provoke this being any further.

"Are you able to speak of the magic on your mind?" Jassyn gathered his courage before taking a step toward the wraith, holding out what he hoped was a placating hand. "I might be able to help you. If you let me try."

The wraith flinched, his shoulders tensing. "No one can help me." Backing into the portal, he vanished.

Jassyn shoved his hands through his hair, grabbing his curls as his thoughts spiraled like a windstorm. *My mind is cracking from the Stardust.*

Vesryn, pulling him out of sleep, hadn't allotted his body time to fully process the drug in his system. *I didn't draw power from the earth or see an Essence-wielding elf-like wraith. I was hallucinating.* That was the only explanation—he knew that was a side effect of the dust.

When this is all over, I need to get help.

CHAPTER 45

SERENNA

Time blurred, burying Serenna in a haze. A disbelieving weariness engulfed her heart, submerging her in a dreamlike trance. Magus Nelya and her squad of menders had found her cradling Velinya.

Their magic was depleting, but they'd stitched what wounds they could to stabilize her friend. Along with others struggling for their lives, Velinya had been transported to the capital for further healing.

Jassyn arrived after Serenna collapsed near the Portal Platform, too exhausted to move. Even shifting her eyes required more energy than she possessed. He offered quiet comfort, clutching her as tightly as she held on to him.

Serenna couldn't think clearly through the shock. Her head was nearly silent, though all she wanted to do was scream. *The wraith attacked Centarya. I almost died, and so did my friends. So many lives have been lost.*

Serenna stumbled as they walked. Jassyn's grip tightened across her shoulders, holding her up. They entered the Citadel's courtyard to join the remaining survivors.

Dried blood coated everyone. One of Ayla's arms was wrapped in a sling, her usual companion Mishryn, nowhere in sight. Every face was blank as grief and despair sank in. How many bodies would they offer to the stars, sending souls to the cosmos on pyres of flame?

Serenna blinked against the brilliant sun. A new dawn vanquished the darkness. The morning light painted the sky in hues of pink and purple—a beautiful sunrise ushering out the hideous night.

Vesryn had released his entire stockpile of bottled Essence to the menders, but everyone used the power sparingly, uncertain if the wraith would return.

The prince spoke stoically to her sire. Scores of Elashor's warriors stood at attention in plated armor.

Armor, Serenna noted, that shined, untouched by the horrors of battle. Someone must've portaled during the attack and alerted the capital, bringing reinforcements to Centarya's aid.

But they came too late. We were here alone, fighting for survival. And they came too late. Their presence would've made all the difference.

Having received orders from the prince, Elashor dispatched ranks to the dormitories to drag out the bodies—of elven-blooded and wraith alike.

Vesryn's eyes found hers over the gathered crowd. He roughly shouldered through the surrounding group, arrowing toward her and Jassyn.

Serenna recoiled at the onslaught of emotion storming through the bond. A primal rage, more intense than anything she'd ever experienced, billowed from him in waves. The black blood spattered over his skin only heightened the savagery radiating from him.

Everyone would've scurried faster out of the prince's way if they sensed the same assault. He swiftly closed the space between them with a desperation to reach her, a thunderstorm of wrath trailing in his wake. Though his eyes were burning, his relief shimmered through the bond.

Serenna felt him waver at a precipice, struggling to stay balanced. She gaped at him as he approached.

Vesryn was utterly unhinged, barely holding himself together. While she wanted to curl up and forget about the night, he was a flame, just waiting on a breeze to send to set the world afire.

Vesryn's attention flicked between her and Jassyn, scanning their faces. The prince hovered a hand near his chest and drew out a light, seemingly restored of magic since the battle. He plunged a portion of his power into his cousin.

Jassyn flinched with a sharp inhale through his teeth. Vesryn frowned at him and tilted his head. Serenna assumed silent communication passed between them, because Jassyn blinked and nodded. Vesryn reached out to squeeze his shoulder.

The prince detected they had an audience. Everyone around them stopped to stare at the exchange.

"Get to work!" he barked at the onlookers. At the command, they scattered like birds shooting into the sky.

Serenna shook when Vesryn drew out another orb of Essence. He sent it spiraling through her veins, fully restoring her Well. His fingers lingered against her chest as if feeling her heartbeat and reassuring himself she was still alive.

I don't want you defenseless, he said telepathically.

He lifted a hand as if to stroke her cheek. Instead, he gently cupped the side of her face. With a shuddering exhale, he rested his forehead against hers.

The fervent gesture, overflowing with more emotion than any intimacy could provoke, expressed far more than words. Vesryn's touch wasn't a mindless frenzy of passion or desire. It was a painful realization that they both could have perished.

But they were here, alive and together.

Serenna leaned into him and grasped his hands. A lone tear trickled down her face as she took strength from the current circulating under the caress of his fingertips.

Stay with Jassyn, Vesryn told her. *I'll get answers from our prisoners. They'll pay a hundred times over for the lives lost.*

Vesryn's lips brushed her forehead before he pulled away. Slowly, as if struggling against the weight of the earth.

I'll return when I can.

His jaw flexed before he straightened, snapping his mental barricades into place, resuming the aura of a commander.

Pivoting, the prince stalked toward the traveling grounds to the gathered wraith prisoners. Rending shadows branched around him as he opened a portal to the capital's dungeons. Serenna had a feeling he was about to expel his wrath on their captives.

Jassyn's hand found hers. He gave her an encouraging squeeze, leading her to his residence hall while crews cleaned up the rest of the island.

Serenna gripped his fingers. Terror had her heart pounding in her ears.

The wraith had attacked their academy, escalating the confrontation to war. Their unbreachable haven wasn't safe anymore. Surely they'd have to respond and hunt the monsters in earnest with the rangers now. If they could find the wraith's stronghold, Centarya would take the battle to them.

And what? Unleash justice for those slaughtered?

But Serenna knew before she had any hope of standing a chance, she needed to be stronger, not reliant on the prince. The only reason she'd survived was because Vesryn had summoned her magic for her. She'd been too afraid, not strong enough to defend herself or call her power. *I would've died if it weren't for him.*

I have to master my magic. I can't be helpless.

Turning around one last time, Serenna watched Vesryn's retreating form. Everything between them was complicated, a tangled string of emotions twisted with their duties to the realm. She trembled, not wanting to think about what would've happened if she'd lost him to the wraith.

Serenna's heart vanished with the prince as he disappeared through the portal.

THANK YOU FOR READING!

If you enjoyed The Aspect of Essence, please consider helping other readers discover this series by leaving a review or a rating on Amazon or Goodreads. Independent authors appreciate word of mouth recommendations—we couldn't spread awareness of our books without your help! Thank you again!

ACKNOWLEDGMENTS

I didn't know what I was getting into when I woke up one day in October 2022 and decided to write a novel. I've learned so much from the writing community as I've embarked on the self-publishing journey. This series, world, and the characters have evolved beyond my wildest dreams but this story wouldn't have been possible without the people I've met along the way.

To my family, who've always supported my crazy dreams. From helping me move to Alaska and then all the way to South Carolina, to being exited about my book—thank you for being there every step along the way.

Michael, thank you for reading my story multiple times and helping transform my developmental edit by picking apart and analyzing every word.

Craig, for being my biggest cheerleader and for encouraging me to share my writing. You read one of my first messy drafts and stuck around for multiple re-reads! Your commentary to my story has been priceless. I appreciate all of the feedback and thoughts from you and Lydia and can't wait to share book 2 with you!

Roxie Cohen, for being my first TikTok author friend! I'm so excited we're on this publishing journey together and I love seeing all of your ideas come to life.

K.L. DeVore for being my first TikTok dark fantasy author friend! Thank you so much for your all of your advice and encouragement and for always being there in the ups in down. I'm so excited to see where your dark fantasy debut *A Touch of Gold and Madness* takes you!

To those readers and authors I've recently connected with and those who've finished this adventure, I hope you'll stick along as the series unfolds. I can't wait to share what's in store for our characters, their relationships, and the new powers awakening.

ABOUT THE AUTHOR

Samantha Amstutz is the author of the Aelfyn Archives and is inspired by Wheel of Time, World of Warcraft, Star Wars, Lord of the Rings, the entire romantasy genre.

In her novels, you can expect immersive magic systems, different races, plot and intrigue, slow-burn romance, diversity and inclusion, and believable characters with flaws.

She is honored and beyond thrilled you're reading her work and she hopes something in her created world resonates with yours.

Printed in Great Britain
by Amazon

22339436-d0a2-4189-9ba4-0784f7978f51R01